Your favourite authors love
Veronica Henry

'As uplifting as summer sunshine'
Sarah Morgan

'Wise, insightful, beautifully written.
A delicious treat of a book!'
Milly Johnson

'An utter delight'
Jill Mansell

'Truly blissful escapism'
Lucy Diamond

'A heartwarming, triumphant story combined
with Veronica's sublime writing – the perfect mix!'
Cathy Bramley

'Veronica Henry has such a deft hand
with families and their complications'
Katie Fforde

'A gorgeous read'
Hilary Boyd

Veronica Henry has worked as a scriptwriter for *The Archers*, *Heartbeat* and *Holby City* amongst many others, before turning to fiction. She won the 2014 RNA Novel of the Year Award for *A Night on the Orient Express*. She lives with her family, by the sea, in North Devon. Find out more at www.veronicahenry.co.uk or follow her on Instagram @veronicahenryauthor

Also by Veronica Henry

A Day at the Beach Hut
A Wedding at the Beach Hut
Escape to The Seaside
Feel at Home with Veronica Henry
A Home From Home
Christmas at the Beach Hut
A Family Recipe
A Country Life
Bittersweet
The Apple Orchard
The Forever House
How to Find Love in a Bookshop
The Anniversary
A Country Christmas
High Tide
The Beach Hut Next Door
An Eligible Bachelor
Wild Oats
Love on The Rocks
Christmas at the Crescent
A Night on the Orient Express
The Long Weekend
The Birthday Party
The Beach Hut

THE HONEYCOTE NOVELS
A Country Christmas (*previously published as* Honeycote)
A Country Life (*previously published as* Making Hay)
A Country Wedding (*previously published as*
Just a Family Affair)

The Impulse Purchase

Veronica Henry

ORION

First published in Great Britain in 2022 by Orion Fiction,
an imprint of The Orion Publishing Group Ltd
Carmelite House, 50 Victoria Embankment,
London EC4Y 0DZ

An Hachette UK company

1 3 5 7 9 10 8 6 4 2

A CIP catalogue record for this book is
available from the British Library.

ISBN (Hardback) 978 1 3987 0616 3
ISBN (Mass Market Paperback) 978 1 4091 8358 7
ISBN (eBook) 978 1 4091 8359 4

Typeset at The Spartan Press Ltd,
Lymington, Hants

Printed and bound in Great Britain by Clays Ltd,
Elcograf S.p.A.

Jacob, Sam and Paddy
who are always there for me through thick, thin
and lockdown.

With love and thanks to you all from Mummer xx

Prologue

It always started with a fluttering in her stomach and a quickening of her pulse. Then a ripple would start on her scalp and run the whole length of her body, right down to her toes: a delicious tingle, like being dipped in champagne and feeling the tiny bubbles burst on her skin.

She knew now never to ignore the feeling. It was as if she was tuning in to a sixth sense; as if her gut, her brain and her heart were all connected, all firing together and urging her on. Like a gambler who knew exactly which horse to back, she always knew she was bet on a dead cert. She hadn't been wrong yet.

As she stood in front of the door, the sensation over-whelmed her. The ancient oak planks were pale as silver; the black iron latch smooth with handling. How many times had she been through it? As a child, a daughter, a teenager, a lover, a mother – so many different versions of herself had found happiness inside these stone walls.

When she'd left home that morning, she'd had no idea this opportunity would present itself. Everything inside her told her it was the right decision. Everything that had seemed so confusing melted away and the answers fell into place. After all, she'd learnt to listen to the signals and trust her instincts. They had never let her down before. She put her hand on the latch and smiled as it clicked and the door opened. As she stepped over the threshold, she felt her past and her future collide.

She smiled. No one would see this coming. Everyone would say she was mad.

It was the ultimate impulse purchase.

I

May was always the best month for parties, thought Cherry. The sun was bright yet soft, the breeze was fresh, everything in the garden was lush and overexcited, and everyone had a spring in their step now the good weather was bedded in and April showers were behind them. In Avonminster, students lay on the grass in front of the cathedral, revising, snoozing, flirting, summer stretching out in front of them as the end of the academic year loomed.

At Admiral House, down by the river, the drawing room was looking its very best. It was situated on the first floor, to take advantage of the magnificent view of the suspension bridge. Full-height French windows gave out onto a wrought-iron balcony, and a long table ran the width of the room. On it, platters and cake stands and wooden boards were piled high with Roquefort tartlets, Parma ham pushed into the midst of purple figs, dark red grapes and ripe rich creamy Camembert, bruschetta with tomato and anchovy, crostini with burrata and blood oranges. The effect was of a Dutch still life, the colours brooding and dark. Stone urns either side of the fireplace spilled acid-green hydrangeas, and between them was a zinc tub filled with bottles of pale pink sparkling wine from a nearby vineyard. Ranks of gleaming glasses stood in wait. The wine would flow. It always did here – it was that kind of house.

As head of the art department, Mike's retirement party should have been held at the university, but Cherry thought having it at home gave it a more personal touch. Over a hundred people had been invited for drinks and substantial canapes and seventy-seven people had RSVP'd yes.

Cherry didn't much care for retirement parties, usually. They felt to her like dress rehearsals for funerals. She and Mike had been to a few in recent years: soggy quiche and warm wine in some faceless function room, topped off by an unimaginative farewell gift and grindingly dull speeches.

So she was determined that Mike's leaving do would bear none of those trademarks. It would be glamorous, relaxed and fun. A glittering celebration of the inspiration he had given to all his students. And a tribute to his career.

On the walls, scattered amidst the nudes, landscapes and abstracts they had collected over the years, were the album covers that had made Mike famous in the early seventies: swirling, intricate, psychedelic illustrations that were iconic even today. He had been the go-to artist if you were a progressive rock band wanting hints of misty mountains and elves and illicit substances on your record sleeve.

And over the fireplace, blown up and framed in black, was the image that had made *her* famous: the photograph of a topless twenty-year-old Cherry astride a Norton

Commando in silver hot pants. She had often thought of taking it down, for it felt a bit inappropriate now, even though her long blonde hair had been covering her chest. She had styled the photo; Mike had taken it and sold the image to a poster company. It had been stuck on hundreds of bedroom walls, becoming almost as famous as the girl with her tennis skirt hoicked up over her bare bum. As photographer, Mike had got the credit, and the royalties were in his name, but as they were an item, Cherry had benefitted and never minded. Nearly fifty years later they were still together, and royalties still trickled in. So the photo stayed, a little piece of art that defined a certain age.

'Hey.' Mike sauntered in, rolling up the cuffs on his denim shirt, untucked over black jeans and Chelsea boots. With his thick-rimmed glasses and his hair expensively scissored to jaw length, he was, thought Cherry fondly, the archetypal professor of art.

'Are you ready for your engraved carriage clock?' she teased as he planted a kiss on her cheek.

'They wouldn't bloody dare,' he grinned, and swiped a tartlet. 'Sorry, I'm starving after my run.'

He still pounded five kilometres every morning, heading out over the suspension bridge. And it paid off. From behind, he looked much the same as he had the day she'd first seen him, that skinny bum in the tight jeans, the mop of curls, though these were now pewter, not gold.

Seventy. How on earth had he got to seventy? It meant she wasn't far behind. There was nothing about either of them that said septuagenarian, unless you had very sharp eyes and could detect the tiny hearing aid behind his left ear.

Despite their wild youth, the last twenty-five years had been respectable. Mike had worked his way up to Head of Fine Art at the University of Avonminster. He was on countless committees, the trustee of several museums and art galleries, and a judge for any number of prizes. Living in Avonminster had been the perfect alternative to London, with its lively arts and music and food scenes. And it meant they were near to Rushbrook, her family home deep in the heart of Somerset. Her connection to the village was as strong as ever. Mike knew how much it meant to her, to go back to the place she still considered home.

Although Cherry had never technically worked, she had probably made more for their pension pot than Mike had. She was the queen of flipping. She had renovated over six of their homes in the past twenty years, culminating in the jewel in the crown that was Admiral House. She could see the potential in the most unassuming listing, the one that estate agents and potential purchasers overlooked as run-down, dark and dreary or downright ugly. The one that needed too much work. She would buy, work her magic and almost double their money every time.

No one had wanted to touch Admiral House when she bought it three years ago, the four-storey student house at the rough end of the river with its overgrown garden and orange pine cladding; the smell of damp that made you gag; the fire doors and cheap carpeting. She had fallen in love with the view, up the gorge to the suspension bridge, and the wrought-iron balconies on each floor, American planter-style. And today demonstrated just how her eye for an up-and-coming area had paid off. Now everyone was scrabbling for a house down here.

'Where's Maggie gone?' Mike asked.

'Getting more ice from the garage. And extra lemons.'

Mike didn't ask if there was anything he could do. There wouldn't be. Cherry and their daughter Maggie would have it covered between them. The dream team. Cherry was in charge of décor and organising and Maggie had done the catering. The fridges downstairs were groaning with more food to replenish what was already laid out. He'd muck in afterwards, of course. Driving boxes of empty bottles to the recycling centre, drying up plates and glasses and moving furniture back.

They both stood at the window for a moment. Cherry's hand reached out for his and gave it a squeeze, sensing his disquiet.

'It's going to be weird,' he said.

'It'll be fine. It'll be over by five.'

'I don't mean today. I mean . . .'

He gave a gesture to mean the future.

'It's going to be wonderful,' said Cherry. 'Just think. No more admin. No more departmental meetings. No assessments.'

It had always driven him mad, the minutiae of being a departmental head. All he was really interested in was spotting talent and nurturing it. Getting his students to push themselves. Getting them to understand both the value of hard work and knowledge and practice, but also risk-taking.

'Talent isn't enough,' he would tell them repeatedly. And the ones who listened to him and responded did well. He had many success stories amongst his alumni, both creative and commercial. And he was loyal to a fault, always going to their private views and opening nights.

They heard the front door on the floor below open, then

a hello accompanied by excited barking and the skitter of claws on the tiled floor. Maggie, Fred and Ginger.

'Up here, darling!' called Cherry, releasing Mike's hand.

Moments later, her daughter appeared in the doorway flanked by two miniature wire-haired dachshunds. The energy levels in a room always went up when Maggie appeared, her smile wide and her eyes bright. She was tall, her long plum-coloured hair cut in layers, her eyes green and laughing. Cherry felt pride that, despite what had happened, Maggie had emerged a beacon of light and strength. There were still dark days, but she fought them with courage. And everywhere she went, Fred and Ginger came too, funny furry bundles of chaos, busy, beetling and beloved of all who knew them. A purchase that had seemed foolhardy at the time, so soon after the funeral, but no one could deny that the dogs brought comfort and distraction and made them all laugh.

'Here!' Maggie held out a box of huge shining lemons with their leaves still on. 'The ice is in the freezer. Hey, Dad, you look smoking hot.'

Mike smiled appreciatively. 'Distinguished and venerable was the look I was going for.'

'That too.' She crooked an arm around her father's neck and kissed him.

'I better get changed.' Cherry was still in a t-shirt and yoga pants. 'It's nearly midday and they'll be arriving from half twelve.'

'You better,' Maggie nodded, running her eyes along the table and nodding in approval. 'No Rose yet?' asked Mike.

'She was just getting Gertie ready. They'll be here any minute.'

'Can I just say,' said Mike, 'how much this means to me? You two organising this.'

He looked a bit overwhelmed for a moment. Cherry and Maggie looked at each other and shared a conspiratorial grin.

'As if we'd let anyone else get a look-in, Dad. You know that.'

Mike snapped his fingers, as something had slipped his mind. 'Oh, yes. The two control freaks. How could I forget?'

'Perfectionists,' corrected Cherry. 'There is a big difference between being a control freak and simply being *in* control. Now, we need the ice topped up in the wine cooler . . .'

Maggie shooed her away.

'Mum. Go and get changed. I'll sort the ice.'

'Ah – here they come.' Mike was looking out of the French windows, waving. In the street below were his granddaughter and great-granddaughter: Rose, gliding along the pavement in a white ruffled midi and Greek sandals, Gertie bobbing along beside her, clutching the string of a helium balloon in the shape of a Tyrannosaurus rex that was bigger than she was. He grinned.

Trex had been his nickname when he was young, a contraction of T. Rex, due to his resemblance to Marc Bolan. Some of his mates still called him Trex. The dinosaur must have been Rose's idea. She was even more about the detail than Cherry and Maggie, but she thought outside the box and trod her own path. Mike's heart still buckled at the thought of what she had been through, losing her father at such a crucial age. Not that there was a good age for tragedy.

He sighed, wishing for a moment that it was just the five of them celebrating, not an enormous rabble. It wasn't rare for them all to be together, for they lived less than a mile apart, but having them at Admiral House today meant the world to Mike. Together, they gave him ballast in an uncertain sea. Even at seventy, Mike often felt he was drifting towards the rocks, about to be swept away by an unseen current. It was the artist in him. He might be a respected academic, but the insecurity never really left you. You needed it, to be the best. And that's why he needed them.

Cherry, Maggie, Rose and Gertie. His girls.

2

Upstairs, Cherry pulled on the outfit she'd laid out on the bed earlier. She eyed it for a moment, wondering whether she should wear a dress, but she needed to be comfortable and practical. She'd be pouring drinks, handing round food, pounding up and down stairs to greet guests and usher them in. Practical didn't have to mean unglamorous, though. She teamed sleek black cigarette pants and an oyster grey silk shirt with silver leather sneakers and mother-of-pearl earrings. She tipped her head upside down and spritzed her hair with salt spray, then flipped it into a French twist, pulling out a few stray ends. A touch of mascara and a caramel lipstick was all the make-up she needed, and a honeyed, smoky cloak of Slow Dance by Byredo.

She checked herself out in the mirror. There was always a moment of trepidation before she looked at herself. Might she be confronted by an old hag in age-inappropriate clothing; a potential laughing stock? She felt relief. She looked cool and classy; nothing was too tight or too short or too shiny. Daily yoga and thrice-weekly swims at the Lido kept her toned and strong. Even she couldn't quite believe she was seventy next year. Seventy!

Though what did they say? Seventy is the new fifty? Actually, she felt better now than she had done at fifty, when inexplicable aches and pains and anxieties had overwhelmed her for some years. The wretched menopause. She batted away the memory. Nowadays, she woke each day feeling optimistic and energetic. And full of ideas. She – they! – had so many plans for the future now Mike was retiring.

Tomorrow, the sale of her mother's house in Rushbrook was due to complete and they would have a beautiful blank canvas. She needed to get today over first. Mike didn't officially finish at the university for another few months, when finals were over and marked and the degrees given out and he'd handed over to his successor, but they'd wanted to do the celebrating before the end of year stress set in.

Happy with her appearance, she slipped back down to the drawing room to add the final touches. She found her favourite French jazz station and connected it to the speakers hidden in the ceiling, adjusting the volume so it was a sultry whisper. Then she lit the half dozen scented candles dotted around the room, their spicy, woody scent soon filling the air. Entertaining was all about layering. Sound and smell were as important as what to eat and drink. Cherry had passed her entertaining skills on to Maggie, though with Maggie the music would be louder, the lights brighter, the drink would be in jugs to be poured into chunky glasses, the atmosphere more casual. Her parties were legendary. At least they had been . . .

Maggie had talked about throwing one this summer.

'I think it's time, Mum,' she had said a couple of months ago, but Cherry hadn't heard her mention it again.

Each summer, Maggie and Frank had thrown 'Frankstock' in their back garden, his record decks set up against the garden wall, trestle tables groaning with food, all the neighbours invited. Everyone dressed in festival wear and danced until dawn, Frank in his element, DJing in whatever ridiculous rig Maggie had assembled for him: a golden cloak, leopard-skin leggings, star glasses ... He had amiably donned his costume, even though he usually wore the sound engineer's uniform of jeans and a t-shirt or a fleece.

They had got through it, somehow, after Frank died in a freak accident – a fall from some rigging at a big event. Cherry's mother Catherine had been a tower of strength, scooping them all up into her house in Rushbrook, their sanctuary. And now she had gone too. Cherry shivered. If the past five years had taught her anything, it was to make the most of people while you still had them.

'Hey, Cherry Bomb.' Rose snapped Cherry out of her reverie, coming in with a tray of water jugs. 'Where shall I put these?'

'Just dot them round the room so people can help themselves. We need to keep them hydrated. You look stunning, darling. Where's that from?'

'Mountville Oxfam. It was all yellow and horrible so I soaked it in whitener and it came up a treat. Eight pounds.'

Rose did a twirl. The column of chiffon ruffles shimmered around her and settled back into place.

'Well, it looks a million dollars.'

It was true. But then, Rose always looked as if she'd wandered off the catwalk. Her style was eye-catching and striking. Most of her clothes were accrued from jumble sales and charity shops then customised. Yet of all the family, Rose was the least enthusiastic partygoer, even though at twenty-two she should have been the most. Some people thought she was shy, but she simply only spoke when she had something useful to say. She put her energy into observing and absorbing. She was the biggest contradiction of them all: rebellious, creative, independent. Fragile.

Cherry had nothing but admiration for her grand-daughter and the unconventional route she had taken. There was something of the undiscovered genius about her, but Rose always bided her time. Cherry had no qualms about her finding her feet in the long term. She was special, Rose. Her moment would come.

Gertie, meanwhile, looked set to be the biggest party animal of all of them. She bounded in after her mother with the T. rex still tied to her wrist.

'This is for Pops,' she told Cherry. 'Can we tie him up?'

Cherry helped her tie the balloon to the big candelabra in the middle of the table. He hovered over the proceedings, out of place yet perfectly in keeping, like the very best art installation.

Trex. Her Trex, with his snake hips and corkscrew curls. Still her hot love since the day she'd met him at eighteen.

Our new life together starts here, she thought.

An hour later, Admiral House was bursting at the seams, filled with laughter and the popping of corks. Greedy fingers reached for the endlessly replenished food. Fred and Ginger shimmied about, weaving between the high heels to snaffle up pastry crumbs. Gertie was given a tin tray piled high with tartlets to pass around. No one could resist her offering.

Mike found himself greeted by a stream of people he hadn't seen for years.

'Mike!' A woman with pink hair swooped down on him. 'Am I allowed to call you that? Or should it still be sir?'

Mike grasped for her name. He was struggling to identify some of his former students. The difference between youthful twenty and middle-aged forty was sometimes significant: weight gain, hair loss, an increase or decrease in confidence or income or cultural capital could alter someone beyond recognition, but he did his best.

'I think Mike's fine now,' he said, gamely embracing her.

Cherry and Maggie were tireless, running up and down stairs to greet people and then getting them to mingle. They were in their element, choreographing the whole event between them with just a nod or a gesture. Rose melted into the background, keeping an eye on Gertie and the dogs and any elderly guests who might need a chair or a glass of water or to be directed to the loos.

Outside the sun shone, beating in through the glass and heating up the room. The suspension bridge shimmered in the distance, a triumph of mankind over nature.

And then Anneka Harding arrived.

Anneka was dressed in layers of pale grey gauzy linen, all asymmetric hems and pointy sleeves. Her ice-white hair was in a thick plait pulled over her shoulder, bound at the bottom with a silk ribbon. She almost floated into the room, serene and confident. There were murmurs of recognition amongst the guests as she stood by the fire-place and pinged the edge of her glass with her fingernail, smiling as patiently as a diva waiting for the applause to stop. The chatter gradually fell silent and all eyes were upon her as she started to speak.

'When Professor Lambert emailed to invite me to Mike's retirement party, I booked my flight straight away. There is no way I would be where I am without him. Twenty years ago, he looked at a shy, nervous art student and saw potential. But he was tough on me. He didn't let me get away with anything. He made me redo my work over and over again. He made me throw away every preconception I had about art. He made me question myself and challenge myself and critique myself. And, most importantly, praise myself, when I got it right. He was . . .' She took in a deep breath and gave a dramatic pause, eyes wide. 'He was my guardian angel.'

There was a smattering of applause. By the door, Maggie and Cherry exchanged glances. Maggie put a discreet finger in her mouth and mimed vomiting. Cherry jabbed her with her elbow, her lips twitching.

Now based in LA, Anneka was famous for painting auras. She would sit with the subject to pick up their vibes, then go home to paint life-size likenesses of what she had seen. They were huge canvases painted in thick layers of white paint run through with streaks of colour, and her work graced endless celebrity walls.

Mike, who wasn't in the least airy-fairy, was neverthe-less very taken by the whole concept.

'It's bloody clever,' he said to Cherry when they saw her work in a copy of *Hello*. 'I taught her well.'

'You don't think it's a con? There's no way she can see their aura.'

Mike shrugged. 'It's her interpretation of the feeling she gets from them. It's perfectly valid.'

Cherry rolled her eyes.

'It's wrong, to make all that money out of people's gullibility.'

Mike just laughed. 'Those people are not victims. They've coughed up quite willingly.'

'The biggest crime,' said Cherry, 'is how awful the paintings are. I bet they don't take her more than half a day. If she even does them herself. She's probably got a studio full of art students knocking them out.'

'Nothing wrong with that either. It's a time-honoured process.'

Cherry hadn't wanted to get into an argument about Anneka Harding's artistic integrity so she'd dropped the subject.

Now, Professor Lambert stepped forward to stand at Anneka's side. The pair of them smiled over at Mike, who was standing by the wine cauldron looking mortified. Cherry could see his fists were clenching and unclenching, a sure sign of stress and discomfort. He hated surprises.

'I'm delighted that Anneka was able to join us today,' Professor Lambert said. 'I was even more delighted when I asked her if we could commission a painting to mark Mike's time with us. We knew it would be difficult, as there wouldn't be time for her to sit with him beforehand and it would have ruined the surprise. But she assured me that she remembered his aura.'

'I held it with me for many years,' said Anneka, pressing a closed hand to her heart.

'It is a testament to his teaching, and how he inspired so many,' Professor Lambert finished, as two men carried in a huge canvas wrapped in sheeting and propped it against the wall.

As the painting was unfurled there was a round of ecstatic applause. Anneka smiled as Mike looked at his aura – a chaotic swirl of deep navy blue and regal purple highlighted with gold. He seemed overwhelmed, totally at a loss for words. Eventually he turned to her with a little bow, his palms pressed together.

'I can't tell you how much that means,' he stammered. 'Thank you. Thank you all.'

'Oh my God,' thought Cherry. 'Where the hell are we going to put that?'

A few minutes later, Mike managed to recover his composure and called Cherry to his side.

'There is one person I couldn't have done all this without. When I first saw her, more years ago than either of us care to remember, riding bareback on a palomino, I knew she was my muse. She's been by my side all this time, cheering me on, supporting me, being the most wonderful partner-in-crime. My life and my career have both been down to Cherry's vision and Cherry's genius and it will be a huge privilege to spend my retirement with her because whatever she turns her hand to is always a huge success. And that includes this amazing party. I have not lifted a finger. This is all down to her. Thank you, my darling.'

A huge cheer rose up and Cherry blushed.

'I'm not taking all the credit,' she protested. 'It was Maggie, Rose and Gertie too.'

She beckoned the three of them over, and they stood in a row, arms around each other.

'I'm the luckiest man in the world, to have four generations of incredible women in my life,' agreed Mike. 'They are quite the lifeforce, I can tell you.'

3

The guests began drifting away afterwards as the sun began to float lazily down towards the gorge. Cherry was suddenly longing for everyone to leave. She felt tired, and her head throbbed from one too many glasses of pink wine. She'd run out of small talk, her legs were aching and she was itching to restore order. The splendour of the table had faded, the flowers seemed to be wilting in the late afternoon sun, and even the dinosaur balloon looked a little deflated.

Mike was nowhere to be seen. She could see Professor Lambert was making signs of leaving and he would want to say goodbye. Perhaps he was in his office? Cherry ran down the stairs and along the corridor to the back of the house and put her head round the door.

There he was, by the window. She was about to call to him when Anneka stepped into view. The two of them were gazing at each other with an intensity she could feel from fifteen feet away. She froze, her greeting stuck in her throat.

'Thank you,' Mike was saying, 'for the most incredible gift.'

'I have a confession,' said Anneka. 'I painted it a long, long time ago. So I could keep you with me. I needed you. My guardian angel.' She echoed the words in her speech.

Mike looked surprised. He nodded. Then smiled. He seemed at a loss for what to say. Moments passed. Eventually he pointed to Anneka's collarbone.

'You've got a sesame seed stuck to you . . .'

'Oh.' Anneka looked down. 'It must be from the sausage roll.' She raised a hand to remove it, but before she could do so, Mike reached out his forefinger and pressed it to her skin, lifting off the sesame seed. His finger hovered in the air between them for a moment, their eyes locked. And then Anneka bent her head and took his finger in her mouth, not leaving his gaze.

Cherry felt her stomach turn over.

Half of her wanted to storm in and confront the pair of them. The other wanted to run away and pretend she'd seen nothing. But in the end, she stood, transfixed, as Anneka put her other hand to the back of Mike's head and ran her fingers through his hair. The gesture was gentle and tender.

'I've never stopped thinking about you,' she murmured.

Mike stared at her, spellbound.

Twenty years ago, Cherry remembered Mike coming home and exclaiming over Anneka's talent. His exultation when she had got a first. How he'd watched her career from afar. Or perhaps not so far . . . She had mistaken it for the pride of a teacher in a promising student.

'Come to LA,' Anneka was saying, urgent.

'How can I?' Mike's gaze didn't leave hers.

'What else are you going to do with all that free time?' Anneka brushed his cheekbone with her thumb.

Cherry almost laughed. It was embarrassing, watching the pair of them. A forty-year-old woman toying with a seventy-year-old man. Distaste curdled with the wine in her stomach. She took in a deep breath, right down to her diaphragm, and put back her shoulders, summoning up courage from deep inside her. She stepped carefully away from the doorway and headed down the corridor. She didn't want them to know she had seen them. She needed time to gather her thoughts. She certainly didn't want drama. The thought of confronting the pair of them made her recoil. Protestations of innocence and denial would be humiliating and undignified. For all of them.

Don't cry, she told herself. Do Not Cry. This was not something to play out in public, in front of family and friends. Dignity, she reminded herself, was a tremendous weapon. The minute you lost that, you were sunk.

She headed back into the drawing room. Maggie was picking up glasses from the mantelpiece and side tables; the table was cleared of dirty plates and the remaining food re-arranged neatly in case anyone was still peckish. The dogs trotted around happily hoovering up crumbs.

'Hey, Mum.' Maggie touched her on the elbow. 'Great job. It was perfect. A really lovely send-off for Dad. I know it meant a lot to him.'

Cherry managed a taut smile. 'It went well, didn't it?'

Maggie gestured over to the painting, leant up against the far wall. 'And that is quite the leaving present.'

She caught her mum's eye, wanting to share a laugh about it, but Cherry wasn't playing ball.

'Mmm.'

'Are you OK?' Maggie frowned.

'Yes – I think it's all caught up with me, that's all.'

'Go and sit down and I'll bring you a cup of tea.'

'That makes me feel ancient!'

'A glass of fizz then.'

'I'll grab some water.'

'Shall we get a takeaway later, all of us?'

'Why not.'

Cherry was glad Gertie thundered into the room at that moment. She was finding it hard to obfuscate. She bent down and opened her arms to the little girl. 'Darling! Have you had fun?'

She scooped her up and turned to see Mike coming back into the room. There was no sign of Anneka. He was smiling from ear to ear. Anyone looking at him might just think it was the smile of a grateful man who had spent the afternoon with his closest friends and colleagues. Not someone who'd just been invited to LA by a woman thirty years younger.

'Just the hardcore left,' he said to Cherry, who managed to nod, her voice stuck somewhere.

'I was just saying to Mum we should have a curry in the kitchen,' said Maggie.

'Poppadoms!' said Gertie, putting a fist in the air.

'Definitely.' Cherry smiled at her great granddaughter.

'Good idea,' said Mike, putting his hand in his pocket for his wallet. 'It's on me.' He pulled out a wad of twenties and handed them to Maggie. 'I better go and say goodbye to the Davenports.'

He moved over to the window, where a couple who owned a gallery in Bath were preparing to leave.

Cherry pulled Gertie a little closer. The little girl was wilting, her head falling onto Cherry's shoulder. Cherry felt like doing the same. She just wanted to collapse into bed and forget what she had seen, overwhelmed by the fact that now she would have to do something about it, and that the future wasn't going to be what she expected. She felt tears building up again, but swallowed them down. How long could she keep up her façade?

She felt a hand on her shoulder, and turned to see Anneka's smiling face.

'Cherry. What a wonderful party.' She reached out and caressed Gertie's curls as she spoke. Cherry had to stop herself from pulling Gertie away. 'Thank you so much. It meant a lot to me to be able to celebrate with you all. Mike was a huge influence on me. I wouldn't be where I was without his input.'

'So you said.' Cherry was ice-cool.

'I said to Mike, if you're ever in LA . . .'

'I very much doubt we will be.'

Anneka smiled gamely at the snub. 'Well, it's an open invitation.'

'Thank you.'

'And thank you for the painting,' Maggie interjected, glancing at her mother, surprised by her lack of manners. 'What a memento. A really wonderful way to mark his retirement.'

Anneka bowed her head. 'It was an honour. There was a time when he was my guiding light. I was very lost as a student. He set me on the path to success.'

'It's so generous of you to acknowledge it.' Maggie was ploughing on bravely in the face of her mother's froideur.

'Excuse me,' said Cherry. 'I need to get Gertie something to drink.'

She left the room, Gertie still in her arms. Maggie and Anneka looked at each other.

'I think today's been more emotional for Mum than Dad,' Maggie said. 'She's been planning this for weeks. And her life's going to be very different now he'll be at home.'

'Of course,' laughed Anneka. 'I expect he'll be quite a handful. There's nothing worse than a bored artist.'

She looked over at Mike but he was embroiled in conversation and didn't catch her eye.

Cherry plonked Gertie down in the kitchen and reached for a glass, filling it from the tap. She sipped at it, as much to quench her rage as her thirst. How dare that woman waltz in and speak to her as if she hadn't had Mike's finger in her mouth? As if she hadn't tried to lure him with her wide eyes and that breathless baby voice?

'Cherry?' Rose was standing in the doorway, looking concerned. 'Are you OK?'

Cherry looked over at her granddaughter. She couldn't tell her what she'd seen. She couldn't tell any of them. They all adored Mike. Was it her duty to ignore what she'd seen? To keep everyone else safe from the truth? Already she felt the burden weigh her down.

'I think I'm dehydrated. Too much running around and not enough water.'

Rose looked at her through narrowed eyes. It was hard to fool her. Rose was hyper-aware. She picked up on the tiniest clues. 'Really?'

Cherry smiled at her. 'It's the end of an era, that's all. The university has been our life for so long. We're entering the next phase . . .'

The final phase. They had both agreed it was their duty

to do as many exciting things as they could, while they could. The list had not included Anneka Harding.

'Hey.' Rose came over to give her a hug. 'It'll be great for you guys. You've got amazing plans.'

'Mmm.' Cherry nodded as enthusiastically as she could.

'You're an inspiration to me.' Rose squeezed her tight, and Cherry nestled into the comfort of her embrace. Beautiful, clever, upside-down Rose, who had dealt with the tragedy of her father's death these past four years in her own unique way.

'*You're* an inspiration,' said Cherry, and she meant it. She had nothing but admiration for Rose.

There was that lump in her throat again. Bloody Mike. How dare he put her in this situation, after everything they had been through? Surely he knew it was family that mattered? Surely he wasn't foolish or vain enough to think that Anneka Harding would bring him anything but a temporary thrill? She imagined him for a moment, whizzing around Hollywood Hills in a soft-top car with his sunglasses on, 'The Boys of Summer' blaring. Was that what he hankered after?

Later, Cherry lay in bed. She could see Mike in the bath-room. The en-suite door was open and he was staring at himself in the mirror. She recognised the ritual. Most people of their age gazed at their reflection, anxious for a glimpse of the person they still felt they were behind the lines and wrinkles – a glimmer of the youth and sparkle they'd once had.

Cherry tried very hard not to focus on the fear of fading looks. To concentrate instead on being a good person, and surrounding herself with beautiful things. Mike worried about it far more than she did. He was ferocious about his daily run, paranoid about losing his hair – she could see him now, running his fingers through it as if to measure how much he had lost since the last time he looked. He turned sideways and tucked in his abs. He needn't worry, she thought. He was in good nick.

But maybe not up to the scrutiny of Anneka. She felt her teeth grind together with the memory of what she'd seen. Why had Anneka moved in on him? Of course, he was an easy target – a vain but vulnerable man on the verge of retirement, about to lose his identity. Why had she done it?

Cherry knew the answer, of course. Because she could. Anneka was that kind of woman. Insecure, despite her beauty and success. She needed affirmation. She needed to know she was irresistible.

Mike snapped off the bathroom light and she shut her eyes. He slipped into bed beside her and she tensed. He reached out a hand to touch her thigh, patting it rather than stroking it. Affectionate rather than suggestive. Usually she wouldn't mind the latter in the least, but tonight – no way.

'You awake?' he whispered, and she gave a sleepy murmur. 'I just wanted to say thank you for today.'

She didn't answer straight away.

'It was all of us,' she said eventually. 'A joint effort.'

'No. You were the mastermind. You always are. I'd be nowhere without you, Cherry.'

It would have been a lovely thing for him to say, and would have mollified her, if he wasn't echoing Anneka's very words to him. Was it conscious or unconscious? And did he mean it?

There was truth in what he said, though. When his work went out of fashion in the late seventies, when punk arrived and wanted brasher graphic imagery, not the whimsical detail he slaved over, she had pushed him into academia and given him the confidence to retrain and use his experience to teach the next generation. Later, when he'd been teaching for a while, she'd seen the vacancy at the University of Avonminster, knew its reputation as a dynamic, innovative seat of learning. The thought of being near to Rushbrook again had been too much for her to resist and she'd gently drawn him away from London and taken them south-west. He had flourished and she had been nearer to the place which still had her heart.

What was the saying? Behind every successful man . . .

She didn't reply. Just reached out her own hand and patted his to acknowledge his gratitude, but at the same time make it clear she wasn't conscious enough to carry on the conversation. Hopefully he would get the hint.

He did. Five minutes later, his breath deepened to a borderline snore/snuffle. Cherry lay there in the dark and allowed the tears that had been welling up almost all afternoon to roll down her cheeks. It was bloody hard, crying without making a noise. The last thing she wanted was for Mike to wake up and ask what was the matter.

It was galling, after working so hard to give him the perfect send-off. She knew he was dreading retirement in some ways, and that he was uncertain about the future. Which was why she'd wanted today to be special. She might never have had a career of her own, but she could see why leaving the university was daunting and she had, as always, wanted to protect him.

Seeing Mike and Anneka together had rocked her to

the core. Normally someone who prided herself on having an answer for any situation, Cherry had no idea what to do. Ignoring what she'd seen meant living a lie and letting him get away with something inexcusable. Confronting him meant drama and ugliness and difficult choices.

After everything they'd all been through, this was so bloody unfair. If only she hadn't gone looking for him. Maybe she was overreacting. She tended to, when she was tired, and it had been a long, arduous day. Perhaps it was just a drunken moment of flirtation, best overlooked.

Go to sleep, Cherry told herself, wiping away the last of her tears. Answers often came to her while she was sleeping; her unconscious scrabbling away and unknotting the tangles that life threw up. The morning might bring clarity. The morning might tell her she was worrying about nothing.

Tomorrow, she would go to Rushbrook. Rushbrook would give her a different perspective. Rushbrook would give her the answer, she felt sure.

4

'Skin a rabbit!'

Rose wasn't quite sure the expression was appropriate for a three-year-old in these days of squeamishness, but it was the one her great-grandmother Catherine had used when Rose was tiny and was getting her ready for bed. And that was how people lived on, wasn't it? By you carrying on their traditions and sayings and little ways. So she would carry on using it, in Catherine's memory.

And Gertie didn't seem to mind. Her arms shot up in the air and Rose peeled off her pyjamas and got her dressed in a stripy long-sleeved t-shirt and needlecord pinafore dress. She had one eye on the clock. They were running late this morning after yesterday's celebrations, and Rose hated having to rush, as it meant she wouldn't have time to go through her mental checklist properly. The ritual would dictate how she felt for the rest of the day. If it was skimped, she would be jumpy, her mind worrying at the details she might have missed. Though of course, nothing dreadful would happen if any of it *was* missed. She had to remind herself of that. Constantly. If Gertie's lunch box was packed in the wrong order, nothing dreadful would happen. If the tyres on her bicycle weren't pumped up in the right order, nothing dreadful would happen.

She had worked so hard at getting on top of her anxiety, but sometimes things crept up on her. She wasn't sure why it had come to the surface today, but she thought perhaps the stress of the party had triggered it. For the party marked a change, and Rose hated change. She liked everything to stay the same, even though her logical brain told her that wasn't how life worked.

She tried to do something new every week, just to get used to new ideas, new people, new surroundings. Yesterday, she had forced herself to speak to three guests she had never met, and had actually enjoyed herself. She'd come home feeling triumphant, but today she was tired and her brain was tetchy. Niggly. She reminded herself to eat properly before they left the house. She didn't get hangry, but she did get what she called hanxious, if she was running on empty.

Of course, the trauma of her dad's death was at the root of it. Before Frank had died, Rose had been quietly re-doubtable, unphased by change or new things. But losing him, aged seventeen, had made her lose her confidence, made her anxious and wary. She had almost got on top of her neurosis, but the recent loss of her great-grandmother had sent her into a spiral. That hadn't been such a shock or tragedy, or even unexpected, for she was well over ninety, but Rose and Catherine had been very close and she missed her.

And, she reminded herself this morning – for finding the triggers always helped her deal with the ensuing spin-out – today was the day Wisteria House was being handed over to its new owners. That must be why she was on edge. It had been such an important part of Rose's life. She knew every nook and cranny, how the light fell in each room, the creak of the staircase, the whir of the grandfather clock. And the garden – she could go round it blindfold and tell where she was just with her sense of smell. The sharp musk of the greenhouse, the dreamy sweetness of the rose beds, the richness of the compost heap. She would never breathe them in again.

It was OK, she told herself. She had taken everything she had learned from Catherine and was putting it to good use. She had her family, tight around her. She was rebuilding herself, gradually. Two A level retakes down last year, and the third about to be finished in the next fortnight. Getting herself match-fit for when Gertie started school at Mountville Primary in September. That thought alone made her tummy turn over several times.

It was Maggie who had gently suggested that Gertie should start nursery in preparation.

'I'm not so sure it's good for her to be constantly surrounded by people who adore her. She needs to learn to share and play by other people's rules and fight her own corner. It would do her good, Rose. And you. You need some time to yourself to do your own thing. You are the most wonderful mother, but you are more than just Gertie's mum. It's not a crime to allow yourself some space.'

Rose knew there was a lot of subtext in Maggie's words. That her relationship with Gertie was possibly a little too intense. Did Maggie think Gertie was spoilt? Overindulged? They all worked very hard not to ruin her, but Gertie was definitely confident that she was adored, and could twist them all around her little finger – Rose and Maggie and Cherry and Mike – if she put her mind to it.

So Maggie had paid for Gertie to go to nursery three days a week and Rose had time to herself. She was putting it to good use, revising for her Psychology A level retake, and also volunteering once a week. But September loomed, for she knew once Gertie was at school she had to step up and become a contributing member of society and get a Proper Job. She couldn't live at home with her mother for ever.

'Come on, darling. Get your helmet and your lunch box.'

Gertie jumped up, putting her banana skin in the compost bin as she had been taught, and gathered her stuff together. Rose shimmied into her backpack and found her keys. Maggie had already left the house. She would lock the door, then give herself a code word to remind herself that she had done it so she wouldn't cycle to the end of the road and have to turn back to check.

'Rhubarb,' she said as she turned the key. It was rhubarb season. Soon she'd be picking the claret-coloured stalks, breathing in the sharpness.

'Rhubarb!' echoed Gertie, who knew the drill, and they climbed on board Rose's bike and set off into the morning sun.

An hour later, Rose was on her knees, digging her fingers into the earth, feeling for the first of the radishes. She could hear the roar of the morning traffic not so very far away from her, for the raised bed she was rummaging in was on the edge of an industrial estate on the outskirts of Avonminster. Once a week she came here to harvest

33

what had been planted then cook up a storm at the Soul Bowl.

The Soul Bowl was funded by a local entrepreneur. It was Aaron's way of paying back society for his success. He'd made a small fortune selling funky sports gear online and had built a kitchen and dining room next to his warehouse. Anyone who wanted lunch could go there, no questions asked. He knew what it was like to go hungry. He'd lost his way in his teens, done things he wasn't proud of, but he'd turned himself around and now it was time to pay it back. He was there, every day, chatting to everyone, eating with them, noticing if anyone was subdued or looked out of sorts, ready with advice. He could always spot the signs of someone in trouble.

Rose had no qualms about giving up her time to garden and cook for him, and it was good for her to be pushed out of her comfort zone and talk to people. What she had been through gave her a natural empathy, for she knew that life could knock you off your feet out of the blue, and that you weren't a bad person for not coping.

She eyed the rest of her haul: lettuce, Swiss chard, carrots and a few fresh peas. And rhubarb, of course, for she had known it would be ready and that rhubarb and custard would be on the menu.

Had she locked the door? She paused for a moment in her work and reminded herself that her code word was supposed to reassure her, not trigger her. Of course she'd locked the door. Of course she had. Of course she had. Of course she had. She picked up her trug, trying to silence the voices in her head, and headed into the Soul Bowl.

In the tiny kitchen adjoining the dining area, she washed all the mud off her hands. Then she began to assess what she might cook, looking in the cupboards and the fridge for the rest of the food that had been donated. A gardener's pie, she thought. There were masses of sweet potatoes she could mash for the topping. Onions, carrots, celery, leeks and parsnips for the bottom. Some of the clients would moan there was no meat, but they always scraped their plates clean. It was part of the ritual – the teasing banter and pretending to complain. She knew they were grateful. And she made sure that what she gave them was as delicious as it could be. Plenty of butter in the mash. Plenty of cheese on the top.

She gave Aaron a high five as he walked in.

'Hey, Rosalita! What's cooking?'

He had the lean physique of the triathlete he was, and was dressed in an orange hoodie with Smashed It written over the back and tight low-slung track pants.

'Gardener's pie,' she told him. 'And maybe mac'n' cheese with some Swiss chard.'

'Some what now?'

'Posh cabbage,' grinned Rose, knowing full well that Aaron knew what it was.

Sometimes, she looked at Aaron and felt something she shouldn't. Though really, who wouldn't? He was successful, kind, funny and pretty damn gorgeous. He wore his wealth lightly. He cycled to work, never flaunting the electric BMW she knew he kept in the garage at the bottom of his apartment block. He never forgot his origins. Went back to his mum for tea several times a week. Hung out with his old mates. She knew he lent money too. To his friends with a band, to record a demo. To his cousin, to start up a food truck selling Jamaican curry goat and rice and peas in different locations around the city. No interest, and no time limit on the repayment.

And something in his spirit reminded her of her dad, which was funny, because they couldn't be less alike. Aaron, young, black, street-smart and achingly cool; Frank, white, middle-aged and a bit of a geek, though they both loved music. Frank hadn't been wealthy like Aaron, but he'd been incredibly generous with what he did have, and with his time. He'd nurtured people and given them confidence. She missed that about him. The way he understood people and how to get the best out of them. Aaron did that too. He made you want to please him.

She set to work in the kitchen. It was simple, but kitted out with everything needed to cater for large numbers: a fridge freezer, a cooker, a double sink and a dishwasher that cleaned everything in five minutes. And plenty of pots and pans and baking trays. She laid out the vegetables then pulled everything out of the fridge and cupboards that she needed: butter, milk, a big bag of grated cheese, pasta... There was enough today to give them a choice, which made her happy.

Five minutes later she was busy peeling the sweet potatoes and dicing the veg for the filling. Aaron flipped on the sound system and some upbeat sixties reggae filled the room. She couldn't help smiling, moving to the beat. By midday, the gardener's pie and the macaroni cheese were in the oven browning. She grabbed a cup of tea and went out into the dining room where the guests were gathering. There were usually about twenty. Half of them were regulars, the rest were people who turned up occasionally and there were always a few she didn't recognise at all.

She moved amongst them, greeting the familiar faces, giving a fist bump or a high five or a pat on the shoulder. She made a point of talking to anyone who looked awkward or shy or unsure. Even though Aaron worked hard to make sure there was no stigma attached to coming to the Soul Bowl, people were sometimes ashamed. The first time they came, at any rate. They were soon put at their ease.

The rule was everyone had to sit at the table. 'Eating together is a really big part of being human,' Aaron said. 'And I want this to feel like family.' Some ate and left as quickly as they could; others lingered, eager for company and chat, and they were never hurried. They were mostly men, but the ages varied. Some were barely out of school; others were clearly of pension age. They were all polite. All grateful. They responded to kindness.

And they all had different reasons for being there. Some were living rough and had been for a while. Others had fallen on hard times and were hoping to get back on their feet. A few were simply lonely, usually the older ones. It was clear that substance abuse was rife, though no one was allowed in if they were visibly drunk or using. Many struggled with their mental health. Sometimes Rose felt overwhelmed by the issues, and didn't know where to start helping.

'You're doing what you can,' Aaron told her when she voiced this one day. 'That's what's important.'

Rose wasn't always convinced that her mac 'n' cheese was going to change anyone's life, but she did her best to integrate and chat over lunch.

Today she was next to Gaz. He was a regular, and the

two of them had bonded over the nineties music he was a fan of. He was impressed with her knowledge.

'How do you know so much about the Stone Roses?'

'My dad,' she explained. 'I've got all his playlists. Seventies, eighties, nineties . . . We talked about music all the time.'

'The nineties were the best,' Gaz told her, though they hadn't done him any favours. He was a drinker, she knew, because he'd been very open about his problem. He'd also had drug problems in the past.

'It was easier to kick the drugs,' he said. 'The booze is the tricky one. It's everywhere.' He gave her a lopsided smile. He had light blue eyes and dark eyebrows, freckles that made him seem younger than his years – about forty, Rose reckoned – and a full mouth. He looked thinner than usual, his face a little pinched, his cheekbones sharp. 'But with the booze, you know . . . Sometimes you think *I'll just have a can, take the edge off.* And before you know it, you're all over the place.' His face clouded over. 'I can't handle it. And I know I can't. So why do I do it? Shell's kicked me out again.'

'Where are you sleeping?'

'Mate's sofa. But I can't kip there for ever.' He picked up his fork and Rose could see his hand was shaking. Was it from last night's excess or because he needed another drink? He saw her looking. 'I always shake,' he said. 'I've done too much. Too much partying.'

He put his fork down again. He'd barely eaten anything.

'Aren't you going to finish your food? Not eating makes me hanxious. You know, hungry and anxious.'

'I don't feel too good,' he admitted. 'It's nice, though. Everyone likes your cooking best.'

She laughed at that, and was touched by his compliment. She didn't feel she could push him to finish. He was looking down at the table, shaking even more. As if he'd got a chill or a fever.

'Where are you staying tonight?' She was worried about him ending up on the street.

'Aaron says I can use the pod.'

Aaron had built a pod in the car park for emergency shelter. You could only stay there one night, then you had to wait another week before you could come back. But it was dry and warm, with a toilet and a basin.

'Cool. Do you want to take some food away with you? I've got some bread. I can make you some cheese sandwiches?'

He looked puzzled, as if he was wondering why she could be bothered with him. Even though he was much older than she was, she felt a strong need to look out for him.

'It's my daughter's birthday today,' he said.

'Oh,' said Rose. 'That's nice . . . isn't it?'

Gaz had come to fatherhood relatively late. His girlfriend, Shell, had talked him into having a baby, against his better judgement. Gaz was more aware of his problems than anyone. Shell had been over-optimistic and had misjudged his ability to lead a quieter life and be a responsible adult. There was no doubt he loved his daughter, but his demons were more than he could manage. Now, he was trapped in a cycle of being on the straight and narrow, falling off the wagon and being kicked out of the house by an exasperated Shell.

His face was bleak. 'I haven't even got the cash to get her something. What kind of a useless dad is that?'

Rose looked down at the table. It was one of Aaron's strictest rules, for the staff not to give out any money. It was too easy to be taken in by a sob story, and the cash could then be misused.

'She wants a plushy unicorn. It's only twenty quid but I don't have it. I'm supposed to be seeing her later but how can I turn up with nothing?' His face twisted, and Rose realised he was going to cry. 'Why am I such a loser? Why can't I get it together? I love them both so much and I let them down. Every time.'

'You can get help. You know that. Talk to Aaron.'

Gaz's eyes flickered over to Aaron, joshing in the corner with a cluster of younger lads who clearly looked up to him. Rose could see him thinking that Aaron was everything he was not. He crumpled in front of her, his head drooping.

'I guess this is rock bottom. Not even having the money to get your daughter a birthday present.'

Rose thought of Gertie, and her bed at home, smothered in more cuddly toys than any child needed. She looked over at Aaron, hearing his warning words in her head. And she looked at Gaz and saw the face of a man humiliated by his own weakness.

'I'm not supposed to give you money,' she said in a low voice. 'But come and get some food off me in the kitchen before you leave.'

Gaz looked mortified she might think he was begging. 'That's not what I meant.' He looked down at his lap. His fingers were twisting round each other. He was shaking more than ever. 'I don't want to get you in trouble.'

What would her dad do? Rose wondered. She thought Frank would probably give Gaz the benefit of the doubt. It was a risk. Her head said no, but her heart shouted louder. Twenty quid for a plush unicorn. How could that hurt?

'No one will know,' she said. 'No one will find out.'

5

An hour's swim at the Lido usually cleared Cherry's head and focused her. But today the water did nothing to wash away her anxiety. She powered up and down, doing sixty lengths, then dried herself, got dressed again, and jumped back in the car. Now she was heading out of Avonminster, over the suspension bridge, compass pointing to the south-west.

She had crept out of bed at six thirty, sunlight streaming through the slats on the white wooden venetian blinds as she pulled on sweatpants and a t-shirt, tied up her hair and slipped on her sneakers. It wasn't unusual for her to leave the house before Mike surfaced – she liked to get to the Lido and get her swim done as early as she could – but she was particularly careful not to wake him this morning. He was face down in his pillow, dead to the world.

Downstairs, there'd been no evidence that nearly a hundred people had partied here the day before, except for the rows of shining glasses waiting to be put back in their boxes now they were dry, and the congratulatory cards lined up on the island. Cherry had taken the tablecloths and napkins out of the washing machine and soon they were whirling round the dryer.

In the drawing room, Mike's guardian angel was propped up against the wall. Cherry looked at it in distaste, tempted to put a foot right through the canvas. Or to take the whole thing up to the suspension bridge and drop it over the edge. How satisfying it would be, to watch it drop down into the water below and watch Anneka's handiwork dissolve in the river, the colours floating away downstream.

She remembered her promise to herself. To be serene. And dignified. She grabbed her bag and headed for the door, anxious to be gone before Mike came down the stairs and began to exclaim about what a wonderful day it had been. She needed a plan before she saw him again.

Now she was whizzing down the M5, sliding down through the Mendips to her childhood home, deep in the heart of Somerset. Once, she had been eager to escape the tiny, sleepy village where you couldn't do anything without everyone knowing, especially if you were the local doctor's daughter. Now, the very air seemed to whisper her name as she drove through the small market town of Honisham, passing the landmarks of her youth. The sprawling secondary school was still there – she hadn't got into the grammar school, and could still feel her disappointment the day the results had been announced. Her mother had comforted her. 'Not everyone is academic, darling. You will flourish, whatever you do. The important thing is to take any opportunities that come your way. And follow your heart. You have a big heart, Cherry. It will serve you well.'

Cherry took some solace from her mother's words,

and in the end she hadn't much cared about failing her eleven-plus, as long as she could carry on helping to muck out the fat brown ponies at the local riding stables every weekend. She couldn't see beyond the joy of a day spent grooming, eating a ham sandwich and a Club biscuit sitting on the fence of the ménage, turning them out into the field at the end of the afternoon.

Of course, by fourteen, the appeal of their soft muzzles and gleaming flanks came second – the secondary modern had something much more exciting to offer. Something that wouldn't have been available at the girls-only grammar. Skinny-hipped, foul-mouthed, warm-handed, the boys of Honisham woke something inside her. They were as hot and weak as the coffee at the Golden Egg where they congregated.

She smiled at the memory. More than fifty years later, the town hadn't changed a great deal. Even Boots was where it always had been. She'd bought her first lipstick there: a pale frosted pink that had tasted chemically sweet and made her lips look even more bee-stung. Everything had changed the summer she started wearing it. Everyone stared at Cherry Nicholson, some with disapproval, some envy, and some naked lust.

Less than two miles further on, she left the main road and was plunged deep into countryside, the lanes becoming more and more narrow until she reached the black-and-white sign announcing Rushbrook.

May suited Rushbrook. The verges were thick with cow parsley, the apple orchards laced with pink and white apple blossom, the air thick with honeyed pollen. The light was still soft, not yet the harsher glare of high summer, and the grass and the trees and the bushes rustled in a hesitant breeze which came and went like a deferential housemaid. Small cottages in colourful gardens eventually gave way to a cluster of larger houses reigned over by a church spire. The heart of the village. And in that heart, Wisteria House.

It was her last chance to say goodbye, and to do the idiot check, making sure there wasn't a diamond ring stuck in a piece of soap in the downstairs loo, even though she knew there wasn't. She and her brother Toby had done the final clean three weeks ago, after months of clearing, making sure every surface shone and every window gleamed. But today she would lock the front door for the very last time. The keys had been handed over to the estate agent ready to pass on to the new owners, except the one she had kept. The key she had had since childhood. The one she had used to let herself in when she came back from school or the stables, with the frayed bit of royal blue satin ribbon tied around the bow. The lock had never been changed. No doubt it would be when the new owners took possession, but that wasn't until midday today.

She had to see inside one last time.

Cherry drove in through the stone pillars that marked the drive to the side of the house. The 'For Sale' sign was still by the wrought-iron front gate, 'Sold Subject to Contract' emblazoned across it. The Bannisters, a couple from London, were buying it; the lure of the nearby train station in Honisham, with a fast train to Paddington, had sealed the deal.

Set slightly back from the road, Wisteria House was square and solid and reassuring, the perfect home for the village doctor. The pale purple blooms that gave the house its name were at their very best. She could smell them as soon as she opened the car door, remembering the scent drifting up to her open bedroom window each spring, heralding summer.

She made her way along the path that led to the front door. It was flanked on either side by drifts of lavender mixed with red and white tulips. Later in summer there would be delphiniums and foxgloves and a carpet of erigeron; rambling roses and then statement dahlias in dark red and purple and orange. She came to a standstill before the front door. She remembered hugging her brother, and the two of them saying goodbye to the house.

It had been therapeutic, going through everything with Toby over the past few months. He had come down from York as often as he could to help her clear the house. They had shared so many memories, and made their peace with each other, all the little misunderstandings of youth cleared up, most of which had made them laugh. He'd finally admitted to scratching her Jefferson Airplane LP, even though he had sworn blind he hadn't been near it at the time. Who else could it have been? She'd admitted to eating the last slice of his birthday cake that he had been saving, starving when she'd come back from mucking out and unable to resist the chocolate icing studded with Smarties that her mum had laid out in the shape of a T. She smiled at the memory. That cake had seemed so elaborate then. Cherry remembered Gertie's most recent birthday cake: it had a tube of Smarties hovering over it, spilling its contents over the top and sides. An anti-gravity cake. Now everything had to be startlingly original, jaw-dropping and Instagrammable. Her heart ached for simplicity and innocent times. And for her mum's embrace.

The day they had cleared the very last item from the house and declared the job done, she and Toby had supper together at The Swan, the local pub tucked into a bend in the river just up the road.

'You know, the thing with Mum was that she was clever,' Toby told her, spearing a chip with his fork. 'Cleverer than Dad, I sometimes think. But she didn't have the opportunity to use it. Fifty years later and she'd have been a rocket scientist. Do you think she was wasted, just being the doctor's wife?'

Catherine had been training to be a nurse when she met the dashing medical student, Nigel Nicholson, just before the war.

'No,' said Cherry, emphatic. 'She did a lot for this village and the people in it. Just because she didn't have a career didn't mean she didn't matter.'

'Oh, I didn't mean that!' said Toby hastily. 'I just can't help wondering what she would have done if she'd been born in a different time.'

'She was happy,' said Cherry. 'And she made other people happy. Isn't that what matters?'

'I miss her so much,' said Toby. 'Even though I was at the other end of the country, I always knew she was there.'

'I know,' said Cherry, hugging her big brother. 'We were so lucky to have her.'

Now, she took the precious key and unlocked the door, pushing it open for what would be the very last time.

6

'I'm so sorry, Maggie, but you know what they're like. The bloody Borgias. I'm the baby of the family. I have no say.'

Mario wasn't looking Maggie in the eye. He was drumming his thumb on the edge of the table he was sitting on. Behind him were towering shelves of tinned plum tomatoes, the very brand she'd recommended they should sell online all those years ago. He still had a hint of Rome in his accent, but it was possible it was just an affectation, as he'd moved to England when he was ten, when his grandfather had started the business. Nevertheless, the music in his voice made everything he said sound much more enticing than it was.

Even today's bad news.

'Spit it out, Mario.' Maggie crossed her arms, admiring his long jean-clad legs despite herself. He was *not* a baby, whatever he pretended. He was a forty-year-old, red-blooded male.

'OK, Maggie. Here's the thing. They're going with a new PR company. They offered us a great deal. Two years at nearly half what you're charging. I couldn't persuade the others to stay with you.'

He shrugged as if to say *what can I do.*

Maggie frowned. The saving wouldn't even cover his sister's fillers.

'At least tell me who have you gone with. Someone out of town? Not someone from London. No London company could charge so little.'

He wouldn't answer.

'Mario. Come on. You owe me that at least.'

'The company name is RedHotStoneCold.'

Maggie shook her head. 'I've never heard of them. I'll google them, I guess, if you won't tell me who's behind it.'

Mario cleared his throat. 'Stone,' he said. 'Stone is the clue.'

Maggie felt a cold chill. 'No. You've got to be kidding me. Zara?'

He gave a tiny nod. 'Apparently her pitch was great. She had a lot of good ideas. Sometimes a change is needed. A fresh eye. We are so grateful for everything you did.'

Maggie's mouth dropped open. If it wasn't for her, the business would be bankrupt by now. She had taken it from a scruffy backstreet importer selling dusty bags of pasta to a string of upmarket Italian destination delis rebranded as When in Rome, with a formidable online presence, four branches in Bath and Avonminster, with two more on the way. It was Mario's mother and older sister who had taken her on. And who had obviously now decided she had outlived her usefulness.

Mario would not be sitting there in his expensive dark blue linen shirt if Maggie hadn't helped them. They had been desperate by the time they had hired her; desperate to get some marketing advice for the business they had inherited, unable to decide whether to ditch it or revamp it. And now they were letting her go.

She couldn't decide whose betrayal was worse. Theirs or Zara's.

She looked again at Mario, who looked genuinely sorrowful. They had hit it off, the two of them, because he was more interested in the food than his sister or his mum, and that was Maggie's passion too. She had kept him at a distance, slightly, because there was no doubt he was a temptation, with his dark tangle of curls, his soulful eyes and his impeccable knitwear. She didn't trust either him or herself if they had gone for dinner, as he had suggested last Christmas. 'An office party for two,' he'd said, but with a self-deprecating twinkle that saved the invitation from being sleazy, even though she knew full well what dinner would lead to. But for a million different reasons she didn't want to – not least because sleeping with clients was a terrible idea.

The one advantage of widowhood was men did tend to take no for an answer. They were scared of grief, so if you flagged it, they backed off. She let her eyes fill with tears as she thanked him but said no, and Mario had taken her refusal with respect. He was Italian. He understood the nuance of death.

'They're insane,' she told him now. 'Zara has no idea. No. Idea. She was a loose cannon when she worked for me. I was endlessly covering up her mistakes. She's all fur coat and no knickers.'

'Eh?' Mario looked confused, struggling with the image.

Maggie rolled her eyes.

'It means everything looks great on the surface but there's nothing underneath. She is a spoilt little princess whose daddy has always picked up after her.'

Maggie knew she was laying it on a bit thick and exaggerating Zara's shortcomings, but she was hurt.

Zara's father would be behind this. Aiden Stone. The one friend of Frank's she'd never really taken to; the captain of the five-a-side football team he played with, and his financial adviser.

To be fair, if it wasn't for Aiden she'd be in a far worse situation. He was the one who had urged Frank to take out life insurance and critical illness cover. It had come as a surprise for Maggie to discover, after Frank's death, that their mortgage had been paid off. Aiden had been good to her, helping her with the nightmare of probate. She started to see what Frank had seen underneath the showy bluster, the electronic gates and the white Range Rover.

Nevertheless, Maggie was wary. Aiden cosseted his wife and daughter in a way that made her feel slightly nauseous. The two women were clones of each other, all swishy hair and eyelashes and tight clothing. That he loved them was apparent, but it was a curious, smothering, controlling kind of love. She knew, because he had told her, how much Zara had cost to conceive. A *lot*. Aiden put a price on everything and that made Maggie uncomfortable.

When Aiden had come to her a year ago and asked her to take Zara on as an assistant, Maggie felt obliged. An extra pair of hands wouldn't do any harm. It was an uphill struggle at first, as Zara had a terrible attention span, no telephone manner, awful time-keeping and kept wanting time off to have her nails done. Maggie had worked hard to get Zara up to speed and make her meticulous, punctual, polite and articulate. After nine months of on-the-job training, Zara was showing real promise. She had a talent for creative ideas, and was a supreme networker. Maggie found herself relying on her more and more and was proud of her protégé. Then out of the blue, Zara had handed in her notice, telling her she was going travelling. Her leaving had left Maggie under pressure, but she hadn't yet found time to replace Zara.

And now she understood the real reason for her departure.

'So that's it,' she said to Mario. 'All those years of us working together disappears just like that?' She pointed at all the goods stacked up on the shelves. 'I created your brand. I made your name something to be trusted and recognised. You were about to go bankrupt when you took me on.'

'Don't make me feel bad, Maggie. If it was up to me, you would be with us for life.'

'This is devastating for me. You're my biggest client.'

'We take up a lot of your time, though, no?' He was doing his best to help her see the upside.

'Yes. Because I work hard for the money you pay me.'

'You'll get new clients, Maggie. You're the best.'

'It's hard to believe that. When your oldest client dumps you.'

'It's not personal. It's saving us a lot of money. Our margins are super tight right now. We're having to make savings across the board.'

Maggie shut her eyes and breathed in.

'You know what they say. Buy cheap, buy twice. You know where I am if you need me.'

She turned on her heel, feeling Mario's eyes burning into her as she walked away. Traitor, she thought, wondering when loyalty had lost its value. She mustn't let it make her become jaundiced and jaded. She shut the door behind her with a defiant bang and headed out into the street.

Caffeine and calories, she thought. Caffeine and calories.

Maggie stalked along the street, weaving amongst the pedestrians making their way through the winding streets of Mountville, the most chichi district of Avonminster, with its artisanal coffee shops and wine merchants and bijoux dress shops. She was tempted to call in to Admiral House and rant to her mum. She knew it would probably be wiser to let off some steam than let her rancour fester. Cherry would calm her down and try and get her to be more objective about the situation. But Maggie couldn't bear it when people behaved badly. She was the first to call someone out if a shop assistant or waiter was mistreated. She couldn't help intervening. Her family cringed but her indignation would always win. She believed in instant justice, and didn't have the patience for karma. Of course, Zara and Aiden would get their just desserts in the end, but in the meantime it was Maggie who was suffering. And her company, Tine, named after the prong of a fork.

She knew exactly where she'd like to stick a fork. In Zara's pert, cellulite-free bottom.

She googled RedHotStoneCold and felt another surge of anger as a slick and minimalist website appeared on her phone. There were some stunning photographs and a selection of soundbites and a stylish Instagram feed. Promises of 'brand strategy', 'content curation' and 'bespoke launch events' were backed up by testimonials that Maggie guessed were from friends of Zara's well-connected father. There were photos of a luxury ski lodge in Zermatt that Maggie recognised from Zara's personal Instagram as well as a glitzy cocktail bar by the harbour that Maggie knew Zara frequented.

She was branding herself as a 'lifestyle' PR. She boasted of unlimited media contacts, and Maggie thought of all the times she'd pulled Zara into a conference to meet a journalist or magazine editor. She had no doubt that she had been through her contacts and copied them into her own address book.

She'd been paying much more attention than Maggie had given her credit for.

It was her own fault. She should have done a watertight contract to ensure Zara couldn't leave and set up on her own nearby. She hadn't thought it was necessary. Silly her, trusting someone.

It wasn't just the betrayal making her feel sick. It was panic. Business was tough these days. People were cutting back on PR to save money, and everyone with an iPhone ran their own Instagram account and thought that covered it. Getting the business was harder than actually doing the job. Maggie found she was spending more and more time pitching for accounts, trying to get her price right so she could undercut the competition but still make a profit. It was becoming harder and harder to persuade people they needed her marketing skills and expertise. She had a horrible feeling that it was because of her age. She was definitely the wrong side of forty. People seemed to value youth and glamour over experience these days. She instinctively knew Zara would be able to dazzle potential clients by looking the part. It was wildly unjust, but that's how it was.

Maggie had become more and more disenchanted of late. She needed to do an audit on her own business. Tine's profits were starting to dwindle yet she was working harder than ever. What advice would she give herself, if she was her own client? Take on more staff and delegate, probably – but then look what had happened when she'd taken on Zara. She didn't want to be a training ground for potential competitors. Should she specialise? In what, though? Coffee? Wine? High-end restaurants? That was a dangerous game, to limit yourself too much by being too niche. Conversely, maybe she should expand her horizons or her catchment?

Or maybe it was time for a complete change? Maybe Tine had run its course? Maybe she should retrain; transfer her skill set? Work for somebody else? That was enticing. The thought of letting someone else take the responsibility. Not that she was lazy. No one could accuse Maggie of being afraid of hard work.

She dodged into a café, ordered a latte and a piece of millionaire's shortbread and tucked herself into a table at the back, then pulled her notebook out of her bag.

She'd bought the first notebook the Christmas after Frank had died. She'd been overwhelmed with work, trying to catch up with all her clients and reassure them that she hadn't taken her eye off the ball. The festive season had been a godsend, and she'd found loads of opportunities to convince her clients she was still on it. But it had meant a lot of markets and pop-ups and parties and events. She felt obliged to attend them all, to get her face back out there. By Christmas Eve, she was exhausted and had done absolutely no shopping.

She'd wandered around Mountville looking for inspiration for presents, wondering how on earth they were going to get through it all without him. They were keeping everything as normal as they could: Mike and Cherry and Maggie and Rose were all heading down to Rushbrook for Christmas to spend it with Catherine, as they always did. They had all agreed that doing something completely different would feel alien and strange and wouldn't bring Frank back. They needed the familiarity of ritual and custom. The kindness of family and friends.

She found the notebook in her favourite stationery shop. It was covered in pale blue suede with smooth cream pages inside, the empty lines waiting for her to spill her thoughts. She hadn't known until she got it home, unwrapped it from the white tissue paper and set it on her desk, what she was going to use it for.

Now, after nearly five years, she was on her eighth notebook. Each time she bought a different colour, and they were lined up on a shelf in her bedroom. In her worst moments, when the insidious grey gloom crept in and smudged over the colours, or when the hard, black grief smacked into her and turned out her pilot light, she wrote to Frank. And somehow, he always gave her an answer. His words came back to her through hers. She felt like a medium, spelling out the truth that was being dictated from the other side.

And now, it was the first thing she picked up every morning. It was the best way to make sense of the mess inside her head without resorting to booze or medication or leaning too heavily on her friends or family. There was a point, Maggie thought, when you needed to move on from your tragedy, when you couldn't monopolise the conversation any more, when what had happened to you didn't set the tone. And rightly so. She didn't want to be defined by what had happened.

The notebook had become her crutch and her ally. Her connection to the man she had loved with all her heart. It was there for her, unconditionally, and she could say whatever she liked – her darkest thoughts, her biggest fears, spilling out at a furious rate, her handwriting erratic: sometimes neat and rounded, if she felt in control of what she was saying; sometimes spiky and illegible if what she was writing was difficult, as if the letters could mask the truth.

She wondered if it had gone on too long. She shouldn't still be writing to him after all this time. What was the cut-off point? When did writing to your dead husband turn from a healthy therapeutic exercise to a weird obsession?

It was private, and a secret, and she had never shared it with anyone else.

Her latte arrived. She took a sip, picked up her pen and started to write.

I know what you're going to say. That I've got a track record and Zara hasn't. That given time she'll come a cropper, and I've just got to be patient. That When in Rome will come back to me in due course, but in the meantime I've got to get out there.

But I'm bloody furious and I just want to sit down with

you and drink too much red wine and swear a lot and for you to take the absolute piss out of me and laugh at how cross I am.

A girl at the next table was staring at her. Was she talking to herself? Sometimes she spoke what she was writing to Frank out loud, when she was at home at the kitchen table. Oh, if only she was there now, with him. If only he could shake her up a martini in his vintage cocktail shaker and put on a record to help her forget. If only he could pull her to her feet and make her dance, and kiss her to stop her ranting.

But he was gone. For ever.

It was always the moment when she remembered this that she couldn't cope. How lucky she had been to have a man like him, and how hard it was to try and be all the things he had been for Rose and Gertie – to inject her life with his moral compass, his quirkiness, his sense of fun and his absolute reliability. She tried to make sure his spirit lived on in their lives. Sometimes it was getting the same takeaway he used to order on a Friday night. Sometimes it was taking them all to somewhere he had loved – like Weston-super-Mare. He'd had a curious fascination for Weston-super-Mare; for slot machines and donkeys and garish ice-creams.

Sometimes she would ask herself, '*What would Frank do?*' when she had a moral dilemma.

Today, she couldn't quite hear his voice. Normally it came through loud and clear, but she was straining to catch his answer. Was it because the Zara conundrum was a tough one, or was it because he was fading? Slipping away? Oh God, she thought. Please don't go.

'Are you OK?' The girl leaned over. 'Can I get you anything?'

Maggie put her hand to her face and realised it was wet with tears. She was crying. She'd had no idea. And now she wasn't sure if she could stop. She was crying more than she ever had – tears of frustration and fury and betrayal and hurt and exhaustion and indignation.

'I'm fine, thank you.' She grabbed a paper napkin and scrubbed at her eyes. Her mum. She needed her mother, right now. Some maternal advice. The cool, calm voice of reason. And a hug. But when she called Cherry, it went to voicemail. She couldn't leave a message. She didn't trust her voice.

7

Cherry's footsteps sounded loud and echoey on the floorboards in the hall. It was still strange seeing the house empty, denuded of all those achingly familiar pieces of furniture, the watercolours on the walls, the floral curtains hanging at the windows. But she nodded approvingly nevertheless. This was a handsome house. You didn't need much imagination at all to recognise its potential. Of course, to do it justice would be expensive – you would need the best tradesmen and materials. As it always did, her imagination ran wild when she thought about what she would do, given free rein.

She stopped herself because it was torture. Today was the day she had to let go. Her eyes flickered to the foot of the stairs, where the grandfather clock had once stood. Toby had taken it back up to York, where it would sit happily in his flat overlooking the Minster, and she felt happy that its tick would give him the comfort of home. Even at their age, losing a parent was unsettling; that person who had been there all of your life, a constant.

She looked at her watch. Less than two hours until the contracts were completed. The thought made her heartbeat falter. She would probably never step over this threshold again. Yet they were all still in here, their spirits, floating in the dust motes. She shut her eyes and breathed. Could she hear them? The laughter, the chatter, the footsteps? Toby's trumpet practice that never seemed to progress, though it must have done for now he was a stalwart in his local orchestra. If she breathed in, she could smell the rich brownness of a Sunday roast, the sweetness of an apple crumble summoning them from whatever they were doing.

She paused for a moment in the door of the drawing room. The fireplace was empty, every last speck of soot had been swept up. The windows stared blankly into the front garden. A single bulb hung from the light fitting in the centre of the room. Its green velvet lampshade was at the tip in Honisham somewhere, too faded to donate to a charity shop. She pictured a three-tiered glass chandelier in its place, the light dancing off its droplets. Or something more stark and modern. What would they choose, the Bannisters?

She shut the door and made her way to the kitchen at the very back of the house. This was her favourite room. Not just in this house, but possibly of all the houses she had ever called home. The thought of giving it up for good made her throat ache. In its current state, especially empty, it looked tired. The kitchen units were ancient, the quarry-tiled floor grimy. But the window over the chipped butler's sink looked out onto the garden, and the scent of the cherry blossom she'd been named after floated in and the whole room was flooded with light the colour of golden syrup.

There was nowhere to sit. Everything had been stripped.

They had taken the dropleaf Formica table to the tip, the black flowers on its pale blue surface so familiar. And the stools, and the circular rag rug that sat underneath them. It had been a huge wrench, but they had to go. There had been plenty of beautiful things for them to keep. You couldn't be sentimental about a stool with a cracked vinyl seat.

Cherry remembered her mum placing a large buff envelope on the table one afternoon a few years before. It had an old-fashioned metal fastening with green string wound around it.

'It's all in here,' said Catherine. 'Everything you need to know.'

'What do you mean?'

'In The Event. I've made it all as straightforward as possible.'

She patted the envelope and Cherry felt a lump in her throat as she looked at her mum's fingers. Mottled and bent, the rings on her left hand swinging loose, but unable to be pulled over her swollen knuckles. She was over ninety. Still sprightly and active and perspicacious, but ninety nevertheless.

'Oh,' said Cherry. 'You mean you've put your affairs in order.'

'So many people don't,' Catherine said with a sigh. 'And it's twice as hard to sort it out when someone's gone.'

'Well, that's very thoughtful.'

'It's just responsible. Anyway, as I said, it's all in here. My up-to-date will, a list of all my accounts and details of all my bills and insurance and council tax. And useful numbers, like the chimney sweep and the molecatcher. In case it takes a while for the house to sell. You must keep on top of things.'

'Of course.' Cherry had quailed then at the thought of the house being sold.

'And it's all straight down the middle between you and Toby.'

'Mum, you don't have to tell me this.'

'Yes, I do. It's fifty-fifty. I'm sure he'll come down and help you sort everything.'

'I'm sure.' Toby came as often as he could. And always at Christmas.

'I can see you don't want to talk about it.'

'No, I don't.'

'Well, no one wants to talk about death. But we have to face up to it. It would be odd if I was the first person in the world to be immortal.'

Cherry had to laugh. Her mother was always forthright.

'I suppose so.'

'I'll only mention it once. I'll leave it in my bureau in the drawing room. There's a copy with my solicitor in Honisham.'

'Great,' Cherry nodded.

Catherine snapped a rich tea biscuit in half and dunked half of it in her tea.

'I think you'll be pleasantly surprised. Your father invested in a lot of pharmaceutical companies. It was his interest, of course, being medical. They've all done rather well.'

'I don't think I'll be pleasantly surprised, Mum. I'll be devastated.'

'Well, it might take the edge off it,' Catherine laughed. The older you were, the less squeamish you were about death, it seemed. Cherry would have done anything to change the subject, but Catherine seemed to relish discussing the inevitable. 'Just promise me one thing.'

She leaned forward, looking serious, and put her hand over one of Cherry's.

'What?'

'This little nest egg is for you. I want you to spend it on something you want. It'll be your chance to put yourself first for once.'

'What do you mean, for once?' Cherry looked puzzled.

Catherine raised her eyebrows. 'You do a lot for everyone else. You might not think so, but you do.'

'Well, of course. It's called being a mum. And a grandmother. And a great-grandmother.' It wasn't like Catherine to be critical. Cherry found it unsettling.

'Of course, offspring have to take priority a lot of the time. But men? Not so much.'

'You mean Mike?'

Catherine put her head to one side and looked at Cherry thoughtfully.

'He would be nowhere without you. You know that, don't you?'

'What's brought this on?'

'I just want the money to go on something *you* want, that's all.' Her mother's tone brooked no argument. 'This absolutely isn't a criticism. You know I think the world of Mike. But I know how much you've done for him.'

Cherry corrected her. 'For us.'

'Please don't take it the wrong way. No one knows more than I do about being the power behind the throne.'

'Did you mind?'

'I have had a wonderful life. And your father needed me. You know things weren't easy for him.'

Cherry nodded. The war had cast a long shadow over so many. Most of his patients had no idea how Dr Nicholson had suffered from the trauma of what he had seen as a medical student during the Blitz.

'Anyway, I'm just making my wishes known.' Catherine patted the envelope. 'This is your nest egg, Cherry.'

'OK,' Cherry nodded. Agreeing was the quickest way to end this morbid conversation. She was puzzled, though, by her mother's insistence. Was it because of what she'd been through herself? Perhaps she felt she had missed out on opportunity, despite her loyalty to her husband. Or was old age making her more opinionated?

What would she say today, if she told her what she had seen at the party? Catherine wasn't judgemental, but she was very good at putting things into perspective.

'Men can be silly buggers,' she would probably say. 'And he's at a difficult age. Your father lost himself for a bit when he retired. Thank God for the fishing, that's all I can say.'

Nigel had spent hours and hours on the banks of the Rushbrook, courtesy of the Culbones who owned the fishing rights along the stretch that went through the village. In the evenings, he had sat tying flies, a fiddly intricate job that kept him absorbed for hours. Cherry and Toby had split the boxes between them as a keepsake.

As she imagined her mother's words, Cherry reminded herself that Mike was probably feeling vulnerable. And Anneka would have sensed that.

Women like Anneka played wide-eyed and innocent but were actually very predatory because they were needy themselves, and they often honed in on men who were feeling a little uncertain. They had a sixth sense for it. Imminent retirement had made Mike twitchy over the past few months. To no longer have that safety net, that cosy environment, the rhythm to life the university gave him, was probably daunting. Anneka had zoomed straight in on his Achilles heel, flattering him, enticing him.

She was excusing him, Cherry realised. But if she knew one thing, it was that people didn't always behave well in life. Generally speaking, they weren't all good or all bad, but a muddy mixture of both, and what they were going through and who they were mixing with and, quite often, how much they had drunk, had a bearing on their behaviour. And forgiveness was a very powerful tool.

She had another choice. She could phone the estate agent. Stop the sale. Tell Mike she wanted to live in Wisteria House. Being back in Rushbrook would feel so right. To be back in the place that was her home. She could go home tonight and pack up what she needed. She didn't want a scene. She would just take herself out of the picture while she got her head around what she had seen. She couldn't bear the thought of Mike's protestations of innocence. She couldn't even bear to tell him what she'd seen and heard. She certainly didn't, at the age of nearly seventy, want couples' counselling.

No, she thought. Going backwards wasn't the answer. And besides, she couldn't do it to the Bannisters. She didn't know them from Adam, but she imagined them piling the last of their belongings into their car. Perhaps a dog being settled into the boot. The doors being closed on the back of a removal lorry stuffed with their furniture.

How could she possibly be so cruel? It would be bad karma.

She walked out of the kitchen and into the hall, pausing at the foot of the stairs for a moment. Then she locked the door behind her and posted the key through the letterbox so she wouldn't be tempted to keep it. She heard it fall onto the doormat, and wiped away a tear with the heel of her hand.

Then she picked a cluster of tulips – white parrot tulips with a ragged raspberry red edge; her mother's favourite – from the path on the right and walked out of the gate along the road to the little church. The grass was still damp with morning dew as she walked through the churchyard amidst the graves, some of them so worn you couldn't even begin to make out the words carved into the grey stone. At the very back were the most recent. She averted her eyes, not wanting to see who else had shuffled off this mortal coil since she had last been here. She would know most of the names, even now. She hated seeing the wilting floral tributes, the words on the accompanying cards blurred from the rain. *Gone from us too soon . . .*

The stone she sought stood out: white marble with jet black letters deeply engraved. A bright new stone to replace the one put up when her father had died fifteen years ago.

IN LOVING MEMORY OF
NIGEL NICHOLSON
AND HIS WIFE
CATHERINE JANE NICHOLSON
TOGETHER AT LAST
RIP

It was simple and understated. They'd agreed that was the best, for where did you stop, once you started trying to say what you wanted to say?

She arranged the tulips in the square stone vase. Their brightness stood out against the white of the stone. It was over nine months since her mother had died. The pain was still visceral. Guilt and regret, the classic post-mortem cocktail. Longing. Overwhelming sorrow. Self-pity, too, though Cherry didn't allow herself to wallow in that very often. She was all too aware that worse things happened than the slipping away of a ninety-something parent. It was her duty to bear her loss without complaint. That didn't mean it didn't hurt.

She breathed in to stop more tears.

'I need you today, Mum,' she said. Were Catherine alive, she would definitely have driven down to see her. They would be sitting at the kitchen table in Wisteria House now, cups of tea at the ready, a packet of biscuits sliced open with a sharp knife.

She turned to see a small creature staring up at her, its bright eyes bulging with silent entreaty. Matilda. The vicar's pug. Left to him by one of his parishioners, the only person she would entrust her beloved companion to. The Reverend Matt had been alarmed by this bequest, for he had not thought himself a dog man. Nor had his husband, also called Matt.

Now the Matts, as they were fondly known, were devoted to the aptly-named Matilda, and she them, although she did have the habit of slipping out of the front door of the vicarage without them noticing.

'Matilda!' Here he came now, racing across the grave-yard in his dog collar and jeans. In his mid-forties, the

Reverend Matt carried the evidence of his husband's cooking prowess in front of him. He swept in front of Cherry and clipped Matilda's lead to her collar, then stood up with a smile, wiping the bead of sweat from his bald head.

'I'm so sorry if she disturbed you.' He indicated her parents' grave. 'This should be a time of quiet contemplation.'

Cherry just laughed. 'It's fine. The sale of Wisteria House goes through today. I'm just here to say goodbye.'

'We do miss your mother.' The Reverend Matt had done Catherine the most charming funeral service. Poignant, personal, uplifting, kind, and he had done the eulogy himself, for Catherine had taught him everything he now knew about gardening. He had come from an inner-city parish and been overwhelmed by the vicarage garden. She had taken him through it, shown him how to tend it, given him her own seedlings and cuttings. 'My almost green fingers are entirely down to her.'

He waggled them.

'I've just thought,' said Cherry. 'If there's anything you want from the garden, it's still mine for the next two hours. So go and help yourself.'

The Reverend's eyes lit up. 'I do not need telling twice,' he said. 'I'll go and fetch a trowel.' He looked at her thoughtfully. 'I don't suppose,' he mused, 'you would consider coming to do the church flowers? Even if it was just once a month? There simply isn't anyone with your mother's touch. And I know you have it.'

Cherry had done the flowers for Catherine's funeral, and remembered Matt's beady admiration. He'd managed to restrain from asking her this favour on the day.

'Well,' she said. 'I'm not sure of our plans, so I wouldn't want to commit. But perhaps I could do Christmas?'

'Would you?' Matt's eyes shone with appreciation. 'That would be a load off my mind. Honestly, the Easter flowers were a dog's dinner. I could have done better with my eyes shut.'

Cherry smiled as she watched him go. Village life, she thought. Everyone in and out of each other's pockets. It could drive you mad, of course, but there was something about it she yearned after. She supposed it was because you knew exactly who you were in a village. Your role within it. And what the rules were. In Avonminster, there were no rules. You could behave exactly as you liked. Whilst it was liberating, it meant a certain loss of identity that she now craved. Here, she was still Dr Nicholson's daughter. Catherine's daughter. She liked the feeling of belonging.

She stood up. She could see someone had arrived to give the grass in the churchyard its first cut, pulling on the starter string of the lawnmower. Eventually it burst into life, shattering the peace.

There was one last place she had to visit before she went home.

8

Cherry left the churchyard and wandered further down the lane, past a row of cottages that would once have housed farmworkers but were now well out of the financial reach of anyone who worked the land. Over the past few years, since Somerset had become the hot new must-live destination, they'd been snapped up, their window frames painted grey-green, the front gardens full of zinc planters and Sarah Raven bulb collections, shiny SUVs parked outside.

While Rushbrook's frontage was aspirational and magazine-perfect, the lanes leading off told a far more interesting story: the sprawling farms struggling to survive, the crescent of council houses, the less attractive houses that had been thrown up in the seventies. Yet as a village, it worked well. No one got above themselves and no one had a chip on their shoulder. Somehow, it just wasn't allowed. A lucky combination of personalities had allowed that to happen. The parish council was broad-minded and pro-active. The Matts, of course, had brought a new energy to the village and the church was fuller on a Sunday than it had been for years.

And then there was the 'big house': Rushbrook House, owned by the Culbone family, which had been dogged by tragedy over the years but was now coming back to life. The youngest generation had turned the land into a boutique glamping site, with safari lodges discreetly nestled along the riverbank. Of course people had grumbled at first, especially about the four-wheel drives seemingly without a reverse gear that cruised the lanes once the weather became fine, but actually, it had provided much-needed employment and a boost to the economy. Dash Culbone was scrupulous about only employing locals to look after the lodges and grounds.

Off the back of the glamping site, Lorraine, the owner of the village shop, had installed a deli counter with charcuterie and local cheese and sourdough bread in one half of the shop, while the other half stuck to baked beans, laundry tablets and lottery tickets.

And the village pub benefitted, of course, being within staggering distance.

It was this pub that Cherry was heading to now. The Swan. Behind a crescent-shaped swathe of grass, it was wide and low, painted cream, with a thatched roof, latticed windows and a stout oak front door. She could hear the rush of the River Rushbrook behind, and it lifted her.

You never step into the same river twice... The saying came back to her, something she'd read in a book that had stuck with her. Cherry knew that nothing in life stayed the same. That you shouldn't take anything for granted. But she had also learnt not to be afraid of change. And that when things did alter, you had to mould things to your best advantage. Embrace the change, and the opportunity it brought.

Only today, she didn't feel like embracing what life had thrown at her. She wanted to go back. To this time yesterday, when she was oblivious and content and looking forward to the future.

She looked up at the pub sign swaying in the breeze. The familiar picture of a single white swan gliding down a river had stayed the same as long as she could remember. Once, the pub had almost been her second home. Maurice the landlord and his wife and all the regulars had been her second family when she worked here. She had learned to add up the cost of several drinks in her head, how to handle unwelcome advances, how to treat everyone the same, from the lord of the manor to the local dustman.

The pub wasn't quite open yet but she knew Alan would be in there. She pushed open the door, and her heart sank, for in the few weeks since she'd last been in, she could feel the deterioration. It felt empty and neglected and sorry for itself. Everything needed a good wash or a good clean. The chalkboard had lines through most of the dishes. It smelled of old chip fat and stale beer. Despite being May, the air felt chilly. She struggled to recognise the vibrant, lively local it had been. No one would want to linger here for longer than necessary.

She peered through the gloom. There were no lights on at all. And then she saw him, with a mop and bucket, dabbing at the flagstones in the lounge bar. She watched him for a moment, looking for clues. The set of his shoulders told her everything, and she felt dread claw at her.

'Hey,' she said, and he turned.

'Oh,' he said. 'I wasn't expecting you.' He managed the weariest of smiles.

'No. It was a last-minute thing.' She leant forward to

73

kiss his cheek. 'This is a little thank you, for everything you did for Mum.' She pulled a soft package out of her bag and gave it to him.

'You didn't need to,' he said.

'But I wanted to. You were so kind. Such a support.'

Every Sunday that Cherry hadn't been able to go to Rushbrook to be with her mother, in the last couple of years when she had become more and more frail, Alan had plated up a roast and taken it up to Wisteria House. He'd stopped to talk to Catherine and reported back. The Reverend Matt had too, of course, but that was his job, to look after his parishioners. As the landlord of a busy pub, Alan had always found the time to go the extra mile, somehow. And Cherry felt she could never repay him.

He pushed the mop back into the depths of the murky water and ripped open the tissue. Inside was a blue silk cravat with yellow spots. He always wore one tucked into his jumper. The uniform of the country pub landlord.

'Perfect,' he said.

Silence hung between them. The elephant in the room could not be avoided any longer.

'How are things?' she said.

'Terrible.'

And she put her arms round him and squeezed him as hard as she could. They stood there for a moment, wordless, for there were no words, really. Eventually Cherry let go and stood back. She cupped his face in her hands, stroking his cheeks with her thumbs. He shut his eyes for a moment, enjoying the comfort.

His skin looked grey, she thought. The bags under his eyes were even more pronounced than the last time she'd seen him. And he seemed to have shrunk. The big cuddly bear-ness of him seemed to have deflated.

Darling Alan. Everyone's favourite landlord. The reason The Swan had once been the most popular pub for miles around. Until fate had intervened.

'I've decided to sell up,' he said to her. 'Marcus Draycott's made me a very fair offer. I'm going to accept it tomorrow. I can't keep it all going.'

'How on earth can you, with everything you've got going on?'

'I've tried the best I can. The bloody chef walked out on me last month. He's buggered off to The Feathers in Honisham. I tried to persuade Tabitha Melchior to come back but she's running the cider business now, at Dragonfly Farm, and everyone reckons she'll marry Dash Culbone. It's just a few locals here now. The odd farmer who comes in for a pint. And Clive, of course. He's keeping me going.'

Alan managed the ghost of a smile. Clive came into the pub at seven o'clock sharp every evening and had a pie and two glasses of Chateauneuf du Pape which Alan kept behind the bar for him. He allegedly made a small fortune trading stamps from a tiny shop in Honisham. Some said he was a money launderer. He was certainly an enigma.

'I'm so sorry,' sighed Cherry. It was so cruel.

'If I sell up, I can be her full-time carer. I don't want anyone else looking after her. I love her to bits, and it breaks my heart watching her. And at least if I sell now, we can set everything up how we want it, and maybe do a few trips before ...

He broke off and Cherry saw his chin quiver. 'Before she gets too bad,' he went on.

Cherry couldn't bear it. She could feel her heart breaking for him. Alan's wife Gillian had been diagnosed with bowel cancer three years ago. She'd dealt with her treatment with grace and dignity, and Alan had spent as much time with her as the pub allowed. She'd had the all-clear after six months. But just after Christmas, a follow-up scan revealed it had come back. The prognosis wasn't good.

Cherry was devastated for the pair of them. How were they supposed to negotiate the next few months? Summer was the busiest time of year for the pub. It wasn't surprising that Alan had decided to sell. Marcus Draycott had been badgering him for years, wanting to turn The Swan into luxury riverside retirement apartments.

She looked around the bar, its walls almost as familiar to her as those in Wisteria House. She couldn't bear the thought of Marcus Draycott ripping out its heart and soul. She could just imagine the little rabbit hutches he would construct inside its thick stone walls. Tiny units masquerading as luxury dwellings, milking the riverside setting, no doubt with an eye-watering management fee. She could see the brochure already: *a prestigious waterside development in the highly sought-after village of Rushbrook, boasting the ultimate in mod cons...* She shuddered at the thought.

How would the village manage without The Swan? Alongside the church and the pub, it was one of Rushbrook's vital organs. Taking it away would cause untold damage. This was where the villagers came to relax, drink, eat, gossip, celebrate; from the Culbones at the big house to the youngsters who came in on their eighteenth birthdays to buy their first legal pint. It was the kind of place you could come on your own and be sure of a welcome, a chat, a drink from someone without being judged, excluded or hit on.

'So how much are you selling it for? Roughly?'

He named a sum, and Cherry looked at him in astonishment. 'That little? Surely it's worth more than that?'

Alan shrugged. 'The business is worth nothing. I'm running at a loss. It's just the bricks and mortar really. It's a good deal more than anyone else would pay.'

'But it's a lovely pub. The right person could soon turn it round.'

'It's bloody hard work. You know what they say. How do you make a million running a pub? Start with two million.' He gave a weary smile. 'And look at it. It needs a major refurb. It's tired and old. People want more these days.'

Cherry looked around the familiar surroundings. Yes, it felt uncared for at the moment. But the bones of it were wonderful. The stone floor. The fish in glass cases, caught in the River Rushbrook over the last century. The thick walls. The huge inglenook fireplace. And she'd seen it at its best not all that long ago, brimming with joie de vivre, flames in the hearth, glasses full, the roar of chatter and laughter filling its walls. People could be lured back.

She suddenly felt that tingling feeling. The one she had when she found a house she wanted to buy. An endorphin rush accompanied by her imagination working overtime, visualising what she could do, the magic she could bring. The feeling had never let her down, and right now it was incredibly strong. She could almost hear the chatter of customers, laughter over the clink of glasses, the creak of the door as it opened to let someone else in along with the night air.

It was an addictive thrill. One she had never been able to resist.

'The boathouse,' she said. 'Does it go with it?'

There was a tiny little stone house at the bottom of the garden, perched on the riverbank. Alan and Gillian had moved out of the boathouse when she was first ill, to a smart new-build bungalow on the outskirts of Honisham.

'Yes. We were planning to tart it up and rent it out, but I haven't got round to it. Marcus can't wait to get his hands on it. I think he wants it for himself.'

Cherry felt a stab of jealousy. 'I'm just going for a wander outside,' she said. 'I'll be back in a minute.'

At the back of the pub, there were a few tired picnic tables, the beer-branded umbrellas down. There were cigarette ends stubbed out on the ground and weeds growing through the brick paving of the patio. She had to admit it didn't look very appealing. No wonder people weren't queueing up to eat and drink here. It had gone from being a jolly, bustling local to a sad, dreary non-entity in a terrifyingly short time. They'd come here after Catherine's funeral, and although it had been a sad occasion it had been an uplifting one. The church had been full, and everyone had been invited to join the family for tea at The Swan. Cherry remembered the bar heaving, silver trays of sausage rolls being passed around and Alan opening bottle after bottle of sparkling wine to toast the woman who had touched so many lives in Rushbrook, ever since she had arrived there as a young woman.

Cherry carried on walking through the garden. Beyond the seating area, the lawn swept down to the banks of the river. It ran, clear and true, bubbling over the mossy stones. A weeping willow trailed its branches on the far bank, and in the distance was a stone bridge. Everywhere bustled with wildlife. Voles, dragonflies, frogs, fat brown trout. Cherry remembered the flash of a kingfisher wing from her childhood. There were rumours of otters further upstream.

There had been a set of swings here when she was small. Her father would bring her down on a Sunday, before lunch, to buy himself a pint of bitter and her a small glass of lemonade. She remembered flying through the air, backwards and forwards, thinking if she let go of the chains she would be catapulted over the river and far away across the fields to the hills beyond.

And the ritual of Boxing Day, when the hunt had once gathered here. Familiar faces beaming with the fug of mulled wine and stirrup cups; gossip and chatter and laughter and season's greetings, everyone wrapped up warm in the sparkling December sunshine. That ritual belonged to another time, of course, but she could still remember the stamping of the horses' hooves and their curls of breath. It had been her job to groom and tack up the hirelings from the stables, and she recalled the scent of leather and hay as if it was yesterday.

And when she was older, and got her first job behind the bar, she remembered a local lad with rough hands and soft lips, kissing her in the corridor outside the loos, tasting of cider, his leather jacket creaking as he pulled her to him. Jim? Jack? She could feel the fire he'd lit inside her even now.

And of course, it was here she had first kissed Mike. She'd woken the next morning in her bedroom reliving the feeling, craving its sweetness, her body teeming with sensation and emotion and longing, none of which she quite understood. All she knew was she wanted – needed – more.

And how many times since then had she and Mike sat in this garden while Maggie was growing up, eating scampi and chips dipped into sachets of ketchup, or one of the roast dinners The Swan had once been known for. And in the months after her mother passed away, she'd been here often with Toby. A quick bowl of soup with crusty bread. Cauliflower cheese with crumbly bacon on top. Or one of the pies they'd been famous for. Chicken and leek was her favourite, the shiny pastry cracking open to reveal a creamy filling. Her mouth watered at the memory.

She wandered over to the little boathouse, fronted by a glade of apple trees, hovering over the river at the back. It was made of the same grey stone as the pub, and had been converted into an open-plan living area with bedrooms tucked into the roof. It was tired now. The pine cladding on the inside walls that had been fashionable at the time was overwhelmingly orange; the kitchen units were burgundy melamine, the sliding doors stuck on their runners. But like the pub, it just needed love and attention. And a bit of imagination. Its setting was idyllic, looking out over the bend in the river. She imagined waking here, hearing the water burbling past and the birdsong.

Cherry felt that warm tingle inside her again. A mixture of excitement and the prospect of taking a risk. Her fingers always itched to get started on a plan and work her magic. Visions of paint charts and fabric swatches floated through her head. Floorboard samples and catalogues for doorknobs.

She knew the money her mother had left was for her. Her nest egg. Catherine had said, 'Do something for you. *You*, not Mike or the girls. You've given them so much.'

The Swan had meaning for her. It had been part of her life for so long. She couldn't bear to think of it being sold off for development. The thought of bringing it back to its former glory, reinstating it as part of life in Rushbrook, the beating heart of the village, sent a thrill through her. She'd seen the pub thriving. The potential customers were all still there. They hadn't vanished. They had just gone elsewhere. They could be lured back.

It was just the challenge she needed. Something to throw herself into after the loss of her mum, something she could be proud of, and that would almost be a memorial to both of her parents. She estimated it would take her less than twelve months to turn the pub around. Once she was sure it was a viable proposition, she could sell it on. To the right buyer, of course. Marcus Draycott would never get his hands on it as long as she had anything to do with it.

She headed back inside. Alan was pulling clean glasses out of the dishwasher, putting them on the shelf, even if the expression on his face denoted what a pointless activity this was.

'I'd like to buy The Swan off you,' she said. 'I can't bear to see this turned into apartments. That's not what this village needs.'

He stood up, frowning. 'What?'

'I might need to ask your advice from time to time.

But I think I could do it. I've got Mum's nest egg. I think she'd approve. In fact, I think she'd insist.'

Alan looked completely flummoxed.

'Cherry. I can't think of a better person to be at the helm here, but it will rule your life. This pub is a demanding beast. And if you don't keep up, look what happens.'

He looked around at the gloomy interior, defeated.

'I've been thinking for a while,' Cherry admitted. 'How much I love Rushbrook. It means the world to me. I'd love to be back in the heart of this village. I wasn't sure how I was going to cope when we sold Wisteria House, but this is the perfect answer.'

'What about Mike?'

There was a brief pause. Cherry put her hand up and tossed back her hair in a gesture of defiance.

'Mike,' said Cherry, 'has got plenty of things to keep him busy.' She tried to shut out the image.

Alan frowned. 'But you two are ...' He crossed his fingers to indicate their closeness.

Cherry hesitated before revealing the truth.

'Something happened yesterday. It was only something small, but it shifted something in me.'

'Oh.' Alan peered at her. 'Are you OK?'

'Yes. I'm too old to take it personally or get upset. Twenty years ago, I might have reacted differently. But I'm nearly seventy. I'm not going to get hysterical.' She smiled.

'Well, I don't like the thought of that. You and Mike have always been solid.'

Cherry waved her hand.

'Oh, we'll be fine, I'm sure. It's just a blip. All marriages have blips, don't they? But I am going to put myself first for once. I'm going to do what I want. I want to do this for *me*.' She put her hands on Alan's shoulders. 'And I want to do it for you, too. So you and Gillian can go off and do the things you need to do.'

Alan cleared his throat. He wasn't sure he could speak. 'Look, go and think about it. It's a big responsibility. You can't just rock up on a Monday morning and buy a pub . . .'

'I bloody well can,' said Cherry. 'If there's one thing I've learned to trust in life, it's my gut. And this village needs The Swan.'

'I'm so ashamed I've let it go.'

'You mustn't feel ashamed.' Cherry couldn't bear the disconsolate look on Alan's face. 'Gillian had to come first. You haven't failed. You've done the best you can with the cards you've been dealt.'

'I'll miss it. This place has been my life for . . . what?' He tried to calculate. 'Twelve years since I took it over?'

'Don't worry – you're not getting away that easily. I'll have you on speed-dial as part of the deal.'

'There's a lot to do. You need to get a licence. You need to get a *chef*.' Alan looked at the mucky water in his bucket. 'And a cleaner.'

Cherry laughed. 'Don't worry. I've got a pair of rubber gloves. I'm not afraid of getting my hands dirty.'

'I know you're not.'

'If we shake on it now, I can take over straight away. Let's not waste any time.'

For there wasn't time. She knew that. They both knew that. Alan put out his big paw. As Cherry slid her hand into his grip, he squeezed it so tightly she almost cried out.

'I feel as if I can cope now. It was all too worrying. I felt as if I was letting the village down, selling to Marcus Draycott, but this is more than I could have hoped for...' He sank into a stool at the bar. 'I can book that cruise. Croatia. She wants to go to Croatia. I was terrified I wasn't going to be able to take her.'

Cherry looked around the room and didn't feel a moment's panic at what she had done. She could see it all so clearly. The room full to bursting as it once had been. Delicious smells wafting from the kitchen. The village with a heart again. The renowned pub quiz resurrected. Roaring fires. Flowers everywhere. Barbecues in the summer, carols at Christmas.

'I've always loved an impulse purchase,' she said. 'Because you make them with your heart and not your head. And I think this is my best one yet.'

9

Cherry walked back to the car at Wisteria House, feeling a bubble of hysteria rise up inside her. But it was a joyful bubble, not a panicky one. She had always been known as the queen of the impulse purchase, but usually she restricted it to kilim rugs or floor lamps. Buying a pub took it to the next level.

Although it hadn't been that impulsive. Like a lot of things done on impulse, there was a deep-rooted logic underneath. She had long fantasised about running The Swan. Every time she went in there, she imagined what she would do if it was hers. It was what she did whenever she went anywhere she liked, wondering how she would keep the good things while putting her own stamp on a place. And she and Maggie had often talked about buying a restaurant and running it between them. There had been a tiny little bar in Mountville they had come very close to buying a few years ago. They'd done all the projections, a business plan, talked to a couple of chefs Maggie knew and organised a business loan. But then Frank had died and of course that put a stop to their plans...

She wondered what Maggie would think of what she

had done. She wasn't going to call her yet, not until she'd spoken to Mike. But she hoped her daughter would be as excited as she was. She would need her help, after all. Maggie was brilliant at brand refreshing and getting the word out there. She would be able to help with finding a chef too. That was going to be key.

She looked at the clock. It was quarter to twelve. She dialled a number. As she waited to be put through, she looked up for a moment at Wisteria House, mellow in the midday sun. The end of an era. A long era, for her parents had bought it a few years after the end of the war, firstly as a weekend cottage to escape to from London, but then as a full-time home when her father had got a job at the practice in Honisham. It had been the perfect place to start a family. Cherry imagined the two of them hand in hand on the path, looking at their idyllic house in the quaint little Somerset village. Nigel and Catherine, the doctor and his pretty pink-cheeked wife, all ready to live the dream . . .

She sighed. At first, Cherry had wanted to buy her brother out and keep it as a weekend home just as it had been when her parents first bought it. But Mike thought she was mad.

'You can't have a weekend home less than an hour's drive away.'

'It'll be a project for me. It's got so much potential.'

'Aren't there more exciting ways we can spend the money? This is a real chance for us to do something new. Together.'

He wasn't being selfish or controlling, because that wasn't Mike's way. He was simply playing devil's advocate, and after they'd talked about other opportunities

– perhaps somewhere in the South of France, or a chic city apartment somewhere – she'd agreed with him that it was time to let go, because Wisteria was *her* home, full of her memories, not his, so she understood that it didn't mean so much to him. Maybe it was unhealthy to cling on to your past? And with his retirement, they would be spending more time together, so it should be a joint project.

But now, after the incident with Anneka, their relationship looked a little different, and it highlighted how important Rushbrook was to her. It was where they had spent every Christmas for as long as she could remember. And every year they decamped to Wisteria House for a week to help Catherine prepare for the summer fete. There were scones and cakes to make and seedlings to pot up from the greenhouse for her plant stall and raffle tickets to sell.

She did not want to let this part of her life go. Of that she was certain.

'Hi, Cherry,' said her solicitor as they were connected. 'Completion day! Congratulations. What can I do for you?'

Cherry knew this was going to be the litmus test: the first time she outlined to someone what she had done.

'Howard. I seem to have bought a pub. My old local, in Rushbrook. The Swan.'

'You've bought a pub?' Howard sounded incredulous.

'It was a bit of an impulse purchase. But you know me.'

'I certainly do.' Howard had done the conveyancing on every property they'd bought since their first tiny house in Kew. More than once he had queried the wisdom of the property she had found, and had to eat his words when she sold it at a profit. 'What are you going to do with it? Convert it?'

'Nope. I'm going to run it. I'm going to turn it round. It's on its knees at the moment but I know exactly what needs doing.'

'Cherry, this is not your usual venture.' Howard felt protective. 'Running a pub can be a fool's game unless you know what you're doing.'

'I know this pub inside out. I know the area and the potential customers. And as you know, I've got the money.' She looked at her watch. Ten to twelve. 'Well, I will have. In ten minutes.'

'This is very sudden. Even for you.'

'Yep,' said Cherry. 'But has my gut ever failed me?'

Howard had to admit it hadn't. So far.

'This is a different ball game though, Cherry.'

'I can do it. I know I can.'

She felt elated. When had she got so bad-ass?

The minute Alan had told her about Gillian, that's when. It didn't bear thinking about. If she could give them precious time together, it was worth it. She briefed Howard, making it clear she wanted the purchase to go through as quickly as possible.

As they talked, the minute hand crept towards midday. Wisteria House was no longer hers. She felt a momentary pang, but it was OK. She had made the most of her nest egg and put herself first, just as her mother had wanted.

She laughed as she saw the Reverend Matt scuttle out of the garden with a full basket. He raised his hand in greeting as he rushed past.

'I've got some lovely bits and pieces,' he told her

through the open car window. 'But best not be found grubbing about in the flower beds by the new owners.'

Cherry laughed. 'Well, I know Mum would be delighted you've got some cuttings.'

The Reverend nodded. 'I hope we'll see you again soon, Cherry. I feel as if you're a part of this village.'

She wondered if she should tell him what she had done, but decided not to just yet. She couldn't tell him before she told Mike.

'I'm sure you will,' she said, and started up the engine.

She drove back slowly past the pub. A thrill went through her at the sight of it, the thatch golden in the midday sun. A pair of wood pigeons high up in a tree cooed their approval, and the old sign swung back and forth gently in the breeze.

Rushbrook was her village. The Swan was her pub. This was her future.

10

The ingredients were all laid out on the island, in little glass bowls. Bird's eye chillies. Galangal. Lemongrass. Kaffir lime leaves. Shallots. Garlic. Turmeric. Bright reds and yellows and oranges, all ready to go into the wok. And standing by were coconut cream, fish sauce, palm sugar and a massive pile of raw king prawns. And a mound of jasmine rice.

Mike took the making of his Thai green curry very seriously. It was always their restorative meal after a late night or a strenuous weekend. Their recovery ritual. Everything was meticulously measured and would be carefully ground to a paste in his pestle and mortar. It was his own recipe, developed over the years with tweaks and adjustments to reach the exact blend of sweet, sour, bitter and spicy. Now he had perfected it, not a grain or a drop was altered. It was written in stone. Or rather, written in his artist's italics with a thick black pen on a sheet of paper. This was pinned to the back wall of the kitchen, which was covered from floor to ceiling in cork board, and where all their recipes hung, whether snipped out of newspapers and magazines, photocopied out of books, written out on the backs of envelopes or scrawled on a scrap of paper.

And amidst the recipes were Polaroids they'd taken whenever a particularly spectacular dish had been created: a rib of beef, a towering pavlova or a groaning cheese board. It was almost a diary of their life: the meals they cooked for family and friends, or sometimes just each other.

Until today, this kitchen had always made Cherry feel happy.

But today as she walked back in, it felt different, in the way that places do when something momentous has happened. It didn't feel as if she belonged here any more. She almost felt like an intruder, excluded from a plan that had been made without her, as she remembered what she had witnessed.

Mike looked up from dicing his chillies as she came in, and for a moment their eyes met and normality hung fragile in the air between them. She realised she had the power to keep that normality. She could forget what she had seen and heard. But she would be living a lie. She would be condoning Mike's behaviour. She would be compromising herself for the remainder of their life together.

'Hey!'

Mike reached out for a bottle of Riesling on the island and poured her a glass. She never had to ask. He was good at all that – very attentive. Or was he covering up for something with his attentiveness? No, she thought. This was usual behaviour for Mike, not guilt. It was funny, once someone had transgressed, how you started judging them on everything.

She sipped her wine, enjoying the cold hint of petrol on her tongue. A wine buyer, she thought – she'd need a decent wine buyer for The Swan. She wanted a great list: adventurous but not overpriced. Again, Maggie would know someone.

Mike tipped his chillies into a big mixing bowl and reached for the lemongrass. He looked over at her.

'So? What's going on?' He gave a light laugh. 'What have you been up to? I was about to send out a search party.'

She took another gulp of wine before speaking.

'I had a bit of a moment today. A light bulb moment, as they say. It made me realise something.' She tried to find the right words. 'I want to come first for once.'

Mike chuckled. 'But you *do* come first. Always.'

Cherry shook her head. 'No. I don't. Not really. I know I'm the big boss. That I'm in control. That everyone in the family looks to me. But I have never done anything for *me*. Ever.'

'I don't understand. I mean, what about this house, for a start? It's got your name written through it like a stick of rock.'

'Yes. Because I put my heart and soul into it. But it wasn't *for* me. We bought it because of you. And your job. Not because I wanted it.'

Mike looked flummoxed.

'I had no idea you felt like this.'

'I didn't know that's how I felt, until today.'

'So what happened? What was the big turning point?' He crushed the lemongrass under the blade of a big knife with rather too much force. 'The *light bulb*.'

'I went to Mum's grave. It was like she was there,

talking to me – you know I don't believe in ghosts or the afterlife or anything, but I could hear her voice, telling me to do something for me. And then I went to the pub and Alan . . .' Her voice broke. She couldn't bear talking about it. 'Gillian's not good. It's spread. She hasn't got long.'

'Oh no. Well, that is awful.' Mike's expression exuded sympathy. 'Poor bugger. How's he going to manage?'

'Well, that's the thing,' said Cherry, and she gave him a bright smile. '*That* was the light bulb. I've bought The Swan.'

Mike laughed, tripping the knife blade merrily through the crushed lemongrass. Bang bang bang bang bang. 'Ha ha ha,' he said.

'Seriously.'

The chopping stopped.

People don't 'visibly pale', thought Cherry. They visibly redden. Mike's face flushed pink with panic.

'What do you mean? You can't just buy a pub on the spur of the moment.'

'Turns out you can.' Cherry felt a thrill of pure exhilaration. 'We've agreed a price. I've instructed Howard. I'm taking over straight away so Alan can go and look after Gillian. I mean, yes, it's a gentleman's agreement at the moment, but we go back years. I'd trust Alan with my life.'

Mike put his knife down.

'Cherry. We need to talk this through.'

'No, we don't. This is what I want.'

'You've done this on impulse. You were probably upset about Wisteria going, after all these years. It's a knee-jerk reaction.'

Cherry took a breath in. 'That might be what it looks

like. But it all gelled this morning. It all came together. Just like that.' She clicked her fingers. 'I love Rushbrook. I can't bear the thought of not being part of it now Wisteria's gone. I love The Swan. I love Alan. And if you remember, Maggie and I looked into buying a restaurant a few years ago, so I know what I'm letting myself in for. And turning things round is what I do. I know what that pub could be like. Everything it used to be and more. Warm and welcoming and cosy and a bit quirky and eccentric with amazing food and an electric atmosphere...'

Mike shook his head as if by shaking it hard enough he could make her words go away.

'Cherry, I'm in no doubt you could make it look amazing. But I don't understand why you didn't talk to me first. We've always been a team. We've always gone into everything together.'

This was the moment when she had to tell him what she'd seen. She had to come clean.

'Ah, well, we're not in this together. This is *my* thing. It leaves you free to do whatever you want.' She spread out her hands. 'Anneka Harding, for example.'

Silence. She lifted her glass to her lips and stared at him as she took another glug. He licked his lips, and she saw his Adam's apple bob up and down as he swallowed.

'Anneka Harding?' He said the name as if he'd never heard of it.

She swirled the Riesling round her glass. 'I saw you, Mike. I saw you with her in your study.'

He looked completely blank. He scratched his head for a moment as if that might help jog his memory.

'I remember chatting to her. Saying thank you. For her extremely generous present. Cherry, what is this?'

'She had your finger in her mouth.'

He looked startled. 'What?'

She would have laughed at the expression on his face, under any other circumstances.

'She had your finger in her mouth and she was trying to lure you to LA.'

'Were you spying?' He sounded outraged, as if this was far more transgressive.

'I came to find you but you were far too wrapped up in her to notice me. So I left you to it.'

She could see Mike assessing his predicament, trying to figure out damage limitation. 'Cherry, I honestly have no recollection. I'd probably had a few drinks by then.'

'Well, I'm not making it up.'

'It didn't mean anything.'

'How do you know, if you can't remember?'

'Because... she doesn't mean anything. Anneka. She's nothing to me.'

He looked terribly flustered. Was it guilt?

'Really? You seemed very close.'

'We were once. She was one of my most gifted students. I was very proud of her and what she achieved. And she was very grateful to me. So I guess we had a bit of a...' He searched for the right word. 'Bond. But that's it. Cherry, please don't make this into something it isn't. That's not like you.'

No, thought Cherry. It's not. She was the mistress of turning the other cheek. Not causing a fuss. Minding her own business. She had never been a drama queen, or possessive. So making a stand like this was a big deal.

She shrugged. 'Well, seeing you together like that, so close, it made me think. And then when I realised Alan's situation, I just thought... go for it, Cherry, if it's what you want. And it is what I want. A challenge, and something that makes me feel as if I matter.'

Mike put his hands to his head and screwed his eyes up, breathing deeply as he processed what she was saying. Then he looked up.

'Cherry, this is awful. I'm so sorry if you got the wrong end of the stick. I thought we were going to go travelling together. See the world. Expand our horizons. This would be a terrible mistake. Don't risk everything we've got because of a misunderstanding. And I don't mean the money. I don't care about the money. I mean us.'

Cherry hesitated. Maybe she'd imagined the scenario between Mike and Anneka? Maybe she was nuts? Maybe what she'd done was nuts? At her age, most women were settling for Pilates and a pension, not taking on a run-down country pub.

'I understand you feel sentimental about letting Wisteria go, and leaving Rushbrook,' Mike carried on, his voice soothing. 'It's a big wrench. But nothing stays the same, you know that. You have to move on.'

'Why?' asked Cherry, finding her mettle. 'Why do people say that? Why do you *have* to move on, if you don't want to and you don't need to? I love Rushbrook. I want it to be part of my life.'

'We spoke about this when we decided not to keep Wisteria House. You said you were ready to let go.'

Cherry walked over to one of the high stools that lined the island and sat down. Her head was starting to throb. The early start, the big day yesterday, the decision. And now, its defence. It was catching up with her.

'I want to do something for me. Something that has

my name on it. Something that makes a difference to people's lives. Something I can be proud of.'

'But you've got loads of things to be proud of. The family, for a start. Aren't you proud of them?'

'Yes, of course!'

'And this house? You must be proud of this house. No one wanted to touch it with a barge pole and look at it now. You've been in magazines, Cherry.'

It sounded churlish to say that it didn't matter a jot. She'd just wanted to create a beautiful house for them all to enjoy, and she'd done it. When it was finished, Maggie had organised a photo shoot, and the house had been in a variety of interior design magazines – the classic before-and-after story, the renovation journey. Yes, it had been lovely to see it all spread out: the beautiful hall with the floorboards painstakingly restored and polished, the staircase with the black-and-cream striped runner like a mint humbug, hot pink silk curtains billowing in front of the landing window. She'd kept the strong architectural lines of the original house but added little surprises with colour and texture: beaten copper work surfaces in the kitchen, geometric wallpaper in the downstairs loo.

'Yes,' she said. 'But I don't want to be remembered for tarting a house up. Anyone can do that.' She knew they couldn't, of course. It was bloody difficult to manage a team of workmen to come in on budget and hit their deadline. But it wasn't enough. She itched for more. 'Call it my swan song, if you like.'

'But you can't run a pub from here. It's a full-time job.'

'No, I know. I'll be staying in the boathouse.'

Mike's eyebrows shot up as he took in this new departure.

'The boathouse? Are you telling me . . . are we . . . over? Is this the end?'

'No. Of course not—'

'Just because Anneka Harding put my finger in her mouth?'

'So you *do* remember?'

Mike shut his eyes, sighing. 'Vaguely.'

Cherry felt a resurgence of the outrage she had felt, watching the pair of them. Mike had just stood there.

'I didn't see you object. I didn't hear you saying *Anneka, please take my finger out of your mouth*. It made my stomach churn.'

Mike flailed for the right answer.

'It was one of those silly things. A slightly drunken moment. I didn't want to be rude or to upset her, not after she'd come all the way from LA. *And* given me that painting. Do you know how much it's worth?' Mike looked desperate. 'Cherry, I'm so sorry. I promise you, I have no intention of going to LA or probably ever speaking to her again. I mean, I hadn't seen her for twenty years. She means nothing to me. I guess I mean something to her, but . . .'

He looked to be on the verge of tears.

'Please. You're taking this too far. It was . . .' He couldn't find the right words. He slumped onto a bar stool and put his head in his hands. 'One of those stupid moments that looks like more than it is,' he managed finally.

Cherry thought for a moment. Maybe what he was saying was true. But it didn't change the fact that it had flipped a switch for her.

'OK. Maybe. But it still made me realise that it's time I did something for me. That's all.'

She was surprised by the despair in his face as he looked up.

'I would never stop you doing something you wanted. You know that. But buying a pub? I can't think of a better way of losing a lot of money in the shortest amount of time possible.'

'So it's about the money?'

'No! I don't care about the money. But I don't want to see you lose your inheritance. I don't want to see you throwing it all down the drain.' He paused for a moment. 'I don't think your mother would want that either.'

Cherry drew herself up. 'That's a cheap shot.'

'It's not meant to be.'

'I think she'd have more faith in me, for a start.'

'I have faith in you. You know I think the world of you. But pubs are notoriously tricky to make profitable. You know that.'

'I think I could make a go of it.'

'Have you looked at the books?' Mike persisted.

'I'm paying for the real estate. Not the business. Alan admitted it's worth nothing.'

Mike held up his hands.

'And he's an experienced landlord. If he couldn't make it work . . . '

Cherry didn't reply.

'Surely you can see why I'm worried?' Mike persisted.

'He's been under a lot of strain, with Gillian. I can make it work. I know I can.'

Mike gave a weary shrug.

'You've obviously made up your mind.'

'I think it's a viable proposition. And I'm really excited

about it. It's the first time I've felt really excited for a long time.'

He looked at her, wounded. 'I was excited about us doing things together. Having proper time to spend with you at last. Don't rush into this, Cherry. Call Howard. Tell him you need to think it over.'

Cherry felt exasperated. Was he being obtuse on purpose?

'The whole *point* is I need to go ahead now. So Alan and Gillian can go away.'

'But what about us?'

Cherry put her face in her hands. Everything had seemed so clear on the drive home. So perfect and logical. She ran back over it. Nothing had changed, except Mike's objection. She supposed it was a shock to him. She needed to get him onside. She certainly wasn't going to go back on her word. But she hated arguing with him. It was unusual for them to disagree. She couldn't remember the last time they had. But they were both strong characters, and now that they were locking horns, someone was going to have to back down.

It wasn't going to be her.

There had to be a way through this.

She smiled, leaning forwards.

'We could do it together. You love The Swan. You'd have some great ideas. Teamwork makes the dream work.'

Mike remained unmoved. 'This is not my dream, Cherry. Far from it. I want to relax. Travel. Have some fun. Enjoy my family. Enjoy *you*. Which I'm not going to be able to do if you're pulling pints.'

'I'm not going to be pulling pints. You're being very

dismissive.' Cherry felt irritated by his attitude. He hadn't given her suggestion a moment's consideration.

'Look, it's your money to do exactly what you want with. But I'm not going to condone something I think is rash at best.'

'You're questioning my ability.'

'I have never questioned your ability. I'm just not sure you're doing this for the right reason.'

'It's not revenge, if that's what you're thinking.' Cherry had never been petty, and felt nettled that he might think she was trying to get back at him.

'No, I think it's sentimentality. Which is far worse.'

'What?'

'I understand you love Rushbrook. I understand Alan's plight. But I don't think it's your responsibility—'

She put up her hand.

'Stop. Now. You're being very patronising.'

He looked up at the ceiling and sighed.

'I don't mean to be.'

'Hello!' A voice swirled in from the hallway. Maggie.

Mike picked up the glass bowl full of translucent prawns.

'Let's talk about it later. But just so you know – I'm only trying to protect you.'

Cherry crossed her arms. It would be interesting to see what Maggie thought. She was always a good barometer. Fingers crossed she was on her side.

11

Maggie swept in with Fred and Ginger, looking ready for combat in her camouflage boiler suit and Converse. She threw her bulging backpack down on a chair and the dogs immediately starting beetling around looking for crumbs.

'Oh my God. I'm so livid, I don't know where to put myself. The bloody spoilt entitled conniving little brat...' She reached out to take the glass of wine Cherry had automatically filled for her.

'Who? Not Rose?' asked Mike. 'You staying for supper? I'll do extra rice.'

'Of course not Rose. Yes, please.' She took a swig and waved her glass around. Maggie spoke more with her hands than her voice. 'Zara Stone. I treated that girl like my own daughter. In fact, better. I wouldn't have let Rose get away with half the stuff she did. And how does she repay me?'

Mike and Cherry both shook their heads. 'How?'

'By setting up on her own. Then pinching my best client. And presumably she'll be after more.'

'Oh, Maggie.' Cherry went round to hug her daughter.

Maggie wilted in her mum's arms with a huff, resting her head on her shoulder. Cherry ruffled her long, shaggy hair. There were a few streaks of grey, Maggie had noticed that morning, in amongst the plum and cherry lowlights. She *was* getting older.

'Does Aiden know?' asked Mike.

'Does Aiden know?' Maggie sat up with a bark of laughter. 'I expect he's bankrolling her. Does she have any idea what hard work it is? Did she learn nothing when she worked for me? It makes me want to give up.'

'Don't worry about Zara Stone. She'll mess up before long.' Mike poured the jasmine rice into the pot. It made a satisfying whoosh as it hit the water.

'She's undercutting me by about fifty per cent. And she talks the talk. And she looks the part. You know how people get taken in. She'll drive up in that car her father bought her and people will think she's a success. They're suckers for a flashy car. They somehow think it means you know what you're doing.'

Maggie thought of Zara's top-of-the-range Mini Cooper with the white leather seats and soft top and her initials on the number plate. She had always felt slightly embarrassed when Zara parked it outside the house next to her own clapped-out Mini that only just scraped through its MOT every year. Not that she couldn't afford to replace it, but Frank had bought it for her, for her thirtieth fifteen years ago. She loved that car.

'I don't know that people are that gullible.' Cherry tried to reassure her daughter.

'Well, Mario sure is.' Maggie looked at her meaningfully.

'Mario!' Cherry looked pained. 'Tell me she hasn't pinched Mario. How could he?'

'It wasn't him, to be fair. It was his mum and his sister. Zara knew exactly how to get round them. But I've lost the account. My biggest account.'

They all loved Mario and his family. When in Rome always had a big Christmas party to promote their wares: tables groaning with bruschetta and crostini dipped in golden olive oil surrounded by platters of Italian cheeses, prosciutto, braesola, panettone, cantucci... There were endless bottles of Franciacorta, which put bubbles in everyone's veins and a sparkle in their eye, while Pavarotti and Placido Domingo belted out 'O Holy Night'. Maggie was always in charge behind the scenes, and ran the guest list, and it was the most wonderful start to the festive season. But that would be Zara's gig now.

'I bet she's stolen all my other contacts. All my guest lists. All my pitches. All my budgets.'

'Can't you sue?' asked Mike.

'Yes,' said Cherry. 'Didn't she sign a—'

Maggie looked at them both with a wry expression. 'Nope. Because stupid me, I trusted her.'

'Turn the other cheek, darling.'

'You can't *eat* the other cheek, though, can you?'

Maggie sat back in her chair, dejected. She hated the bad taste in her mouth. The double betrayal. She was scrupulous in her dealings with people. She couldn't understand why or how you could go behind someone's back.

'Well, I've got a new client for you,' said Cherry with a smile.

'Who?' Maggie looked expectant. Mike didn't say

anything. Just flashed Cherry a warning glance, which she ignored.

'Me.' Cherry held out her arms. 'You are looking at the new owner of The Swan.'

'What swan?'

'In Rushbrook. The pub. I've bought The Swan off Alan.'

There was silence while Maggie took in the news. She wrinkled her forehead in consternation, wondering if this was some sort of joke or trap.

'How long have you been planning this?'

'I haven't. It was one of those spur of the moment things. I was in Rushbrook this morning and...'

'What – you bought it just like that?'

'Pretty much.' Cherry laughed.

'Wow.' Maggie shook her head in disbelief, then started to laugh. 'Do you know what the weird thing is? I don't think you're that crazy. That place has so much potential.'

Mike turned round from stirring the curry, raising his eyebrows. 'Is this a conspiracy?'

'Every time we go in there, we talk about what we'd do if it was ours. I mean, it used to be great but you have to admit it's gone downhill.'

'It's not Alan's fault. It's because Gillian was ill. And she's not good again, Maggie.'

Maggie's face fell. 'Oh no. Oh God. Oh, it's not fair.'

'I know. And that's part of the reason I bought it. He wants to look after her. She probably hasn't got long.'

Maggie's eyes glistened. 'Oh Mum...'

Maggie remembered Alan coming to see her at Wisteria House, just after Frank's accident, in that awful first few days when they were in a washing machine of numbness, not knowing which way was up. They'd gone straight to Catherine, her and Cherry and Rose, and Alan had knocked on the door the night they arrived, his face wet with tears. He had held Maggie in his arms, made her promise that whatever she needed, she was only to ask. Some of the villagers had been scared of their grief, and had stayed away, but not Alan.

'I bloody loved Frank,' he said. 'He knew more about my beer than I did.'

That was Frank. Expert in beer, music and random facts.

Alan had shown them all such kindness, and now Maggie couldn't bear to think of what he was going through. But she felt excited by her mother's revelation. It shouldn't feel right, buying a pub on impulse, but in this case, it did.

'So,' said Cherry. 'I'm going to need your skills for the relaunch. Can you fit me in?'

'One hundred per cent,' said Maggie. 'This is perfect timing. And at least I don't have to worry about Zara poaching you. Not that I'll charge you,' she added hastily.

'No, I'll pay you properly. And I'll need to pick your brain about lots of other things. Staff, suppliers. I might need you to interview the chef. You know way more than me. Obviously.'

Maggie had trained at Leith's, and had been running a tapas bar in Mountville when she met Frank, who was working as a sound engineer at the BBC studios nearby. In her mid-twenties, when Rose came along, she had given up her career as a chef – Frank worked away a lot, and the antisocial hours didn't fit in with a small baby, so she had set up Tine. It had seemed the perfect compromise; her training meant she had excellent inside knowledge of most aspects of the food industry, and she could work from home.

'Anything you need, Mum. You know that. Wow. I can't help thinking how thrilled Granny would be. She loved The Swan.'

Cherry avoided Mike's eye. She had to admit it almost looked as if she had primed Maggie in advance.

'The beauty of it is we've got a blank slate. There's not a single member of staff left. Poor old Alan's run everything right down. But he'll be on hand to advise us. I mean, I know it's gone downhill but he does know what he's doing.'

'When do you take over?'

'As soon as possible. I've got loads of ideas but we need a strategy.'

'Strategy is my middle name. You need a business plan. A budget. And a timetable.' Maggie scrabbled in her backpack for a notebook.

In the background, Mike ran his knife through a pile of fresh coriander. The noise made them both look up.

'Sorry,' he said.

The two of them stared at him. It was almost as if they had forgotten he was there.

'What about you, Dad? Are you going to be behind the bar? Mein host?' Maggie mimed pulling a pint.

'I doubt it.' Mike wiped his knife clean and swept the coriander into a bowl.

'Dad's not entirely convinced it's a good idea.' Cherry made a face.

'That's an understatement,' said Mike.

Maggie frowned. There was a chilliness between her

parents she hadn't detected at first, in all the excitement. It unnerved her. They rarely disagreed on anything, but it really looked as if Mike wasn't on board with this at all.

'Oh, come on, Dad. You know how good Mum is at this stuff.'

There was a pause, and Maggie tensed. Something was amiss. The atmosphere was off kilter. She glanced around the kitchen. Everything was in its place. It smelled right – aromatic coconut and the soapy scent of coriander. But there was a tension that hadn't been there the day before. Her parents were keeping their distance from each other, keeping the island between them. This was odd. Usually there was a touch, an embrace, a kiss – they were very tactile with each other. They might not be married – they came from an era who had turned their back on the institution – but their relationship was stronger than any marriage.

'Dad?'

Mike sighed. 'I just don't think it's that simple. I know she'll make it look amazing. I know it will feel like the most wonderful place in the world, somewhere you never want to leave, because that's what she does. But . . .'

He trailed off, obviously uncomfortable about pouring cold water on their enthusiasm. It wasn't something he ever had to do.

'I can help with all the business stuff,' said Maggie. 'I've worked in enough kitchens, and dealt with enough restaurants. I know what goes on under the bonnet. I know it's not just about what colour paint you put on the walls. I know about pricing, and employment law, and quality control, and suppliers, and health and safety. And cash flow.'

'I know, Maggie. It's not that I don't trust you or Mum. But I think it's a massive risk. It's a lot of money.'

'Isn't it my risk, though?' asked Cherry, looking defiant. 'My money. My problem?'

Mike shrugged. 'Sure. You can do whatever you like. But I can't help worrying. And I'm not going to stand here and watch you walk into something you can't handle without saying something.'

'But maybe *we* can handle it?'

'I've got faith,' Maggie said. 'We can totally make it work. And if it fails, Mum can put the pub on the market. What has she got to lose?'

'Exactly,' said Cherry. 'At the end of the day I'll still have the bricks and mortar.'

Mike didn't reply but his face said it all. He undid the apron he was wearing and threw it down on the island in a gesture of defeat.

'Dinner's in fifteen minutes,' was all he could find to say in the end, and left the room.

'It's not like Dad to be so anti something.' Maggie pulled open a bag of prawn crackers and began to munch.

'I think it was a bit of a shock.'

'But it's a no-brainer. Can't he see that?'

'I guess not,' said Cherry, knowing there was more going on between her and Mike than she felt comfortable letting on. But she had Maggie on her side. Together they could take over the world. As a team, they were unbeatable.

12

That evening, Rose couldn't settle once she'd put Gertie down to sleep. She lay on the bed with her, staring at the stars of her night-light projector swirling across the ceiling. They usually calmed her, but Rose couldn't shake the feeling of unease she'd had ever since leaving the Soul Bowl. She couldn't get Gaz out of her mind. He was so vulnerable, and she wanted to help him, but she knew the only person who could help Gaz now was Gaz.

Aaron had stopped her as she was leaving. He could see she was troubled. He pointed a warning finger at her.

'Don't take it home with you, Rose,' he said. 'It's wasted worry. You can only do what you can do.'

'Gaz is on the edge,' she said.

Aaron nodded. 'He knows this is a safe space. He's in the pod tonight, so he doesn't have to worry. He'll be OK.'

'I've given him some food.' She didn't mention the money. The money was what was worrying her. What were the chances of it going on a present? Of Gaz heading to a toy shop instead of the off licence? Why had she given in so easily?

'We've got his back.' Aaron touched hers, and she felt his warmth and tried to feel reassured. He was exactly the kind of person she needed in her life. Frank would have approved of him; she knew that too. She smiled at the thought of them together: powerful Aaron towering over her wiry, geeky little dad. Chalk and cheese and yet not so very different. Big hearts, big souls.

She missed her dad so much. She would be able to talk to him about what she had done, and he would understand her anxiety. Maggie would just worry if she confessed what she'd done, and Rose didn't want to stress her. She was trying to detach from her mother a little, conscious that she relied on her a bit too much. Some would say that it was OK, after what had happened, because that was what mums were for, but she knew she should start standing on her own two feet.

On good days, that thought didn't seem too daunting. But today, after what she had done, she could feel anxiety building inside her, like a swarm of bees. She could almost hear it buzzing.

Idly, she sat at her computer and started looking for Gaz's girlfriend Shell on Facebook. There couldn't be many 'Shells' around Avonminster. She found her, and started looking through her page for clues about the sort of person she was. She was a bit younger than Gaz, early thirties, Rose estimated, but she looked pretty cool. She had a fifties vibe, with some intricate tattoos, and a whole lot of attitude. There was a little girl with her in some of the photos. They posed together, in their mother/daughter camaraderie, their fingers held up in defiant peace signs. Don't come between us, they seemed to be saying, and Rose recognised their chemistry.

She felt a niggle of concern for Gaz. Was he too weak for these strong women? She could see how Shell might have been attracted to his bad boy image once upon a time, but perhaps that was wearing off, now they had a child? Maybe his partying was wearing a bit thin now they had responsibilities?

She remembered his remorse at being kicked out yet again. She hoped against hope he had gone to buy the unicorn, and hadn't reverted to type. She remembered the anguish on his face, and his self-loathing. Would the temptation to blot that out have been greater than the need to buy his daughter a present?

She couldn't leave it to chance a moment longer.

She phoned the next-door neighbour to ask if she would come and babysit for an hour. It didn't look as if Maggie was going to be back for a while. Mrs Elkins was always delighted to help out with babysitting, especially as Rose and Maggie had a much bigger telly than she and her husband, so Rose didn't feel guilty about asking her at short notice. Ten minutes later, Rose ushered Mrs Elkins in and settled her into the depths of their pink velvet sofa. She left a plate of chocolate digestives for her to munch while she watched *Eastenders*.

Then she jumped on her bicycle and cycled as fast as she could to the industrial estate. Her thighs were burning as she turned into the car park. It was empty now, but she could see the bright blue pod like a little beacon. It was made of wood, with just a strip of window to ensure privacy, and a sturdy padlocked door. Inside was a bed, a chemical toilet and a phone charger. Enough for a comfy night's kip away from the elements.

She jumped off her bike, leant it against the wall and knocked on the door.

'Gaz?' she called. 'Gaz, it's Rose. From the Soul Bowl. I just wanted to make sure you're OK?'

As long as he was all right, she wouldn't try to find out what he'd done with the money. She'd learned her lesson, though. No more cash. She cursed herself when there was no reply. Maybe he wasn't in there? Maybe he'd never checked in? Maybe he'd gone to his mate's? Maybe he'd gone to see Skye? But somehow she felt sure he was inside.

Should she open the door? She had the code. Aaron had entrusted her with it, just in case. It was changed every week, for security, but she always got the email with the new number.

'Gaz, it's Rose. I'm going to open the door. Is that OK?'

Her heart was hammering as she pressed the number into the keypad. She had no idea what she might find but she couldn't walk away now. She pushed the door open. The smell hit her as soon as she looked inside. Pure alcohol. And there was Gaz, stretched out on the bed, still and silent. The bottle on the floor said it all. A big bottle of cheap vodka. Empty. Anyone who said vodka didn't smell was kidding themselves.

She ran over to him.

'Gaz!' she cried. 'Gaz! Can you hear me? Wake up.'

She grabbed at his shirt and shook him but he was comatose. His eyes flickered slightly then rolled back inside his head. With shaking hands, she dialled the emergency services.

'Ambulance, please,' she said, trying to stay calm, trying not to get hysterical. She needed to get him into the recovery position. 'I've got someone here – he's drunk a bottle of vodka. He's passed out.'

She wanted to shake him. How could he be such an idiot? It was his daughter's birthday. He couldn't do something like this on his daughter's birthday. She swallowed a sob and dialled Aaron. He would want to be there.

'Hey, Rose. What's up?' Aaron sounded surprised to be called.

'I'm at the pod,' she said. 'It's Gaz.'

'What?' He was instantly alert.

'He's drunk a whole bottle of vodka. I've called an ambulance.'

'Shit. I'll be right there. Ten minutes.'

'I'm sorry.'

'What for?'

She looked at the empty bottle and Gaz's inert body and felt a horrible wave of fear.

'Just get here.'

She quailed at the thought of what she was going to have to admit to Aaron. It was all her fault. She had given Gaz money, when she knew he was an alcoholic. And what had he gone and done? Drunk it away. Of course he had.

She saw his phone on the floor and picked it up. She pressed it out of curiosity. He didn't have a password. Gaz's screensaver was a photo of him and Shell on holiday somewhere with a deep blue sky and lots of palm trees. Majorca, maybe, or Lanzarote. It must have been long before things went wrong. Maybe before Skye came along, with the added pressure a child brought to a relationship. Gaz looked fit and well and happy, his arms toned and muscular, probably two stone heavier than he was now.

Shell's head was resting on his shoulder. She was smiling dreamily, the picture of a woman in love. The perfect couple.

'You bloody idiot,' Rose shouted at his inert form, but she was shouting at herself really, for being the idiot and handing over her cash. She pushed at his arm to try and rouse him. There was a groan, but he didn't open his eyes.

'Hey.' She looked up to see Aaron in the doorway, standing there in his grey camo joggers, a black quilted waistcoat and a yellow beanie, not a bead of sweat on him though he must have raced to get here. 'What are you even doing here?'

'I had a feeling.' Rose stood up, but she couldn't quite look him in the eye.

'A feeling?' Aaron frowned. She was going to have to confess. But Aaron was more concerned about Gaz. He shook his arm.

'Hey, buddy. Come on. Wake up, dude. Gaz.'

There was no response. Rose and Aaron looked at each other as the sound of an approaching siren broke the evening air. Aaron picked up the vodka bottle, weighed it in his hand, staring at it, and Rose felt the guilt writhe in her stomach.

'Oh God.'

'He's going to be OK, Rose,' said Aaron gently. 'He's lucky you found him.'

He put an arm around her and she leant into him for a moment, grateful for his reassurance. His embrace was like iron, his biceps rock hard, his chest bulletproof underneath the down of his gilet; hours and hours of resilience and training went into his physique. Rose wondered if he had ever had a moment of weakness, and cursed herself for her own.

The paramedics didn't waste time.

'Oh dear,' said the driver, with the world-weary tone of someone who had seen this with monotonous regularity. 'Let's get him sorted.'

Within minutes, Gaz was on a trolley and in the ambulance.

'Either of you want to come?' asked the driver.

'I've got to get back for Gertie,' said Rose, torn.

'I'll follow in my car,' said Aaron. 'I'll keep you in the loop.'

He headed to his vehicle. It was sleek, black, silent and quietly expensive – he rarely drove it to work, preferring to walk or cycle. As he opened the driver door, his eyes met hers for a moment. She gulped as he gave her a reassuring smile, then indicated he would phone her. She felt another wave of shame. It was Aaron's single-mindedness that made him successful; his ability not to give in to temptation but to stick to the rules he made himself. How weak she was in comparison.

The driver slammed the door shut then ran around to the front and got into his seat. He flipped on the siren again as he drove away and headed out of the industrial estate onto the main road. Rose watched it go with her hands clasped, not in actual prayer, because she didn't believe in God, but begging to anything, any power that might be up there, to let Gaz be all right.

It was only when Rose went back into the pod to check the window was shut that she noticed the plastic bag under the bed. She pulled it out. Inside was a toy unicorn. A white plush unicorn with a pink satin horn and pink satin hooves and big eyes. She imagined Gaz picking it out, squeezing it for cuddliness, stroking it for softness. He'd chosen well. It was the softest, cuddliest unicorn she'd ever felt.

She felt her heart tumble. He had been out to get it. He'd had every intention of taking it to Skye, but somewhere along the way he'd gone on a bender. God knows how he'd got the vodka. Nicked it, maybe?

And now Skye would never know about the present he'd got for her.

She turned the unicorn over in her hands, imagining Skye's face when she saw it. It belonged with her. She needed it now, on her birthday. It was up to Rose to make sure she got it. She didn't trust anyone else to understand its importance. She still had Gaz's phone. She scrolled through to Google maps and clicked on Home. An address down by Babbington Brook came up. Not too far. She grabbed her bike, threw the unicorn into the basket and set off.

13

It took Rose fifteen minutes to cycle along the river to the house where Shell lived. And, presumably, where Gaz had lived until recently. It was a modern maisonette, one room wide and three storeys high, clad in cedar, in a pedestrianised enclave full of young families. A cool, vibrant place. It wasn't what Rose had expected. Somehow, she'd imagined something more desolate and hopeless. A place for a relationship to crumble and despair to set in. This was full of life and hope.

Rose locked up her bike to the lamppost outside and strode up the path, knocking on the glass door. She watched as a shadow approached, unsure quite what she was going to say. It would depend on the reaction she received. She stroked the plush fur of the unicorn, digging her fingers into the softness, holding it tight for courage as if it was a talisman.

The door opened. She recognised Shell straight away from the photo on Gaz's phone. She was in a halterneck dress covered in palm trees, her hair backcombed and tied in a ponytail.

Rose felt dowdy in comparison. On Soul Bowl days, Rose wore jeans and a t-shirt, and she was sweating from the bike ride.

'Hi.' Rose held up the unicorn. 'I brought this. For Skye? It's for her birthday. From Gaz. He left it at the Soul Bowl.'

Shell looked uncertain. Rose could tell she was surveying her for clues but couldn't put her into a category. Too young to be police or a social worker. Too posh to be a friend of Gaz.

'Who are you?' she asked.

'I'm a friend.'

Shell looked doubtful. 'Really?'

A figure appeared at the top of the staircase behind Shell. Rose saw the little girl before her mother did. A little girl with a bird's nest of blonde hair and yellow pyjamas.

'Is it Daddy?' The child's voice was full of excitement and anticipation as she began to make her way down the stairs, one hand on the wall, one step at a time with both feet. Shell turned around.

'No, darling. I'm afraid not. Go back to bed, sweetheart.'

'Oh.' Skye's face fell as she stared at Rose. 'Who is it? What's that?'

'It's a unicorn. For you. From your daddy.' Rose held the unicorn up. Skye's face brightened. Shell's lips tightened but she stepped back and let the little girl come down the stairs and take it off Rose.

'I love him.' Skye buried her face in the toy's fur, and Rose felt her heart melt.

'Isn't he lovely?' said Shell. 'Now take him up to bed with you, poppet.'

'Thank you.' Skye turned to Rose with a smile, and Rose felt her heart crumple a little bit. She was adorable.

'You're very welcome, darling. I'll tell Daddy how much you liked it.'

'When's he coming?'

'I'm not sure,' said Rose. 'As soon as he can, I expect.'

Skye seemed happy with that answer, and made her way back up the stairs.

'Right, well, thanks,' said Shell. 'It was kind of you to bring it.'

She was obviously eager to get rid of Rose as quickly as possible.

'I thought you should know—' Rose put out her hand to stop Shell shutting the door on her. 'Gaz drank a bottle of vodka tonight. He's in hospital.' She spoke quietly so Skye wouldn't hear.

'Again?' Shell sighed, and gave a world-weary shrug. 'We haven't seen him for a couple of weeks. He just walked out.'

Rose frowned. 'He said you'd thrown him out.'

Pain flickered across Shell's face. 'No. I wouldn't do that. He's Skye's dad at the end of the day.'

'Oh,' said Rose, realising with a sinking heart that Gaz had lied to her.

'It's what he does, when he's on a bender. Lies to people. Don't take it personally.'

Rose's heart was pounding. Had she been a fool to be taken in by Gaz? She had seen the anguish on his face. The knowledge that he was letting everyone down, including himself, and the battle he was going through.

'He really struggles,' she told Shell. 'He really tries. I see him every week, and I know how hard he finds it. And he loves you. You and Skye.'

'I know,' said Shell, with a weary smile. 'We love him too. But sometimes he loves the booze more than he loves us.'

Rose hesitated. 'I don't think he does,' she said. 'I think he hates it. What it does to him. And all of you. But it's a disease. There's help you can get...'

She stopped. Shell was a good ten years older than she was, and looked worldly wise. She had probably tried everything under the sun to sort Gaz out. What must it be like, to lose someone like this, over and over?

'All I want is for us to be a family,' said Shell. 'And every now and then, it's perfect. I don't know what happens to make him smash it all up again. But I'm tired. And it's not fair on Skye.'

'I'm sorry,' said Rose, suddenly stricken with guilt. 'I've got to go. I just wanted Skye to have her unicorn...'

'Thank you.'

A moment shimmered between them. Rose felt the urge to reach out and hug Shell, but it wasn't appropriate. She had already stepped over the boundary.

She turned back along the path and unlocked her bicycle, looking up at the window she thought was probably Skye's. At least, whatever happened, Skye would know that her dad had cared, on her birthday. She shivered at the memory of Gaz lying on the bed in the pod, the moment she had thought she was already too late.

Rose climbed on her bike just as fat drops of rain began to fall as she wound her way through the evening traffic. She reached the bottom of Mountville High Street, the steep hill with its independent coffee shops, vintage boutiques and record stores. It was a challenge to get to the top but the trick was not to stop. Her dad had taught her that. Frank had got her into cycling as a way of getting around the city. Avonminster might be full of hills, but if you got yourself fit enough, it was much easier to cycle than to drive. You always beat the traffic, you could always park.

As she cycled, she felt the familiar signs of anxiety creeping back. The funny deals she made with herself to prevent catastrophe. *If I get to the zebra crossing before the lights turn red . . . If I can count to ten before that car turns left or right . . . If I see three red cars before I get to the university building.* She knew the rules didn't make sense, but it didn't stop her mind playing games. She'd worked so hard to get out of the habit, but it didn't take much to be sucked back into the depths of a dark world where she had no control.

By the time she got home she could feel the signs she dreaded. Her chest felt tight and her tongue went numb. She stood with her bike on the pavement, trying to breathe in and out, trying to control the panic. It felt as if a tiny bird was trying to get out of her chest, wings flapping, claws scratching. Only oxygen would calm it.

Eventually the bird was still. It was always inside her, but she had learned to manage it. She took one last breath in and pushed her bicycle down the side of the house and put it back in the shed. She was home. She was safe.

Half an hour later, with Mrs Elkins thanked and despatched, Rose sat curled up on the sofa with a cup of cinnamon tea, replaying the events of the day over and over. Whether Gaz had used her money to buy the unicorn or the vodka was immaterial – she had enabled him. Without her contribution, he might have stuck at the toy and resisted the temptation. Either way, he had used emotional blackmail. But Rose didn't hold it against him. He was ill. She blamed herself, for not seeing he needed help.

Her phone rang, and she jumped. She stared at the screen: Aaron. She felt filled with dread. She hated her phone at the best of times, remembering that afternoon in the café with her friends when Maggie had called her. *You need to come home. Who are you with?* She swallowed, her mouth dry, listening to the ring until it cut off.

And then it rang again and she mustered up the courage to answer.

'Rose. It's me.' Aaron sounded his usual cool, together self. 'They've got Gaz in A&E. He's going to be all right. He's not going to feel too clever tomorrow though.'

'Oh,' was all Rose could manage, flooded with relief.

'He's got you to thank.' Rose winced at the irony of Aaron's words. 'You did good tonight, Rose. Trusting your instincts.'

No, I didn't, she wanted to say. It was all my fault. As they said goodbye, she hung up and sat with her arms curled around her knees, wondering where Maggie was, shame and panic building inside her, the events of the day whirling around inside her head, trying as ever to figure out what was fate and what was down to her and what she could have, should have, done differently. This was always her internal monologue as she battled to keep disaster at bay, but today was one of those days when her worst fears were realised, so she knew her anxiety was not unfounded.

Terrible things happened and there was nothing you could do about it.

14

Cherry couldn't get to sleep that night. The spices in the Thai curry made her heart race and the stone-washed linen duvet cover was too heavy and hot now it was May and her brain was doing overtime. It was funny how calm she felt underneath about what she had done – she hadn't a moment's regret about buying The Swan – but she kept thinking of all the things she would have to do if they were to reopen as soon as possible. Punctilious Howard had already emailed her a list of questions that made her mouth go dry at the very sight of them, and she was waiting for the Fabulous Builder Brothers to get back to her. The pair had done all her building work in Avonminster and they knew just how to work to her specification – she'd trained them pretty well over the years. She was hoping she could lure them to Somerset as soon as possible, but they were very booked up.

Really what she should do is get up and write a list, to settle all the random thoughts that were whirling around, but she didn't want to wake Mike. They had gone to bed with their differences unresolved, a polite froideur separating them. It was, she realised, their first real disagreement.

She supposed that was an achievement after so many years together, but it was also sad and discomfiting.

She turned to find him staring at the ceiling, an expression of bleakness on his face.

'Hey,' she said softly. She knew he wasn't happy about what she had done, but she didn't want to hurt him more than necessary.

'I need to tell you the truth,' he said, his voice strangled, and she shut her eyes. Was this going to be another bombshell?

'Go on,' she said, bracing herself.

'Anneka Harding,' he said, 'made my life hell for nearly three years. When she first arrived, I was electrified by her talent. She was the most exciting student at the university for years. But she misunderstood my interest in her. She thought there was something between us. I never, ever did or said anything to lead her on, but she convinced herself we were in love.'

'Oh my God.' Cherry sat up. 'Seriously?'

'She was completely obsessed with me. She wouldn't leave me alone. She did anything she could to be with me. When I tried to keep her at arm's length, she got hysterical. I was at my wit's end. She was so volatile. I thought about going to the university to explain my predicament, but I didn't trust her not to make trouble. She could so easily have turned on me and made out it was me obsessed with her. Because everyone knew she was my protégée. And I did give her a lot of attention, because she was so talented.'

'Why didn't you say anything to me?' Cherry asked.

'Because I didn't trust her not to lie to you as well. Because I was scared. Because it was easier not to. I just had to wait until she graduated and I'd be free. And you were ... not yourself at the time.'

'Oh,' said Cherry, thinking back twenty years to the fug of the menopause: the self-doubt and insecurity and hypersensitivity. 'Yes, I would not have taken that well.'

She remembered those difficult few years, when she'd struggled to be herself amidst the mood swings and hot flushes, until a sympathetic GP had prescribed HRT. The relief had been palpable.

'And you were very tied up with Maggie. Rose had just come along. I didn't want to bring my problems home. Home was my escape. My refuge.'

'You should have trusted me.'

'I was petrified,' said Mike. 'I was worried that you would make me report her and she would be thrown out. I didn't have it in me to be that cruel.'

'Even though she made your life hell?' Cherry looked at him in disbelief. 'This is awful, Mike. How could you have kept this quiet for so long?'

'I know. Looking back, I should have taken control. But I kept putting it off, hoping she would calm down and leave me alone. And eventually, of course, she left. I can't tell you what a relief that was.'

Cherry slumped back on her pillows. 'So you hadn't seen her since. Until yesterday?'

She couldn't help a hint of accusation in her voice. Had he seen her in the intervening years?

'God no,' said Mike. 'Her turning up was like a recurring nightmare. When she cornered me in the study, I was terrified she might bring everything up again. I just went along with everything she said to keep her quiet. My finger in her mouth, the invitation to LA ... I just went

along with it, hoping she would go away. And she did.'
He gave a half laugh. 'She's out of the city now. I feel as
if I'm out of danger. You have no idea how awful it was,
seeing her turn up.'

Cherry remembered Mike's face, and how he had been
lost for words after Anneka's speech. She had put it down
to the emotion of the situation, and him being the centre
of attention, which he hated.

'So why tell me now?'

'I'm telling you,' he went on, 'because if the thing with
Anneka was what made you buy The Swan, if it was some
sort of . . . revenge, then it's not too late.'

'Too late?'

'To back out.'

Cherry didn't speak for a moment. She turned over in
her mind the events of the day and tried to analyse her
motivation. Sure, if she hadn't still been angry at what
she'd seen, she might not have been so impulsive. She
might not have done it on the spur of the moment, but
after a period of reflection. But all her reasons for buying
it still stood. Mike's revelation didn't change anything. She
wanted to buy The Swan.

And she felt hurt that he had kept such a momentous
secret for so long. It unsettled her, to think she had been
oblivious. She believed what he had told her, but she
couldn't quite come to terms with being kept at arm's
length about the situation.

'Well,' she said. 'I'm glad I know now. Though I feel
sad that you didn't trust me enough to tell me.'

'It wasn't that—'

She held up a hand to stop him.

'It's OK. I don't want to go over it. What's done is

done. And anyway, it doesn't change anything. I'm still going ahead.'

He looked at her. 'But it's not what we planned. And where do I fit in? You'll be in Rushbrook. We're supposed to be travelling. Hanging out. Making plans. Mexico. Vietnam. Berlin . . .' He listed some of the places they'd talked about visiting.

'I know it's not what we planned. But it's something I've got to do. For me. And if you want to get involved, you can. You love The Swan.'

'For a pie and a pint!' His indignation was almost comical. 'There's only one side of the bar I want to be on.'

'It's a really exciting project and I think we could make a huge success of it.'

He crossed his arms. 'I think you're mad.'

'Just give me six months, Mike. Let's look at it again at Christmas. If it's not working, I can think again.'

He turned away from her without replying, pulling the duvet over him, indicating the subject was closed.

Cherry lay back down on the pillow. She wasn't going to let Mike make her feel guilty. He would come round, she knew he would. He would, eventually, realise what a brilliant idea it was for all of them.

15

Maggie, too, found it hard to sleep. She woke at half six the next morning and crept down to the kitchen, putting the Moka on the stove and opening her notebook to capture some of her thoughts. Writing to Frank sometimes crystallised things. She felt as if there was a sparkler inside her head, firing off ideas. And she still hadn't dealt with her anger towards Zara. The whole Swan thing had diverted her from the issue, but this morning her fury burned brighter than ever. She wasn't going to take it lying down.

She began to write.

I know what you'd say. Turn it to your advantage. Figure out what Zara wants and manipulate her to your own end. But I'm just not sure how. And I know she's going to decimate me. Maybe I should just let her? We're going to be pitching for the same jobs. I don't think I can put myself through the humiliation. Would I be a coward to roll over and let her take it all from me? Then I can concentrate on The Swan, with Mum. God, I wish you were here. I wish we could go down to Rushbrook and have a celebratory drink. I can see you, sitting by the fire with a pint of Melchior cider and a pork pie... You used to say it was one of the places you felt happiest. Maybe that was the cider talking?! It was magic though. We didn't have a care in the world, did we?

She stopped for a moment, swallowing down her tears. When would she stop missing him? She could see his dear bespectacled face, hear his sing-song Black Country accent that made everything he said sound funny because he was so dry, so quick, so observant.

'The Art of War, Maggie,' she heard him saying. 'He will win who knows when to fight and when not to fight.'

She reread her words, looking for clues, a signpost towards a solution. Sometimes, the answer was staring her in the face. As the coffee came to the boil, she gave a little squeak.

'Oh my God. Of *course*! That absolutely solves everything. The Art of War, baby!'

She did a karate chop in the middle of the kitchen and started laughing.

By nine o'clock she was marching towards the elegant Georgian house in Mountville where Aiden Stone had his office.

'I need to see Aiden right now,' she told the sleek receptionist.

The receptionist opened her mouth to say he wasn't available, but Maggie cut her off. 'I'm not going until he's seen me, so he might as well get it over with. Maggie Nicholson, tell him. From Tine PR.'

Less than three minutes later she was stepping onto the thick white carpet in Aiden's office. She refused his outstretched hand and strode over to the window that looked out onto a beautifully landscaped courtyard with clipped box hedges.

'You know why I'm here,' she said. 'Zara isn't capable of doing what she's done off her own bat. I'm really shocked that you think it's OK to behave like that, given your friendship with Frank. Or don't you have loyalty to friends once they are dead?'

Aiden was dressed in a three-piece tweed suit that wouldn't have looked out of place on Bertie Wooster. He even had a gold watch chain draped across his breast.

'She is my daughter. I want her to succeed. This is the first time I have seen her throw herself into a project. She's determined to do well. We appreciate everything she learned from you, but there was nothing in her contract to stop her setting up on her own.'

'No,' said Maggie. 'Because there's this weird thing called trust that decent people adhere to.'

'That's just naïve, Maggie. You know it is.'

He was right. You had to protect yourself in this day and age. You couldn't leave anything to chance.

'She didn't even have the balls to tell me what she was doing. So she knows she's done wrong. And you must have known, too. I'm guessing you've bankrolled her?'

He nodded, quite unashamed. 'I'm an investor in the business. I'm her father, Maggie.'

'And you think that's being a *good* father, do you? Encouraging her to stitch me up?'

Aiden stared at her. He wasn't going to admit that his daughter was guilty of anything.

'She's been working very hard since she left you. I'm very impressed with the campaigns she's put together. I wouldn't invest in her if I didn't think she could do it.'

The awful thing was, Zara probably would make a success of it. She'd pull in her dad's contacts, spend his money, blag her way through meetings, carbon-copy everything she'd learnt from Maggie and use everyone she knew to get what she wanted.

'Did you know she was going to set this up when you asked if she could work with me?'

Aiden looked wounded. 'Maggie . . . I don't know how you can say that. It wasn't pre-meditated.'

'That's how it looks to me.'

'Look, Zara had a wonderful time with you. She respects you and everything you do. You should be flattered you inspired her. We went skiing not long after she left you – she was telling the people who owned the chalet how to market themselves and they asked if she'd take it on. It grew from there.'

He was thoroughly convincing. Maggie reminded herself that he was a salesman.

'She's nicked one of my best clients. One of my favourite clients. I don't understand how you can condone what she's doing.'

'This is the first time she's showed any interest in anything other than clothes and make-up. She's my daughter and I'd do anything to help her achieve.' He shrugged. 'She's not like Rose. I used to listen to Frank talk about Rose and I was jealous of how proud he was of her. I was never proud of Zara because she never *did* anything. But I am now. She's finally got her act together. And I'm not taking that away from her.'

'Wow.' Maggie shook her head in disbelief.

'Maggie, you can handle the competition. Avonminster's a big place. There's room for both of you.'

This was the moment. This was the moment to go in for the kill.

'How about if I made it a whole lot easier for her?'

'What do you mean?'

'You could buy Tine off me.'

His eyes widened in surprise and something that looked like amusement.

'It would save her trying to steal my clients. I can just hand them over to her. It would save us all a lot of time and effort. And it would be better for the clients in the long run. They wouldn't need to feel guilty about abandoning me.'

Aiden walked to the other side of the room and leant against the mantelpiece of the fireplace. Over it was a huge photo of his wife and Zara, all dressed in white, sitting on a sofa with a beautiful silver-grey dog at their feet.

'How much?' he asked.

Maggie had always known how much she was worth. She never undersold herself. It was why she knew Zara would always be able to sabotage her by undercutting.

She named her price. She knew it was a risk.

'Why do you want to sell?' Aiden's eyes bored into her. He was suspicious.

'I'm going into business with my mother. Nothing that will be in competition,' she assured him. 'A totally new venture.'

His eyes gleamed.

'Interesting. Tell me more.'

'Absolutely no way,' Maggie grinned. She had the measure of him. She wouldn't put it past him to go and gazump them if he took a fancy to The Swan. Her pulse was galloping with the adrenaline of the confrontation and the thrill of the deal.

'I want two days' consulting a month from you as part of the deal,' he said.

So Aiden wasn't that confident in his daughter's ability. Or was it a control thing?

'For six months,' agreed Maggie. She didn't want to be tied for ever. And that would make *her* feel less guilty about abandoning her clients.

'OK,' he said finally, and held out his hand.

Maggie tried to steady her breathing. She held her hand out to take his, remembering that Frank had always said, laughingly and fondly, that if you shook hands with Aiden you should count your fingers afterwards.

When she walked out into the street ten minutes later, she couldn't believe that she had done something almost as rash as Cherry the day before. She believed in them as a team. She had absolute faith in her mother's ability to bring about The Swan's renaissance, and she knew she was the perfect wing woman, but she needed to give it her full attention. Relaunching a pub was not a part-time job.

She felt a tingle of excitement. It was a long time since she had got her hands dirty, literally and metaphorically. She loved the buzz of a kitchen and its elaborate dance with the dining room; the tight choreography. Her head was already in the depths of The Swan, calculating covers, estimating how many staff they would need. *Start small and simple. Don't be overambitious or try to show off.* She must heed her own advice, the advice she gave to clients.

She stopped off at her favourite bakery to buy a trio of Portuguese custard tarts. She'd done their launch, three years ago, and now they were flying – or rather, their goods were. She looked at the logo she'd helped them design, and the thick brown paper bags that graced every kitchen worktop in Mountville and beyond. Maggie had put their signature custard tarts at the forefront of the publicity campaign, sending them out to local influencers and business people and asking them to take a picture. Her favourite had been the hot boys at the local car wash, stripped to the waist, holding their tarts aloft. Now they sold out by midday every day.

She was good at her job, she thought, but it was time to move on. Change was important in life, and she was aware that she had become a little stale, finding it harder and harder to think up new strategies. Maybe Zara would breathe new life into Tine, once it was in her care? She would have to notify her existing clients, assure them that she was still going to be there in the background and that they were in safe hands with Zara. She had, after all, learned from the best.

She reached her car and jumped into the front seat. She needed to get back home. Rose had been in bed when Maggie had got back last night, and she and Gertie had still been fast asleep when she left the house, but Rose needed to know what was happening. Rose didn't like change, Maggie knew, and for a moment she thought perhaps things were moving too fast, that there hadn't really been time to think things through properly.

But she'd needed the element of surprise with Aiden. *He will win who knows when to fight and when not to fight,* she reminded herself, and felt the thrill of victory once again.

16

Rose was glad that Tuesday wasn't a nursery day. She had slept in until eight, letting Gertie sneak into bed next to her and play on her phone. Every time the phone beeped she jumped, thinking it might be a text from Aaron saying Gaz had taken a turn for the worse in the night. Part of her was longing to call Aaron and confess what she had done, but she couldn't bear the thought of his disappointment in her.

And in the cold light of day, she realised she shouldn't have been to see Shell either. That was breaking all the rules of confidentiality. She'd looked at Gaz's phone, for a start. Found his home address. What should she have done instead? Called Aaron? Given him the unicorn to deal with?

What had possessed her to take matters into her own hands?

Then she reminded herself of Skye's face when she'd seen the toy. She'd done the right thing. Aaron didn't have kids. He might not have understood how important it was for Skye to get it on her birthday.

Of *course* he would understand. Aaron was the most

empathetic person she had ever met. She should have gone to him straight away and now it was too late. She'd committed so many crimes she couldn't start to unravel them, from the moment she'd given Gaz the twenty pounds.

She went downstairs to give Gertie her breakfast. She didn't even feel like getting dressed. She hadn't had a day like yesterday for a long time. Maggie always told her it was OK to feel like that sometimes, but Rose knew that in battling anxiety it was important to head it off at the first sign. To recognise your own traits.

For her, that meant not going over and over things she couldn't change, and instead to offset it with some positive action. So she tried to put all thoughts of vodka and unicorns and ambulances to the back of her mind. Today, she was supposed to be revising for her final Psychology exam next week. That was one of the building blocks for New Rose. She must not sabotage herself.

She was surprised to hear Maggie coming in the front door. Once she'd left for work, her mum rarely came back until the evening. She looked up to see her bouncing in, holding a brown paper bag aloft.

'Oh good, you're up. I nearly woke you last night to tell you. You will never in a million years guess what?'

'What?' Rose couldn't help smiling as Maggie pulled a plate from the rack and tipped out three custard tarts. 'Oh my God. Custard tarts. It must be something big.'

'It is. Mum has only gone and bought The Swan.'

Rose blinked. 'The Swan? Our Swan? The Rushbrook Swan?'

'Yep. She went down yesterday, to say goodbye to the house, and Alan told her he was going to sell it to that awful developer, so she made him an offer on the spot.' She pushed the plate of tarts towards Rose. 'She wants to do it up, get its old reputation back. Maybe sell it on once it's back on its feet. Or maybe keep it – she's not sure yet.'

Rose took a tart over to Gertie, who was engrossed in her Sylvanian family.

'There you go, darling.' Rose turned back to her mother. 'That's insane! But kind of brilliant. And classic Cherry. Oh my God, she would make it amazing.'

'And,' said Maggie, sitting down at the breakfast bar, 'here's the best bit. I'm going in with her. We're going to run it together.'

'What?' Rose stared at her.

'It makes much more sense than taking on a manager. We can keep it in the family. But don't worry,' she added hastily, seeing Rose's look of panic. 'You and Gertie will be OK here on your own. I'll be backwards and forwards. It's only an hour away.'

Rose could feel the prickles starting – the sensation she got when she felt out of control. She tried to assimilate what Maggie was telling her. It wasn't a disaster. Rushbrook wasn't far. She and Gertie would be fine. They were perfectly safe on their own at the house. She'd be able to manage. Maybe pop down to Rushbrook at weekends ...

She looked over at Gertie. How would they cope without Maggie and Cherry nearby? Not that she lived in their pockets, but knowing they were there was her safety net.

Of course she could cope. What could go wrong? She had everything under control. Only she didn't, did she? Yesterday had proved that.

She started wringing her hands. One of the things she did when she felt uncertain.

'Oh,' was all she could say.

'I'm so sorry,' said Maggie, noticing her agitation. 'I shouldn't have just sprung this on you, but it's happened rather quickly. Cherry only told me last night.'

'It's OK,' said Rose, but her voice sounded a little tight. 'I'm just getting my head round it.'

'I think Dad's struggling to get his head round it too. But you know Mum, when she has a plan . . .'

'Yes. And it's a great idea.' Rose managed a smile. 'It's amazing. It'll be wonderful.'

She nodded her assurance, but her eyes looked wide with panic and her breathing was shallow.

Maggie looked at her daughter. She had underestimated her fragility. She cursed herself for getting carried away in the heat of the moment and all of the excitement. She knew Rose was doing her best to be independent, working towards the day when she could stand on her own two feet, but she was vulnerable.

Sometimes she wondered if they all made life too easy for Rose, if they mollycoddled her because of what happened. But wasn't that called being a mum? Or a grandparent? And Rose was perfectly capable of looking after herself, most of the time. She was acing her retakes, she was a brilliant mother to Gertie, and she wasn't spoilt or overindulged.

But she had suffered, after Frank died, from anxiety. Which was totally understandable. Maggie didn't want this to be a setback. How thoughtless of her, she realised, for Rose not to have been her first concern.

'You could come too?' she suggested. 'It's not as if there wouldn't be anything for you to do.'

'Could I?' Rose's face lit up.

Maggie thought about the boathouse. Three tiny bedrooms. It would be a squeeze.

'You and Gertie would have to share a room in the boathouse.'

'We wouldn't mind.'

Summer in Rushbrook, thought Rose. One last summer before Gertie started school and she had to knuckle down and get a proper job. She would never have the freedom to do something like this again.

Hang on, she told herself. Don't let your emotions take control. Think. Is this the best thing for you?

She thought about Rushbrook, and how it felt like home just as much as this house did. She used to go there at least once a month. It was part of her, and she still hadn't found a way to replace the comfort it gave her: the smell of wood-smoke, pungent wild garlic, autumn leaves. Swimming in the river in summer and sledging down the big hill in the winter when it snowed and everyone pretended to be cut off even though most people had a four-wheel drive that would get them out. Yes, part of her was a city girl, for her home and her friends were in Avonminster, but deep inside she felt more like a country girl in her heart of hearts. Happiest with the sun on her back and her fingers in the earth.

'I finish my A levels pretty soon. I could give notice at the nursery. It would be wonderful for Gertie to spend some time in the countryside before she starts school in September.'

If she went to Rushbrook, she could just slip away from the Soul Bowl. She would never have to tell Aaron what she had done, or face Gaz – she still wasn't sure how she felt about him deceiving her. Would running away to Rushbrook make her a coward?

'It would be really good for us all,' said Maggie. 'To do something like this together. A project for the summer. I know Cherry would love you to be part of it. And think how proud Granny would have been.'

Rose's heart gave a little jump. This wasn't running away, or being a coward. This was a wonderful opportunity to spend the summer somewhere she loved, before real life kicked in.

Moving to Rushbrook was the perfect solution. To everything.

HELP WANTED

Hi everyone,

We are Cherry, Maggie and Rose.

We are delighted to have taken over The Swan.

We have lots of exciting plans but we want to hear what you want from your village pub. It's your local, after all. And we're going to need lots of help to bring our ideas to life.

We're at the pub all day at the moment, giving it a bit of a makeover, so swing by and have a glass of cider on us and tell us your ideas.

If you'd like to work for us, tell us what you're good at.

If you've got a crazy idea, let us in on it.

We've got a very open mind – the only thing we are sure of is we want The Swan to be a second home for everyone.

It's up to you to tell us what that means!

Specifically we need: a head chef, two KPs, a pastry chef, wait staff and bar staff and two cleaners.

17

Not long after dawn – he slept with the curtains open these days, for out here who could see that he slept naked? – Russell rolled out of bed and pulled on the blue overalls he'd left in a crumpled heap on the floor the night before. He had four pairs, on rotation, bought from the feed merchant. He had to admit that he would happily wear them all day, every day, for the rest of his life and be free from the tyranny of deciding what to wear. There was nothing to stop him, except the thought of his daughter's disapproval. He grinned to himself. She would know – Jen missed nothing, even from the other side of the world.

He shivered as he snapped up the poppers. Dawn's fingers had an icy pinch still. What was the saying? *Ne'er cast a clout till May is out*? It was bloody June, and the frost still lingered some mornings in the valley, on the north-facing slopes, glittering defiantly until the sun nudged it away.

He risked a glance in the mirror and winced. His hair had grown thick and wild since Christmas, the last time he'd been anywhere near a barber, and it was well past his shoulders. Working outside had reddened his skin and chapped his lips. He was almost unrecognisable from the traffic cop of five years ago, sleek in his pristine uniform behind the wheel of a high-powered BMW. He liked this wilder version of himself. He was still fit though. Running round after pigs was more demanding than chasing after criminals. Though pigs, it turned out, were equally wily and eager to escape him.

He glanced out of the window to remind himself why he was here. The rolling green fields outside were lanced by a shaft of golden sunlight as the sun rose, forcing its way through the drifts of mist. Giant oak trees loomed through the last traces of silvery white, casting long shadows over the hill. There was a sow waiting for his attention; the possibility of a wriggling litter of ginger piglets, and he smiled at the prospect. He loved every truffling snout and whiskery chin and curly tail on the farm. His charges' frisky natures and their knowing eyes. Their mischief and gung-ho attitude to life.

They lifted his heart after the slump he went into after his perfectly amicable divorce. Amicable or not, it was still hard not to take it personally when someone said, 'It's not you, it's me' after twenty-five years of marriage. Actually, Trudy had been brave to call it, otherwise they would still have been lumbering on pretending they had something in common and he was grateful that he had found what made him, if not ecstatically happy, then content. And wasn't content better than happy? Happiness was a hungry beast, requiring constant feeding, while contentment was placid, undemanding.

After the divorce, he took early retirement from the force and decided to do something completely different, somewhere completely different. He'd searched for over a year for the perfect piece of land and had found this little smallholding, further south than he had ever been. It had an agricultural tie, so it was affordable. It meant he had to prove he was earning a living off the land, which after nearly three years he just about was, with his little herd of Tamworths, wrangling clients' orders, loading up the truck to go to the farmers' market in Honisham on a Thursday, handing over sausages and bacon wrapped up in brown paper and tied with red-and-white butcher's string, weighing out gammon, slicing his Stanley knife through the skin of a pork loin.

Russell looked sharply at the furthest field. A sudden movement had caught his eye. His heart sank. The little terrors. They'd got out again. He could see them more clearly now, a cluster of piglets making a bid for freedom, tearing across the ground and towards the woods, ears streaming behind them. Shit.

He flew down the stairs and paused for a second to stuff on his boots by the back door, then charged across the yard and out into the fields. He had checked and double-checked the electric fence the night before, but this latest lot was a group of absolute rogues. He loved every single last one of them, but they would be impossible to catch. Thank God he'd taken to running around the lanes at twilight, breathing in the scented evening air and taking in the hedgerows, the trees and the riverbank. He powered up the slope through the paddock they'd escaped from, the churned-up mud slowing his progress, spied the bit of fence where they'd broken out and made their egress, smothered a smile at their daring and searched the field beyond for glints of copper, ginger and rust.

He dive-bombed on the first escapee, holding its squirming, furious little body as tight as he could.

'Right, you,' he said. 'We're going full lockdown after this. There will be no escape.'

The only response was a disgruntled snort and a look of indignation from a pair of small eyes.

It took him a full hour to retrieve the rest and block up the fence temporarily. When he got back to the house, he pulled open the fridge to get the milk for a well-deserved pot of tea.

There was none.

He thought about having black, but he wanted milk for his cornflakes too. He sighed, and went out to the flatbed truck to drive to the village shop. At least there was one. Lots of the places he'd looked at had been truly isolated, and he was glad now that he'd found somewhere reasonably near civilisation. He was emotionally self-sufficient, but he'd lived in a buzzing city all his adult life. He needed people, even if he kept them at arm's length. It was enough to know they were there.

Outside the shop, he stopped to read the adverts. New owners at The Swan. That would be interesting. He hoped it wouldn't be spoiled. He liked a quiet pint on a Friday night, or perhaps Sunday lunchtime or evening, and The Swan was one of those places you could go on your own. There was always someone to chat to if you felt like a conversation, but at the same time people would leave you alone if you set your shoulders in a certain way. He'd been sad when Alan had told him he was thinking of selling to a developer.

'Swan's had a reprieve, then,' he said to Lorraine,

plonking a loaf of bread, a pint of milk and a packet of Polos on the counter.

'What a bloody relief,' she told him, cashing up. 'I couldn't bear the thought of that crook Marcus Draycott getting his hands on it. Retirement apartments!'

She gave a toss of her blonde mane. Russell had no idea when she had the time to get it done, for she was at the shop from six until eight every day. She looked more like a croupier than a shopkeeper, but she could get you anything you wanted and was relentlessly cheerful. And a mine of very useful information.

'So who are they then? The new lot?'

'The family from Wisteria House. Catherine Nicholson who lived there – she died last year – it's her daughter that bought it. And her daughter's helping her. So they're not outsiders. Not that there's anything wrong with outsiders,' she added hastily.

Russell smiled. He knew he would be an object of suspicion for many years to come. 'Sounds great.'

'Dr Nicholson delivered me, you know.' She pointed upwards. 'In the bedroom up there. My mum wouldn't have let anyone else near her. So we'll be in safe hands.'

Russell wasn't sure that being descended from someone who delivered babies qualified you to run a pub, but he wasn't the quibbling kind. 'All women, then.'

Lorraine flexed a bicep. 'Girl power. We just need a female vicar and we're sorted. Though I love the Matts.' She pointed at him. 'And don't say anything about women not being able to change a barrel properly – Cherry Nicholson worked at The Swan before you were a twinkle in your mother's eye.'

'I wouldn't dream of it,' said Russell, who wouldn't. He

had a lot of respect for women. In his view, they made the best traffic cops. A woman had got him out of trouble more than once over the years. They were more interested in getting the job done than proving themselves.

'Rushbrook will be on the up if they get it right. Did you see how much they got for Wisteria House?'

'No.' Why was everyone so obsessed with property prices down here?

'A lot.' Lorraine raised her eyebrows and nodded. 'It's the river that does it. Anything riverside – ker-ching. The new owners get five newspapers on a Sunday. Who has the time to read five newspapers?'

'I don't know, Lorraine,' Russell chuckled.

It was hard to keep up with her sometimes. Lorraine loved dissecting Rushbrook and the changes in it. She was usually the first to know anything, being on the parish council as well.

'Will we see you at the opening night? Midsummer's Eve?' Lorraine looked at him from under her lashes as she handed him his change. She was pathologically incapable of not flirting, even though she was perfectly happily married to Don. 'Two weeks' time, according to Maggie.'

'Depends what's on telly.'

'You're a dark horse.'

'Aye,' he said, sending himself up by playing the taciturn Northerner. He gave her a little salute and left.

Back in his kitchen, he poured a hefty bowl of cornflakes and made himself a brew. Halfway through his breakfast, his phone burbled at him. Jen. She FaceTimed two or three times a week. She worried about him, but she didn't need to. He accepted the call and smiled at the sight of her, sitting on her balcony in Adelaide, the dark hair she'd inherited from him tumbling to her shoulders, her freckles out in force.

'How's it going, Dad?'

He shook his head. 'The little buggers got out again. Talk about high-intensity interval training.'

'Didn't you check the fence?'

'Listen, they could get out of a maximum-security jail if they put their mind to it.'

'What are you up to today?'

'Well.' He poured himself another handful of corn-flakes. 'I thought I'd head down to The Swan. It's been taken over. I thought I'd see if they'd let me supply them again.'

'Good for you.'

'Try and get in there before anyone else.'

'That would be a nice contract. And on the doorstep.'

'That's what I thought. It was a good bit of bread and butter when Alan was still doing food.'

'I thought the pub was going to be apartments?'

'Apparently not. There's a grand reopening in a fort-night.'

'Well, that's good. Maybe you'll meet someone down there.'

He looked up from his bowl and gave her a wry smile. It was her mission to get him back in the saddle.

'I'm all right.'

'No. You deserve someone lovely. You can't spend the rest of your life surrounded by pigs and listening to Black Sabbath.'

'Hey. It's bloody paradise, I'm telling you.'

'No, Dad. You need to have some fun. You're turning into a boring old fart.'

'Thanks. Love you too!'

'I'm only saying that because I know you're not one. But you've got to get yourself out there. It's been nearly five years, Dad.'

'I've been busy!'

'Have you signed up for that app yet?'

'No fear.'

'It's how everyone does it, Dad. It's nothing to be afraid of.'

'It's Russian roulette.'

'You have to learn to trust. Take a few risks.'

'You can't accuse me of not taking risks!'

'Not emotional ones, you don't. You've shut yourself away on that farm. It's a waste, Dad. Someone out there deserves you.'

His heart buckled for a moment.

'OK. I'll give it a go. What should I say? Miserable old pig farmer seeks Kristen Scott Thomas/Minnie Driver?'

Jen rolled her eyes. 'You're not old. You need some nice pictures. Get your hair cut first, though. It's gone beyond a joke.'

He pulled a beanie out of his overall pocket and put it on, pushing his curls inside. 'How about that?'

Jen sighed.

'You're hopeless.'

He carried on shovelling in his cornflakes, but he was smiling. She badgered, nagged and cajoled him, but that she loved him there was no doubt. She was his life, Jen, and she was too far away. Sometimes he dreamt she came home and he converted one of the barns for her to live in, but that was a selfish fantasy and not likely to happen, and nor should it. She had to live her own life. As soon as he had found someone he could trust with the pigs, he would get on a plane and go to visit her.

In the meantime, there was mucking out to be done, fencing to be repaired and sausages to sell. He hadn't taken the easy option when he retired. Chasing a nicked car down the motorway was a breeze in comparison to running a pig farm. But would he go back? Not on your life.

She was right though, because Jen knew him better than anyone in the world. As much as he adored his pigs, deep down he craved companionship. But he was not going on a dating app for any money, no matter how much she tried to persuade him it was what everyone did. Russell might be adept at assessing the road ahead and putting his foot down to overtake a speeding criminal, but when it came to affairs of the heart, he was deadly cautious. He wasn't going to take a risk on a random smiling face on his phone screen. No way.

18

Chaos. It was always chaos, no matter how hard she tried to organise it. No matter how hard she tried not to shout. They were only kids, and it was hard for them too, so she tried not to raise her voice, but it was impossible to get them out of the door otherwise. If they missed the bus to Honisham, they would be at home all day, and that wasn't good – for lots of reasons but mostly because Chloe was desperately trying not to attract attention. She didn't want anyone sniffing around.

Of course, they were old enough now to go to the bus stop themselves, but she didn't trust either of them. Especially not Otis. He was starting to get a look in his eye she didn't like. And whatever Otis did, Pearl would follow. If he didn't get on the bus, she wouldn't either. So Chloe had to march them there and see them on. She actually had to wait until the bus had left because if she didn't, they would hop off as soon as her back was turned.

She had to get up at six thirty to make sure everything was sorted. If they weren't out of the house by twenty past seven, it was all over. She packed up their bags, made sure their homework books had been signed, did their lunches (peanut butter sandwiches, carrot sticks, a Penguin), quadruple-checked for any letters heralding a trip or bloody World Book Day. There was always something missing at the last minute, no matter how organised she was. Shoes, usually. She tried to get them into the habit of taking them off when they came home and leaving them by the door, ready to put on as they left, but somehow they forgot and one always got kicked under the settee or left behind the bathroom door.

There was a blood-curdling shriek from upstairs. Chloe felt her heart turn over. She ran to the stairs and looked up to see Pearl holding up a perspex cage.

'It's Beyoncé. She's just lying there. I think she's dead.'

The bloody hamster. Chloe raced up the stairs. Maybe it would be a good thing if it *was* dead? Traumatic, but at least that would be the end of the constant anxiety over Beyoncé's health. She peered into the cage at the small lump of ginger fur.

'No, she's breathing, look. She's probably tired.'

'She's ill. We need to take her to the vet.' Pearl's voice was shrill.

'I'll keep an eye on her. If she's not better by lunchtime, I'll take her. I promise.'

She wouldn't, of course. A trip to the vet was pro-hibitively expensive. It would be cheaper to replace the hamster with a new one.

'I want to take her to school.'

Ah. So that was the game-plan. Pearl had a beseeching expression on her face that Chloe knew only too well.

'It would be way too noisy for her. And what if she escaped? What if someone let her out?'

Pearl looked at her, weighing up whether she was being fobbed off.

'Come on,' said Chloe. 'Put her back on your dressing table. We're going to miss the bus.'

Please don't have a meltdown, she begged.

Pearl hovered for a moment, looking at the hamster, then decided that co-operation was the best tactic for now and went to put the cage back in her bedroom. Chloe breathed a sigh of relief and ran back downstairs. Out of the corner of her eye she saw that Otis was still in front of the telly in his pants.

'Otis! We're leaving in two minutes. Do you want to go to school in your crackers?'

His eyes didn't leave the screen. He had headphones on, so he couldn't hear her. She grabbed the remote and pressed off. That soon got his attention. His head swivelled round and he glared at her.

'Get dressed!' She knew he could hear her now. 'We're leaving in *two*.'

She held up two fingers to emphasise her point.

He gave a world-weary sigh and stumped over to the settee where she had laid his clothes half an hour ago. She knew she shouldn't run around after them quite so much, that they should be able to look after themselves, but it made her life easier if she made their lives easier. The important thing was to keep life as normal as possible for them. They were the priority.

By some miracle the three of them made it out of the house without any more drama or shouting. She herded them along the pavement and out of the crescent, then along the lane. The sun was warm, and she thought what a shame it was they had to go to school, how much nicer it would have been to walk down to the river and muck about.

She heard a car approaching from round the bend.

'Get in, kids.'

The lane was narrowest here, just before it met the main road, and she flattened the three of them against the hedge to let it pass. She recognised the car as soon as it rounded the corner. The dark green Defender, with *Rushbrook Safari Lodges* emblazoned on its side. Her heart sank as she saw the driver. Dash Culbone. There would only be one reason for him to drive up this road. He wound his window down, and she held up two fingers just as she had done to Otis.

'I'll be two minutes. Can you wait?'

He nodded, and gave her a sympathetic smile. 'You're OK. Don't rush.'

Two minutes. Why was it her life always seemed to be measured in two minutes? Why didn't she ever have any longer?

Her heart was pounding as she hurried Otis and Pearl onto the main road and along to the bus stop, praying it would be on time. The pressure felt relentless. You got over one crisis and another lurched along. She wasn't sure how much longer she was going to be able to keep it up.

'She's going to be all right, isn't she?' Pearl was looking up at her, her eyes rounder than ever. For a moment, Chloe wondered if she meant Mum, then realised she was talking about Beyoncé.

'Of course,' she said, smoothing down the little girl's hair, wishing she'd had a chance to do a proper French plait instead of a rushed ponytail. Maybe they'd do one tonight. And here was the bus. It rumbled to a stop, the doors wheezing as they opened.

'Have a good day,' she said to them both, but they were up the steps without a backward glance. She didn't wait for the bus to leave before she retraced her steps, running as fast as she could back to the house. Number five was almost in the middle of Kerslake Crescent, half a dozen pairs of semi-detached council houses in yellowing pebble-dash that backed onto open fields, with woodland and the river beyond. They'd landed with their bums in the honey, getting this house. Mum had found it by some miracle – there wasn't much to rent in this part of Somerset, as anything nice went as a holiday cottage, but number five needed money spending on it that the landlord didn't have so there they were, quite happy to have a kitchen with the doors falling off in return for fields on the doorstep.

She saw that Dash was there, parked up on the other side of the road by the old phone box. She was grateful for his discretion. She didn't want anyone knowing anything. She felt sweat trickle under her arm pits from the stress and the exertion. It was going to be a hot day.

'Hey.' Dash had wound the window down and was leaning his elbow on the door jamb. He had a baseball cap on over his dark curls, and a polo shirt with the RSF logo embroidered on it.

'I'm really sorry,' gasped Chloe. 'Mum's not very well today.'

Dash sighed. 'We've got five lodges that need turning around. I'm relying on her.'

'It's OK. I can do it. No problem.'

Dash frowned. 'What about school?'

'I'm on study leave. For exams.' GCSEs were proving to be a godsend. She didn't have to come up with endless excuses.

'Shouldn't you be revising, in that case?'

'I can catch up later.'

'I don't want to get you into trouble.'

'I won't get into trouble.' The trouble would be if they didn't get this money in. There was precisely fourteen pounds left in the kitty. Enough for maybe three days' food.

'Is your mum OK?' Dash was looking up at Nicole's window. The curtains were still drawn.

She wished she could trust him. Dash was kind, for a posh bloke. He paid good wages and looked after his staff. For a moment she was tempted to confide in him. Tell him what her life was really like and what she had to put up with. Tell him how tired she was. How sick she felt every morning.

'It's one of her migraines again. I gave her some tablets first thing. She should be OK by tomorrow with a bit of luck.'

He looked at her thoughtfully. Chloe gulped, nervous he was about to probe further, but he seemed to swallow her story and smiled, nodding his head at the passenger seat.

'Hop in, then. I'll give you a lift.'

The sooner she went and turned around the lodges, the sooner she could get back. She had Beyoncé to deal with. Hopefully she wouldn't cark it while she was out. Pearl would never forgive her. If Beyoncé died, she'd have to get the bus to the pet shop in Honisham and buy another hamster the same colour before Pearl got home.

It was possible, but it would be so much easier if she just stayed alive . . .

She'd take Beyoncé with her. That way she could keep an eye on her and head into town straight from Rushbrook House if she needed to.

'Can you hang on two minutes? There's something I need.'

'Sure.' Dash seemed happy now he knew he had cover.

Chloe rushed into the house. Everything was quiet. She ran up the stairs to the kids' bedroom. Any minute now Pearl would have to move into Chloe's room. She was twelve, and Otis was fourteen – it wouldn't be right for them to keep sharing. They both needed privacy. Mind you, they were lucky to have three bedrooms. Chloe had to keep reminding herself to be grateful.

She picked up the cage – Beyoncé was looking a bit brighter. How long did hamsters live? Not long, probably. Beyoncé had been one of her mother's impulse purchases. On one of her good days. Nicole had totally ignored Chloe's warnings that the hamster would be a responsibility the family couldn't manage, given they couldn't look after themselves most of the time. Who was going to clean it out and feed it? And what would happen when it died? Nicole had been swept away by the novelty and Pearl's undying devotion to her once Beyoncé had been procured.

Chloe crept out of the bedroom. She hovered on the landing outside the closed door. She had to check. For all her mother's shortcomings, she did still care about her.

The room was pitch black. It smelt stale, with an underlying sweetness that was Nicole's trademark scent of alcohol and perfume. Chloe picked her way across the floor carefully, knowing it would be strewn with discarded clothes and shoes: a silk kimono; a pair of boots. At the bedside, she peered at the shape under the duvet.

'Mum?' A loud whisper should be enough to wake her but not cause alarm.

Nicole groaned. 'Mmmm?'

'I'm going to Rushbrook. To do the lodges. Dash is here.'

A pale arm stretched out as Nicole wiggled her fingers in a request for contact. Chloe took her hand and squeezed it, appreciating the squeeze her mum gave back. A squeeze of acknowledgement, appreciation and love. It was the most she could expect in her mum's current state.

'Do you want anything?'

'Mm-mm.'

'I'll be back as quick as I can.'

'OK.' It was half croak, half whisper.

She might be up and about by the time Chloe got back. She might not. She might sleep through till the next day. Chloe didn't know which was the best option.

There was no best option.

Outside she scrambled into the front seat of Dash's car.

'All good?' asked Dash, putting the car into first gear and setting off.

'Yep,' said Chloe, setting the hamster cage on her lap. 'I've got to bring Beyoncé with me, if that's OK. She's looking a bit peaky, so I need to keep an eye on her.'

One bright eye peered out from the depths of the shavings.

'That's a big responsibility,' smiled Dash.

Chloe managed to smile back. Beyoncé a big responsibility? He had no idea.

'I expect she'll be fine. She's probably had too many sunflower seeds. They always overfeed her.'

Maroon Five drifted out of the radio. The sun was shining and the air smelled sweet with apple blossom. She wished she could enjoy the drive, sing along, but there was a knot in her stomach. There always was.

19

Nicole could hear the Defender pull away down the road. She rolled onto her back with a groan. She'd done it again. She groped on the bedside table for some water to swallow down some painkillers. Chloe would have left her a glass before she went to bed. She would make it up to her. It was her prom soon. She'd make her the most wonderful outfit – create something amazing. Nicole was a genius with a pair of scissors and a boxful of sequins and feathers. She was very, *very* good at silly things that made people happy. Like building a papier maché castle for Beyoncé to scamper about in. Or making a *Game of Thrones* cake for Otis. Things that made people gasp with admiration, but weren't actually useful. Or profitable.

The only other thing she was good at was getting drunk. She could win Olympic Gold for it these days. She wished, more than anything, she could stop. Wished that she didn't have to wake filled with self-loathing and panic, and stumble through the day avoiding mirrors and bright light and other people.

She hadn't always been like this. Once she'd been able

to leave it to Saturday nights, or holidays. But that was before the world had shown her up for what she was. A failure. How else had she ended up losing everything?

She had loved teaching English at Meadow Hall. The kids were bright, smart and funny and she'd pushed them, got excellent grades. But schools like Meadow Hall didn't like scandal. And a teacher's husband having an affair with another parent was beyond the pale. Even though it hadn't been her fault when Rich went off with Elizabeth Spring – though obviously it had, for happy men didn't stray, did they? – she had felt the disapproval, from both the staff and the other parents. In the end, she couldn't cope with the humiliation, so she had resigned, thinking she could be a supply teacher while she found something else more permanent.

And then she'd lost her licence. She'd got into the habit of a couple of glasses of wine in the evening. And when Chloe had missed the bus home one evening and needed a lift, she hadn't thought she was over the limit. She'd told herself she'd only had two glasses, not taking into account the glass she used was the size of a goldfish bowl, so she'd probably had the best part of half a bottle. So of course she'd failed the breath test when she was pulled over after pulling out a bit too sharply on a roundabout.

Thank goodness for this house which she'd found to rent. Space was a little tight but she had just been able to afford it, and Rushbrook seemed the perfect place to hide away and lick her wounds. She just wanted to hide away from the embarrassment of it all – no husband, no job and no driving licence – and the kids had been able to stay at the same school, thanks to the bus to Honisham. She'd got the job at the Safari Lodges, and although she had never imagined herself ending up as a cleaner, the surroundings were so glorious and Dash was such a wonderful combination of handsome and kind that it took the sting out of it.

It would be easier once she got her licence back, if she could afford a car, to get a better job. A librarian, perhaps? She'd thought about private tutoring, too. She knew her stuff, knew what the exam boards wanted, and Skype made it easier. Nicole resolved to check out the competition online later. It was too late for this year, as exams were nearly over. But she could start afresh in September. A new leaf, for autumn. Yes! Something like a plan was gradually starting to form in her head.

She had to pull herself together if she was going to survive. She didn't have to live like this any longer, she told herself. Of course she didn't. The trick, she knew only too well, was not to have the first drink, with its deliciously deceptive cloak of comfort, because that led to the second, and then the third, and it was the third that was the very devil himself and made you completely forget your resolutions.

Just. Don't. Start.

She had seen the look on Chloe's face last night. She'd had enough. Wonderful Chloe, who blamed herself for the drink-driving thing, for needing a lift that evening.

'How can it possibly be your fault?' Nicole had tried to reassure her over and over again.

'If I hadn't needed a lift,' Chloe argued, 'it would all be fine.'

It wouldn't, though, because losing her licence was the tip of the iceberg. She should have stopped drinking there and then, but it was too easy to buy a couple of pretty bottles of pale pink rosé from the village shop. It looked so innocuous. And it was so easy to quaff the lot.

What she should do is ask Lorraine not to sell it to her. Sometimes she caught the shopkeeper's eye and saw questions she didn't want to answer. Lorraine could count. Lorraine knew how much she got through. She was reliant on the shop because she had promised herself not to add wine to the weekly supermarket delivery. Once it was there, in amongst the baked beans and Rice Krispies, there would be evidence.

Get it together, Nicole, she told herself. Get up, get showered, get dressed. Make dinner for your beautiful children. She needed them, for they were the only thing keeping her going. Her funny, nutty, gorgeous kids.

She pushed herself up and slid her long, pale legs out of bed. She picked up her kimono from the floor and wrapped it round her body. She'd lost more weight, she realised. She could almost wrap it round herself twice. The room shifted a little and she put a hand to the wall to steady herself. She couldn't do this yet. She had all day to sort herself out before the kids got back. She'd go back to bed, just for a while. Sleep it off. If she got up at midday, she'd get it all done.

20

Cherry, Maggie, Rose and Gertie left for Rushbrook in convoy the morning of the pub handover. Cherry had piled up her car with an assortment of paraphernalia from the basement of Admiral House – ornaments and lamps and fabric remnants; anything she thought might come in useful for the revamp – as well as gallons of carefully chosen paint. Maggie had all her favourite kitchen equipment. It was a strange feeling, like setting off on holiday, but also the thrill of the new venture infected them all. Rose was worried that Gertie might be sick, she was so hyper, and had to sit next to her in the back of Maggie's Mini to calm her down.

'I'm coming back up at the weekend,' said Maggie. 'So if anyone's forgotten anything I can pick it up.'

Space was going to be at a premium in the boathouse, so they were travelling light.

As she drove over the suspension bridge, leaving Admiral House behind her, Cherry's excitement was dampened by the fact that Mike hadn't been there to see her off. She had thought he would come round to her buying The Swan after the shock had worn off, but he still wouldn't discuss anything to do with it. He wasn't sulking, exactly, or hostile to her – only the idea. Over the past weeks, with emails back and forth between Cherry and Howard and Alan and his solicitor, he had refused to talk any of it through with her. She found it unnerving. Not that she couldn't make her own decisions, but she valued his opinion and his point of view. He was adamant he was staying out of it.

'I can't pretend that I think it's a good idea,' he told her one night. 'So I'd rather say nothing.'

So the atmosphere between them was strained. They didn't argue, and he still cooked her lovely meals and they still curled up in bed together at night, but somehow The Swan had become the elephant in the room. Mike's downer on it didn't deter Cherry, though. The more she dug into the idea, the more excited she was and the more convinced they would make a success of it.

She felt sure that once they had turned it around, he would relent.

'I'm only protecting you,' he told her again, and she knew he wasn't being patronising, just caring, but there was nothing she could say to change his mind. And she did feel a little hurt that he had shot off to the university early that morning, and not stayed to wave them off. Maybe he was right? Maybe she was making a terrible mistake?

But as she pulled up in front of the pub, she felt her resolve return. The Swan was looking demure in the mid-morning sunshine, as if butter wouldn't melt, as if it didn't hold any nasty surprises or horror stories inside its thick stone walls, but would emerge when they reopened as resplendent as a blushing bride at the altar.

Behind her, the others pulled up and tumbled out of the car. They stood on the lawn, the four of them, surveying the place that would be their raison d'être for the foreseeable future.

'Two weeks,' said Cherry. 'Do you think we can do it in two weeks? Or are we mad?'

'Two weeks . . .' Maggie quailed. Being in charge of the kitchen, she had the most to organise. The food could make or break a pub, and you had to get it right from the start. You didn't want any disgruntled customers wandering off grumbling about half-cooked chips or greasy lasagne.

'Course we can,' said Rose, uplifted by the scent of apple blossom. 'There's not much wrong with it, after all. And it will be a work in progress. We don't have to get it all right first time.'

'At least summer's here,' said Maggie. 'People will forgive a lot if it's sunny, and they've got a glass of cider in their hand.'

'Well, the Fabulous Builder Brothers are coming tomorrow, so we need to be ready with a plan,' said Cherry. 'I don't want them standing around with nothing to do.'

The Fabulous Builder Brothers had dropped everything to rearrange their diary for Cherry as she'd given them so much work over the years. A chippy and a sparks by trade, they could turn their hand to anything and didn't look at her as if she was mad when she told them what she wanted. They had agreed to come down in their campervan and stay in the car park till the job was done. It would be a bit of a holiday for them.

'We can try out our new menus on them,' said Maggie. They would be harsh critics. They were bearded, tattooed hipsters who took their coffee and their sourdough very seriously. If the menu got past them, they'd be on the right track.

'Here's Alan.' Cherry put her hand up and waved as they all watched Alan's beaten-up burgundy Volvo rattle along the road and swing into the car park. None of them could believe how quickly things had moved. Nothing had been officially signed and sealed yet, but he and Cherry had agreed there was no point in prolonging the takeover, that it was best for all of them if it happened straight away. The pub licence was being transferred; Maggie already had a personal licence from when she had run the tapas bar, and Cherry had applied to the council for her own licence, for good measure.

Alan parked and got out of his car, a country pub land-lord to the end in his beige cords and checked shirt and big cardigan with the leather buttons. They hung back for a moment as he looked at the building that had been his life for so long, until Fred and Ginger raced around from the garden at the back where they had been exploring, to discover who the interloper was, and broke the spell.

Alan walked towards them all, a wide smile on his round face, dangling the keys aloft.

'My beautiful Swan,' he said. 'I can't tell you how pleased I am to be leaving her in such safe hands.' He stopped and blinked. There were tears in eyes. 'It's going to be the pub it should be.'

'We want it to be everything it was in its heyday,' said Maggie. 'We have such fond memories, all of us.'

'Oh, the glory days,' said Alan. 'There were times when I was fully booked every night of the week, and no one left till gone midnight.' He smiled at the memory.

'I'm not sure my liver will ever forgive me. I've run the pub into the ground, though,' he went on, darkly. 'She deserves better.'

'We'll do our very best to get The Swan back on her feet,' said Cherry. 'We'll resurrect her in your honour. We'll make you proud.'

'I can't thank you enough.' He was choked with tears. This was an emotional morning for him. 'We're setting off tomorrow. Three weeks in Croatia. I'm just hoping . . .' He coughed and cleared his throat. 'Anyway, here you are. The keys to the kingdom.' He passed over the tasselled fob. 'Forgive me if I don't come in. But I'm on the end of a phone whenever you need me.' He put up his hands in a gesture that encompassed farewell, thanks and good luck, but which also told them not to come near him. They could see it wouldn't take much for him to break down. 'Farewell.'

He turned and walked back to his car. They all looked at each other.

'I can't bear it,' said Rose. 'It's not fair.'

'We're doing a good thing,' said Cherry. 'Here, Gertie.' Cherry handed her great-granddaughter the key. 'Go and find the keyhole, darling. You can be our lucky mascot.'

The four of them marched over the gravel chippings to the arched front door of the pub. Gertie stood on tiptoe and inserted the key, looking up at her mum to help her. Rose put her hand over her daughter's and twisted until they all heard the lock click back. Rose pushed open the door, and they all stood for a moment on the threshold, filled with anticipation. In the end, Fred and Ginger barged in first, barking with excitement at the thought of what might be inside, so they followed.

It was dark and gloomy and smelled stale. The stools were up on the tables. Despite the warm weather outside, it was damp and cold; the air stagnant. It felt hostile and unwelcoming. It wasn't a place you'd want to be in for more than five minutes. Maggie shivered.

'Get the curtains and the windows open,' commanded Cherry. 'I'll light a fire. Put some music on, Rose. It just needs some life in it. All pubs look awful first thing in the morning.'

And she was right. In twenty minutes, with fresh air and light streaming in, and a fire blazing away, and some tinkling piano music coming out of the speakers, the atmosphere felt completely different. It was strange, though, sitting in the empty pub, at the table they always used to commandeer if they could, with a large window to one side and the fireplace to the other. Despite the music, the quiet was disconcerting. The Swan had always been so lively. Rowdy at times. To get all those people back was going to be a tall order.

Maggie poured them coffee and Cherry lifted her mug.

'I want to propose a toast,' she said. 'To my mum, for giving me the means to do this. Her nest egg gave me the courage to make the biggest impulse purchase of my life. It might seem foolhardy, but I'm convinced we will do great things. So this is to Catherine, for making this happen. For all of us.'

'To Granny,' said Maggie.

'To GG,' said Rose, her nickname for her great-grandmother.

'GG,' crowed Gertie, clinking her mug carefully with each of the other's in turn.

Cherry could picture Catherine, in her Liberty blouse

and faded jeans and old tennis shoes, her white hair held back with a tortoiseshell hairband, ordering her favourite Cumberland sausage and mash. Cherry couldn't stop wishing she was here to see them all. Today was a turning point, an exciting new venture for all of them that Catherine had gifted them, even if she didn't know it.

'So,' she said. 'The grand reopening is the Friday after next. How do we do this?'

'Right,' said Maggie. 'Roughly speaking, Mum is front of house, I'm in charge of the kitchen and Rose—'

'Just call me the groundsman,' grinned Rose.

'I suggest we spend today drawing up a game plan and a shopping list. We can't just go nuts and spend our way through this. We've got a budget to stick to and I'm going to be strict about it from the start because it'll be tempting to splurge. We want it to be beautiful but anyone can make somewhere beautiful if they splash enough cash.'

'I'm very good at doing things on the cheap,' Cherry protested.

'Hmm,' said Maggie doubtfully. 'I know you can spot a bargain but you do love an expensive light fitting.'

'OK, so that Murano glass chandelier thing was about a gazillion pounds, but I can rein it in. I'm the queen of compromise.'

Rose smiled to herself and pulled out a colouring book for Gertie. Her mum and grandmother could go on like this for hours. Cherry was spontaneous and impulsive while Maggie tended to be very exacting and organised. 'Mum. You've got to give Cherry free rein and not be controlling,' she said.

'It's OK, darling,' said Cherry. 'I've got to remember this is a business and not my home.'

'Exactly,' said Maggie. 'Though we do want your magic touch. Tell us your vision again.'

They'd discussed it often enough, but somehow hearing it in situ would bring it all to life.

'I want The Swan to keep everything that we loved about it,' said Cherry. 'Its quintessential country pub-ness. The way it's the heart of the village, but also welcoming to outsiders, strangers, visitors. A place to eat, drink and be merry. A place for quiet contemplation or a rowdy party, depending on your mood. But I want it to be so much more than that. Something softer, warmer, more inviting. Something that's in the spirit of us three. Something...' Cherry struggled to find the word. 'Nurturing? Does that sound pretentious?'

'No,' said Maggie. 'I think that's lovely. Something for everyone. Inclusive, not exclusive. And timeless.'

'Yes. I want people to feel as if they are stepping into another world. One where they feel at home.'

'That's it,' said Rose. 'They need to feel at home, but also as if they are a special guest. Looked after.'

Cherry clapped her hands. 'Do you know, it's weird, but I've never felt so excited about a project. I guess because this feels as if it's got a point to it. For the first time in my life, I feel as if I'm doing something constructive. Not just choosing wallpaper.'

'Don't be so hard on yourself, Mum,' Maggie frowned.

'You know what I mean. This is a real challenge. It's not just about deciding where to put an RSJ or whether to have seagrass or coir. This is about people. Creating something they want to be a part of. It's pretty scary, too, because what do I know about running a pub?'

'We're pretty sussed between us. And we've got Alan

on speed dial, remember. Loads of people who run a pub have never done it before.'

'Yes, and loads of people run them into the ground and lose a fortune.' She echoed Mike's sentiments, feeling his absence once again. He should be here, she thought wistfully.

'Don't get cold feet now. There's no time for panic.' Rose turned to Gertie, who was doing some careful colouring. 'Gertie? What do you think the pub needs?'

'Chickens,' said the little girl, decisively. 'Can we have chickens?'

Maggie laughed. 'I suppose we'll need eggs.'

'Chickens would be amazing,' agreed Rose.

'We need a chef first,' said Maggie. 'Bar staff. A cleaner. I've put an advert up in the village shop. It would be nice to use local people where we can. And as many women as we can.'

'That would be cool,' said Rose. 'To have an all-woman team.'

'We'll probably have to take what we're given. A female chef would be great, though.'

'Let's get hiring,' said Cherry. 'We want to open the doors in two weeks' time and have some sort of menu up and running, even if it's just really basic. Do you reckon we can do it, Maggie?'

'One hundred per cent,' said Maggie. 'Even if I have to get in the kitchen myself.'

Cherry swept her gaze around the bar. There was a limit to how much they could change in two weeks, but she was determined to give it a really fresh feel, whilst keeping it comfortably familiar.

She felt a thrill rush through her. The challenge was

daunting but exciting, but the stakes were high. And underlying it was the quiet unease she felt at the state of her relationship with Mike. She knew what he feared: that in six months' time they would be standing in a cold, empty pub teetering on the brink of bankruptcy.

She was not going to let that happen.

21

Maggie braced herself to walk into the kitchen. She knew Alan's chef had walked out on him and he'd had to rely on a temporary chef brought in from an agency, so her hopes of finding a clean and orderly kitchen weren't high. In the end, it had all got too much and Alan had got rid of the chef and simply stopped serving the food that The Swan had once been so well known for. Her heart went out to him – the captain of a sinking ship struggling to keep afloat, while also battling the nightmare of Gillian's illness. At least now he didn't have to worry about how to keep the pub buoyant, or feel he was letting the village down. He could focus on his darling wife. Maggie's throat went tight when she thought about them heading off to Croatia.

The kitchen was even worse than she'd expected. Alan had freely admitted to shutting the door on it, and it was just as the temporary chef had left it. There were piles of dirty pans next to the sink, and she didn't dare open the dishwasher. The burner was coated in grease, and the walls around it were spattered with fat. Nothing was where it should be. The fridge was full of unidentifiable rotting produce and she slammed the door shut. The floor was grimy; the strip lights coated in dead flies.

It needed a deep clean, and some new shelving, and proper organisation. Everything was piled up haphazardly, with no sense of order, no labelling. She resolved to throw every item of food out and start again. She knew she was being a little draconian, but if she was in charge, she needed the kitchen immaculate. She had only got where she was today by being obsessive and organised.

The more she investigated, the more she felt rising panic. Eventually she shut her eyes and counted to ten, running through her options. She could call an agency to do a deep clean. Or she could get over herself and get her rubber gloves on. If she opened the windows, put on the radio and sang her way through it, she could save several hundred pounds that she could then spend on new equipment.

She didn't want to think about what might be hiding in the corners. Cockroaches, mice or even worse, rats.

She went out to the car. She'd had the foresight to bring as many cleaning products as she could with her: bleach, surface cleaner and scouring pads. She lifted the box out of the boot and put it on the draining board. She grabbed an extra-strength bin bag and flung every bottle and every jar she could find into it. Every packet of pasta and rice, every box of salt. It might seem wasteful but she couldn't risk using any of it. She steeled herself as she opened the fridge and flung out bags of decomposing greenery, packets of rancid cheese and butter, and cartons of sour milk, shuddering and trying not to retch.

She opened the dishwasher and was relieved to find it empty, so she put it on its hottest wash to freshen it up so she could load it. Each pot, pan and plate in the kitchen was going to go through twice.

Then she filled the sink with hot soapy water and snapped on a pair of bright yellow rubber gloves so she could scrub down every surface and every shelf.

She was halfway through the pile of pans when her phone rang. Mario. She frowned. What did he want? Curiosity got the better of her, and she pulled off her gloves and answered.

'Maggie.' His voice trickled down the line like warm extra virgin olive oil.

'Yes,' she said, cautious.

'I just found out from Zara. You sold the business to her.'

'I did. Not that it makes any difference to you.' The betrayal still stung.

'Maggie.' His voice was full of reproach. 'Listen. Have dinner with me. I miss you. And I want to say thank you for everything you did for us.'

'Well, I don't know if that's a good idea.'

'I can get us a table at Ottantadue.'

He named her favourite restaurant. It was an offer she couldn't refuse. Not least because she was going to need him as a supplier. For oo pasta flour, for olive oil, for cheeses, for cans of ripe Italian tomatoes – she was not going to cut off her nose to spite her face. More to the point, she was going to use his guilt to nail him down on price.

'How about dinner on Friday?' She was going to go back to Avonminster at the weekend to get the rest of her kitchen equipment.

'OK then. Friday at eight o'clock.'

He rang off and Maggie couldn't help smiling. She liked how Mario went about getting his own way. She pulled her gloves on, plunged her hands back into the water and started to think about her plans for resurrecting the food.

It went without saying that they would use local produce as much as they could. Everyone did these days. It was almost a given. But Maggie wanted the pub to represent the true heart of Rushbrook, and reflect that in its dishes and ingredients. After all, the fare on their doorstep was mouth-watering and more-ish: there were producers doing amazing things with cheese and charcuterie and cider. And further down, along the coast, there were Porlock oysters. Maybe crab and mussels too. And there was game – venison and pigeon – and of course trout from the river. Simple, unmucked about with, unpretentious country cooking.

She would bring back the pies, too. The pub had once been famous for them, made by a local girl, Tabitha Melchior, but somehow when she left, no one had her light hand with pastry. Maggie remembered them vividly, the crust golden and glistening, the insides moist with sauce or gravy. Who didn't love a pie? She made a note to track down Tabitha and persuade her to part with her recipes.

The door opened and Cherry stuck her head round.

'There's someone here to see you. Russell, from Pepper Wood Farm? He saw the ad in the village shop.'

Maggie headed out into the bar. There was a tall bloke in blue overalls and wellingtons, a beanie pulled over his head. He'd obviously come straight from the farm. Mind you, she thought, she didn't look much better, in her boiler suit, her hair stuffed into a catering hat and rubber gloves on. Not a good look.

'Hi – Russell?' she said. 'I'm Maggie.'

'Hi,' he said, looking a bit awkward. 'Um – Alan used

to buy pork from me and I wondered if you'd like me to supply you again?'

'Oh my goodness – absolutely! If those were your sausages, they were amazing.'

'Still are, I hope.'

'Why don't you send us down some samples? We could trial some dishes then set up a regular order.'

'Great,' said Russell. 'I was thinking too – I'm going to be doing hog roasts this summer. Maybe they'd be good for bank holidays?'

Maggie's mouth watered at the very thought. 'I tell you what,' she said. 'Could you do us a hog roast for the opening night? It's on Friday week. It would take the pressure right off us. And it would be a perfect way to get everyone in the village up here. Who doesn't love a hot pork roll?'

'Well, vegetarians, I guess,' said Russell.

Maggie looked at him. He was very dry, very deadpan, and she wasn't sure whether to laugh.

'Sorry,' he said. 'It's my sense of humour. Or lack of.'

They both laughed then, slightly nervous.

'Let's give it a go,' said Maggie. 'If it goes well, maybe we can do one every Friday.'

'Deal.'

Maggie held out her hand, then pulled it away, remembering she had been elbow-deep in grease. 'I'd shake on it, but you don't want to touch my hands.'

'Don't worry. I'm sure you're as good as your word. I'll come along on the Friday morning to set up.'

They nodded at each other, then he raised a hand in farewell and strode out of the pub. Maggie watched him go, admiring his broad shoulders for a moment, then headed back into the kitchen.

As she scrubbed and scrubbed, she went through menus in her head: of West Country chicken bubbling in cider and tarragon, of butternut squash and fragrant sage melting into Arborio rice, of trout stuffed with orange and dill baked in butter. The customers would be back, she told herself. They would be back.

Russell walked back over to his truck feeling pleased. He was pretty sure that supplying The Swan would be a done deal and it would be something to tell Jen when they next spoke. He knew his pork won people over as soon as they tasted it. It was persuading them to try it that he hated. He wasn't a salesman; hustling made him feel awkward. That transaction hadn't been so bad, but he'd been halfway to success given that he used to supply Alan.

As he reversed out of the car park, he caught a glimpse of himself in the rear-view mirror. Jen was right. He had let himself go and he needed to sort himself out. He'd felt an absolute shambles talking to . . . what was her name? Maggie? He almost felt ashamed. She hadn't even wanted to shake his hand, he was so unappetising.

He'd go home, have a shower and drive into Honisham. Get himself a haircut and a new pair of jeans. Spend the hog-roast money on making himself look like a decent human being. He used to take pride in his appearance. When had that changed? OK, so he didn't need to dress up to look after the pigs, but there was no excuse for going out in public looking like Worzel Gummidge. He needed to get a grip.

22

Rose took Gertie's hand and wandered out into the pub garden. She was a little bit daunted. After all, her hands-on gardening experience wasn't that extensive. She had spent most of her childhood trotting around after her great-grandmother, helping her with potting, planting, weeding. She'd learned the names of all the plants in the garden and how they needed to be treated. As a teenager, she'd lost interest a little, but the year before, she'd done up their courtyard garden in Avonminster for Maggie's birthday, because she'd had no idea what else to get her. She'd made her a herb garden for cocktails, upcycled loads of pots she'd scavenged from various sources and planted them up, repainted all the woodwork in chalky paint and thrown around loads of chippings. It had reignited her childhood fascination, and then she'd volunteered to look after the garden at the Soul Bowl, and that had cemented her interest.

But the garden at The Swan was much bigger than anything she'd dealt with. Bigger, even, than the extensive garden at Wisteria House. The grass had run away with itself, so the first thing she needed to do was to mow it.

There was nothing more pleasing than an English lawn, perfectly cut, with immaculate velvety stripes. Alan said there was a ride-on mower in one of the sheds.

She looked at the rest of her surroundings with a critical eye. A large brick patio ran along the back of the pub, then the lawn, dotted with trestle tables, ran down to the riverbank. There were nobbly apple trees and weeping willows, which added a softness, and with the water burbling in the background, the rustling of the trees and the clouds scudding past the sun overhead, it felt like a lovely place to be. But Rose knew that with a little imagination and hard work, it could be transformed into something truly magical. At the moment, it was a little stark and a bit bland – you could be in any riverside pub in England. And it was somewhat neglected. The half barrels were empty, waiting to be filled with bedding plants, and there were weeds starting to poke through the patio.

She imagined it at dusk, lit up with twinkling lights and candles in storm lanterns, the sweet scent of nicotiana drifting across the grass. Striped cushions and parasols; dolly tubs planted up with fragrant lavender. A sundial, perhaps. A swing! A herringbone path made of old brick. Some pergolas or arches to break it all up, and lots of trailing honeysuckle and clematis in a tangle. It didn't have to cost a fortune, and Cherry had taught her well. They had often scoured the charity shops together, Cherry picking up vases and soup tureens and cocktail glasses, while Rose plundered the clothes rails for vintage treasures: tea dresses in crepe de chine, cashmere cardigans, tweed coats. She had learned a lot from her grandmother, about getting a good eye, about spotting quality. And how to look after things properly and give them a new lease of life.

Now she was here in Rushbrook, she felt herself starting to relax, her shoulders dropping downwards and her jaw less clenched. It had been a while since the incident with Gaz, and it was only now that she could remember it without feeling sick. She had emailed Aaron the day after and given in her notice. He didn't need her, not when she couldn't even follow his most basic rules and had put one of the clients in jeopardy.

Aaron had phoned her the minute he got it. She'd been tempted not to answer his call, but she didn't want to be rude.

'Rose. I'm not accepting this. You can't abandon us.'

'It's a family thing,' she told him. 'We're moving to Somerset for the summer.'

'Oh.'

'We're all going. Me and my mum and my grandmother. So I won't be able to help any more.'

'But you're my right hand – I can't do without you.'

'Yes, you can.'

'I don't think you know how special you are, Rose.'

She wasn't special at all. She had let him down. She wasn't even brave enough to tell him what she had done.

'Sorry,' she said. 'I know the rest of the team will step up.'

'Somerset's not that far. You could still come—'

'Sorry,' she repeated. 'My family need me. Sorry to let you down.'

She hung up, riddled with guilt for letting him down, but he was better off without her.

And this was what she had needed. A change of scene. An escape from the city which, much as she loved it, fed her anxiety. The cars, the people, the pollution, the queues: they all rolled off her when she was on top of things, but as soon as she went under, she became almost agoraphobic.

Here, the air was sweet, apple blossom replacing the choking fumes; the drone of bees replaced the distant hum of a city traffic jam. A breeze caressed her cheek and ruffled her hair, playful, affectionate. She lay down on the moss of the bank and shut her eyes for a moment, the sunlight trickling through the branches of the willow. It was her favourite time of year. Her and her dad's favourite. It was nearly festival time. Glastonbury. It was four years since she'd been. She couldn't believe it, but there was the evidence: little Gertie, bounding around with the dogs, having the time of her life.

'Goosey duck!' Gertie was pointing across the lawn, down to the river. Rose laughed, for there was a swan, gliding silently past.

'It's not a goosey duck, darling. It's a swan.'

And not just one swan, but two. No, three! Three elegant, graceful creatures as dazzlingly white as Alpine snow. Rose and Gertie lay on the riverbank and watched, transfixed, as they reached the bend in the river.

'Oh!' said Rose, as an idea came to her. 'Come on, Gertie. Let's go and find the others.'

The two of them scrambled to their feet, raced back up the lawn, through the back entrance and into the main bar where Maggie and Cherry were surveying the bar and deciding if it needed remodelling or if, as it had been the same for decades, they should just paint it. They looked up as she rushed over.

'I've had an idea,' said Rose. 'Let's change the name. Let's change it from The Swan to The Three Swans. For the three of us.'

'That's brilliant,' said Maggie. 'And perfect for a re-launch. It gives us a story. A hook.'

'What do you think, Cherry?' asked Rose.

'The Three Swans,' said Cherry. 'Like the Three Musketeers. All for one and one for all. I love it!'

23

Chloe set to work at the Safari Lodges, determined to do a good job so Dash would overlook Nicole's absence. Her mum couldn't afford to lose this job. She'd already lost her driving licence so it was hard for her to get anywhere else to work. She could see Dash was at the end of his tether with her. The thing was, everyone loved Nicole – until she let them down. And these days, she seemed to be letting everyone down.

If Dash did give Nicole the sack, maybe Chloe could take over as soon as her exams were over? She only had another week to go and it didn't really matter who did the work as long as they had money coming into the house. And Pearl and Otis were old enough to leave during the day. Weren't they? She'd never forgive herself if something happened to one of them while she was out, but what else could she do? There was, after all, only one of her. She couldn't bring in the money and do the childcare.

It suddenly occurred to her that perhaps that was why her mum found it so hard to cope? Knowing, as a single parent, that you were responsible for absolutely everything and there wasn't enough time. But turning your back on your responsibilities and getting drunk hardly helped matters. She'd been over and over it all in her head. Why was her mum so useless? She hadn't always been. With a sigh, Chloe thought back to the days when her mum and dad were happy, when they were all happy. What had gone wrong?

She buried herself in her surroundings to try and forget. The lodges were all cosy inside, with lots of sheepskin and fairy lights and low beds covered in velvet bedspreads. Outside each one was a cedarwood hot tub with a view overlooking the valley. And Dash kept the land beautifully, with everything rewilded: new trees planted, and meadow flowers, and the hedges re-laid. He'd even built a natural swimming pool. There were fishing lessons, and yoga, and stargazing. Any cocktail your heart desired delivered on a silver tray. A therapist to come and give you a massage or pedicure or even a tarot reading. It was back-to-nature with every luxury you could think of. A chance for hard-working city types to kick back and relax.

Chloe stripped the bed, put the duvet outside to air, and bundled up the linen. Everything was given a thorough scrub, clean, wipe and polish until the surfaces gleamed – every tap, every window, every table top. Then she replenished the scented candles, the eco-friendly soap and shampoo and stocked the fridge up with cider from Dragonfly Farm – Dash's girlfriend Tabitha lived there – and local cheese, jam, chutney, yoghurt, milk and butter. Last of all she made up the bed – hospital corners and the pillows as plump as a sleeping honey bear – and folded the freshly laundered towels. She left the packet of wildflower seeds and the welcome card on the bedside table – *These seeds are for you to scatter during your stay.*

Please let us know what we can do to make your time here even more magical – and locked the door.

There were three more lodges to do. She checked on Beyoncé – she'd left her cage outside on the deck. The little hamster seemed to have perked up no end, so she lugged the cage to the next lodge. She stood looking out at the view for a moment, the long grass studded with wildflowers swishing in the breeze, and tried to imagine having the kind of life where it was possible to book a week away in paradise, to not have to lift a finger, to have your every whim attended to.

What did you have to do to deserve that?

When she'd finished, she took all the linen back up to the main house and set it going in the washing machine in the laundry. Dash came out of his office just as she was about to make her escape.

'Chloe.'

She stopped and turned. He had a grave look on his face.

'Thanks for today. But you shouldn't have to cover for her, you know.'

Chloe tried to keep her face expressionless but inside she was starting to panic. She didn't know what to say.

'It's not fair on you,' he went on.

'She'll be fine tomorrow. It's one of her migraines.'

'So you said. Only I'm not sure it is.' Dash's voice was gentle, but Chloe wasn't sure who she could trust. 'Is everything OK, Chloe?'

It was so tempting. He was so kind and solid and reassuring. But once she'd told him, that would be it. She couldn't un-tell him, and there was no way he would do nothing about the situation because that's the sort of

189

person he was: responsible, law-abiding. And Mum would probably lose her job and all hell would break loose and she would drink even more. God forbid they might have to go and live with Dad and horrible Elizabeth.

So she pushed back her shoulders and looked him straight in the eye. 'Honestly. It is. She's had them ever since she was my age. Sometimes it's cheese that sets it off, and sometimes it's chocolate and sometimes we don't know, it just happens. She has to stay in a dark room for a day and then she's fine.'

Detail. People liked detail. Dash smiled and nodded at her, understanding that she didn't want the conversation to go any further for now. He pointed at the hamster cage.

'Do you and . . . Beyoncé want a lift home?'

'No, I'll be fine. Thank you.'

As she walked away, she could sense him watching after her, wondering. Should she turn and give him a little smile and a wave, to convince him everything was fine? No, she thought. Just keep walking. She felt awful lying to him. Dash was so lovely. Why couldn't her mum find a man like him? She was pretty enough. And clever enough. Her mum was *really* clever.

But Dash had Tabitha Melchior. Chloe had seen a photo of her in *Somerset People*, sitting on top of a mountain of apples, in a scruffy jumper and jeans and wellies, her blonde hair tumbling in a wild mess. There was an interview with her, about how she was turning Dragonfly Farm around, which she and her cousins had inherited from her great uncle. Melchior Cider was winning medals after just two years in production.

Chloe sighed. Some people had uncles who left them farms. Just as some people had mums who got out of bed in the morning and made them breakfast. You had to make the most of what you were given. She was just grateful they were in Rushbrook, when they could have ended up somewhere dreary on the outskirts of Honisham. It was the summer holidays soon. Life should get easier.

She was nearly at the village shop. She'd go and buy some sweets for Pearl and Otis and meet them off the bus. She stopped outside to read the notice board, out of habit. Her mum always combed through the flyers because you never knew what you might find for sale, or what opportunities might come up. When she was on it, Nicole could be shrewd. She was great at upcycling people's unwanted possessions and flogging them on eBay.

A notice in the middle caught Chloe's eye. It was on brown recycled paper, in an old-fashioned typewriter font. Not the usual biro on a tatty index card, advertising a litter of ferrets or a window-cleaning service.

Hi everyone
We are Cherry, Maggie and Rose.
We are delighted to have taken over The Swan...

Chloe read the rest of the advert and looked down at the cage in her hand. For a moment, she thought the little hamster was giving her a meaningful wink.

'Well,' said Chloe to Beyoncé. 'What do you think of that?'

24

At the end of the first day, the four of them piled into the boathouse. Alan had left most of the furniture for them, and they had brought the bare essentials with them for the time being: their own bedding, clothes and toiletries, Gertie's toys.

Cherry's heart sank slightly. Without anything in it, it looked rather bleak and smelled damp. It had been converted in the seventies, and there was a lot of orange pine cladding and a rather stained grey corded carpet in the living area. It needed gallons of white paint and the carpet pulling up at the very least. But their accommodation wasn't a priority at the moment. And it did overlook the river at the back. They sat with the French doors open – the sweet summer air flooded in, despatching the fustiness, and they ate a macaroni cheese Maggie had made the night before and brought with her.

Cherry and Maggie sat on the little balcony while Rose put Gertie to bed, watching the river flow past.

'I've got three possible members of staff to interview tomorrow,' Maggie told her. 'A cleaner, a waitress and a kitchen porter. And the pig farmer up the road is going to bring us a hog roast for the opening night. People can help themselves and go and sit in the garden.'

'If the weather holds.'

'It will. It's Midsummer's Eve! It wouldn't dare rain.'

'Maybe we could do that every weekend, if it goes well?'

'It would save us a lot of work. Even if it's just for this summer, while we get on our feet. I'll ask the pig farmer when he drops it off. I can't remember what he said his name was. God, that's a bit rude. Lorraine will know. I'll ask her.'

Maggie was starting to realise she was going to be leaning quite heavily on Lorraine for intel. She was very useful for background information and had sent two of the three potential members of staff down to The Swan. That was how villages worked: an elaborate network of gossip, recommendation and favours. Which was great, as long as it worked in your favour.

Cherry put down her fork. 'Do you know, I think I'm going to get ready for bed. The Fabulous Builder Brothers will be here at eight so I want to hit the ground running.'

Maggie looked at her. Her mum looked tired, and she had to remind herself she was nearly seventy. Cherry was such a lifeforce, it was impossible to believe that officially she was retirement age. She hoped she had an ounce of her energy at that age.

'Have you heard from Dad?' she asked.

'Oh, he had a private viewing tonight. I'll chat to him in the morning.'

'When's he coming down to have a look?'

'I want him to wait till it's all done.' Cherry gave her daughter a bright smile. 'We'll knock his socks off.'

'I hope he's not too lonely without us.' Maggie looked at her mother thoughtfully.

'He's fine. You know what the end of term is like at the university. He's probably glad to have us out of his hair.' Cherry stood up. 'Come on. Let's get those beds made up.'

Come midnight, Cherry lay in bed still wide awake. Perhaps she was overtired – it had been a long and exhausting day – but she couldn't sleep for worry. For all her enthusiasm and optimism, for all her vision and planning, suddenly The Swan felt daunting. She panicked that she had wildly underestimated what needed doing, and how many staff they needed, and how long it was going to take to turn it around.

She reminded herself that she always felt like this when she took on a project. That there was always a moment of gloom and doom when it seemed impossible. But a little piece of her wondered if she should have done something more sensible and less risky with her nest egg. Taken some advice, spread her investments around. Maybe she should have bought Rose a flat? Or just sat on the money for a while. Had it gone to her head and made her reckless?

She picked up her phone for the tenth time. She had texted Mike earlier. *All safe and well. Big day tomorrow. We miss you. xx* The empty screen stared back at her. It was odd for him not to reply at all. Was he trying to prove a point by blanking her? That wasn't Mike's style. He wasn't petty. Or unkind. He was hurt, though. She knew she had hurt him by what she had done.

She got up and went over to the window. Outside, a bright moon lit up the river, an everchanging silver thread. She told herself not to panic. The Fabulous Builder Brothers would be here tomorrow, and they always gave her back her confidence. By the end of the week, the place would look very different. And then, perhaps, she could concentrate on bringing Mike round. If he could see what she saw, he might relent.

She went and checked on Maggie, fast asleep in the other bedroom, and felt a surge of gratitude for her daughter. Maggie had more clarity than anyone she knew. She wouldn't have let her mother go into this if she didn't think it had potential. Maggie was redoubtable. Cherry still didn't know how she had managed to get back to work so quickly after Frank died. It didn't mean she wasn't affected by his death, far from it, but work had definitely been her anaesthetic. Better that than wallowing in booze or drugs, thought Cherry. Perhaps being in the country-side would allow Maggie to relax a bit more, and have some time for herself. Though perhaps not – running the kitchen was going to be quite a workload, but if anyone could do it, Maggie could.

She peeped into the room Rose and Gertie were sharing to check they were OK. They were curled up together, as Gertie had abandoned her little truckle bed.

Was this the right place for Rose, she wondered? A small rural village, away from the buzz of the city she'd grown up in? With Gertie still so young, it was hard for Rose to have many choices, but that she had talent and potential was undeniable. Rose had always loved coming to Rushbrook, but surely she was going to miss her friends? They all knew how fragile she was beneath her robust exterior. They dreaded the anxiety that visited her when things got on top of her. They knew the signs now, knew how to bring her back quickly so she didn't plummet. And they were all very open about her mental health. She and Frank had been so close, it was no wonder she had been suffering silently while they had all presumed she was coping. It was a surprise to them all that Gertie had been her saving grace. Rose had taken to motherhood effortlessly. She had never complained about lack of sleep or freedom. Though to be fair, Gertie had been the very best of babies, sunny and funny, and both Maggie and Cherry had been on hand to help out.

Cherry couldn't believe that Gertie would be starting school in September. That wasn't so far off, and then Rose would have time to take stock and make plans and carve out a future for herself. She would succeed in whatever she chose to do.

Though she couldn't shake the feeling something had happened lately. Rose had been very quick to join them. Was she running away from something? Cherry made a mental note to take her to one side and do a little probing. She was not going to let renovating the pub take away from the most important thing in her life: the people she loved. She went back to her own bed knowing that if she didn't get to sleep by midnight, she would be good for nothing in the morning.

She was just drifting off when her phone chirruped. She grabbed it and read the message from Mike. *Just got in. Glad all well. Night.* And then, a few seconds later, a single kiss. An afterthought. Normally, if they were apart, which was rare, they would have a conversation before bed, but his text didn't seem to invite a cosy bedtime chat.

How strange, she thought, to feel as if she couldn't phone him. She'd never felt that before, but she was unsettled by his continued ... what? It wasn't quite stoniness, but she didn't feel she could regale him with the events of the day. She really had thought he would have thawed by now.

She sent back a single kiss, mirroring his. It felt insufficient, and almost seemed to cement the stiff formality between them. The chilly reserve that was unlike the warm, loving easiness they'd shared during their life together.

She lay there worrying at the problem with the moonlight beaming in on her. She finally fell asleep at four, and woke at seven to a flurry of texts from the Fabulous Builder Brothers. *Cherry! We're here! Where are you?*

25

The Fabulous Builder Brothers were waiting in the car park with their orange campervan, and Cherry felt a flood of relief wash over her. Now they could get things rolling. Tom and Ed were never fazed by anything she asked of them. She had utter confidence in their ability to bring about her vision. Yesterday's anxiety melted away as she led them in through the door and showed them round the pub, excitedly outlining her plans as they walked.

'We're all going to be fighting over you, I'm afraid,' she said. 'Let's get a coffee and sit down and you can work out a timetable. Or tell me if we're making any awful mistakes. Or being too ambitious?'

'You, ambitious?' teased Ed. They were used to Cherry's demands. But nothing she had wanted done had ever been a disaster. They loved the challenge of working for her, and were relishing the luxury of working in the countryside for a fortnight. Avonminster could be stressful for a builder, with endless traffic issues and complaints from disgruntled neighbours. Rushbrook looked like heaven in comparison.

Half an hour later, Maggie, Rose and Gertie had

arrived, coffee and bacon rolls were on the go and the plans and drawings were spread out on the table.

'I'm right in thinking we've got less than two weeks?' Ed was looking at the wish list Maggie had printed out. 'Opening night is Midsummer's Eve?'

'Tell me honestly. Do you think we can do it all?'

The brothers looked at the list and then at each other.

'It's a good job we're not going back to Bristol. And the days are long,' said Tom.

'Raised beds? Wooden jetty? Thatched gazebo?' Ed raised his eyebrows. 'I'm not sure we can do thatch. You'll need a specialist for that.'

'We want an outside kitchen. For the wood-burning pizza oven. I guess it doesn't have to be thatched,' Maggie laughed.

'And what do you think about knocking that out?' Cherry pointed to the wall separating the dining area from the snug.

'It's not load-bearing,' Tom assured her. 'It's only a stud wall. So it should be easy enough, and you can always put it back up.'

Cherry nodded, pleased. She wanted an open feel, not the slightly claustrophobic traditional pub atmosphere. It would let more much-needed light into the low-ceilinged bar area.

'What about the bedrooms upstairs?'

'Oh God. Those are phase two,' said Maggie. 'They're unfit for human habitation right now. Otherwise we'd have let you sleep in there.'

There were four potential letting rooms on the first floor, but they were shabby and dusty with hideous carpet and wallpaper, ancient cracked sinks and very tired furniture.

The brothers conferred for a moment, poring over the lists, nodding, shaking their heads, agreeing, disagreeing. Maggie, Rose and Cherry waited in trepidation for their verdict. Would this be the moment they would be told their expectations were unrealistic?

'I think we can do it,' said Tom finally. 'It's going to be like *DIY SOS*. Or *Grand Designs*. But you know we like a challenge.'

Half an hour later they were standing in masks and goggles, surrounded by drop cloths, tarpaulin and dust sheets. The Fabulous Builder Brothers were on the case!

The sound of the ride-on mower started up outside. Rose was making headway cutting the lawn. Gertie had gone off with Catherine's old daily, Mrs B, for the morning, so it was a race against time. Mrs B had been with Catherine for as long as they could remember, and had retired when Catherine had died, but she'd told them she would come back to work as soon as she heard they had bought the pub. She had been a terrible cleaner towards the end, so they'd asked if she would help with Gertie instead, so as not to hurt her feelings.

By mid-afternoon, everything was covered in a thick coat of dust. The wall was down, and the light that flooded in highlighted the tiredness of the bar's interior. It looked naked and exposed, its flaws no longer disguised.

'What do you think?' she said to Maggie. 'Do you think it was a mistake?'

'Mum, you never make mistakes. You know you don't. Once we've got decent lighting and new paint it will be fabulous.' Maggie was concerned, but only because it wasn't like Cherry to doubt herself. There was a tightness to her jaw this morning, and shadows under her eyes. 'Are you OK?'

'Yes. I didn't sleep well, that's all. This is a big challenge.'

'I know.' Maggie's eyes sparkled. 'That's the fun of it.'

Cherry told herself to hold her nerve. It was vital not to panic.

'Hello?'

They turned to see a girl standing in the doorway looking nervous. She had the sweetest round face and big glasses and a cloud of strawberry blonde ringlets.

'I've come to see about a job? If you're still looking for people?'

'Definitely,' said Maggie. 'Come on in and let's have a chat.'

The girl ventured in, looking a bit alarmed by the chaos.

'In fact, no, let's go outside. We can't hear a thing in here. What's your name?'

'Chloe.' She followed Cherry and Maggie out into the garden, where Rose was still driving hell for leather across the lawn, dressed in cut-off dungarees and a straw hat to keep the sun off.

'That's Rose,' said Cherry. 'My granddaughter. And I'm Cherry, and this is Maggie. The first thing we need to ask is how old you are. For our licence.'

'Sixteen.'

'Well, that's perfect for waiting. Have you got experience?'

'No.' She looked anguished at this.

'Don't worry,' Maggie assured her. 'We can train you up. We're looking for confident, friendly staff who are quick to learn. So tell us a bit about yourself.'

'I'm just about to finish my GCSEs,' said Chloe. 'So

I'm looking for a summer job. And this would be perfect. I live just round the corner. So it will be easy for me to get here.'

She knew transport was one of the difficult things for both employers and employees round here. Apart from the school service, buses in Rushbrook were infrequent and unreliable and certainly didn't run late at night.

'That's perfect. Do you live at home?'

'Yes. With my mum and my younger brother and sister.' She paused. 'In Kerslake Crescent.'

This was the moment they would pigeonhole her, no doubt. She was conscious that Kerslake Crescent was the rougher end of Rushbrook. Everyone knew that. But they didn't say anything.

'What's your favourite meal?' asked Maggie.

Chloe looked as if this was a trick question.

'It's OK,' said Maggie. 'There's no right or wrong answer.'

'Pizza,' confirmed Chloe.

As soon as she said it, she knew that it was the wrong answer. She should have said something exotic. Something French or Italian. Mum used to cook amazing food, but she never bothered any more.

'Who doesn't love pizza?' said Maggie kindly.

'I mean – aubergine parmigiana,' Chloe corrected herself, remembering how Nicole used to make it on a Friday, all stringy mozzarella and rich tomato sauce. It seemed like a lifetime ago.

'Yum,' said Maggie. 'Do you like cooking?'

Chloe nodded her head. 'Yes,' she said. 'But there's never enough money for proper food. So everything I cook tastes horrible.'

'OK,' said Maggie, surveying her thoughtfully. 'And what do you want to do?'

Chloe looked at her as if no one had ever asked her this question before.

'I don't know, really. There's not much choice around here.'

Maggie frowned. 'But you don't have to stay in Rushbrook. Not for ever.'

Chloe opened her mouth, closed it, and then looked as if she might cry.

'I suppose not,' she said eventually. 'I'll be going to college for sixth form. In Honisham.'

Maggie handed her a notebook and pen.

'Can you put your name and phone number in here?' she asked. 'Then we'll contact you if we need to.'

'And thank you so much for popping in,' said Cherry. 'We'll be in touch.'

When Chloe had gone, they looked at each other.

'She's quite shy,' said Cherry.

'Well, she's very young. Weren't you shy at sixteen?'

'Actually, no,' admitted Cherry. 'I worked here and I was very sure of myself.'

'Maybe because you were the doctor's daughter? You had status. I doubt Chloe has.'

'Maybe not, if she's from Kerslake Crescent. Though I think it's changed since my day.' Cherry remembered its reputation from when she was younger, but the council houses had all been sold off and now it was a decent place to live.

'The good thing is she will know people, which is useful. People like a familiar face,' said Maggie. 'And she can give us all the inside gossip about what's going on the village.'

26

They wouldn't be in touch. Of course they wouldn't. She had completely and utterly blown it. Chloe had been so overwhelmed by Maggie and Cherry, she hadn't been able to find her tongue. And she was devastated. They were so very much what she wanted to be. Cool. Confident. Kind. Interesting. Together. Exciting. Funny. She loved how they were a team: mother, daughter and granddaughter. How amazing was that? She craved that kind of bond. The way they all looked out for each other and bounced off each other. The way they looked as if they could do anything they wanted.

Chloe brushed away her tears angrily. It was the first time in her life that she had seen something *she* wanted. The first time she had come close to feeling a shred of ambition. But she was never going to get even close to that kind of a lifestyle. Not while she had to step in for her mother. Not while she felt responsible for Otis and Pearl. She was trapped.

She arrived back at Kerslake Crescent. The curtains to the front room were closed. She knew she had opened them that morning before she left for school. She tried to keep things normal so the neighbours didn't speculate. It meant Nicole was up, but had closed them, which meant she hadn't gone to work. She felt filled with dread.

Inside, Nicole was lying flat out on the sofa, watching telly. Not even watching telly. She just had it on, and was staring into space.

'Hey, sweetie.' She smiled up at Chloe, who looked around the room in despair. It had been tidy when she left. Now there were empty cups and cereal bowls dotted around, the pillows from Nicole's bed brought down. Tissues on the floor. An empty Coke can on the coffee table – classic hangover remedy. 'How was your Maths exam?'

Chloe was surprised she'd remembered.

'Aren't you supposed to be at work today?' she asked, her voice tight with panic.

Nicole tapped her forehead. 'Bloody migraine won't shift.'

She wouldn't look Chloe in the eye. Chloe looked down at her shoes. She wanted to cry. She'd thought her mother was going to make it to work today. She had to say something. Everything was going to fall apart if she didn't.

Chloe tightened her fists. She went and stood in front of her mother. 'It's not a migraine, Mum,' she said. 'You know it isn't. I know it isn't. Dash knows it isn't.'

Nicole slumped back onto her pillows, sighing.

'He won't give you another chance,' Chloe persisted. 'You'll lose your job.'

'He can't sack me for being ill.'

'He totally can.' Chloe knew how zero hours contracts worked. Dash was very fair and would never abuse them, but there would be a limit to his patience. He couldn't afford to have a member of staff who didn't turn up.

'I'm sure I'll be better tomorrow.' Nicole managed a wan smile. 'I'll get back to work and everything will be fine. Now why don't we make a cake? For Pearl and Otis?'

She held up her hand. Chloe took it reluctantly and gave it a squeeze. It always seemed to be her job to reassure her mother, not the other way round. She did understand it was hard. It must be awful for Mum, Dad being with Elizabeth. But why did she have to drink? How did that solve anything? Couldn't she see they were struggling to survive as a family? Chloe did her best to keep it all together for the little ones, but it was at the expense of her own future.

She had seen what she wanted, this very afternoon. She was not going to let the situation they were in stop her from getting it.

'I'm sorry. I've got to go out.'

'Where?' Nicole sat up, frowning as Chloe headed for the door. 'Chloe? Please. Let's make a cake together. We've got all the stuff...'

Chloe headed for the front door, ignoring her mother's pleas, slamming the door behind her. She ran back up the road to The Swan, arriving red-faced and out of breath. She found Maggie in the kitchen.

'I'm sorry,' Chloe said. 'I was rubbish earlier. I didn't know what to say. But I'd really like to work for you. This is the most exciting thing to happen in Rushbrook since for ever and I want to be part of it. I'll do anything. Even just the washing up.'

'Oh,' said Maggie. 'Well, that's funny because we were just about to call you. I need someone to help me over the next week or so putting the kitchen back together, running errands, basically being my right hand. Would you be interested?'

'Oh my God,' said Chloe. 'Yes. Yes, please.'

'When can you start?'

'Right now if you want. I'm on study leave and I've only got one exam left.'

Maggie laughed at her enthusiasm. 'How about to-morrow? Come in scruffy clothes. You'll probably get filthy. We'll give you lunch.'

'What time would you like me? I have to drop my brother and sister off at the school bus at half seven.'

'Any time after that. The Fabulous Builder Brothers start at eight so we can hit the ground running.'

Chloe gazed at her. 'Were you really going to phone me?'

Maggie thought back to her conversation with Cherry after Chloe had left.

'Yes, I promise you. You'll be a valuable addition to the team.'

Chloe looked as if she was about to cry. Maggie had to remind herself that she probably was a bit overwhelmed; that opportunities like this didn't pop up in the middle of a village like Rushbrook very often. Rose had been lucky, living in Avonminster. She'd had her pick of Saturday jobs and holiday jobs.

'It's going to be hard work,' she warned her. 'I hope you don't mind getting your hands dirty.'

'I get my hands dirty all the time,' Chloe assured her. She didn't add that it would be nice to be paid for it for once.

27

Later that afternoon, Cherry went for a walk to get away from the noise and dust and to clear her head. She always needed thinking time on a project, and there wasn't the luxury of much of that on this one. But she felt better now things were under way and they had momentum. She hated standing still. Tom and Ed were into the swing of things, and what they had already achieved gave her confidence. If you told them to knock a wall down, they did.

As she walked, she found herself magnetically pulled to Wisteria House. If she half closed her eyes, she was transported straight back there. The picnic blanket rough underneath her. Out would come the tray with the silver teapot and the bone china cups and saucers and the plate of home-made shortbread, crisp and buttery and dusted with caster sugar. The scent of freshly mown grass, cut into perfect stripes with her dad's Ransomes Marquis. The buzzing of bumblebees feasting on nectar in the rose beds. And always the gentle noise of the river in the background. You could feel it wherever you were in Rushbrook, whatever the time of year: a ghostly gelid glide in the depths of winter, a jubilant torrent after heavy autumn rain, a languid drift in high summer when the levels fell. The river curled around the village as if protecting it, a maternal embrace, the last bend before it headed for the coast on the other side of the moor.

As she walked past the house now, Cherry's eyes were drawn to the windows, raking them for clues – a shadow, a profile, a light on. She couldn't help herself. She told herself it was rude, and nosy, and a little bit stalky. The new owners wouldn't want her peering in at them, but she was longing to know what they were like. And more importantly, what they were going to do with it.

No one moved into a house these days and left it as it was. They were only too eager to put their own stamp on it, and congratulate themselves on having a good eye for seeing potential. Walls would be knocked down or put up, fireplaces unblocked, kitchens and bathrooms ripped out and staircases moved. Cherry knew this only too well for she had done it herself, countless times.

It was her rule never to do anything to a house until you had lived in it for two months and worked out its rhythm – where the sun rose, which rooms you gravitated towards, where the heart of the house was. It was a massive mistake to go in with the wrecking ball on day one. A house could surprise you with its hidden secrets. It could whisper things to you that you'd never thought of, beckoning you to an unloved corner.

She hadn't seen signs of anyone yet, which was a mystery. When she bought a new house, she could never wait to get there, but perhaps the new owners of Wisteria House had more patience. She knew they were from London, so perhaps they were there during the week working.

Today, though, there was a sleek grey Jaguar F-Pace parked at the side and a man standing with his arms crossed looking up at the façade. He had on jeans and a dark blue linen blazer. When he turned, she saw he was probably in his late fifties. She saw, with approval, a deftly knotted scarf with frayed edges tucked round his neck. Nice car, nice scarf – so far, so good.

What was he thinking as he looked at the house? Was he thinking – big mistake? Or was he delighting in its perfection – the mellow red brick, the light bouncing off the glass in the sash windows, the eponymous wisteria tickling the top of the door frame?

She slowed down deliberately so he would see her, and managed to catch his eye. He tilted his head upwards with a drift of a smile but she could tell he was absorbed in his thoughts, so she raised her hand in greeting. She slowed to a halt, her heart thudding. If he showed any sign of disinterest, she would move on, of course, but she longed to connect with him.

'Hi,' she said, lingering by the gate. 'I hope you don't mind me intruding. But this was my mother's house. I hope you'll be very happy here.'

She wondered if he was someone who'd been pulled in to do a quote, for a new roof or new windows. But to her relief, he smiled, and walked towards her, quite eager to engage.

'Thank you,' he said. 'I'm Theo. Theo Bannister. I was just thinking how very lucky I am.'

He stretched out a hand and Cherry took it.

'Cherry. Nicholson. You are lucky. This was my family home.'

His face clouded with empathy.

'I'm sorry. It must have been a wrench, selling up.'

'It was. But it's OK. It didn't really fit in with my life plans. It's a beautiful house, though. And there's so much you could do.' She grinned. 'As I'm sure the estate agent told you.'

'Yes. Though I want to keep all the period detail. I can't bear it when people go in and smash a house to smithereens.'

Cherry felt a rush of relief. Wisteria House was in safe hands, it seemed. She warmed to Theo immediately.

'Oh, I am glad. I'd have hated to see her spoilt. There're so many lovely features . . .'

She thought longingly of the fireplaces, the pantry, the old bread oven, the alcoves and hidey-holes . . .

'Are you still local, then?'

'Ah, well, thereby hangs a tale. I've just bought the village pub. Rather on impulse.'

He looked impressed. 'Wow. Just like that?'

'The opportunity came up. I was looking for a challenge. And selling Wisteria House gave me a bit of a nest egg.'

'If it's The Swan you've bought, it looks full of potential.'

'It is.'

'Well, good for you.' He seemed genuinely admiring.

'I still can't quite believe it. Though it's not just me. My daughter and granddaughter have come in with me.'

'Three generations. That's quite unique. And rather lovely.' He seemed very taken with the notion.

'We've got lots of experience between us, and I've been going to The Swan for . . . well, let's put it this way: I was a barmaid there when I was at school. Back in the dark ages.'

'So what will it be? Scampi and chips – or everything served with achingly hip foam?' His eyes were dancing. His tone was teasing.

'Oh, it'll be proper pub food. Down to earth but nicely done. Nothing pretentious, but no deep-fried frozen rubbish.'

'Sounds just up our street.'

Our street. So it wasn't just him. Cherry was curious. Wife? Husband, perhaps? Family? He wasn't giving much away. She flicked her gaze behind him, where the front door was slightly ajar. She longed to push on the gate and walk up the path, enter the cool of the hallway.

She pulled her attention back to him.

'Well, we've got a grand reopening next Friday. As much cider as you can drink and a hog roast. Do come.'

'Oh, perfect. Amanda will be really excited to meet you again.'

'Again?'

'Yes, she's from Rushbrook. She remembers your family. Your dad was the doctor, right?'

'Yes.' As the doctor's daughter, Cherry was used to people knowing who she was, even if she didn't know them.

'And she's always been obsessed with this house. The minute it came on the market she put in an offer.'

Cherry remembered the call from the agent, telling her they had the asking price from a cash buyer, and the relief she and Toby had felt. They had accepted it straight

let her ride bareback on one of the ponies when
them back out into the field at the end of the day.
had hung on her every word, gazing at her from
her thick glasses. Those eyes had missed nothing.
er remembering Cherry meeting Mike.
gh it had been an extraordinary day. She could
er it as if it was yesterday.

away. Holding out for more would have been greedy and
stressful and the agent had assured them the offer was
copper-bottomed.

'You have to act quickly round here these days.'

He looked proud. 'I'm very glad we got it. I've been
trying to get Amanda to slow down and I'm hoping this
will do the trick. She's producing a massive period drama
at the moment – a sort of Georgian *Eastenders*.'

'Oh. That sounds very high-powered and glamorous.'

He made a face. 'It's bloody hard work but she's very
good at it. She's promised me this is her last gig but I
know she's lying. She'll carry on until her dying breath.'
They both looked up to see a woman standing in the
doorway. 'Hello! Speak of the devil and she shall appear.'

'Oh my God.' The woman started heading down
the path. She was probably about ten years younger
than Cherry, with a curly shoulder-length bob, dressed
in skinny jeans and an expensive-looking jumper. 'It's
Cherry, isn't it? You don't look any different.'

Cherry felt awkward. She had no idea who this woman
was. Amanda, her husband had said. Amanda who? She
searched her features but there was no clue, just a tan that
said winter holiday, electric blue mascara, well-manicured
eyebrows and quite a lot of silver jewellery. Money,
London, successful.

'Mandy,' said Amanda eventually as she joined them.
'Mandy Fryer? You must remember me from the stables?
I never left your side. Bill Fryer's daughter. The postman?'

Cherry was lost for words. The last time she'd seen her,
she must have been about eleven, with stubby bunches
and National Health spectacles, trotting round a field
picking up horse poo.

'Mandy,' Cherry managed at last. 'Of course I re-member you. How lovely to see you again.'

'Amanda now.' Amanda shook back her curls. 'I can't tell you how great it is to see you. Tell me, are you still with Mike?'

Cherry couldn't equate the tubby little girl she remem-bered with this groomed, confident woman.

'Yes, actually. Though he's not here at the moment. He's up in Avonminster. He's Head of Fine Art at the university. Or was – he's just retired.'

'I remember the first day you met him.' She turned to Theo. 'Honestly, it was love at first sight. I remember thinking I wanted to find someone who looked at me the way Mike looked at Cherry. Totally smitten.' She clapped her hands. 'And how wonderful that you've stood the test of time.'

'We're not actually married,' admitted Cherry. 'But we're still going strong.'

She didn't need to share any doubts about their rela-tionship at this point.

Amanda smiled. 'It's taken me three goes to find Mr Right but I think I've finally nailed it.'

She tucked her arm into Theo's.

'Did you know it was Cherry who's bought The Swan?' Theo asked her.

'No way!' Amanda looked thrilled. 'I am so far behind on village gossip. This is the first time I've had the chance to come down to the house since I bought it. Good for you. We'll probably be your best customers. I'm a terrible cook.' She ruffled Theo's hair. 'And it's not fair to keep Theo chained to the stove.'

Theo rolled his eyes and Che
who wore the trousers.

'Well, we reopen next Frida
the builders to get on with it,

'We'll be there. And as soon
must come for supper. If you

'I am. And we'd love to.' C
ate that things were straine
sooner or later, they'd be ab

Cherry had mixed feelin
pub. Seeing Amanda and T
House was like seeing an e
same time, she'd been pl
were definitely the sort of
money in the pub. They'

Mandy Fryer, though
lieve. Bill Fryer, the p
rabble of children – five
remember. They lived i
too many of them crar
had treated the mot
Cherry remembered
when she'd been fou
blamed himself, but
doctor he was, and
everyone in his car

And the younge
lost soul. Like m
refuge at the loca
following her ar
her under her w
properly, or ho

always
they le
Mandy
behind
Fancy
Thou
rememb

away. Holding out for more would have been greedy and stressful and the agent had assured them the offer was copper-bottomed.

'You have to act quickly round here these days.'

He looked proud. 'I'm very glad we got it. I've been trying to get Amanda to slow down and I'm hoping this will do the trick. She's producing a massive period drama at the moment – a sort of Georgian *Eastenders*.'

'Oh. That sounds very high-powered and glamorous.'

He made a face. 'It's bloody hard work but she's very good at it. She's promised me this is her last gig but I know she's lying. She'll carry on until her dying breath.' They both looked up to see a woman standing in the doorway. 'Hello! Speak of the devil and she shall appear.'

'Oh my God.' The woman started heading down the path. She was probably about ten years younger than Cherry, with a curly shoulder-length bob, dressed in skinny jeans and an expensive-looking jumper. 'It's Cherry, isn't it? You don't look any different.'

Cherry felt awkward. She had no idea who this woman was. Amanda, her husband had said. Amanda who? She searched her features but there was no clue, just a tan that said winter holiday, electric blue mascara, well-manicured eyebrows and quite a lot of silver jewellery. Money, London, successful.

'Mandy,' said Amanda eventually as she joined them. 'Mandy Fryer? You must remember me from the stables? I never left your side. Bill Fryer's daughter. The postman?'

Cherry was lost for words. The last time she'd seen her, she must have been about eleven, with stubby bunches and National Health spectacles, trotting round a field picking up horse poo.

'Mandy,' Cherry managed at last. 'Of course I remember you. How lovely to see you again.'

'Amanda now.' Amanda shook back her curls. 'I can't tell you how great it is to see you. Tell me, are you still with Mike?'

Cherry couldn't equate the tubby little girl she remembered with this groomed, confident woman.

'Yes, actually. Though he's not here at the moment. He's up in Avonminster. He's Head of Fine Art at the university. Or was – he's just retired.'

'I remember the first day you met him.' She turned to Theo. 'Honestly, it was love at first sight. I remember thinking I wanted to find someone who looked at me the way Mike looked at Cherry. Totally smitten.' She clapped her hands. 'And how wonderful that you've stood the test of time.'

'We're not actually married,' admitted Cherry. 'But we're still going strong.'

She didn't need to share any doubts about their relationship at this point.

Amanda smiled. 'It's taken me three goes to find Mr Right but I think I've finally nailed it.'

She tucked her arm into Theo's.

'Did you know it was Cherry who's bought The Swan?' Theo asked her.

'No way!' Amanda looked thrilled. 'I am so far behind on village gossip. This is the first time I've had the chance to come down to the house since I bought it. Good for you. We'll probably be your best customers. I'm a terrible cook.' She ruffled Theo's hair. 'And it's not fair to keep Theo chained to the stove.'

Theo rolled his eyes and Cherry smiled. She could see who wore the trousers.

'Well, we reopen next Friday so I'd better go. I've left the builders to get on with it, which is always a danger.'

'We'll be there. And as soon as Mike comes down, you must come for supper. If you're allowed a night off.'

'I am. And we'd love to.' Cherry wasn't going to intimate that things were strained between them. Hopefully, sooner or later, they'd be able to take up the invitation.

Cherry had mixed feelings as she walked back to the pub. Seeing Amanda and Theo in the garden of Wisteria House was like seeing an ex with a new lover. But at the same time, she'd been pleased to meet them. And they were definitely the sort of people who would spend proper money in the pub. They'd buy a decent bottle of wine.

Mandy Fryer, though. She still found it hard to believe. Bill Fryer, the postman, was a widower with a rabble of children – five or six of them, she couldn't quite remember. They lived in the middle of Kerslake Crescent, too many of them crammed into a tiny house. Her father had treated the mother for post-natal depression, and Cherry remembered how desperately upset he had been when she'd been found dead from an overdose. He had blamed himself, but everyone knew what a conscientious doctor he was, and how he had done his very best for everyone in his care.

And the youngest, Mandy, had always seemed such a lost soul. Like many girls in those days, she had found refuge at the local stables. Cherry remembered Mandy following her around like a little shadow. She'd taken her under her wing, showing her how to do up a girth properly, or how to pick out a horse's hooves, and she always let her ride bareback on one of the ponies when they let them back out into the field at the end of the day. Mandy had hung on her every word, gazing at her from behind her thick glasses. Those eyes had missed nothing. Fancy her remembering Cherry meeting Mike.

Though it had been an extraordinary day. She could remember it as if it was yesterday.

28

Fifty years earlier

School was finished, at long last. Cherry never had to darken its doors again. She had no idea what she wanted to do with her life, but at the moment it didn't matter. Summer stretched in front of her, and she was working every day at the stables, albeit for a pittance, but supplementing that pittance by working behind the bar at The Swan at the weekends.

This Saturday morning she lay curled up on her bed, flipping through a magazine and hearing her parents' voices drift up through the open window where they sat drinking tea on the lawn. She knew she had only scraped through her exams. The only subject she might have done well in was art, but she had no idea what to do with that. Some of her friends were going off to university or polytechnic, and now she felt a stab of panic that even though they were committing themselves to another three years of studying, at least they were going on to pastures new when she still didn't have any idea about her future. She knew that with a little more effort she could have done better in her exams, which would have given her more options.

Her parents had been kind, and her father had offered to ask the pharmacist in Honisham if she could have a job.

'It might be a career worth thinking about,' he suggested.

But she didn't like the idea of going to work at the chemist, shaking out pills and pouring out medicine for the sick and infirm of Somerset. Not even if it meant being able to get discount on a new lipstick. She didn't want to work anywhere in Honisham. There was nothing to get excited about there. There wasn't even a record shop; just a small section of LPs in WHSmiths that she flipped through every week, but the stock never seemed to change. The only dress shop was laughable. Even her own mother wouldn't be seen buying anything from there. It sold shapeless dresses in thick material in horrible dreary colours. And the shoe shop only sold shoes fit for children or grannies.

She felt unsettled. On balance, she loved her life in Rushbrook, but she couldn't stay here and work at the stables and the pub for ever. She wasn't even *that* mad on horses any more – they weren't the passion they had once been – but working at the stables suited her for now, mucking out, grooming, exercising the liveries.

Her mother had made a few suggestions – typing school was the most practical.

'It can get you in anywhere. And you never know where you might end up. Lots of very successful women have started off as secretaries.'

But Cherry couldn't see herself as a secretary. She hoped

she wasn't too much of a disappointment to her parents. Her mother had even suggested nursing, but Cherry felt quite ill at the thought. She wasn't cut out for it. You couldn't be squeamish when you were dealing with patients. She had nothing but admiration for her father and what he dealt with on a daily basis, but she had not inherited his cold blood.

'Something will pop up, darling,' her mother consoled her. 'It always does.'

She thought that secretly they were hoping she'd find herself a suitable husband, for that would solve everything, but Cherry wasn't pinning her hopes on love and marriage. She had decided she would spend the summer putting away as much money as she could, and come the autumn she would make a plan. In the meantime, she leafed through magazines, listened to records and had as much fun as she could, galloping over the fields and flirting with boys in the pub. A curious mix of childhood and adult pleasures.

It was time to go to work. She pulled on her jodhpurs and an Aertex shirt, plaited her hair and grabbed her boots, running down the stairs and out of the front door then jumping onto her bike.

At the stables, Lorna the owner was halfway down her tenth cigarette of the day. She spent most of her time smoking and bossing the staff around, and never lifted a finger except to teach the clients she liked. There was a cluster of ten- and eleven-year-old girls hovering around her, waiting for the chance to be given a useful job that might mean getting nearer to a horse. She greeted Cherry with relief.

'Thank Christ you're here. I need you to groom Pia

then take her into the ménage. We've got a photographer coming to take some pictures. You know Pia better than anyone. She'll behave for you. I'd do it but I'm teaching four lessons back to back.'

'OK.' This made a change. And Pia, a palomino mare, was Cherry's favourite. 'What's it for?'

Lorna frowned and shrugged. 'Oh, the cover of a record or something. I don't know really. All I know is they wanted a golden horse with a white mane and tail.' She rolled her eyes. 'Who will stand still.'

She cackled and threw her cigarette butt to one side. Lorna was weather-beaten and hard-bitten and like a lot of horsey people, didn't suffer fools. She was quite keen on money, though, so this was probably a quick earner. Cherry raised her eyebrows. Pia was not known for being placid. But she felt a shiver of excitement. A record cover?

Pia was waiting in her stable, sixteen hands of highly strung perfection. She knew something was afoot, and was eyeing Cherry suspiciously, dancing from side to side. Cherry slipped back the bolt and put a head collar on her, feeding a few pony nuts into her mouth to win her over, relishing the feel of the horse's soft, bristly muzzle on her fingers. Then she set to work with a curry comb brushing the mud and grass stains off her coat, then going over and over it with a body brush until it shone like rose gold. Then she untangled her mane and tail with a comb until they were snow-white.

She stood back and admired her handiwork. Pia looked as if she'd stepped out of a fairy tale.

'Good work, Cherry. The circus is here. You deal with them. I'll only be rude.' Lorna opened the stable door.

'I'm doing my lessons in the top field so they can use the school.'

Cherry's heart was pounding as she led Pia out of the stable and over to the cluster of people waiting in the ménage. They looked like something off the telly. *Top of the Pops*. The cluster of girls who'd been hovering around Lorna had moved to the fence of the ménage, hanging on to the top rail and watching the proceedings wide-eyed.

A man came forward, curls almost past his shoulders, green bell bottoms, a cheesecloth shirt unbuttoned half-way down his chest.

'I'm Mike,' he said. 'I'm the photographer. And the driver. And the art director.' He laughed, and Cherry relaxed straight away. He was wearing dark glasses, but as she took his hand, she saw he wasn't very old. Not all that much older than she was, maybe a year or two. 'This is Alouette, our model. She's going on the horse.'

'You can ride, can you?' Cherry asked, looking at the girl. She was in a high-necked silk wedding dress with bare feet and a lot of make-up: heavy eyes and very shiny lips. Her hair was a cloud of curls the same colour as Pia's mane.

'Oh yeah,' she said. Despite her exotic name, she sounded straight out of London. 'We always go riding on our holidays.'

Cherry had heard that claim countless times. No one who said it could ever ride.

'And this is Pam, who does make-up and hair.'

Pam had a bright red urchin cut and was wearing a paisley tunic over suede hot pants. She gave Cherry a reassuring grin and waved a hairbrush at her. 'I'm going to be a ruddy nuisance, I'm afraid. I'll have to touch up her make-up every two minutes in this heat.'

'OK. So what's the plan?' Cherry was dubious. This lot didn't look as if they knew one end of a horse from the other.

'I just need some nice shots of Alouette on the horse,' explained Mike. 'It's going on an album cover, so there'll be lots of illustration around her. I want to make it look as if she's coming out of an enchanted forest.'

'Right,' said Cherry, then frowned as Alouette lit a rolled-up cigarette. A heady, spicy scent rolled towards her on the breeze.

'Anyone?' asked Alouette, holding it out. 'I need to chill out before I get on.'

'Never when I'm working,' said Mike, pulling a huge camera out of a box at his feet.

Pam grabbed it and took a hit, laughing. 'Don't mind if I do.'

She held it out to Cherry, who shook her head. She wanted to try it more than anything, but Pia was her responsibility. 'Maybe later,' she said with a smile, as if she turned down marijuana on a regular basis.

At last they were ready. Pam perched a crown of flowers on top of Alouette's head and put another layer of gloss on her lips.

Alouette just stood and stared at Pia. 'How am I sup-posed to get on?'

'I'll give you a leg up,' said Cherry, holding out her forearm, but Alouette looked at her askance and took another toke on her next joint. Cherry sighed. 'Let's use the mounting block.'

She led Pia over to the mounting block and kept her

steady while Alouette finally managed to climb into the saddle and picked up the reins, gripping so tightly her knuckles were white.

'Where did you ride, exactly?' asked Cherry.

'Blackpool,' said Alouette, defiant.

'Donkeys, then?'

'It's all the same, isn't it?'

'I'm not going to be able to let go of the lead rein,' murmured Cherry to Mike. 'This is not a beginner's horse. She'll bolt.'

'Her agent swore she was an experienced rider.'

'She hasn't got a clue,' said Cherry.

'She's way higher up than I'm used to!' Alouette wailed, jerking on the reins every time Pia moved. 'She's going to run off.'

'I've got her,' said Cherry.

'I can't have you in the shot, though,' said Mike.

'I am not letting her go.' Cherry shook her head. She patted Pia's neck, smoothing down the velvet fur. She could feel the horse's panic through her fingertips. Pia didn't like being made to stand still. She was born to fly across open fields and over stone walls. She was skittish, dancing on the spot, breaking out in sweat from the stress of all the people standing round her, and the imbecile on her back. Cherry sensed that before long Pia would take matters into her own hooves and throw the model off.

'Alouette,' said Mike. 'If you relax for one minute, the horse might. The sooner we can take the pictures, the sooner you can get off.'

'I can't relax,' whined the model. 'I'm bloody petrified. This thing's mad.'

'She's not mad.' Cherry snapped. 'You're making her

223

nervous. You're squeezing her with your legs but you're pulling too tight on the reins. How's she supposed to know what to do?'

'I'm trying not to fall off.'

'Loosen the reins and take your legs off. She'll stand still then.' Cherry was getting impatient.

Mike ran his hand through his hair in despair.

'This is hopeless. Let's forget it. Get off, Alouette.'

Cherry watched as Alouette leant over the horse's neck and cocked her leg over the saddle behind her, then slid to the ground.

'That's a waste of a day.' Mike glared at her. Alouette shrugged.

'Don't blame me. Blame Dobbin. They should never have given us that crazy animal.'

Cherry felt outraged on Pia's behalf.

'Don't blame Pia. She was confused, and that made her nervous.'

Mike looked at Cherry. 'Can you ride her?'

'Of course I can. I can make her do anything you want.'

He pointed at Alouette. 'Take off that dress.'

'Fuck off. This is my gig.' Alouette was lighting up again.

'You'll still get paid. Come on.' He turned to Pam. 'Can you do her make-up? Do something with her hair?'

'Sure. Same sort of look? Blue eyes, plum lips? I've got hair pieces.'

'Anything that makes her look like a fairy-tale bride.' He turned to Cherry. 'Sorry, love. I don't even know your name. Are you happy to do this?'

'I'm Cherry. Yes, of course.

The little audience at the fence exchanged glances.

Cherry tied up Pia then dodged into a nearby stable, pulled off her jodhpurs and Aertex and wriggled into the dress. It was a bit too big and a bit too long, trailing along the ground. She lifted up the skirts and came out into the yard.

Mike looked at her in delight. 'I think,' he said, 'this is what's known as a happy accident.'

'Shush,' said Pam in scandalised delight. 'Alouette will flip her lid. Come here, let me pin that up at the back for you.' She started adjusting the dress with deft fingers.

'I don't care,' said Mike. 'She wasted my time and my money. You've got ten minutes, Pam.' He looked up at the sky. 'I don't like the look of those clouds. We need to get a wiggle on.'

Half an hour later (she was to learn that everything took three times as long as it should on any kind of shoot), Cherry was fully made up, with her hair bulked out by half a dozen hair pieces and topped with the flower crown.

'Can you ride bareback? Barefoot?' Mike asked.

'Sure. I just need a leg up in this dress. I don't want to tear it.' She took off the saddle, put it over the fence of the arena, then Mike made a stirrup of his hands. She hitched the dress up and put her foot in his hands, then threw herself onto Pia's back, rearranging the layers of silk and lace behind and in front so her legs could be seen.

'Perfect,' said Mike in reverence. 'Now look at me like you were looking at Alouette earlier. With total contempt.'

Cherry laughed, then composed her features into a haughty scowl. Mike started snapping his camera.

'Amazing. Relax your shoulders a little bit. Turn your

head towards me. Now imagine I'm the man your father wants you to marry. A fat horrible stoat of a man who makes your skin crawl. You're about to gallop off into the sunset leaving him standing at the altar.'

For the next quarter of an hour, Cherry was that girl. She found it easy. She didn't need to pretend. She slipped into the role as if she had born to it. She felt admiring eyes on her as she did everything she was asked.

'OK. Can you canter round the school on her? But this time I want you to look happy. As if you've just had a lucky escape.' He turned to Pam. 'Can you get some more powder on her? She's a bit shiny.'

By the end, Cherry was breathless and her hair was all over the place and Pia was sweating, but she had a trick up her sleeve that she wanted Mike to see.

'How about this?' she said. 'Are you ready?'

As he put his camera up to his eye, she gave Pia the instruction 'Up, up.' The horse reared up obediently, and Cherry flashed Mike a triumphant smile filled with all the defiance she had been saving for her imaginary husband.

'Jesus!' Mike exclaimed. 'That's the money shot. Baby, you are a star. Can you do that for me again, once more? This is worth a million dollars. They are going to be over the moon when they see this.'

'Alouette is going to be seething,' said Pam. Alouette was having yet another smoke in the stable yard, sitting in an old armchair Lorna used to sit in and bellow instructions.

'I'll deal with Alouette.' Mike finished off the roll of film as Cherry fell onto Pia's neck and hugged her.

'You're such a good girl,' she murmured, then walked her round the school a few turns to cool her down and calm her.

She rode her back into the yard where Mike was putting his gear away.

'You're a natural,' he said. 'Have you ever thought about being a model?'

'No way,' said Cherry. 'All that standing around must be so boring. And not being able to eat. And being bossed around by photographers.'

Mike laughed. 'Yeah. We are tyrants. Bloody impossible. You'd do well to keep out of the business if you want to stay sane.'

'I'm more interested in behind the scenes. How you pull it all together.'

'Ah, well, that's where the dark arts come in.' Mike looked up at her, unscrewing the lens from his camera. 'This is only about a tenth of the creative process. But it is the most complicated.' He looked over to Alouette. 'Especially when not everyone's on the same wavelength. And they've told you a massive porkie.'

'She could have wasted the whole day.'

'She was an expensive mistake.' This reminded him of something and he dug in his pocket, pulling out a wad of notes. 'Which reminds me.' He peeled off two fivers and held them up to her. 'Will that do? As your fee?'

Cherry looked at it in amazement. 'I wasn't expecting anything.'

'You did a great job. You saved the day. I'd have had to find someone else and do it all over again. And I can tell you, I wouldn't have found anyone as good. Like I said, you're a natural.'

Cherry leant down and took them off him. He held her gaze as she sat up.

'Thank you,' he said, and his smile was as warm as the sun on her back. She gazed at him, thinking she had never seen anyone like him in Honisham. He looked like someone, but without being too full of himself. He was with it and confident but best of all, he was nice. He didn't make her feel awkward or uncomfortable or like a country bumpkin. On the contrary, he made her feel like a queen. A fairy queen.

'You're OK with being on an album cover?'

'Yeah. I suppose so. What band?'

'You won't have heard of them. Not yet. But they're going to be massive when the LP comes out. They're called the Silent Whisper.'

Cherry nodded. 'You're right. I've never heard of them.'

'This cover is really important. For them and me. This could be my lucky break.' Again that smile, that ray of sun. 'And if it comes off, it's all down to you.'

Cherry felt a little overwhelmed by his praise. She wasn't used to compliments, but found she rather liked the recognition. But she wasn't sure how to react, so she swung her leg over the back of Pia, slid to the ground and tied her up.

'I need to get my boots back on,' she said. 'Don't want my feet trodden on.'

She could feel his eyes following her. She turned to look at him and he laughed and gave a shrug at being caught out. She grinned back and disappeared into the stable to change back into her jodhpurs. Her heart was beating fast and her blood felt warm and it wasn't from the exertion. She felt a surge of urgency – these people were going to disappear from her life as quickly as they had arrived. She couldn't bear the thought. She wouldn't mind never seeing Alouette again, but Pam had a combined sense of fun and professionalism that Cherry had felt drawn to: she knew exactly what she was doing but was totally laidback and relaxed. As for Mike – had she imagined that there was something between them? Or did he treat everyone the same?

She folded up the dress carefully when she took it off, and put her jodhpurs back on. She felt ordinary again. When she'd been on Pia, playing the role she'd been given, she felt like another person. Almost powerful.

The seconds were draining away. They would be gone, and her brief foray into another world would be a memory. It made her even more determined to find herself a future. There must be another life out there. She had seen it.

She left the stable and walked slowly to fetch Pia. There was nothing she could do to prolong their stay. She couldn't bear the thought of the three of them piling into the car and heading back to London. But she could hardly go with them.

'Hey,' said Pam. 'We don't want to drive all the way back to London tonight. We need somewhere to stay. Do you know anywhere?'

Joy surged through her. Here was her chance. Would they jump at it, if she told them? Or would they decide to go further afield?

'There's The Swan,' she said. 'In the village. They have a couple of rooms upstairs. I expect they're free.' She prayed they were. 'I work there, on a Saturday night. Behind the bar.'

Mike looked at her, and Pam looked at him, then Alouette.

'That would do. I don't fancy travelling far now. I just want a shandy in the beer garden and pie and chips. Me and Alouette can share. Can't we?'

Alouette shrugged. She was still sulking. 'I suppose so. If you don't snore.'

Pam laughed. Cherry held her breath. Mike smiled.

'That sounds just the thing. The shandies are on me. We'll see you there.'

And he gave Cherry a wink.

Back at home an hour later, Cherry got ready for work. She usually didn't make a lot of effort – a plain blouse and a skirt – because it was hot and dirty work behind the bar in the summer. If she dressed up it would be strange and she would feel awkward. In the end she settled on a white seersucker blouse and a corduroy skirt that showed off her legs. She felt grubby and sticky and felt sure she still reeked of horse, but she didn't have time for a bath or to wash her hair so she did her best with a damp flannel, a dusting of talc and a squirt of Yardley. She brushed the dust out of her hair and put on mascara and lipstick, which again she never usually bothered with. She surveyed herself in the mirror. She didn't look anything like as hip as Pam or Alouette, with their heavy eyeliner and dangly jewellery, but not too bad.

'That's your birthday blouse,' said her mother in the hall as she left.

'Yes,' said Cherry.

Catherine smiled. 'You look lovely.'

Cherry was so excited she gave her a hug. 'Thanks, Mum.'

*

Alouette, Pam and Mike were the liveliest thing to hit The Swan in living memory. After a couple of drinks and some food, Alouette got over her sulks and was actually quite funny. She and Pam spent the evening pumping money into the juke box, taking requests and dancing with anyone who wanted to join them. The atmosphere was electric, and the bar stayed busy all night.

'We've made more tonight than we have done in a week,' Maurice the landlord told Cherry. 'You can bring your friends again.'

Cherry felt proud to be associated with them. And when it was closing time, she was allowed to stay for a few drinks because they were residents.

'I'm sorry if the rooms are awful,' she told them. 'I don't think they get cleaned all that often.'

Pam waved a hand at her. 'We don't care. We always just collapse into bed after a long day and a few drinks. Don't we, Mike?'

For a moment, Cherry felt her insides turn to ice. Was Pam going to bed with Mike? She didn't think they were together but maybe they did, sometimes? That was the way these days. People didn't ask too many questions or make too many commitments. She found she couldn't bear the thought of them together.

'Go and dance with Cherry, Mike.' Alouette had noticed her crestfallen expression. 'Poor girl's been stuck behind the bar all night. She needs some fun.'

Mike reached over and took her hand. 'What's your song, Cherry? The one that makes your heart beat faster?'

She couldn't think. All she could feel was the blood rushing to her head at his touch. She couldn't have named a song if her life depended on it.

'I don't know,' she said, feeling lame, and Alouette came to her rescue, jumping up and pressing the buttons on the juke box. 'Jumpin' Jack Flash' leapt out and soon they were all dancing, arms waving, hips swivelling, hair flying. Maurice stood in the doorway, smiling. They could dance all night as far as he was concerned. This trio from London had covered his wages for a month.

Then the mournful notes of 'Nights in White Satin' floated around the room. Alouette grabbed Pam, laughing, and they danced cheek to cheek, hamming it up. Mike put up his hands and took Cherry's, drawing her closer to him, and suddenly she was in his arms, her head resting on his shoulder, feeling his curls brush her cheek, smelling his warm sandalwood scent. Across the room, Alouette gave her a wink. Cherry realised the model had been her champion all evening, and thought better of her. It was a lesson, she thought, in not judging people too quickly.

Then she saw Maurice watching her, and he raised his eyebrows towards the clock, then with a rueful expression jerked his thumb towards the door to indicate she should leave. She knew why. He was afraid of her father's disapproval if things got out of hand. Dr Nicholson might go on the warpath if he thought his daughter had been sullied on Maurice's premises. It was a bit late for that, thought Cherry, remembering her encounter on the riverbank a few weeks ago one moonlit night. She'd wanted to know what it was like, and now she did, and next time she would know what to expect.

But Maurice was right, she realised, looking at the clock behind the bar. It was half past one. She was usually home by eleven o'clock. Her parents would be wondering where on earth she was. Granted, they were usually already in bed by the time she got home, so they might not have noticed her absence, but she couldn't leave it any later. She was torn between the thought of worrying them and her longing to stay.

'I have to go,' she whispered to Mike.

He pulled her in tight and brushed her lips with his. A fleeting kiss, but she thought she might die from the thrill of it. She felt as if her insides were filling up with the soft, sweet ice cream that was pumped into a cone from the van that came round every Friday.

'Must you?' he said.

'My parents will be worried.'

He nodded, and took her hand. She couldn't tell what he was thinking. He seemed enraptured, but no doubt he was inhibited by the steely gaze of Maurice on him.

'If you ever come to London,' he said, 'look me up.' And out of his pocket, he pulled a card and pushed it into her hand. 'I think we could have a lot of fun.'

His words echoed around Cherry's head as she walked back along the road. She had never been out this late before. The air was cool on her skin, the moon above lit her path, the air smelled sweet and pungent. She imagined hundreds of tiny eyes in the hedgerows, watching her, wondering, judging.

We could have a lot of fun . . .

She stopped just outside the house. The scent of wisteria drifted over to her on the breeze. The red-brick façade and the windows, blank with black night, gave nothing away. She could hear the river behind, but there was no judgement in its murmur. With luck, her parents were deep in slumber. She crept in, hoping the floorboards wouldn't squeak and the door wouldn't slam. The grandfather clock tutted reproachfully. It knew better than anyone what the time was. She pulled off her boots, leaving them by the doormat, and headed for the stairs, stepping on each one carefully.

Just as she reached the top, the landing was suddenly flooded with light. She looked up to see her mother, her hand on the light switch.

'Darling!' Her mother looked startled, standing there in her pink quilted dressing gown with her curlers in her hair. 'What time is it?'

'Sorry. I stayed to chat after work. I didn't realise what the time was.'

Her mother looked at her. She gave a funny little smile, and Cherry wondered if she knew what had happened, somehow.

'I couldn't sleep. Fancy a cup of tea?'

'OK...'

They sneaked back down to the kitchen, and Catherine boiled the kettle, busying herself with the teapot, while Cherry sat and realised she could still smell the faintest trace of sandalwood on her skin. Every time she breathed it in, it made her head spin.

'So,' said Catherine. 'Tell me about tonight.'

She sat down, putting two mugs of tea on the table and looking Cherry straight in the eye. But the smile on her face was kind, and she had never been one to judge. She probably wouldn't approve of everything that had happened today, but Cherry could leave out those bits.

'Oh, Mum,' she said, and took the card out of her skirt pocket. 'I've had the most amazing day. And I've met this...'

She wasn't sure whether to say boy or man, because she wasn't sure how old Mike was.

'Guy,' she said eventually. 'He lives in London.'

'Oh,' said her mum. 'Well. What does he do?'

It was the first question any parent worth their salt asked.

'He's an artist. A photographer. He's designing an album cover.'

'Wow.'

'He's very nice,' Cherry assured her.

'Of course he is, darling.' Catherine put a hand over hers and squeezed. 'Just be careful, that's all. You know your dad and I trust you, and would never stop you doing anything you wanted. But you must look out for yourself.'

Cherry looked at her. 'Do you mean I could go to London? To visit him?'

Catherine Nicholson, despite her cosy village life, was very much a woman of the world. She saw everything through the lens of her husband's work and had no illusion about the sort of things that could go on behind closed doors. But she also knew that to keep a young woman on a tight rein was asking for trouble. She knew that if she gave Cherry her head, she would get into less trouble. A girl had to learn by her own mistakes, not be stopped from making them.

'If that's what you want to do.'

'The girl he works with – Pam – said I could go and stay with her any time.'

'Well, that's a very kind invitation.'

Cherry thought of all the places she had seen in magazines. The Kings Road. Chelsea. Kensington. The shops – she felt faint with longing at the thought of actually going into Biba. And perhaps a haircut. She could get rid of her waist-length mane. It had become something of a trademark, but now she had seen Pam's crop, she wanted shot of it.

She looked outside at the moon, and it seemed to give her a nod of encouragement. Nothing will change if you don't make a change, it told her. She knew any change she made had to be a big one. And today had happened for a reason. She would never get this opportunity again.

'Come on,' said her mother. 'We really must go to bed. It's nearly three in the morning.'

Cherry thought she would never sleep, but before long she had been plunged into dreams of pirouettes and flower garlands and spinning turntables, all to a jumbled soundtrack. And when she woke in the morning, her watch told her it was half past ten and she could hear voices in the garden. She ran to her window and looked out and there she could see Mike, sitting at the table with her father, a tray of tea in between them. She listened more closely and grinned as she heard them discussing the cricket, one of her father's passions. Mike sounded very enthusiastic and knowledgeable and the discussion was very intense indeed.

What was he doing here? How did he know where she lived? She supposed it wouldn't have been too difficult to find out. He only had to ask Maurice. She scrambled into a pair of jeans and the white blouse from the night before, washed her face and teeth quickly at the sink, and brushed her hair before running down the stairs barefoot and into the garden.

'Darling,' said her mother, who was bringing out a

plate of her shortbread. 'Look who's here. Mike's come to ask you out for lunch.'

He looked up and the smile he gave her was so familiar, so easy, so confident. She felt as if she had known him for ever. She couldn't believe her luck. A man like that, so cool and with it, with his wild curls and his shades, but who had the nerve to seek her out *and* the common sense to charm her parents? He was her future, right there.

Something inside her told her they were going to be together for a very long time.

29

At the end of the week, Maggie headed back to Avonminster. She drove up the motorway on a bit of a high. Only days ago she'd been panicking that they wouldn't be able to find a decent chef, but inspiration had struck and she had phoned the college in Honisham to see if they had any promising students on their catering course about to graduate. It didn't look as if she was going to get anyone experienced, but someone with promise would be second best. And it might be easier to mould someone than do battle with a chef who had strong ideas about what to do in the kitchen. Maggie's ideas were strong enough, she thought. But she didn't want to be doing all the cooking. She needed someone capable and she needed them fast.

The college sent over their most able student. Winnie O'Neill was five foot nothing with a blue-black bob and a mass of tattoos over her tiny frame.

'She's quite a little powerhouse,' the tutor told her. 'You won't keep her for long if you do get her.'

Maggie didn't want to do a formal interview. She had a raft of things to be getting on with the morning Winnie turned up. So she sent her into the kitchen and gave her free rein.

'Surprise me,' she said. 'I don't care what you make. Just make me swoon.'

'Okey doke,' said Winnie, cool as a cucumber, and sauntered into the kitchen with her knife roll under her arm.

Twenty minutes later Maggie felt a tap on her arm as she sat at her laptop wrestling with the invoicing program she'd downloaded. Winnie slid a small bowl over to her, filled with warm, salty cashews and macadamias, roasted in maple syrup and a mixture of hot, sweet, mellow spices.

'Oh my God,' said Maggie, unable to shovel them in fast enough. Winnie disappeared, laughing.

Over the next hour, she brought out dish after dish. A delicate but crisp potato basket filled with smoked trout and crème fraiche. A perfectly cooked omelette, pale yellow with just the right amount of runniness. A bavette steak with a soy and mirin dressing, topped with seared scallions. And finally, an exquisite blueberry clafoutis, as light as a feather, with a hint of fiery ginger to stop it from being too dainty.

Maggie was blown away. The girl's technical skills were impeccable, and she had a lightness of touch that couldn't be taught. She knew when to stop, knew when to let the ingredients speak for themselves and which method would serve them best. She would pay double to have this girl work for them.

'I want to travel,' Winnie told her. 'I don't know if I want to be tied down.'

'Work for me and I'll teach you everything you need

to know to take you to the next level,' Maggie promised her. 'You'll get the best jobs that way.'

Winnie looked doubtful.

'Give us six months of your time,' Maggie persuaded her. 'You must be secretly interested or you wouldn't have come here.'

'I was interested because my tutor told me about you. I liked the idea of a family team. A female team.'

'Let me introduce you to Rose.' Maggie led Winnie out into the garden, where Rose was digging in compost into the raised beds Ed had built for her. Maggie knew that Rose and Winnie would hit it off. They weren't far apart in age, and they had that same wildness of spirit that meant they didn't do things the usual way.

She was right. An hour later Winnie came back in and agreed to start work the following week.

So as she headed back home, she felt jubilant. Things were falling into place. With Winnie on board, she could feel the ethos of the kitchen taking shape, and it excited her. It added to the anticipation of her dinner with Mario. She supposed it was the novelty of actually going out for dinner with someone, one to one. She couldn't remember the last time she'd done that.

She stood in the shower for at least a quarter of an hour, washing out all the grease and the grime from the week, relishing the heat and the pressure. The shower at the boathouse was an ineffective trickle that had done nothing to combat the filth from the kitchen that seemed to have ingrained itself into her skin and hair over the past week. She felt like a human fatberg, and still shuddered at the clods of grease she had found clinging to the work surfaces. At last she emerged smelling sweetly of neroli and geranium, her hair squeaky clean and treated to a nourishing mask.

She flicked through all the dresses in her wardrobe. She had quite a selection, as her job meant lots of launches, award ceremonies and corporate entertaining. She chose a black silk shirt-waister with mother of pearl buttons, and spent a long time deciding exactly how many of them to leave undone. One at the bottom, three at the top, in the end.

She blow-dried her hair. The ludicrously expensive hairdryer that she'd bought made it look a bit too immaculate, so she tousled it up with a bit of wax. She didn't want to look overdone. Black suede kitten-heeled ankle boots finished it off. Sandals or courts would be too dressy.

She looked at herself in the mirror. This was the moment Frank would pad across the room in his pants, drop a kiss on her shoulder and tell her she looked like a fox. She realised she hadn't had time to write in her notebook over the past few days. And there wasn't time now – her Uber would be here any minute. She would find some time to write tomorrow.

'So.' Mario snapped off a piece of carta di musica and dug it into the artichoke dip on the sharing platter between them. 'Zara's good. You trained her well. But she's not you. And I'm still trying to work out how to get you back.'

He sat back, popping the loaded flatbread into his mouth.

'Oh, I think it was better that I went.' Maggie was distracted, too busy looking at the sharing platter to see what ideas she could use at The Swan. Sharing platters were a bit of a catering cliché but people loved them and they were a gift for a busy restaurant. They could keep punters quiet for hours. 'I used every trick in my repertoire. I was getting stale. Zara is full of energy and enthusiasm.'

Mario shrugged. 'She doesn't have your class, though.'

'Ah, yes, well. You can't buy class, can you?' Maggie teased.

She looked at Mario. He was slight, in his white linen shirt and Armani jeans, but she could see the outline of his toned arms through the fabric.

'Well, I just wanted to say thank you. You taught me a lot. About how to look at food. And the world. And how to treat people. I would never have done what my sister and mother did. I still can't speak to them.'

Maggie knew he was exaggerating. He loved to drama-tise.

'Oh dear. I don't want to cause a family rift.'

'They are power-crazy. They don't listen. And that scares me sometimes. I wonder maybe if it's time to leave the business.'

'And do what?'

'I don't know. I just feel like if I don't go now, I'll be with them for ever. And I'm not sure that's what I want.'

Maggie was intrigued. She'd never seen this side of Mario.

'Do it! You know your stuff.' She laughed. 'It's funny, isn't it? You're trying to leave your family and I've just gone into business with mine.'

'You still haven't told me what you're doing.'

'My mum's bought a pub. We're running it together. Me, Mum and Rose.'

'A pub? What pub? Where? Are you insane?'

'Maybe. It's the pub in the village she was brought up in. We've gone there for years. Mum worked there when she was a teenager. It's kind of a dream of hers.'

Mario whistled softly. 'That's cool. Three generations of women. Running a pub. That is great PR. Smart.'

'Of course.' Maggie smiled at his teasing.

Mario ran his thumb over his bottom lip, looking thoughtful. 'You know there's one good thing that's come out of this.' He leaned forward. 'Because while I was working with you, I couldn't ask you out.'

'Oh?' Maggie raised an eyebrow.

'I never mix business with pleasure.'

Maggie picked up a plump black olive and put it in her mouth. She didn't know what to say. Mario sat back in his chair.

'I think you're amazing,' he said. 'You're so smart and you care so much and you're such a great mother and a great daughter. And now you're not working with us . . .' He looked down at his wine glass, swirling the liquid round, then looked up again. 'Maybe I have a chance?'

Maggie didn't answer straight away. She was a little taken aback, not thinking she would be Mario's type at all. She imagined a size eight goddess in Gucci sunglasses, sultry, sulky, high maintenance. But Mario wasn't her type either. He was charming, entrepreneurial, engaging – but a little too smooth for Maggie.

'I'm really sorry,' she said softly. 'But I'm not ready for a relationship yet.'

He reached for the bottle of wine from the bucket next to the table. There was a chink of ice cubes as he lifted it out, and Maggie watched a trail of water splash onto the tablecloth as he filled her glass.

'Maggie,' he said. 'It's been four years. More than four years.'

'I know,' she said. 'But I can't help how I feel. I'm just not ready.'

'OK,' he said. His smile didn't quite reach his eyes, but it was disappointment rather than petulance. Maggie was surprised at how crushed he seemed. Maybe he wasn't used to not getting his own way?

'We can be friends though.' She lifted her glass to him. 'And no hard feelings.'

He gave a tiny shrug, and his mouth twisted into a half smile. 'Friends.'

After that, the tension eased and dinner was fun. Maggie realised how starving she was. Apart from Winnie's feast, none of them had really eaten a proper meal all week; she'd served them all up her staple ramen bowls to keep them going. Now they had laid down the ground rules, the conversation flowed as smoothly as the wine – they talked about the plans for The Swan, and Mario promised to supply everything she needed from him. And he talked about how difficult it had been for him to leave Rome when he was small, but how he had come to love Avonminster nevertheless. And Maggie talked about her fears for Rose, how worried she was that the life she was leading was never about her, that everyone else seemed to come first.

'Does she complain?' asked Mario.

'Never,' said Maggie. 'But sometimes I want her to behave like a normal kid her age. She knows I will always have Gertie for her. Though it's going to be hard with the pub.'

'I think Rose is really lucky. Being young isn't always a picnic. All those hangovers and comedowns and broken hearts. She's safe and secure and loved. Isn't that what we all want?'

'You're right. I guess I feel guilty.'

'How is any of it your fault?' Mario shook his head in disbelief.

'I don't know. A mother's default position, I guess.'

They finished off with cantucci dipped into vin santo. Maggie felt completely relaxed after the mayhem and physical rigour of the week. And spoiled – the food at Ottantadue was lusciously indulgent and Maggie knew they were VIPs from the little extras that had come from the kitchen for them to try: truffle porcini arancini and pumpkin tortellini with sage.

'Do you want to come back for coffee? My apartment is two minutes' walk.'

'I never do coffee. I won't sleep.'

There was a pause. 'Then I'll make you decaf. Though it is against my religion.'

'Oh.' Maggie blushed.

Suddenly, sitting there in the comfort of the banquette, in the glow of the lamplight, filled with delicious food and not a little wine, Maggie felt a shoot of desire. Mario was as tempting as the tiny little cups of tiramisu they had just devoured: sweet, dark wickedness. He was crumpling up his napkin, studiously ignoring her until she answered. She knew if she refused he would accept her refusal graciously. But suddenly she didn't want to refuse. They had bounced off each other all evening, laughing and teasing each other, but also sharing some intimate details about their fears and worries. Mario had revealed a depth she had never appreciated before. As the evening drew to a close, she felt herself warming to him.

More than warming.

She reminded herself that they'd had a bottle of Amarone on top of several glasses of white wine. And the vin santo. But she wasn't insensible. She just suddenly felt the need for a pair of arms around her, the warmth of a body. She hadn't felt that for a long time.

'OK then,' she said, and burst out laughing at his astonished expression. 'Let's go.'

They walked out onto the little cobbled street and along to the harbourside. She tucked her arm into his, and it felt strangely familiar, walking amidst the Friday night throngs of drinkers and diners moving from bar to restaurant to club. This was Avonminster at its best: the river gleaming black under the moon, the music spilling from doorways, the lights of the city twinkling behind. He led her to an apartment block in a converted warehouse.

'That's a lot of tins of tomatoes,' said Maggie, looking up at it in wonder, then thought perhaps she'd been a little rude. Mario laughed.

'I guess I'll be selling tomatoes until my dying breath.' He punched in the code and the door swung open. He held out an arm. 'After you.'

This was the moment she could change her mind. She knew he wouldn't protest. She trusted him. They understood each other. And maybe that was why she smiled and walked straight inside.

The apartment was as sleek and expensively dressed as Mario. A flick of a switch lit the living room with a soft warm glow, and Maggie made her way over to the sofa and sank down into its velvety depths with an appreciative sigh. And realised she'd forgotten this feeling. Anticipation, uncertainty and that delicious corkscrew of lust. She had buried so many feelings out of necessity, and now they were unleashed she relished the relief. They were red-hot against the grinding grey of her grief. The grief had once been black and harsh, but was a softer constant now, though no less wearing. To feel something different was a release.

Mario walked behind the sofa to put on some music. Some smooth seventies soul. As he made his way back past her, he ruffled her hair affectionately. Without thinking, she leant back into his hand, like a cat asking for more affection. He didn't say anything, but began to massage her scalp with the most gentle touch, his fingers playing with her hair, lifting strands of it and letting it fall. She felt as if her head was covered in a million tiny pinpricks of light.

'Oh,' she breathed. 'That feels wonderful.'

He still didn't speak, just let his fingers dance over her head and down her neck, touching the top of her spine, skittering up behind her ears until she was almost melting. To be touched like this after so long was exquisite but almost unbearable. She was hypersensitive, and Mario was as deft as a virtuoso piano player, knowing exactly how much pressure to apply. She almost couldn't bear it but at the same time she didn't want him to stop.

She put her hands up to her face and gave a sigh.

'I can stop if you want.' He took his hands away and she longed for him to put them back.

'Don't stop.'

He bent down and she felt his lips on her neck, just

beneath her hairline, and she gave a whimper that she hated herself for. God, if she couldn't control herself when he kissed her neck, what chance did she have if—

She stood up. He looked up, mortified. 'I'm really sorry. I thought...'

She held out her hand to him. 'I presume you have a bedroom?'

His eyes widened. 'Strangely enough, I do.'

'Then come on.'

She felt bold as she followed him, trying not to laugh at herself. What was she doing? *What the hell*, she thought. If his head massage was anything to go by, she was in for the time of her life.

His room was just as she imagined it might be. Just a seven-foot bed visible. Everything else hidden behind sliding walnut doors. Subdued lighting. A grey velvet bedcover and crisp white sheets. They stood at the foot of the bed, staring at each other for a moment.

'On your back,' said Maggie, gently pushing his chest with her palm.

'Oh my God,' he said, falling backwards with his arms spread out and a wide smile on his face.

She kicked her boots off and pulled her dress up so she could put one leg either side of him, and began to un-button his shirt. When he went to touch her, she tapped his hand.

'You're quite the dominatrix,' he said admiringly.

She smiled as she reached his bottom button and revealed the top of his jeans.

And then the track changed and she recognised the intro. 'Lowdown' by Boz Scaggs. And she froze. All she could see was Frank, in their kitchen, doing his smooth

Studio 54 dance, friends doubled up with laughter as he pointed his fingers in the air and strutted his stuff.

And then she looked up and saw the full-size mirror over the bed, and a dishevelled woman staring back at her, her hair wild, her skirt pulled up and her legs either side of a man who until ten minutes ago she had never even thought about kissing.

She was jerked back into reality. What on earth was she doing? Who was that crazy woman? She was a grieving *widow*, for heaven's sake. Suddenly all she could see was Frank's shocked face. His crushed expression at the sight of her rolling around with the Italian Stallion, as he used to call Mario. This was wrong, no matter what her body might be telling her.

'I'm sorry,' she said, and scrambled off him as elegantly as she could.

'What's the matter?' Mario sat up, leaning on his elbows, his shirt falling away to show his chest.

'I can't do this.'

He looked puzzled. 'Oh.'

She couldn't vocalise her feelings. She just shook her head.

'I'm sorry. I really thought you were up for it. I wouldn't have...'

'Oh God. I was. I totally was. Don't think I wasn't. It's just...' She sat on the bed with a sigh. 'I'm sorry. I can't help it. I can't stop thinking about Frank.' She was surprised at herself for telling him, but to her surprise Mario looked sympathetic.

'I get it. It feels like a betrayal?'

'Totally.'

'But it's not. You deserve to feel good. This doesn't mean anything, Maggie.'

'Oh. Right. No. I mean, I know it doesn't. But it's still—'

'It's just a physical pleasure. Like the food and the wine. The perfect end to a wonderful night. We're not fucking with our minds, Maggie. Or our hearts. Just our bodies.'

She couldn't help but look shocked. 'Right.'

'I don't expect anything from you. No strings. *Amici con benefici*. Friends with benefits.'

'It's sounds so much better when you say it in Italian,' Maggie murmured, but she was drawing away. The moment was gone. The desire had evaporated.

'Don't do this to yourself, Maggie.' Mario was gazing into her eyes. 'Don't keep yourself on ice for ever.'

'It's how I feel. I can't help it. I'm so sorry.'

'I'm not saying this for me. I'm saying it for you.'

She stood up.

'I'm really sorry. Please don't take it personally.'

'No, no – I do understand.'

'You're very lovely, Mario, and I would love to . . .' she gulped, '. . . you know, under any other circumstances, but it doesn't feel right and that isn't fair on you.'

'Hey, listen, I can handle it.'

He smiled at her, wry. In the lamplight, he looked like a model posing for Italian *Vogue*, his dark hair tousled, his shirt undone, his abs smooth and hard.

'Can we forget this ever happened?' she asked.

He stared at her.

'There's no way I'm ever going to forget it,' he said. 'But I won't mention it again, I promise.'

*

Maggie fled the apartment, heading out into the harbourside, which was still heaving with people. She tried to make herself look as unflustered as she could while she called an Uber. Her head was starting to throb from the unaccustomed drinking – she didn't usually mix her drinks like that. She tried to add it up, and thought it was no wonder she'd behaved how she had.

Back at home, she drank three glasses of water and swallowed two paracetamol. She took her notebook out of her bag. She let the pen hover over the page for a few seconds.

You will not believe the chef we've got for The Swan. She's only Rose's age but she's awesome. And I really hope the two of them will be friends. I feel like all Rose's friends went off the radar a bit when she had Gertie. Not that they don't love her still, but she doesn't see them so much any more. But Winnie would be great for her. She's smart and sassy and sorted. Anyway, a good end to an amazing week. I really think it's going to work, this mad venture of ours. One more week to go before we open. Shiiiiiit!!!!

Mario took me out for dinner to say thank you for everything I did for When in Rome. Which was sweet of him. He's not as . . .

Then she put the pen down. She was still drunk. And she wasn't sure what she should say. Whether she should confess what happened. Frank might think it was funny. But he might be hurt . . . up there, wherever he was.

She shut the notebook, ran up to her bedroom and put on Frank's Nirvana t-shirt over her pyjama bottoms. Straight away she felt comforted. She remembered him wearing it the day Rose was born, sitting with her in the delivery room for fourteen hours of unfruitful labour, until they wheeled her off for an emergency Caesarean . . .

She could see him now, blue scrubs over his t-shirt and jeans, and a sort of shower cap over his hair. Most men, she knew, would blanch at the prospect of watching their wife undergo a C-section, but Frank suffered from an insatiable curiosity. To him, the prospect was fascinating. The chance to see inside someone didn't come along all that often. Not in his line of work, anyway.

He stood as close as he could to the operating table, at Maggie's head, because the team liked to keep partners on that side of the screen, away from the business end of things. After all, he was there to give her support and comfort, not be a spectator. But he peered as closely as he could, mesmerised by the deft ballet, the incision, the gleam of the knife.

'Stop gawping. I haven't given you permission to look at my gizzards.' Maggie was holding tightly on to his hand.

As the team prepared for the incision, Frank was doing a Groucho Marx waggle with his eyebrows, running through a series of expressions: quizzical to disapproving to shocked to outraged.

'Don't make me laugh,' Maggie pleaded. She didn't want her belly shaking when someone was about to cut into it.

He grinned, and settled for a final nod of approval.

'They're going in,' he said, and Maggie winced – at the thought rather than any feeling. Although she couldn't feel pain, she could feel tugging and pulling.

Frank watched intently, and she watched his face rather than the surgeon's. He was riveted, and her heart buckled with love for him. His pale heart-shaped face with the too-thick eyebrows, the Tintin quiff, his eyes the pale green of old-fashioned lemonade bottles. Her quirky, eccentric husband with his eye for detail and his never-ending ability to see the sunny side, the funny side. His party trick was to sing 'The Joker' by Steve Miller, complete with the wolf whistle on his guitar, and it always made everyone gleefully weak with laughter.

'My gangster of love,' she called him, giddy with a fondness that was so much more nourishing than the unhealthy passion she'd had for the bad boys before him.

He was the least likely person for Maggie to end up with. Geeky, bespectacled, uncool – yet somehow super-cool, with his chivalry and his forensic understanding of how everything worked, from the Hadron Collider to her hair straighteners. He would be identifying all her body parts as they were revealed, nodding sagely as he recognised them.

Suddenly she saw his eyes widen, then mist over.

'Oh my God,' he breathed. 'Oh, my dear God.'

Her own eyes shot towards the screen, to see the surgeon's eyes crinkle with delight above his mask as he lifted out a baby. Their baby. A bundle of lilac streaked with red, little legs bunched up.

'A little girl. Congratulations,' said the surgeon.

'A little girl,' Frank breathed as a fat tear rolled out of one eye and down his cheek. 'Oh, Maggie.'

She squeezed his hand, weak with joy.

The baby was whizzed through the air to the waiting

arms of the midwife to be weighed and checked over as the rhythm of the theatre ploughed on, the quiet acknowledgement of a newly arrived miracle implicit in everyone's smiles and nods. Maggie willed them to hurry as they stitched her up. She wanted to be alone, the three of them. She felt passive, which was not what she was used to. It felt odd, having no say in what was happening. She shut her eyes for a moment, shutting it all out, for if she thought too much about it, she panicked. She realised how tense she had felt, how there had been a curdle of fear in the pit of her stomach since the moment an emergency section had been mooted.

An hour later, there was a bed on the ward, a floral curtain, tea in a white plastic cup. Frank sat in the uncomfortable chair provided for visitors with the baby in the crook of his arm, close enough for Maggie to reach out and touch her. She stroked the baby's cheek with the back of her finger, marvelling at its softness, its delicate pink and cream.

'It's like a rose petal.'

'Rose,' said Frank. 'How about that for a name?'

They both stared at their daughter.

'Rose?' breathed Maggie. There was the faintest little sigh of satisfaction in response.

'It suits her, I think,' said Frank.

'Rose Amelia,' said Maggie. Amelia was the friend who had introduced them to each other, outside the tapas bar. 'Rose Amelia Nicholson-Fuller.'

'Perfect.'

'Well, now that's settled, we'd better do the phone calls.

'You call your mum first.'

'Really?'

'I know Cherry is trying to be all cool and laidback about it, but she'll be beside herself,' he laughed. 'My mum can wait.'

Maggie gazed at Frank. He was so unbelievably kind. Always. She could never believe quite how lucky she was.

She would never be able to replace him. Never.

30

There were five of them. Bewildered, bald and bedraggled, they huddled up in the enormous box Rose had found for them. She and Gertie had cut horizontal slits for them to breathe through on the journey home from the rescue centre. For Rose had decided, on discovering the dilapidated hen house at the far end of the garden by the compost heap, that Gertie's wish should come true and what The Three Swans needed more than anything was chickens.

She had spent two days restoring the hen house, painting it periwinkle blue and making sure there wasn't a single hole in the fence where a fox could get in. And now she was the proud guardian of five battery hens, rescued from slaughter by the Chicken Lady, as Gertie had christened her, as their egg production was no longer sufficiently bountiful.

'They should lay quite happily once they've settled,' the Chicken Lady assured them, when they went to pick them up. There were queues of people waiting to collect their own little cluster of hens from the pick-up point. A swift and efficient procedure that ensured a new life for the poor creatures.

All the way home from the rescue centre they sang 'There Ain't Nobody Here But Us Chickens', and Gertie kept her little hand on top of the box to stop it sliding on the back seat. Back at the pub, they carried the box down the garden, set it down gently inside the run, opened the lid and tore down one of the sides to make them an exit.

Rose was nervous about releasing them. The Chicken Lady had warned them the hens might be overwhelmed by their new surroundings at first.

'It will be a shock for them, going from being cooped up to having space to roam. It takes a while for them to acclimatise and get used to their freedom. And they will need to get used to each other, as well. It's a gradual but delicate process, but very rewarding. You won't regret your girls for a moment.'

They sat down to wait and watch, letting them emerge into the sunlight of their own accord. They were tentative at first, stretching out their scrawny necks, beady eyes darting hither and thither, stepping out with one clawed foot after another. They were like prehistoric dinosaurs, on high alert for predators in a hostile world.

'Aren't they beautiful?'

'I love them,' said Gertie. 'I love them all the same.'

Rose held Gertie on her lap, her heart simultaneously breaking for these misused beings, but also filling with joy at their chance for a new beginning. It made her feel happy, to have made a difference and to have something to care for. And she wanted to teach her daughter to do the same. It would be Gertie's job to feed and water them every morning, under Rose's supervision. You were never too young to learn to care.

Soon their new charges were making their way around the run, pecking at the grass, stretching out their poor featherless wings and enjoying the sunlight.

'Billie, Ella, Amy, Peggy and Nina,' said Rose, naming them after her favourite jazz singers, and Gertie recited their names after her, pointing to each chicken in turn. They each looked identical at the moment, but no doubt when they emerged into full bloom, they would develop identifying characteristics.

Rose rested her chin on Gertie's head, thinking how very much at home she felt here. She loved Avonminster, but the city was full of memories and shadows and here, somehow, her anxiety receded and it felt like a fresh start she hadn't known she needed. Of course, Rushbrook had always been a sanctuary, pottering about the garden with Catherine, pruning roses and picking raspberries. It was the smells she had loved more than anything: the warm sun on the earth, the scent of lilac and jasmine and honeysuckle on the breeze, the sharp tang of tomatoes in the greenhouse. Now, as she set about bringing the garden at The Three Swans to life, she was trying to remember everything she had learnt.

'Gardening's all about trial and error,' Catherine had told her. 'If it doesn't work one year, you try again differently the next. The great thing is it doesn't matter!'

Rose couldn't help wishing that Catherine was still around to advise her when to plant, when to water, when to pick. But, she supposed, if Catherine was still alive they wouldn't be here. They would still have been running around in their old lives, instead of being given this wonderful opportunity to start a new venture together.

It was funny, she thought. Most of her school friends were making their way in the world, finishing uni, getting as far away from their homes and families as they could. Not that they didn't love them, but it was natural to fly the nest. Yet that was the very last thing Rose wanted. She wanted everyone around her, as close as they could be. The thought of flying the nest made her feel quite ill. Even the thought of Gertie going to school in September made her pulse quicken. But she knew she had to dig deep and build a new life for herself and not define herself by her loved ones. She needed to make new friends, get a social life and broaden her horizons. She already felt stronger here; she sat with Gertie by the river each morning and did her own version of meditation to set her up for the day, and they had all got into the habit of a swim before their evening meal, to wash off the dust and the grime and the sweat. Working in the garden had made her fitter, and she had colour in her cheeks. This place was a healing place, she thought.

She stood up to go and take the box out of the coop, now the birds were finding their feet. Birds of a feather, she thought, and scattered some corn on the ground for them to peck at.

'Hey!' Rose looked up to see Winnie coming out of the pub with a coffee for her. 'Oh, look how happy they are.'

'All they've ever known is a cage they can't even stretch their wings out in,' Rose told her, feeling proud.

'Imagine what it must be like. To be free after all that time.'

The two of them made their way over to the bench on

the banks of the river to drink their coffee. They watched Gertie pottering about, delighted with her new charges, careful not to alarm them.

'She's a cutie,' said Winnie. 'I've always wondered whether I'd want kids, but if I could have one like Gertie I'd go for it, for sure.'

'I worry that we spoil her. She's always the centre of attention. But I think we've done OK with her.'

'So – what's the story, then?' Winnie was disarmingly blunt. 'Where's her dad?'

'Oh!' said Rose, surprised. 'Well. Do you want the short version – one-night stand, didn't get his number – or the long one?'

'The long one!' Winnie's eyes gleamed. 'I want *all* the detail.'

'Gertie,' began Rose, realising she had never told her story to someone she didn't really know, 'is a Glastonbury baby . . .'

31

Maggie had been worried about Rose going to Glastonbury on her own.

'I don't think you should go.'

'Mum. I've been every year since I was twelve. I know the ropes.'

'At least go with someone. I don't like the thought of you in a tent on your own.' Maggie could feel panic bubbling up inside her, then remembered she didn't have Frank to appeal to, the voice of reason.

'Mum, I know loads of other people who are going. I'll hook up with them when I get there. And I don't want anyone else in my tent. Have you any idea what it's like sleeping next to someone who hasn't washed properly for days?' Rose made light of the situation to put her mum off the scent. She didn't want to go with anyone else. That was the point. She wanted to go and remember her dad, her own private memorial.

Maggie wasn't happy. It wasn't that she thought Rose was in any real danger. She wasn't an idiot. But Maggie was worried that once she was there, she might find it overwhelming. That she might become too emotional.

That she would feel her dad's absence even more keenly and might not be able to handle it.

Glastonbury had always been Frank and Rose's thing; their sacrosanct annual outing. Every year when they went to buy tickets they asked if Maggie wanted to come, and she knew they would have been more than happy if she'd said yes. But the answer was always no. She didn't like camping and she didn't like queueing and she didn't like hot sun or pouring rain. Maggie had always been content to stay at home and watch the festival on the telly, grateful to have a fully functioning bathroom, a well-stocked fridge and chilled wine at her disposal while she enjoyed the music. Maggie felt her heart burst with love for them both as she waved them off in Frank's beloved VW campervan packed with everything they needed, whatever the weather. She made them samosas and flapjacks to snack on even though part of the fun of it for them was the food on offer: burritos and katsu curry and Alpine street food...

This year, she was seriously tempted to go with Rose, to keep an eye on her, but she knew her daughter wouldn't want her, and anyway she wouldn't be able to get a ticket now. She understood that it was a ritual for her, and that in some way it might be healing; might make her feel connected to Frank and unlock her emotions. It was over three months since he had gone, and so far Rose had seemed to have taken his death in her stride, quiet and composed and determined, but somehow Maggie found that more worrying than overt displays of grief. She hadn't even seen Rose cry very often. She just seemed to hold it all in, determined to carry on with life, with her exams, with her Saturday job, and with supporting Maggie. She seemed to instinctively know what her mum needed: a cup of tea, a hot bath, a takeaway pizza. More than once she'd climbed into bed with Maggie and held her through the night while Maggie sobbed, curled round her protectively. It was almost as if she was the mother.

Maggie worried that as a result *she* wasn't being a good mum, that she was neglecting Rose's needs, but she was blindsided by her own grief. How could Frank not be here any more? Why was he not here now, to drive Rose to Glastonbury, to push the B52s tape into the cassette player and play 'Rock Lobster' as they set off? In the end, she accepted that she had to let Rose go. She was, after all, eighteen. An adult. She would drive her there – Rose hadn't passed her driving test yet – and she would pick her up late on Sunday night.

Look out for her from up there, will you, darling? she wrote to Frank that evening. *I think it's going to be really intense for her. I shan't sleep all weekend until she's back home. Shit, I wish you were here and you were going. I know how much you were looking forward to Sigur Rós.*

A lump rose in her throat. They'd played Sigur Rós at Frank's memorial. Even people who'd never heard of them were moved to tears. By the end, everyone had their arms around each other, eyes closed, remembering the man who had meant so much to them. The son, the husband, the father, the friend.

Usually, Maggie watched the whole thing on the telly, but she didn't think she'd be able to handle it. She could only hope that Rose would be OK.

*

Arriving at Glastonbury on foot on her own was a totally different experience from rocking up in the campervan with her dad. Rose had expected that. It wasn't just that her dad wasn't with her physically, with all the usual anticipation and thrill of arriving. He wasn't here at all. She felt as if she was on one of those glass platforms you see on the internet, the ground thousands of feet below. Although she knew she was safe, if she looked down she felt terrified. So she kept looking ahead. Taking everything one step at a time. In this case, quite literally, dragging her luggage trolley through the mud to the field she had pinpointed as being neither too rowdy or too dull or too far away from the action. It was a fine balance, choosing where to pitch your tent. She wanted to feel the atmosphere but she knew she would need sleep.

She'd printed out the timetable of what they'd been planning to see: a complex criss-crossing of the site timed to the last nano-second, going from tiny, almost unheard-of, debut artists to international stars. Frank loved to mix it up, taking a risk and discovering new acts but also revelling in the headlining legends. She looked at it before she folded it up, and she felt a wave of sadness as she remembered them debating the merits of ZZ Top versus Editors (ZZ Top had won on the grounds of best beards. They both agreed the beards could not be missed.)

Ever since she was tiny, Frank had made Rose playlists. He'd played her Vivaldi and Van Morrison in her crib. Then moved on to Chet Baker, Erykah Badu, Elvis Costello, Paul Simon, Nirvana, Roxy Music, The Beach Boys, Rachmaninov. Where her friends tended to get fixated on one band and play them over and over to the exclusion of all else, Rose had a different artist for every mood or occasion. Frank told her endless rock-and-roll anecdotes: tales of excess, destructive love affairs, drug abuse and creative genius. He told her the stories behind the songs. 'Music will teach you everything you need to know about life,' he would say. 'There is a song for every occasion. Music will always give you the answer.'

Every year, a few weeks before they went, Frank would make a playlist with all the best songs from the bands they were going to see. Part of the thrill was the expectation of hearing a song you loved, and trying to guess what track a band would finish with. This year Rose had made the playlist herself, digging into each band's backlist and immersing herself in their history.

It had got her through the dark hours. At night, she would take to her bed, clamping on the earphones he and Maggie had got her last Christmas, and lose herself, half awake, half asleep, until another day without her dad had passed. Everyone exclaimed how well she was doing. No one knew it was just a façade. They would find out, eventually, that despite outward impressions, she had sabotaged her future. That despite her calm exterior, inside there was a nihilistic creature who didn't see the point to anything. She did her best to keep that Rose hidden from the world. From school and from her family and her friends. That Rose frightened her.

To keep that Rose hidden, she was spending more and more time on her own. Company and conversation jarred with her. It was too exhausting to keep up. The trick was to withdraw without being seen to withdraw. Without anyone suspecting. She created endless mirages, pretending she was with people, or going somewhere, or doing something. How easy it was to create an alter ego. An alternative Rose: sorted, coping, together.

Inside, her thoughts and feelings were out of control.

As she made her way along with the crowds of other festival-goers, she prayed this weekend would be healing and help her move on. That the fug of grief might lift and allow her to be who she knew she should be. Right now, she thought, she was not someone her father would be proud of. Her stomach tilted as she thought about what she had done. She tried to push the shame away. She needed a pint of Somerset cider and a burrito. Then she'd be good to go.

You can do this, Rose told herself. *He is here with you. His spirit is in you. Enjoy it for him.*

By Friday evening, Rose was starting to feel like her old self. It was impossible not to be infected by the atmosphere. You had to run with it, cram in as many experiences as you could. She did some power-ballad yoga, watched a tiny acoustic set by a girl she'd seen in Avonminster a few times; listened to an intense debate on feminism; had some orange and pink braids put in her hair; ate a huge portion of mac and cheese with crispy bacon and fresh basil washed down with some Voodoo Rum Punch. She had managed, somehow, to avoid seeing anyone she knew, deliberately steering clear of the bars and the bands where her peers might be hanging out. She didn't want to get pulled into their agendas, have drinks forced upon her and be endlessly hugged.

And then it was night-time and she knew she was going to have to face her biggest challenge yet. Her dad's favourite band, Sigur Rós, were playing. As soon as the sun started to leave the sky, she imagined how excited Frank would be about seeing them. She remembered how emotional he would get when he listened to their music; how his eyes would swim with tears. 'It's the closest I'll ever get to believing,' he would say.

She found a place in the audience where she felt comfortable, as near to the front as she could get without getting squashed. She pulled her jacket round her as the night air began to cool and darkness fell. And with the dark, everyone dropped down a gear and became more mellow. They were languid, sweaty, affectionate, expectant. They closed around her and she felt safe. A surge of anticipation bubbled up inside her, sweet and intense, and as the first notes began, her heart swelled with joy.

She could feel, she realised. She thought she was never going to be able to feel again. She had been numb for weeks. The only thing she had felt was a grinding despair. But as the music began, she was enraptured, completely enveloped by the hypnotic beat, the soaring, dreamlike chords, the angelic vocals, the darkness soft around her. Song after song lifted her higher and higher. Frank had always told her that music had more power than anything to change you, to heal you. As the final song began, there was a shaft of silver light shining up to the sky, and she felt as if she could climb up towards heaven, as if she could reach out and touch her dad, touch her fingertips to his and feel his warmth.

'Hey.' There was a warm voice in her ear, and she felt a hand on her shoulder. 'Are you OK?'

She looked up in surprise, into an unfamiliar face. A pair of deep green eyes under thick, dark brows, wild curly hair, a five o'clock shadow and a Cupid's bow mouth. He wore an emerald velvet jacket, his chest bare underneath, skin-tight jeans and snakeskin boots.

She didn't know him, and yet she did. He stared at her for a moment, grave with concern. 'It's OK,' he whispered, and with his thumb gently wiped away the tears she had no idea had been streaming down her face. Then he turned her round to face the stage again, putting both his arms around her from behind, cradling her as the music increased in intensity and she leant against him. They swayed gently in unison as the song reached a crescendo. She could barely breathe for emotion yet she felt safe and warm for the first time in months, wrapped up in a stranger's hug. She could feel his heartbeat against her back. She had never felt so close to her dad, to another human, to a piece of music. She felt as if she was the music. She never wanted it to end. The song, the night.

The audience erupted into applause as the song faded away, but the stranger held on to her tight. They stood like ballet dancers, their breathing in rhythm, as if waiting for their own applause. Rose thought if she moved he might disappear, that she might turn round to find he had vanished, that he had been a figment of her fevered imagination. As the audience started to melt away, she turned to face him.

'Thank you,' she whispered.

'They do that to me too,' he said. 'Make me want to cry.'

'They were my dad's favourite band. We played Glósóli at his funeral.'

'Oh.' Anguish and sympathy flickered across his face.

'We came here every year. Just me and him. He was really excited about seeing Sigur Rós...'

'Oh, baby,' he said with a sigh, and he squeezed her hand. 'He must have been a very cool dad.'

Rose smiled at the thought of Frank being described as cool. 'No. He wasn't cool. Definitely not. But he was the best. He was funny. And kind. And everyone loved him.'

'I'm really, really sorry.' He was looking straight into her eyes as he spoke. Most people avoided eye contact when she talked about him. 'He sounds amazing.'

Rose nodded her agreement, unable to speak any more. She felt odd, as if she was stepping from darkness into light. They were facing each other holding hands. She didn't want to let go. She kept staring at him. He had appeared from nowhere, a complete stranger, yet he felt so reassuringly familiar.

'I feel a bit funny,' she said, and he put his palm on her forehead. She shut her eyes and leaned into him. He smelled of cinnamon and oranges and burning candles.

'I'm going to stay with you, as long as you want me to. But if you want me to leave you alone, just say.'

'Thank you.' She squeezed his hand.

The crowds around them had melted away. They were standing almost alone.

'Is it me,' Rose ventured at last, 'or is this weird?'

He didn't answer for a second, but his eyes roamed her face, taking in every feature. And she didn't worry that her make-up might be smudged, or her face too shiny, because he seemed to be drinking her in as if she was perfect. 'It's kind of weird,' he said with a sigh.

Rose laughed. 'We can't just stand here all night. Shall we go and get a drink?'

'Sure.' He put his arm around her and led her through the last straggles of people. Rose snuggled into him, relishing his warmth and his Christmassy smell that made her head swim a little. For the first time in months that cold, hard lump at the very core of her seemed to melt away as they wandered through the crowds, with no real idea of where they were going. There was no need to know. People seemed to part for them as they walked by. She shivered with the thrill of it all and he thought she was cold.

'Let's stop here,' he said outside a bar. 'Sit down and I'll get something to warm you up.'

She sat on a rough wooden bench and he disappeared into the crowd at the bar. She felt a little dazed, but confident he would return. How on earth had this happened? It was completely unexpected. She'd never had a big love. Her boyfriends were usually mates of friends who she mucked about with until they drifted apart amicably. And she'd made a decision at Christmas to stay single until her A levels were finished.

At the memory of her exams, a tiny dart of anxiety needled its way back in but she flicked it away. And then he emerged from the melée with an espresso martini cradled in each hand.

'Oh wow,' she said. 'How did you know that's my favourite?'

'Because it's mine,' he said with a shrug, and they both

laughed. The martinis were good ones – dark and not too sweet and loaded with shots of vanilla vodka.

'You've got coffee fluff on your top lip,' he told her, laughing, and before she could put her hand up to wipe it away, he leant forward to brush it away with his thumb. She drew in a sharp breath and he rested his thumb on her mouth and she shut her eyes and leaned in to kiss him, bold with vodka and their electricity. He tasted of sugar and cream and coffee and she wound her fingers in his hair, pulling him in tighter, and she didn't want this magical night to end. She would never have believed it was possible for her to feel like this, bursting with light and energy and something that felt very potent and intoxicating. She had thought she would be cold and hard and dead inside for ever.

It was starting to rain. Gentle drops, but insistent, falling in a way that hinted they were just a prelude to a downpour.

'Come on.' He jumped up and held out his hand. She took it without demur and followed him back to his tent, too wrapped up in the wonder of it all to really notice where they were going.

'I'd carry you over the threshold,' he said, unzipping the front. 'But it's a bit too low. You'll have to crawl inside.'

There was nothing cosier than being tucked up inside a tent while the rain fell. He draped a spare blanket around her shoulders and magicked a bar of Fruit & Nut from a rucksack while he made them a nest on his sleeping mat, turned on a lantern and put some music on a little portable speaker. Goldfrapp. She smiled in recognition and approval. Then he dug around and found a couple of cans of cider. They sat huddled together, sharing the chocolate and sipping at their drinks, until both their cans were empty and there wasn't a crumb of chocolate left. There was a silence, and Rose wondered if perhaps she'd imagined the bond between them, and she was about to suggest that she'd better go and find her own tent before it got too late when he put both arms around her and pulled her to him.

'I just want to hold you,' he said. 'All night long. You make me feel so warm. Inside and out.' Then he laughed, and she loved the way his eyes turned down, and a little dimple appeared high up on his cheek. 'I've just realised. I don't even know your name.'

'Rose,' she told him.

'Rose,' he said, as if it was the most intriguing and unusual name he'd ever heard. 'It suits you perfectly. I should have known that's what you were called.'

'And yours?'

'Oh,' he said. 'They call me Ziggy. It's my nickname. My mum's a massive Bowie fan. My real name's too boring for words.'

'That's a great name. It suits you.'

Rose and Ziggy, thought Rose. Ziggy and Rose. It sounded good, whichever way round you said it.

She woke up next to him, the two of them entwined inside his sleeping bag. His arms were around her, possessive, reassuring, and she lay for a few moments, enjoying the heat and the closeness, remembering the remains of the night before with a quickening heart. Had she dreamt it, or had it been perfect? She didn't think it was a dream, given that their clothes were in a discarded tangle on the floor. She felt a flush scamper over her cheeks. She wasn't in the habit of jumping into bed with strangers. But he hadn't felt like a stranger. Far from it.

She needed the loo, and she needed to wash and brush her teeth at the very least. She couldn't bear the thought of leaving him, even for a few minutes, but if she was quick, she could be back inside his arms before he'd even noticed she was gone. She unzipped the sleeping bag quietly and rolled out. He stirred, gave a groan, reached out for her hand without opening his eyes.

'I'm going to the bathroom,' she whispered, and he nodded, squeezing her fingers before drifting back to sleep.

She pulled on her clothes as quickly as she could. Outside there was a steady drizzle. The rainbow bright colours of yesterday were nowhere to be seen. Just rows and rows of khaki and navy and grey in the half light. The sun had no intention of making an appearance yet. She shivered in the chill of early morning, keeping her head down in a fruitless attempt to stay dry, heading for the wash area she knew to have the best facilities. It was quite a walk, but it would be worth it to feel clean and fresh.

The queue had a dawn camaraderie: everyone sleepy and dishevelled and damp. Rose hugged herself to keep warm and realised she was smiling at anyone who caught her eye, still wrapped up in the thrill of Ziggy.

'Good night?' one girl grinned at her, and she blushed and nodded.

When she came out from her makeshift wash and brush-up, the rain was falling even harder. She tried to get her bearings, and realised with disquiet that she'd been in such a daze she'd forgotten to take note of exactly where Ziggy's tent was. She started to head in what she thought was the right direction and then stopped. Was it the other way? Think, she told herself. Which direction had she approached from? She was light-headed from lack of sleep and a tiny bit hung-over. She tried to think back to the night before, and where they had headed, but she hadn't been taking any notice. She had followed him blindly.

This way, she reassured herself. Definitely this way. She huddled under her jumper as the rain doubled its efforts, so torrential she could barely see in front of her. The world seemed to be dissolving as she walked into a sludgy mixture of grey and brown. Walking became difficult as the ground beneath her feet turned to thick mud, pulling her under, wrapping her boots in heavy clay. Within minutes she was soaked to the skin, shivering. She walked past tent after tent, but she couldn't remember what colour his was. She hadn't been able to see it in the dark, hadn't noticed when she left for the loos. Everyone was rushing for cover, charging past her. The sky was glowering and offered no hope. The entire mood had changed. All the joy and laughter of yesterday seemed to be washed away by the rain.

She didn't know what to do. She couldn't knock on every tent to see if he was inside. Could she? She told herself to keep calm and have a system. Use her common sense. That's what Frank would tell her. Find a fixed point and work your way around. But it was impossible. There were acres and acres of rain-soaked tents, all identical. All the landmarks were hidden by the mist that seemed to have descended.

She slipped in the mud and fell over. She stayed still for a moment, crouched on all fours, humiliated, but no one seemed to notice her. They were all intent on escaping the deluge. No one cared about a silly girl who'd fallen over in the mud. She got back up again and trudged towards the gate.

Maybe she should go back and find her own tent? She knew where that was because she'd made a note of its exact position. Maybe she should go back and get dry and warm, then go out and look again when the rain stopped. Ziggy would be asleep for ages, probably. It was still early in the morning. No one got up early if they didn't have to.

In the end, she decided that was the only logical thing to do. Her own tent was right the other side of the site, and it took her nearly an hour to find it, by which time she was exhausted and tearful, her clothes heavy with rainwater. She fell inside, relieved. It took ages to pull off her clothes and get herself dry. She pulled out a fresh set of underwear, leggings and a t-shirt and a hoody. No fancy dress today, she just wanted to get warm.

And find Ziggy. She felt panic. She could wander around all day and not find him. She pulled out her mobile. They should have swapped numbers. That would have been the sensible thing to do. But she'd been so loved up when she left the tent, drifting along on a tide of elation, that she hadn't had practicalities on her mind. All she'd wanted was to get back to him as quickly as she could so they could plan their day.

Of course it was too good to be true. Of course she wasn't allowed to have someone who made her feel safe and happy. Of course he was going to be snatched away from her.

She remembered his touch. His mouth. His voice. His laughter. *Their* laughter.

She pulled a waterproof poncho from her rucksack, slipped it on and pulled up the hood. She was starting to shiver despite her dry clothes. Then a moment later she felt hot, and too weak to stand. She collapsed onto her mat and lay for a moment. There was a dull ache inside her bones, followed by shooting pains. She was sweating but freezing.

Tears streamed down her face. She wanted her dad. He would come along and get her back up on her feet. Jolly her along. Why wasn't he here? He was always up early. He'd be crouched over his little gas stove, making her a comforting cup of tea, boiling some eggs, pouring water into pots of instant porridge with golden syrup.

'An army marches on its stomach,' he would tell her, and she would protest at first but would always feel better afterwards.

Her teeth were chattering now. She was sweating inside the poncho and pulled it off. She missed him so much it hurt. Was that what this was? Was her grief literally making her ill? Maybe she should go to one of the first-aid tents and get checked out?

Or maybe she should just go home? She was never going to be able to find Ziggy. The chances of bumping into him were remote – a hundred thousand people. And she didn't want to be here a moment longer without Frank.

She dialled her mum's number, praying she had enough signal.

'Mum?' she said as Maggie answered. 'Can you come and pick me up?'

'Are you OK?'

She could hear the panic in her voice.

'I just don't feel very well.' She tried not to alarm her.

She packed away her things as quickly as she could, loading them onto her luggage trolley and covering them in a bin liner to keep dry. Then she battled to take down the tent and fold it back up. A spiteful wind made this even more difficult, snatching the canvas out of her hands, and the whole thing was soaked through by the time she'd finished. She shoved it on top of everything else and began to drag the trolley through the mud.

'Oh, sweetheart.' There she was, her mum, in her weekend joggers and a denim jacket, jumping out of the car to help her and giving her an enormous hug. 'Hey, it's OK. You were so brave to go and I'm so sorry it didn't work out.'

Rose got into the car without telling her mother any more.

As they left the festival and started on the winding road back to Avonminster, Rose felt as if she had left a piece of her heart behind. She knew now she would never see Ziggy again. If she couldn't find him at Glastonbury, she certainly wouldn't be able to find him afterwards, once they'd made their way back into the real world.

Maggie bundled her into a hot bath filled with lavender bath salts as soon as they got home. Rose gradually felt the heat make its way back into her core, then slipped into a pair of pyjamas and into the bed her mum had made up with fresh linen. She took the shirt she had been wearing into bed with her. If she breathed in really deeply, she could smell Ziggy, and it brought him back so vividly. She remembered the very weight of him on her.

She felt more tired than she had ever felt. Her curtains billowed slightly with the breeze from the open window, and if she listened really hard she could hear music. What was he watching now? What had he thought when she hadn't come back? Had he understood, or had he thought she'd done a runner? He would never know how hard she had tried to find him.

She felt cold again. She began to shiver and curled up into a ball. When Maggie came back to check on her half an hour later, she was burning up.

'I'm never going to see him again,' she said to her mum, wild with despair.

Maggie thought she was talking about Frank. The agony of seeing her child in pain was almost too much to bear, for she knew herself how much it hurt.

'Shhh,' she said, smoothing Rose's hair back from her sweating forehead.

And then Rose remembered something. She had left their list behind, in Ziggy's tent. The list she and her dad had made together. The one she kept in her bag, but had taken out to show Ziggy. The list that had been folded and unfolded so many times; that had her dad's handwriting on it, with his star system, and his unique timetable, and the little pictures of drinks and hot dogs for food breaks. And she couldn't bear the thought of never seeing it, or her dad, or Ziggy again. And it was as if all the grief she had been saving up inside her came out all at once. The tears she hadn't cried.

Maggie did her best to console her, but she knew this outpouring was essential, that all that sadness had to come out, for it wasn't good for Rose to carry it around inside her heart. And if she could have had Frank back on this earth for five minutes, she would have handed him straight over to their daughter, for Rose to feel his arms around her.

On the morning of her A level results, Rose didn't need to log on to the school website to find out how she'd done. She knew exactly what grades she'd got.

Maggie was in the kitchen pretending to be bright and breezy but obviously dying of curiosity, like every parent across the country anxious to know how their son or daughter had done.

'Don't worry if you didn't do as well as expected,' she said to Rose. 'It's understandable. The great thing is you did your best and I'm so proud—'

'Mum.' Rose cut her off. She had to tell her now. 'I didn't pass. I didn't get any of my subjects. I got three Us.'

'What?' Maggie was astonished. 'That's impossible. Three Us? How?'

Rose looked her mum in the eye.

'I didn't write a word in any of the exams. I just wrote my name at the top and that's it. I sat there for two hours, pretending to write.'

There was anguish in Maggie's face as she realised Rose was speaking the truth. 'Darling. Why? I mean, you worked so hard.'

'I couldn't face it. I didn't have the energy. I know everyone thought how amazing I was and how brave and I wasn't. Not at all.' She screwed her eyes up to stop the tears. 'I'm not the person everyone thinks I am. I'm scared. Scared about the future. I don't want to go to university to be the girl whose dad's just died. The girl who's too afraid to have fun because it doesn't feel right.

The girl who feels like half a person. Who feels like she will never be herself again.'

'Oh Rose.' Maggie pulled her to her. 'It doesn't matter. It doesn't matter at all. You've got all your life ahead of you. You can go back and do retakes. It's just another year. We'll get you through it. Please don't feel bad.' She patted her back. 'You've done all the hard work. We just need to get your confidence back. I'll phone the college.'

'No,' said Rose. 'I can't go back to college.'

'Of course you can. Loads of people do retakes. It's nothing to be ashamed of.'

Rose sighed. She might as well get all the revelations over in one day.

'I can't,' she said. 'I'm pregnant.'

Maggie blinked. Frowned. Looked at Rose, uncertain, not sure if she was teasing her or not.

'What?' she said. 'How? Who? When? Where? *What*?'

Rose couldn't help laughing.

'At Glastonbury. I met someone. But I don't know his real name. I don't know how to find him.'

Maggie sat down at the kitchen table. 'Oh. Shit.'

'The thing is,' said Rose. 'I should be bricking it. I should be thinking I've ruined my life. But it's really weird. I feel as if this baby is meant to be. I feel as if it's been sent to us. To make up for taking Dad away.'

Maggie knew she had to be careful before she answered. She wasn't going to judge, or scold, or panic. She tried to think about what Frank would say or do. He wasn't the archetypal shotgun-toting father – not that there was anyone to brandish the shotgun at, it seemed.

She looked around the kitchen for guidance. He was still here, in its very walls. In the wi-fi code he'd written on the chalk board. In the takeaway leaflets he'd tucked behind the recipe books – he would pull them out on a Friday afternoon and leaf through them, then put in a much bigger order than they needed, then invite people round to help eat it all. In the cans of craft beer piled up in the alcove, the labels an art exhibition in themselves. And he was there, in the little jars of spices that he made labels for with the Dymo gun he'd had as a teenager. Maggie would never have had the patience, but Frank had relished the task, painstakingly turning the wheel and pressing out the white letters onto black tape.

They'd made their own dhal blend one afternoon. There was one tablespoon left. It was just what they needed, a big bowl of spicy golden-yellow lentils, while they talked through Rose's options. Maggie did her best thinking whilst she was cooking. It allowed her brain to freewheel. She froze if she had to make decisions in the spotlight, with no distraction.

'I'm going to make dhal,' she said, and Rose understood. She knew her mum wasn't dodging the question. That this was her way of giving it the consideration it deserved, as well as providing comfort.

Maggie picked up the jar, smiling. They hadn't been able to agree on the spelling, so he'd made a label for each way: dal, daal, dhal. That was Frank all over: keeping an open mind, happy to compromise to keep everyone happy, accepting that there wasn't always a right answer.

She opened the jar and breathed it in: cumin and coriander and turmeric and paprika.

The two of them worked together. Maggie pulled out a big onion, some garlic and a red chilli and began to chop them while Rose poured water into a pan and added a stream of pale orange lentils, then heated some oil.

'What do you think Dad would say?'

'I think he would stay calm. He'd talk through it all from every angle. And he'd trust you to make your own mind up, and he would stand by your decision. And so that's what I'm going to do.'

Maggie threw the onion into the warmed oil and put her arms around Rose's neck.

'This is hard, without him. I've got to be both of us, for you.'

The hardest thing of all was being both her and him without Frank there to support or encourage her, or re-assure her. He had always had more faith in other people than they had in themselves, and somehow found a way to unlock that faith. He had given Maggie so much self-belief. Not that she had been insecure, but he somehow found a way to make you dig that little bit deeper and go that little bit further. He never let you doubt yourself, that was the wonderful thing.

She looked at Rose, stirring the lentils as they came to the boil. Her heart buckled as she thought of her scratching her name on the top of her exam paper, then leaving it. A wholly premeditated act of self-sabotage that made Maggie terrified for her. For Rose to be that destructive was much more terrifying than announcing she was preg-nant. It indicated a fragile state of mind, while getting pregnant was just... a mistake anyone could make.

Or had she done that on purpose too? Taken a reckless risk? Seen it as an escape route?

'I think,' she said, 'a baby is just what we all need.'

32

'What a beautiful story,' said Winnie, her eyes glassy with tears. 'But didn't you ever find him? Ziggy?'

Rose sighed. 'I tried to.'

How could you find someone when the only information you had about them was a nickname? There was so little to go on. She knew nothing concrete about him. They hadn't talked about themselves at all that night. They'd talked about music, the bands they had seen, the bands they wanted to see. And films. Their favourite films: *Eternal Sunshine of the Spotless Mind* and *Napoleon Dynamite* and *Spirited Away*. She thought perhaps he had mentioned a hometown beginning with C – wherever it was it didn't have a big music venue, was all she could remember, and he envied her Avonminster. Colchester, Cheltenham, Chichester – she wracked her brain but it didn't come back to her. She knew nothing about him – whether he had brothers and sisters, what his parents did, what he was studying or if he had a job. Nothing that would provide a shred of a clue.

And then she'd found him. David Jefferson, the 'Ziggy' hidden away in quotes, deep in the far corner of Facebook.

She sent him a friend request, holding her breath, longing for a chance to explain to him what had happened that morning so he didn't just think she'd done a runner.

'He blocked me,' she told Winnie. 'The next time I looked him up, his name had disappeared, so I couldn't even message him to tell him about Gertie. I guess he was hurt. I don't blame him.'

'Oh,' said Winnie. 'He should have given you a chance.'

'Maybe he had someone else by then? Maybe it would have been awkward?'

'I guess.' Winnie shrugged. 'So that's it? He'll never know about Gertie? Man, his loss.'

'I know. What makes me feel sad is that she'll never know him. How wonderful he was. He was very special. And I feel terrible that he thought I'd abandoned him because I didn't care. When I couldn't have cared more. I dream about him sometimes...'

'Oh, babe,' said Winnie, wrapping an arm around her.

Rose sighed. 'It's OK. I'm used to it now. And I had loads of people around me. I've been really lucky.'

Rose looked over at her daughter, picking daises off the lawn. They had all done it, between them. Brought Gertie into the world and looked after her. She might not have a father, but she had Maggie and Cherry. And Mike, who was the kindest, coolest great-grandfather you could wish for.

Having a baby had been the making of Rose. It had given her purpose and confidence and made her feel rooted again. It was probably the last solution anyone would have suggested to an eighteen-year-old who had lost her dad, to drop out and become a mother, but it had helped her make sense of the world, finding Gertie snuggled up in her cot each morning, and lifting her out, a snuffling, warm bundle of scrumptiousness.

Now, she felt she'd told Winnie enough. She wasn't used to talking about herself.

'So tell me about you,' she said. 'How did you get into cooking?'

'I was a complete nightmare at school,' Winnie told her. 'I think I'm probably a bit dyslexic but I never got diagnosed. I didn't get any exams. I thought I was such a rebel, but I was just an idiot. I got in with a bad crowd and did some dumb things for a while. Then I started watching Anthony Bourdain on Netflix and I thought – he's cool.'

'Oh,' said Rose. 'My dad loved him. We watched them all. There were so many places we wanted to go.'

'I know, right?' said Winnie. 'I mean, where would you even start? Anyway, it made me think maybe food could be my ticket to a great life. So I finally got my act together and went to college. And here I am.'

She held out her hand, smiling. She looked genuinely happy. Rose stood up.

'Come and tell me what herbs you want planted.'

'Oh wow,' said Winnie, her eyes lighting up. 'Where do I start? Mint – lots of kinds. Chives. Acres and acres and acres of chives. Lemon thyme. Purple sage. French tarragon. I am such a herb geek. You're going to wish you'd never asked.'

Rose felt reassured that someone else her age hadn't taken a conventional route and was a late developer. Sometimes she thought she was the only person who had screwed things up. To know Winnie had a rocky start, and was now flourishing in the kitchen, was an inspiration to her. It gave her the courage she needed to start moving forwards.

33

'We nailed it!'

The morning before the opening, Maggie spread open that day's copy of the *Somerset Daily News* on the bar. There was a photograph of the three of them standing in front of the pub, with a quarter of a page write-up underneath. Maggie read it out loud.

'Three generations of women have taken over the helm at The Swan in Rushbrook. The pub has undergone a revamp ready for its grand reopening as The Three Swans this Friday. Cherry, Maggie and Rose are mother, daughter and granddaughter, and have combined their skills to inject a breath of fresh air into this popular village local. The interior has been given a contemporary twist while still nodding to the trout-fishing heritage of the pub, which is idyllically set on the banks of the River Rushbrook.

***"We very much want The Three Swans to be the heart of the village, a place for everyone to call their own,"* Cherry explained to us.**

Head chef Winnie O'Neill has devised a mouth-watering menu. Try Somerset ham hock with home-made piccalilli, or smoked trout rillette with green goddess dressing. Dinner might be duck glazed with local honey, pork with apples and cider, or you could go for one of The Swan's famous pies. They're firm believers in pudding too: treacle sponge, lemon meringue pie and toffee apple crumble will all be on the menu, served with clotted cream from the dairy just up the road.

With Melchior cider on tap, a huge range of craft beers and a wine list to satisfy the most discerning connoisseur, The Three Swans looks set to be the destination pub of this summer.

Cherry, Maggie and Rose look forward to welcoming you, whether you want an early evening drink on the riverbank or a candlelit three-course dinner.'

Maggie set the paper back on the bar with a contented sigh. Even with her contacts and her experience, you could never guarantee the response from a press release. It depended what else was going on that week. A quarter-page was worth its weight in gold.

The only weird thing was Cherry not asking Mike to come and take the photos. What was the point in having a photographer in the family if you didn't use him when you needed him? There was definitely something up between Cherry and Mike. Maggie had sensed it the night after the retirement party and there was still an unfamiliar tension in the air, and Cherry had refused to let Maggie ask him.

'You know Dad doesn't approve of me buying the pub,' Cherry reminded her.

'Yes, but he doesn't want it to be a failure. I know he'd come and take the pictures.'

Cherry shook her head. 'He's very busy at the university, getting ready for the handover. Please don't bother him.'

Maggie let it drop. It didn't matter in the grand scheme of things. The important thing was they were in the paper.

'Right,' she said, clapping her hands. 'Let's not rest on our laurels. We've got a lot to do before tomorrow night. Has that skip man been in touch? I want those skips gone by the end of today. Rose, go down to the river and see if you can get some footage of the swans to share on Instagram. Anything that will get us some likes and shares. And where are the FBBs?' This was her nickname for the builders. 'I've got a snag list as long as your arm.'

Rose and Cherry looked at each other.

'Be afraid,' Rose said to her grandmother. 'She's always a nightmare before a launch.'

'Damn right,' said Maggie.

'Cherry Nicholson?' A delivery man hovered in the doorway.

'Oh,' said Cherry. 'The lamp shades. At last.'

'I don't think so,' said the man. The package he brought in was far too big. It was large and flat, the shape of a painting, but Cherry wasn't expecting any artwork.

She signed for the parcel, although there was no clue on the paperwork. It was heavy, so she laid it on a table and cut open the packaging with a Stanley knife. She pulled away the bubble wrap and gasped.

It was a sign. A double-sided sign, painted in a dark

green-black, with three impressionistic swan heads, their snow-white necks entwined, their beaks orange, and a little crown on each head. And underneath in gold was written The Three Swans. It represented Cherry, Maggie and Rose, captured in a few deft brushstrokes. If she had briefed an artist herself, she couldn't have come up with a more striking image.

There was only one person who could have painted something so perfect. How had he known exactly how big to make it, and where to put the brackets so it could be hung? There must be a spy in the camp. Or had he driven down in the darkness to measure it up?

It was exquisite. Of course it was. But it was a message too. A message of support, despite their rift. Cherry felt overwhelmed. Mike knew exactly how to convey what was needed. An image that represented them perfectly.

She looked for a note but there wasn't one.

'Oh, Mum.' Maggie had come up behind her. 'Wow. I didn't know you'd got Dad to do that?'

She didn't need telling it was Mike who had done it. It was so clearly his work: stunning, stylish, impactful.

'I didn't. And how did he know that we'd changed the name?' said Cherry. 'I hadn't told him. It was going to be a surprise.'

'I told him,' said Rose. 'He rings me nearly every night, to see how Gertie is. I think he's really missing us.'

'He's coming to the opening, surely?' said Maggie.

Cherry turned away, her eyes filling with tears, flooded with guilt.

The truth was she'd felt awkward about telling Mike about the name change, wondering if it might make him feel even more aggrieved. They had barely spoken over the past week. A few cursory texts and the odd phone call where they had discussed domestic matters. Stiff little conversations that made the distance between them seem huge, not just an hour's drive.

This sign was a sign, surely. An olive branch. An indication that he wished them well.

'Let's get it up,' said Maggie. 'It'll be the perfect photo to post tomorrow. Ed!' She called to a passing FBB. 'Can you put this up for us?'

'Bloody hell,' said Ed admiringly. 'That's a beauty. I'll get my ladder.'

An hour and quite a lot of swearing and messing about with a spirit level later and the work of art hung, resplendent. In the sunlight, they could see every detail, the shimmering green and the bright white and the gold.

'It's wonderful,' said Cherry, feeling choked. He should be here, seeing it go up. He might not be a swan, strictly speaking, but he was still one of them. They wouldn't be where they were now without Mike behind them over the years, supporting them, encouraging them, loving them with all his heart.

She walked away to phone him. She couldn't let this gesture go. And maybe, just maybe, it was a turning point. She had been so busy, she hadn't acknowledged how very much she missed him. She took a photo of the sign to send to him, then dialled his number.

His phone rang but he didn't pick up. His voicemail kicked in. Cherry shut her eyes and left a message.

'Mike. I can't tell you how much this means. It's absolutely beautiful. Thank you. And I really hope you can make it to the opening tomorrow night. It would mean the world to all of us.' She paused for a moment. 'Love you.'

She hadn't, she realised, said that to him since his party. Once upon a time, they'd said that to each other countless times every day. But she did still love him. Of course she did. She sighed for a moment, looking at the sign swinging gently in the breeze, and wondered if the price of what she had done was a little too high.

The sun was blazing in the sky. Flaming June. She walked back over to the others.

'Come on,' she said. 'We've all been working insanely hard. Let's go for a swim. We deserve a break.'

Maggie and Rose didn't need a second telling. The three of them dashed through the pub and out through the French doors at the back.

'Look at my lawn, though,' cried Rose, glowing with pride and exertion as their bare feet sank into the springy grass. 'It's a work of art.'

She had transformed it from overgrown and straggly to velvety and inviting, the immaculate stripes leading down to the riverbank.

They arrived at the water's edge, panting.

Cherry started laughing. 'Look at us all. What a state we are. Come on. Let's get all the muck and dust off before Gertie gets back.'

She started stripping off.

'Oh my God. It's going to be freezing in there.' Maggie looked uncertain.

'Come on. We won't be able to do this much longer. Not when we've got guests.' Cherry stepped out of her boiler suit and stood in her bra and pants.

'Oh, come on, we've got to do it properly. Kit right

off!' Rose threw off her dungarees and shimmied out of her t-shirt, then threw off her bra and pants. The three of them followed suit and stood on the bank of the river, stark naked, laughing. Under the willow tree, the river widened out into a deep pool. On the pub side, there was a shallow stony edge, making it easy to get in. Cherry waded in first, not even flinching as the icy water hit her. In three strides she was up to her thighs, then she reached forward and dived into the middle.

'It's wonderful!' she said. 'It's like swimming in liquid silk.'

'Liquid nitrogen, more like,' said Maggie, dipping a toe in tentatively. Beside her, Rose took the plunge. Not wanting to seem a coward, Maggie followed, gasping with the shock.

The three of them floated on their backs, their hands gently sculling the water. They could see peeps of blue sky through the branches of the willow tree, and the occasional sunbeam wound its way through the leaves, turning the surface to gold.

'Do you think we look like a Pre-Raphaelite painting?' asked Maggie.

'Ha!' Rose cackled. 'I should think Rosetti would run a mile.'

'Cheek!' Maggie hit the water with her hand and splashed her daughter.

Cherry felt the stress of the last fortnight melting into the water as her limbs relaxed. This was heaven, she thought, floating beneath the twisted roots and the tangled branches, the coo of a nearby woodpigeon soothing her. Her mind drifted back to the summer days of her childhood, when she and her friends would roam the riverbanks with a sandwich and an apple in their pockets. And later on, adolescent gatherings under the bridge, with cider and cigarettes. How lucky she was, she thought, to have this river flowing through her life. She had been right to come back here. But as she gazed up at the tiny wisps of cloud, she knew that more than anything, what she wanted was Mike by her side. What they were doing was incredible, but without him it felt wrong.

Maggie gradually got used to the icy water on her skin and felt the lists that were whirling around her head trickle away. She had done so many launches over the years, but never her own, and her perfectionist nature had always taken over. She knew there were things she should be letting go, but she found it hard not to expect every detail to be spot on. She hoped she was being kind to everyone, but sometimes she knew she was a bit – well, brisk was probably the best word. She made a mental note to get everyone together the next morning, before the opening night, and give them a pep talk, one that made them feel valued. You were, after all, only as good as the people carrying out your orders. And she loved the people she had taken on so far, especially Winnie, who had already made her feel ten times calmer with her cool head and kitchen skills.

And she had a good feeling in her gut about Chloe. She was a little reticent and inexperienced, but she only ever needed to be told anything once, and she asked all the right questions, and handled people with such a gentle touch that they warmed to her immediately. She thought Chloe had the potential to go far. Maggie loved to nurture people, even if the last person she had taken under her wing had stabbed her in the back, though perhaps that had been for a reason – part of a master plan? Either way, her team was starting to gel. With a few key people in place, she could begin to build.

Rose noticed how the cold of the water made her think more clearly, as if she had been shocked into focus. Spending time with Winnie had been a real wake-up call for her. She fed off her energy, and talking to her about what they were going to grow in the garden to use in the kitchen made her feel excited and empowered. More importantly, she found her anxiety had receded, that she had fewer intrusive thoughts and didn't feel as if she was keeping a panic attack at bay. The self-loathing of a few weeks ago had faded, along with the memory of her transgression with Gaz. She ignored the tiny whisper that still insisted running away was the act of a coward. The Soul Bowl was better off without her; she had learned from her mistake and she was moving on.

She had found it therapeutic, working outside, working with a purpose, and Rose acknowledged the feeling with interest. It was physically tough tending the lawns and hedges, weeding the flower beds, digging in the new roses she'd ordered from the nursery near Honisham that her grandmother had used. She'd filled a dozen zinc dolly tubs with allium and agapanthus to range along the back of the pub, rich deep blues and purples that stood out against the green. Alternate sun and rain meant the garden was looking at its most lush, the grass and the foliage at their most verdant, and the scent, especially in the warmth of the early evening, was almost narcotic: sweet and heady and overpowering.

She remembered Catherine saying that if her great-grandfather had been able to prescribe gardening to his patients, they would have been a lot healthier and happier. The memory of those words planted the seeds of something in her mind. As she drifted on the surface of the water, she wondered if what she was thinking was unrealistic, or if the idea had legs. She would start to investigate, she decided, once the opening night was out of the way.

For the next half an hour, the river held them. A dappled light shone through the trees and the reeds on the riverbank swayed in a hypnotic dance as the three floated on the surface of the water, serene and regal. It was as if they belonged there; as if this was their kingdom, three swans bound together for all eternity.

34

Midsummer's Eve dawned sulky and brooding, a bruised lilac dawn drawing a veil of rain along the riverbank. Its soft hiss woke Maggie at six, and she ran to open the window. Everything was hiding: the birds and insects, the rabbits and squirrels, the swans on the river. There was no sign of life, and her heart sank. If even the ducks and the dragonflies couldn't make it out, what hope did they have of anyone turning up tonight? People would take one look at the inclement weather and stick with whatever they were bingeing on Netflix.

But as she breathed in the irresistible scent of warm grass and leaves and earth dampened by rain, she realised there was time, plenty of time for the sun to come out, and a dawn deluge would be good for the garden. There was no point in worrying about it, she decided. She had no control over the weather, so she must focus on what she did have control over. She pulled up her lists on her iPad, a colour-coded chart of strict timings, and ran through them again, still with the nagging sense that there was something vital she had forgotten. Every time she did a launch she always had that feeling, and nothing awful had ever been missed. She was too experienced to make a mistake. It was her equivalent of stage fright: that last-minute dread that some kind of nightmare scenario would unfold, something that was of your own making.

She did what she always did when she felt unnerved, and opened her notebook to write to Frank.

Well, it's peeing with rain, which doesn't bode well. If you have any influence up there, could you pull a few strings?!! Otherwise we are poised to find out whether we are going to be a raging success or fall flat on our faces. If it's the latter, at least we've had fun doing it. It's been so good for us all, being here together, working together. We bounce off each other in a way that must be very annoying to outsiders; the Fabulous Builder Brothers know us well enough to laugh at us, but I can see them looking at each other when we get carried away. Though I think you can remember what it was like! You used to tease us when we had one of our projects. Like when we were decorating the Christmas tree – I can see you and Dad making a hasty exit, disappearing off to the pub, knowing you were both better out of the way or you'd get roped into something you didn't want to do . . . The poor old FBBs haven't had any choice but to do our bidding. But they've done us proud. No TV makeover show could have had a more dramatic transformation.

I wish you were here to see it. I think you'd really love it. I keep imagining your face when we bring you in to show you what we've done . . .

Though the biggest transformation has been Rose. She has lost the tight-lipped, wide-eyed look she got after you went, the one that came back again after Catherine died. Understandably, I suppose – they were so close. But the

Somerset air and the sunshine have turned her to gold, and her smile reaches her eyes again. You would be incredibly proud.

I must stop rambling. I need to kick ass. And I need to decide what to wear tonight. Something wildly impractical, I hear you suggest. Something that makes you look like the queen you are.

Maggie laid down her pen, Frank's imagined words ringing in her head. There was a silk dress hanging in the wardrobe she had bought in the sales last summer: smothered in red and orange and hot pink flowers, it had a tight bodice and bell sleeves and a skirt that swirled as you walked. It was not a dress for a shrinking violet. Today, it was the armour Maggie needed to feel in charge, both of herself and everything else. She jumped out of bed and pulled it from the wardrobe. As she hung it up to look at it, she pricked her ears. Was it her imagination or was the rain subsiding?

35

Rose was in the little kitchen, slicing up a banana to mix into raspberries and yoghurt for Gertie's breakfast.

Gertie was having a trial day with the Dandelions. Rose had seen the advert in the village shop, and as soon as she saw it, she remembered that it was Catherine who had set up the playgroup for the mothers of Rushbrook all those years ago. As the doctor's wife, she often came into contact with the mums, and realised there was little support for them in the village; that being a new mother was daunting and lonely. So she had commandeered the village hall and ran the toddler group three times a week, raising funds for toys and books and playground equipment. It was still on the go, but it was a fully fledged nursery now, and fed the village school.

Now they had moved, Gertie was entitled to a place. And while Mrs B had been a godsend, Gertie needed the stimulation of other children and clearly missed her old nursery. So Rose had plucked up the courage to see if there was a space, and there was, so they had agreed she would try it out.

'Come on Friday,' said the vibrant young woman who ran it. 'We're going for a picnic in the orchard at Dragonfly Farm. We go every year. They get bread and cheese and apple cake, and they get a ride on the donkey. Honestly, she will love it. Pick her up from there at half three.'

Rose put the bowl in front of her daughter and for a moment she felt overwhelmed with emotion. Gertie had picked out her own clothes this morning – jeans and a gingham shirt and rainbow wellies and a baseball hat. Rose loved the fact that by going to the Dandelions, she had a connection with Catherine. She could still feel the legacy of her great-grandparents woven through the village, even though Wisteria House now belonged to someone else. People still stopped her and spoke to her about them. She relished that sense of history. It made her feel strong.

Maybe this was where she truly belonged?

She filled a water bottle and popped it into Gertie's bag. If she picked her up from Dragonfly Fly farm at three thirty, there would be time to get back and for them to get ready for the opening. Gertie was to be allowed to attend for the first hour or so, then Mrs B was going to come and babysit. She looked out of the window at the rain. She had asked for it the night before, just enough to give the garden a thorough soaking. Hopefully it would stop in time for the picnic, in time for the lawn to dry and the roses to unfurl and the lavender in the border to be warmed enough to throw off its scent.

It was going to be perfect.

'Guys, you are miracle workers. This is beyond anything I imagined. I don't know how you did it. It's as if you climbed into my head and brought it all to life.' Cherry's eyes were shining with appreciation. She couldn't quite believe that yet again the Fabulous Builder Brothers had pulled it off.

'Oh, man,' said Tom. 'We've had a great time. We don't want to go home.'

They'd made the most of their fortnight in the countryside. Cherry had got them permission to go fishing from Dash Culbone, who owned the rights from Rushbrook House all the way to the bridge beyond, and they'd wandered off with their rods every evening, sitting on the bank for hours amidst the midges, putting the world to rights.

'And you are great to work for,' Ed admitted. 'We wish we had more clients like you. Ones who know what they want but trust us to get on with it. Usually it's the other way round – they haven't a clue what they want but keep trying to tell us what to do.'

'*And* you muck in more than anyone we've ever worked for. You don't mind getting your hands dirty.'

They'd been full of admiration of Cherry's energy as she set to with her roller, covering wall after wall with a deeply pigmented paint that was completely transformative.

Now, they were doing a deep clean, wiping the last traces of plaster dust from the windows and woodwork and polishing the floor until it gleamed. It was this level of care that made Cherry value them so highly. Lots of builders would have left her to do the clearing up, but they had pride in their work and wanted to see it at its best.

She looked around the inside of the pub with wonder. It was one thing having a vision, it was another thing seeing it realised, and the results were more spectacular than she had dreamt. The walls of the bar were a rich, lacquered green, the colour of the river at its deepest. The cases of fish caught from its banks that had hung on the pub walls for decades had been cleaned and re-hung. She'd had the yellowing photograph of the Rushbrook cricket team from the 1920s blown up to almost life-size and put up on one wall so it almost looked as if the players were in the room. Her father's collection of fishing flies was mounted inside vintage bamboo frames.

Beyond the bar was a cosy area for people to come and sit with their laptops if they wanted to come to the pub to work. There was a thick oak counter with high stools and plenty of plugs on the wall behind, and two sofas in ochre velvet faced each other next to shelves brimming with books and pots trailing greenery. The cushions on the oak settles in the dining area were re-covered in grain-sack linen with a black stripe. Tables had been dipped and stripped and a zinc top hammered on; chairs were painted a black-green several shades darker than the walls. Richness, texture and the occasional burst of colour were layered up, and here and there was something unusual that caught the eye: a leather pommel bench tucked into an alcove with a kelim underneath; a six-foot wrought-iron candelabra stuffed with church candles in an otherwise dark corner.

And now Cherry was adding the finishing touches. She had goldfish-bowl vases stuffed with bright orange tulips. Every other table was laid up with a soft linen tablecloth, bone-handled cutlery, cream plates with an embossed edge, sparkling etched glasses and a napkin tied with garden twine, a sprig of rosemary tucked in. And she'd found the perfect scented candles: a delicious blend of lavender, sage and bergamot that would cover up the inevitable pub smells.

She felt nervous. She was delighted with the turn-around, but this was just the beginning. It was all very well creating an interior that looked magazine-worthy, but what it needed more than style was people. That was going to be the challenge. If it was still empty and picture-perfect in a month's time, she would have failed in her mission.

Invitations had gone out to everyone in the village, and Maggie had put sponsored posts on Instagram in a five-mile radius to promote the opening. Winnie had concocted a welcoming cocktail: a Rushbrook Swan, made from elderflower liqueur, milk vodka from a local distillery and bubbles from a nearby vineyard – and Melchior cider on tap. If that didn't make the evening go with a swing, nothing would.

In the garden the Fabulous Builder Brothers had created an open-fronted gazebo for the hog roast, so food could be cooked and served even if it was raining. The beast was already cooking, turning slowly. In the kitchen, piles of bread rolls were standing by waiting to be filled with slices of hot pork, buttery apple sauce and melting onions. There would be puffed-up salty crackling, too loud for conversation, and bowls of slaw made with red cabbage, fennel and apples.

The idea was that food and drink was free from six until eight, when there would be (brief!) speeches and Maggie would bring out her celebratory pièce de résistance: she and Winnie had worked on it all morning and Cherry wasn't entirely sure that it was the best use of their time but she had to admit the results were spectacular.

After eight the bar would open and hot pork rolls would be five pounds. Cherry prayed that everyone would stay, happy to put their hands in their pockets.

'You are coming tonight, aren't you?' she asked Ed and Tom.

'We wouldn't miss it for anything,' they assured her.

At least they'd be assured of two guests, she told herself. Although Dash Culbone had definitely said he would come with Tabitha, and Lorraine from the shop would be dying to see what they'd done. Oh, and of course the Matts. Curiosity would get the better of the rest of the village, she felt sure.

She smiled as a text came through from Toby, sending her all the luck in the world.

I can't believe you've pulled it off. I'll be there later in the summer – you know I hate big parties. But Mum and Dad would be tickled pink.

She headed out into the garden. Rose had left a bucket of fallen rose petals by the French doors, for it was Midsummer's Eve. Folklore said that young girls should scatter rose leaves before them, reciting the poem, and their true love would visit them.

> *'Rose leaves, rose leaves*
> *Rose leaves I strew*
> *He that will love me*
> *Come after me now.'*

Cherry bent down and picked up a handful, their soft silkiness gentle on her skin. Would it work, she wondered, if you had already found your true love but had mislaid him, rather carelessly, somehow?

36

In the Ladies' loo, Chloe looped the apron over her head. It was dark green, with The Three Swans embroidered in white across the front. She felt an incredible sense of pride as she tied a bow behind her back. She had fallen into a world she had no idea existed. A world of strong, capable women trying to realise their dream, working together, supporting each other, bouncing off each other. She wished her own mother had an ounce of their determination and energy. But Nicole had lost all her drive and ambition. Somehow, she had lost herself.

Chloe remembered that Nicole had once been someone. Her pupils at Meadow Hall had loved her. They had loved how she had sat them all down and made them listen to 'Wuthering Heights' by Kate Bush when they were doing it for GCSE. She had made books come alive for them. She'd been respected. But her dad had ruined it all. Somehow, he'd walked away with everything he wanted – Elizabeth and her witchy green eyes and her silver sportscar – and now Mum was drowning, in misery and cheap pink wine, and couldn't find her way back to herself.

She'd been better this week, after last week's horrible episode. She'd worked every day, and didn't look as dishevelled or red-eyed. But Chloe still felt uneasy. It was a cycle, she knew that. Binge. Remorse. Apology. A week on the straight and narrow, where they all started to feel as if things might be OK. And then...

She wasn't going to think about it tonight, decided Chloe. She needed to focus all her attention on the opening. She was Maggie's right hand, ready to do her bidding, ever alert to what needed doing, in tune with the rest of the team. It was, she decided, almost like a football game, everyone match-fit with their eye on the ball, and each other, moving seamlessly to certain victory.

She looked at herself in the mirror. She'd treated herself to some expensive conditioner and her curls were under control, not exploding into the ridiculous wedge that made her despair. She'd put on enough tinted moisturiser to make sure her cheeks weren't flushed, and behind her glasses her lashes were thick and long, just as the mascara had promised.

She pushed back her shoulders and gave herself a double thumbs-up. She was part of the team. She deserved to be here. She was one of them.

37

Of course the sun came out. Of course it did – that had been its plan all along. 'You shouldn't have worried,' it seemed to laugh, as it heaved itself into the sky just before midday and set to work coaxing out birds and blossom and blooms, and with it came the sweet song of thrushes and the scent of honeysuckle. Trout hurtled along the river, ebullient with rainfall, and the banks teemed with activity, beetles and voles and damselflies. On the far bank, a cluster of solemn cows grazed, their black-and-white flanks gleaming, their tails flicking away unwanted flies.

By six o'clock, everything was set fair.

'I just want to say,' said Cherry, as the three of them lined up under the sign for Chloe to take a picture, 'that if this is a disaster, it's all been worth it. To spend this time with you, as a team, working together. It's been wonderful.'

'It's not going to be a disaster,' said Rose. 'They were all talking about it when I went to pick Gertie up from the picnic. They're all coming.'

She was still gratified at how welcoming the other

Dandelion parents had been. She'd felt a bit awkward and shy at the pick-up, but they had all made a fuss of Gertie the new girl, who'd had several invitations to tea, and they'd been wide-eyed to discover that Rose was part of the team taking over at the pub.

'We're all so excited,' one mum had told her. 'It's a drag going into Honisham if you want something to eat. And we all really miss having somewhere to go for a drink.'

'We're going to reinstate our TGIF ritual,' said another. 'We always used to take the kids into The Swan after pick-up on a Friday. We'd give them tea and we'd have wine. You are going to allow kids, aren't you?' she added, suddenly worried.

'Oh my God, totally,' Rose laughed. 'It's a family pub. For everyone.'

'You'll have to join us.'

Standing under the apple trees at Dragonfly Farm, watching her daughter racing around with her newfound friends in the afternoon sun, Rose felt her heart fill with happiness.

Now, with the opening only an hour away, she stood smiling for the camera. She had on an old cashmere cardigan of Catherine's, on which she'd sewn dozens of tiny satin rosebuds, and wide cream palazzo pants. Her mum looked sensational in a silk dress splashed with red and pink flowers, and Cherry was in a pale green satin kimono over skinny jeans.

The three of them put their arms around each other, and Gertie sat at their feet – Rose had washed all traces of donkey and apple cake and grass off her, and put her in a clean dress.

'Everyone say Rushbrook,' said Maggie, who knew all

the tricks, and that an 'o' sound would make your mouth look more natural while your photo was being taken: money, prunes, Wogan.

'Rushbrook,' they chorused, and Chloe did a burst of photos and then scrolled through them to check they were OK. There they were, the three swans, poised on the brink of something truly special that was going to change everyone's life. Including hers.

By seven o'clock that evening, it felt as if everyone in Rushbrook had come to check out the pub. It was a gloriously golden evening, and people were hugging each other, clapping each other on the back, shaking hands, clinking glasses, thrilled to have somewhere to congregate again. There was a mix of ages and backgrounds: dressed-down pensioners, dressed-up youngsters, farmers fresh from the field, young mums glad to get out of jeans and into a dress, office workers glad to get out of suits and into jeans. The cocktails were going down alarmingly quickly and the cider pump was doing overtime.

Cherry recognised nearly everyone. The two Matts, of course. Lorraine from the shop already on her second Swan cocktail, getting ever more garrulous. Dash and Tabitha, who congratulated her effusively.

'This is just in time for our high season,' Dash told her. 'You are going to be overrun with our guests.'

'I need these builders at Dragonfly Farm,' added Tabitha. 'I can't believe this has only taken them two weeks. Do you think they'd do my renovation?'

'If you let them fish all summer,' laughed Cherry. She pointed over to Ed and Tom, who were dressed up in plaid shirts and baggy jeans nursing pints of Melchior cider. 'You'll have to ask them. They do get booked up.'

'I'm not surprised,' said Tabitha. 'We've just finished the barn conversions, but I want to do the house next. And I'll be honest, the guys I was using nearly made me tear my hair out. We should have been finished six months ago.'

There was a melee of dogs, ruled over by Fred and Ginger, with Matilda as their lady-in-waiting. An enormous Dogue de Bordeaux lay slumped by the fire, the size of a small sofa. There were border terriers, a Dalmatian, two black Labradors . . . Gertie was in her element, Rose desperately trying to stop her patting every dog that came in.

This was exactly what she had envisaged, thought Cherry. The Three Swans as the beating heart of Rushbrook, once again. For a moment she was tempted to film the throngs on her phone and send it to Mike, just to prove that her instincts hadn't been wrong. But she didn't, because she knew that any fool could fill a pub up with free drinks and hot pork rolls. The proof of the pudding would be in whether they came back and put their hands in their pockets.

38

Maggie noticed the man as soon as he walked in. He was on his own. Tall, well over six foot, in a collarless linen shirt, untucked, and faded jeans. Dark curly hair, quite long, but with the kind of messy, artful layering that only a good hairdresser could achieve. And a beard that had the same feel: a little more than a five o'clock shadow but not full. The overall effect was sexily dishevelled, as if he had more important things to do than stand in front of a mirror. He stood looking around for a moment, his eyes roaming over all of the revellers. He was, she felt, observing them rather than looking for someone.

Maggie moved forwards with her best hostess smile. 'Welcome to The Three Swans,' she said. 'I hope you like what we've done.'

He swept his gaze around the walls. He didn't look like the sort to be moved by interior decoration.

'Yep,' he said. 'Though I'm not really bothered about what colour the walls are as long as you've still got Inarticulate on tap.'

His voice was vaguely familiar – low and slow, slightly

laconic. And as Yorkshire as a treacly, gingery slab of parkin.

'Of course.' She paused for a moment, not quite sure what to say next. 'Are you a regular, then? From round here?'

'I'm from Pepper Wood Farm.' He frowned at her, and she was worried she'd offended him. 'Russell? The pig man? We met last week.'

'Of course!' said Maggie, mortified. 'I'm so sorry, I didn't recognise you.'

'With my glad rags on?' He smiled, fleetingly, and his eyes gleamed as warm as a conker. 'It's been good to get out of my overalls. It's all I seem to wear these days. I might as well not bother getting changed and wear them in bed.'

Maggie blushed slightly at the thought. 'Yes, I've been in scruffy clothes for ages. It was nice to put a dress on.'

His eyes flickered over her silk dress, but he didn't comment and she wondered if it was too much. Too bright, too clingy, too low-cut.

Maggie wanted to bring back his smile, so she held out the tray.

'Have a Swan cocktail. Or are you more of a cider man? We've got both on tap until eight. Or I can get you a pint of Inarticulate at the bar.'

'I'd rather have a pint, to be honest. It's OK, though, I'll get it myself.'

He gave her a nod as he went to move away. Sean Bean, thought Maggie. There was a hint of Sean Bean in there. Terse, rugged. A little stony. But when the warmth came out . . .

'I'm so thrilled we're going to be using your pork,' she

said, not wanting him to go. 'Winnie says it's the best she's tasted.'

'Thanks.' He looked at her, thoughtful. 'By the way, I'm sorry about your husband.'

Lorraine in the shop had told him Maggie was a widow. As a traffic cop, Russell had learned not to be afraid of talking about death. He knew the importance of condolence.

'Yes. A while ago now. But...' Maggie shrugged.

'It doesn't get any easier?' He seemed to read her thoughts.

'Not really,' she said. 'But you learn to live with it. Because you have no choice.'

'Well, I'm sorry. What was his name?'

Maggie was surprised. Most people changed the subject as quickly as they could. 'Frank. He was a sound engineer. And a bit of a geek. And bloody hilarious. And kind. But he wouldn't take crap from anyone. He never let anyone think they were better than anyone else.'

Oh God, why was she going on about her dead husband? He wouldn't want to know.

'He sounds grand.' He leaned in, conspiratorial. 'You do know,' he said, 'that the whole village will be dying to set us up. All eyes are upon us.'

He had already seen Lorraine give him a thumbs-up, her micro-bladed eyebrows waggling.

'Oh God,' said Maggie. 'That's awful.' She blushed. 'I don't mean the thought of being with you is awful. I mean...' Oh dear. What did she mean? She just kept putting her foot in it, whatever she said. 'I mean, why do people think they need to interfere? Why don't they understand that you're perfectly OK as you are, and you don't need anyone else?'

He looked at her, and she couldn't tell what he was thinking. 'Well, quite,' he said at last. 'They should just mind their own bloody business.' He touched her on the arm in a farewell gesture. 'Very nice to see you again, and good luck with the pub. A village needs a decent pub.'

He walked off and headed to the bar. Maggie watched after him. Nice arse, she thought, then shook herself.

What a totally inappropriate thing to think.

39

At seven thirty, once the ice had been broken and everyone had a drink in their hand, they all gathered around as Cherry began to speak.

'It's so wonderful to see all of you here tonight. I can tell you we all had The Fear earlier. We convinced ourselves that no one was going to turn up. But I guess curiosity got the better of you all. Of course, the trick now is going to be making sure you come back now you've had a look. So I just wanted to tell you all that we want this pub to be a place for everyone. At any time of the day.' She looked round the room. 'More importantly, there is a host of people I want to thank for this transformation. Not least the Fabulous Builder Brothers, who loved their time in Rushbrook so if you have a project, please keep them in mind.'

There was a round of applause and the FBBs held up their tankards of cider.

'And of course, huge thanks to lovely *lovely* Alan, the best landlord a pub could hope for. I'm hoping we have kept the spirit of everything he ever did here. I really wish he was here tonight but he and Gillian are cruising round

Croatia and I think we all agree that they both deserve the holiday of a lifetime.' She could feel tears welling up in her eyes at the very thought. She cleared her throat. 'Anyway, this pub has been a part of my life since the first time my dad brought me in for a bottle of lemonade and a bag of salt and vinegar crisps when I was about eight. And I probably served some of you when I was a barmaid here back in the sixties. And I can't begin to count how many Sunday lunches we've eaten here over the years. It's been a home from home for us and so that's what we want it to be for you. Oh, and before I forget – Clive is bringing back the pub quiz. The first one is next Friday.'

She smiled as a burst of applause broke out and Clive stepped forward to raise his glass, nodding proudly.

'Teams of six, sixty pounds a team to include a sharing platter and half a bottle of wine a head,' he said. 'If you don't have a team just let us know and we'll match you up.'

As the speech came to a close, Maggie brought in a silver platter. On it floated a huge white meringue swan. Surrounding it were dozens of tiny meringue cygnets. Amidst thunderous applause the tray was passed amongst the crowd for everyone to help themselves to a mouthful of sugary fluff.

'If that doesn't get us some Instagram followers,' Maggie said to Cherry, 'nothing will.'

'Very cunning,' said Cherry, popping a cygnet into her mouth. 'I think this has gone well, don't you?'

Maggie looked around the room. The queue at the bar was already three deep. The whole place looked and felt completely different now it was filled with people. Outside, the sun was starting to nestle into the branches of the trees that lined the river, as if it could leave the party now it was happy it had got started.

'I think we've smashed it, Mum.' She put her arm around Cherry's shoulders.

Across the room, Cherry saw Theo and Amanda arrive, and she lifted a hand in greeting.

'Oh look,' she said. 'It's the Bannisters. The people who've bought Wisteria House.'

Maggie turned to look. 'Is that the TV producer?'

'Yes,' said Cherry. 'Mandy Fryer that was. The postman's daughter.'

Amanda was dressed in drainpipe leather trousers, high-heeled boots and a cream silk shirt, accessorised with a lot of statement jewellery.

'She doesn't look very Somerset.'

'No,' said Cherry. 'But that's OK. They'll bring interesting people. I must go and say hello.'

She moved across the room and Theo and Amanda both greeted her warmly, as if they were old friends.

'This is a triumph,' said Amanda. 'I would never have recognised the place.'

'It's fantastic,' said Theo. 'I can see us spending a lot of time in here.'

'You are so clever,' said Amanda, her eyes drinking in all the detail. 'Is this your design or did you get someone in?'

Her eyes were everywhere, taking in every detail, and Cherry remembered her being a watchful child. Remembered her hanging on to the top of the ménage fence as Cherry got Pia to rear up on her hind legs, desperate to impress.

'It was a joint effort, between us,' said Cherry. 'But interiors are my thing.'

'You'll have to give us some inspiraton for Wisteria.' Amanda's eyes were round with admiration. 'We're starting to think we've bitten off more than we can chew. We're used to London flats. The amount of space we've got is suddenly very daunting.'

'As for the garden,' said Theo, 'I can already feel the eyes of disapproval upon us. I think it's running away with us. But we haven't a clue what's what.'

'I've kept Mum's planting plans, if you want to know what's in the garden,' offered Cherry. 'If you want to have a look, I'd be happy to lend them to you.'

Catherine had done a planting plan every year, painstakingly drawing and colouring everything onto graph paper, every rose, every salvia, every geranium, and annotating it with a Rotring pen. The plans had given Cherry huge pleasure when she found them – she loved the names: Alberic Barbier, Ghislaine de Ferigonde, Adelaide d'Orleans, but they weren't actually of much use to her now, only as a sentimental keepsake.

'I'd love that.' Amanda's eyes sparkled at the prospect. 'I'm a pretty useless gardener but I'm very eager to learn. And I'd hate to dig up something valuable by accident.'

'I'll drop them in next time I'm passing.' She saw Rose passing by. 'In fact,' she touched Rose on the shoulder and drew her in, 'this is the girl to ask for gardening advice. She learned everything she knows from my mother. This is my granddaughter, Rose. Rose, this is Amanda and Theo, who've bought Wisteria.'

'Hello.' Rose smiled at them, and Cherry thought again how she had blossomed in such a short time. Her eyes looked brighter and she seemed to hold herself taller. 'You're the luckiest people alive. How is the garden?'

'Well,' said Amanda, 'probably not up to standard. The only plant I've ever managed to keep alive is a pot of supermarket mint for my mojitos.'

'We could do with some advice,' added Theo.

The thought of being able to go back to Wisteria House made Rose's heart beat a little faster. Cherry smiled at the pleasure on her face. 'I'm sure Rose would help.'

'Can you spare her, though?' asked Amanda. 'We'd pay.'

'Oh, you don't need to pay me,' said Rose.

Amanda tutted in mock disapproval. 'Darling, never ever turn down money.'

Rose looked embarrassed. 'Well...'

Then a strange expression came over Amanda's face. She had spotted something in the distance. At first, she frowned, then she smiled, then she clapped her hands, almost jumping up and down like a child.

'Oh my God. I don't believe it!' she exclaimed. 'He hasn't changed a bit either. What on earth are you both on?' she said to Cherry, who turned to see what she was looking at.

He was there. In the doorway, looking around at the jostling throngs with a smile, in jeans and a new pale suede jacket that suited him down to the ground. She pushed through the crowds to join him, putting her arms around his neck, overwhelmed with the joy of seeing him here, the very place she had first held him. If she shut her eyes, the jukebox was playing, and the scent of sandalwood was in the air.

'Trex,' she breathed, and he pulled her to him.

For a moment they held each other. He could feel her rib cage rise and fall, the deepness of her breath, her heart thudding deep inside her.

'I can't believe you're here. I'm so glad.'

'Of course I am.'

'The sign. Did you see your sign?' She looked up at him, her eyes shining.

'I did.'

A moment later and Rose was beside them. She looked, he thought, like a woman suddenly. There was something more confident about her. He sometimes thought of her as still a teenager, even though she wasn't.

She slid her arms around her grandfather's waist, kissing him on the cheek.

'You made it,' she said. 'Cherry was so worried you wouldn't. She'd quite convinced herself you had a thing on.'

'I wouldn't miss this for the world,' he laughed.

'Gertie's in bed,' she told him. 'I could get her up, though? Or you can see her tomorrow, if you're staying?'

'Oh, don't wake her,' he said. 'There's far too much going on. It wouldn't be fair.'

And then there was a flash of scarlet and fuchsia and Maggie appeared. 'Dad?'

She looked for a moment as if she might cry.

'Hey,' he said, ruffling her hair.

He stood in the middle of the three of them, looking around the room in awe. It was familiar yet strange. Familiar because he had spent so much time here over the years, from that very first evening with Pam and Alouette to the last Sunday lunch they'd had the weekend after Catherine's funeral. Strange because it was like seeing someone you loved in a brand-new outfit that was a little different from what they usually wore – more daring, more colourful. Yet he recognised Cherry's hand. The décor had her DNA in it. The bold colours, the luxurious touches, the witty twists, the bones of the original concept – not that The Swan had ever had a concept, exactly, it had just evolved – allowed to shine through.

He gave a nod of approval. 'Not bad.'

'Is that it?' said Maggie. 'Not bad?'

'It's bloody wonderful,' he said. 'But I knew it would be.'

'Michael!' The Reverend Matt always called him Michael, probably the only person who ever had. The two men shook hands warmly. 'You must be very proud.'

'Yes,' said Mike, although he hadn't really had time to take it all in yet. The pub was buzzing, more crowded than he ever remembered it, even after Nine Lessons and Carols at Christmas when everyone came in for free mulled wine.

'Oh my goodness.' A woman descended on him. He didn't recognise her at all. He frowned, trying to place her.

'You won't remember me. But I was there the day you met Cherry, at the stables. I was one of those podgy little girls who used to hang around, like flies. My dad was the postman.' She put out a hand. 'Amanda Fryer. I just want to say what a legend Cherry is. She's such an inspiration. I wish I had an ounce of her talent.'

'Amanda's bought Wisteria House,' Cherry added.

'Oh!' said Mike.

'You've both got to come round for supper. Reminisce about the old days.'

'Right. Only I don't remember that much about them. You know what they say, if you can remember the sixties, you weren't there,' he joked.

'Well, what we can't remember we can make up. Let me find Theo. He'll be very glad of a drinking partner.'

Amanda hooked her arm through Mike's and led him away. He looked at Cherry and she shrugged, smiling.

'Sorry,' she mouthed.

As he disappeared into the throng, she breathed a sigh of relief. It was all going to be OK. He wasn't blanking her, or nursing a grievance. He had come round, in the end.

It was getting towards half past nine. Rose was about to go and check on Gertie. She wanted to make sure she was asleep; she was quite capable of twisting Mrs B around her little finger and stalling bedtime, which would make her grumpy tomorrow as she always got up at the same time no matter what time she went to sleep.

And then she looked over at the door, and her heart turned over. There was a figure standing in the doorway, searching the crowds. She felt her mouth go dry at the sight of him. What on earth was he doing here? How on earth had he found her? She wasn't sure if she could deal with this, with no warning. She looked around to see if she could make her escape before he noticed her, but just as she was about to head for the French doors, their eyes met.

He smiled, his whole face lighting up, and she knew she couldn't run away. Not this time.

40

Chloe paused for a moment in the kitchen to catch her breath. She hadn't stopped all evening, and she was swept up in the atmosphere. To her surprise, she felt completely confident, as if she'd been part of the team for ever. That was down to Maggie, who had put her at her ease, talking her through exactly what was expected of her, and reassuring her that she couldn't really make a mistake. Her job was simply to move amongst the crowds and make sure everyone had what they wanted and to take dinner bookings on the iPad, ensuring they came back again.

Of course, it helped that she knew so many of the guests. Dash and Tabitha for a start, who seemed really pleased that she was working there. Although Dash had complained to Maggie in jest, 'We were hoping Chloe would come and work for us this summer.'

Chloe blushed, not wanting Dash to think she had betrayed him in some way.

'This is much more up Chloe's street,' said Tabitha kindly. 'I worked here for ages. You'll love it. It'll be great fun. Hard work, but never a dull moment.'

'She's my right-hand girl,' said Maggie, and Chloe felt proud.

She washed her hands in the sink and splashed a bit of water on her face. She had a tendency to go red, and it was hot and crowded out there. She pushed her way back through the door, and her heart sank.

Her mother was here. In very tight jeans and high-heeled boots and a white shirt with a ruffled neckline, her hair pinned up loosely, a pair of vintage earrings flashing. She looked ravishing, like she had done in the old days before Dad left, a hint of New Romantic in her style. She was far more beautiful and interesting than Elizabeth, who looked like a mannequin.

Chloe felt a burst of pride. And fondness. She wanted her old mum back, the bright, lively, vibrant mum, not the punctured, spiritless version who drowned her sorrows.

And then Nicole caught sight of her and her face lit up. She made her way over to Chloe and put her arms around her neck.

'Isn't this wonderful? I can't believe it. And look at you!' She stood back and looked Chloe up and down. 'You look the part. I'm very proud of you.'

'Oh,' said Chloe. 'Thank you. Yes, it's brilliant. I told you it was going to be brilliant.'

'Yes, but I didn't realise *how* brilliant.'

She had a cocktail in her hand. Chloe bit her lip as Nicole raised it to her lips and took a sip. Her mum saw her looking.

'Don't worry. I'm just having one. Just to celebrate. It would be rude not to.'

She laughed, a little too loudly, and Chloe realised that

it wasn't her first drink. She could tell she'd probably had a couple of glasses of wine before she arrived. She sighed. At least the free bar was over.

'You look great, Mum,' she said.

'I thought I'd make an effort for once,' said Nicole. 'I don't often get the chance to dress up.'

She looked around the room at all of the other revellers. For a moment, she looked out of place and vulnerable, a woman on her own at a social gathering. Chloe felt a sudden flash of understanding for her mum's situation. It must be very difficult for her. She didn't really have anyone to support her, not in the way Cherry and Maggie and Rose did. Chloe did her best, but she sometimes thought Nicole felt judged by her.

Nicole's glass was empty. They both looked at it without saying anything.

'Shall I get you an elderflower pressé?' Chloe asked eventually. 'It's very hot. You must be thirsty.'

'Thank you.' Her mum smiled. 'That would be lovely.'

41

Play it cool, Rose told herself as she made her way over to him, although she'd never been much good at playing cool. She might look the part, but inside she was always a writhing mass of doubt and uncertainty. She raised a hand and smiled, gathering her thoughts as quickly as she could.

'What on earth are you doing here?' She leaned forward and pressed her cheek to his. Warm but polite.

Aaron put his hand on her arm and gave it a squeeze. Affectionate. Reassuring. She felt filled with unexpected warmth. As unexpected as his appearance.

'We always take a whole page in the *Somerset Daily News*. I always have a look through when I'm checking the ad.' He grinned. 'I was pretty surprised to see your face. I couldn't resist coming to have a look.'

Rose gave an uncertain smile. 'Welcome to The Three Swans.'

'It's wicked.' Aaron looked around approvingly. 'But I don't understand why you didn't tell me this was what you were doing.'

'It all happened so quickly. I wasn't thinking straight. I'm sorry.'

It was so wonderful to see him, thought Rose. He wasn't in his usual sportswear, but in black jeans and a grey cashmere sweater and tortoiseshell glasses. He looked so cool. She could see people glance over at him, wondering who he was. He looked too glamorous for Rushbrook; like a celebrity.

She felt nervous. She had to tell him the truth. She had been ashamed, ever since she had run away. She had lied to him, but now he was here in front of her, she realised she had also been lying to herself about how important he was to her. She couldn't keep what she had done a secret any longer, if they were to salvage their relationship. Their working relationship.

'Come outside and see the garden,' she said to him. 'And the river. It's still light, just about. The longest day.'

They wove through the crowds and out of the French doors, pushing through the stragglers eating the last scraps of hog roast. Long shadows threw themselves across the lawn as the sun set, and the night air was heavy with promise and pollen. She babbled as she walked, telling him about her plans for the polytunnel to grow the more fragile herbs, the raised beds she'd already planted up with salad stuff, the long-term plans for fruit cages and cucumber frames.

They were walking across the lawn down towards the river. Rose screwed up her courage. Full disclosure, she decided.

'I've got a confession,' she told him in a small voice, as they reached the riverbank.

He searched her face for clues.

'I did something terrible.'

'What?' he asked, his face even more anxious.

'I don't know that you'll ever forgive me.'

He shook his head. 'Forgive what? Rose, you can't have done anything that bad. I mean, I know there's no money missing . . .' He laughed, but stopped when he saw her face. 'Not drugs?'

He had zero tolerance with any kind of substance in his workforce.

'Worse. I gave Gaz money.' She looked down at the silver water gliding past. The river didn't stop to listen to her confession. It stopped for no one.

'What do you mean?'

'The day he went on a bender.'

Aaron frowned. 'Oh.'

The expression on his face told Rose there was no coming back from this. She'd broken the golden rule. The rule that was there for a good reason.

'He wanted to buy a unicorn for his daughter. For her birthday. And I couldn't bear the thought of him not being able to get her a present. So I gave him twenty quid.'

She was not going to cry. She wasn't going to cry to get his sympathy.

'Shit, Rose. You know the rules.'

'I know I do. I let you down. I went against everything you stand for. Everything you've worked so hard for. I knew as soon as I gave it to him, I'd done the wrong thing.'

'He never said. He never told me.'

'I guess he knew I'd get into trouble. And you wouldn't let him back, if you knew he'd taken it off me.'

There was silence. Rose could sense that Aaron's opinion of her had changed in that moment. It made her feel sick. His opinion of her mattered so much.

Aaron wouldn't have given in to Gaz in a million years. Aaron would have sat down and talked to him, made him confront his issues. He wouldn't have slid him a couple of crumpled notes because he would have known exactly what he would have done with it. Why hadn't she been able to see it?

'Gaz would have found a way to get the drink.' Aaron's voice was as soft as the night air. 'Whether you had given him the money or not.'

'Don't excuse me,' said Rose. 'I did a terrible thing. I knew the rules.'

'You aren't the first to fall for a sob story. And I promise you, I was a soft touch, back in the day. Until I figured it all out. Don't be too hard on yourself.'

'There's more, though.' She had to tell him everything. He had to know what she was capable of. 'He did buy the unicorn with my money. I found it under the bed in the pod. After you'd gone to the hospital.'

'Oh.' Aaron looked surprised. 'Well, there you are. I rest my case. He must have nicked the vodka, or got money off someone else. So please stop feeling so guilty.'

She could leave it at that. But she wanted a clear conscience. He'd come all this way. It must mean something. She couldn't risk him finding out from someone else. Gaz or Shell could easily tell him the truth.

'I took it to his girlfriend. I wanted his daughter to have it. In case something happened.'

There were tears flowing down her cheeks now.

'Rose!' Aaron went to put his arm around her, but she stepped away, putting her hands up.

'I broke every rule of confidentiality. I got the address from his phone.' She looked up into Aaron's anguished face. 'I'm really sorry. That's why I left without telling you where I was going. I couldn't face you, knowing what I'd done. That I'd broken all the rules and interfered in his life.'

For a moment, she thought Aaron was going to turn and walk back up the lawn, leaving her there. She couldn't make out his expression. What was he thinking? There was a slash of coral across the sky on the other side of the river, the sun disappearing completely, slowly turning the world navy blue. Above their heads, something small and fast skittered. A bat?

Rose shivered. What should have been a wonderful evening had turned bone-chillingly cold. How had she thought she could run away from what she had done?

'Rose...' Aaron's voice was deep and serious. She couldn't look at him. He put a hand on her shoulder and turned her to face him. 'Rose, you did what you did for the very best reason. Gaz would have gone on a bender anyway, whether you gave him that money or not. That was where he was, in his head. He was on a spiral, and it was you who saved him. Your intuition.'

'My guilt.' Rose wasn't going to let herself be absolved that easily.

'You gave him that money for his daughter. Because you knew how important it was for him and for her. You understood.'

'I should have handled it differently. I should have gone to you.'

'Shoulda woulda coulda.' Aaron shrugged the words away. 'You care, Rose. That's what makes you special. You don't walk out of the Soul Bowl and forget about those people until the next week. They get under your skin. And you get under theirs. It's not the same without you. Everyone asks where you are.'

Rose tried to smile.

'And he's good now, Gaz. He's got himself dry. He's doing a programme and he's managing to stay on track.'

'Really?'

'He's sorted. And that must be down to you, in part. You should come and see him.'

'No, no . . .' She felt a flutter of panic at the thought.

Aaron took her hands, and her stomach looped the loop.

'I came here,' he said, 'to ask you to come back. I need you. We all need you. For a start, the cooking's not as good on a Monday. Everything Shona cooks is brown. There's a lot of lentils.'

She laughed shakily.

'I can't come back,' she said. 'They need me here.'

'Just once a week. Surely they can spare you?'

'I can't,' she said. 'Mum and Cherry need me here. And besides, there's Gertie. I'm really sorry.'

Aaron dropped her hands and sighed. 'At least I know where you are. I was very worried,' he said. He looked up at the lights spilling from the pub, a stream of gold spread over the lawn. They could hear laughter trailing across the night air and a drift of music teased them. 'I can see why you've all moved here. It's a way of life, isn't it?'

'It wouldn't suit a city boy like you.' Rose felt able to tease him.

'You don't know that. I like change,' said Aaron. 'I like a challenge. I never want to stand still.'

Rose knew that. Aaron was restless. Always in pursuit. He wouldn't last two minutes in a place like sleepy Rushbrook, even if they were doing their best to bring some life back into the village. But it was nice he appreciated why they had made the move. He was staring at her. What was he thinking? It was intense. Too intense.

> *'Rose leaves, rose leaves*
> *Rose leaves I strew*
> *He that will love me*
> *Come after me now.'*

The words resounded in her head. She was being ridiculous. He'd come down to check on her, that's all. Professional interest. Nothing more.

'I'm really sorry. I've got to go. I need to go and check on Gertie,' said Rose, panicking. 'Thank you for coming, though. It means a lot.'

And she turned away from his gaze and fled across the lawn to the boathouse, unable to bear the way her thoughts were heading a moment longer.

42

By the time Rose got back from giving Gertie her goodnight kiss, Aaron had gone. She felt a mixture of disappointment and relief, but also very touched that he had come all this way to see her. The pub was still pretty busy, even though it was a paying bar now. The crowds had fallen into their little groups: the young farming lot with their pints of cider, the Sauvignon Blanc brigade, the trendy craft ale drinkers. Maggie and Cherry were circulating, and outside Winnie was packing up the hog roast. Every last scrap had gone.

Then Rose noticed a slight commotion at the bar. She could see a woman barely able to stand, remonstrating with Chloe. By the intensity of their altercation, it must be her mother. She was stunningly attractive but absolutely hammered. Poor Chloe looked mortified, and was trying to persuade her to go home.

Rose made her way straight over. Chloe shouldn't have to deal with this on her own, but she wouldn't want a scene either.

'Hey,' said Rose. 'You must be Chloe's mum. I'm Rose.'

'Rose?' Nicole looked at her blankly. Her eyes were bloodshot and her mascara was starting to run.

'I can't tell you how much we love Chloe. Um, Chloe, if you want to go home with your mum, that's cool. We've got enough hands on deck.'

'I'm not ready to go,' protested Nicole. 'I want another drink.'

'We've actually stopped serving, I'm afraid.'

Rose was so certain and authoritative that Nicole couldn't argue. 'Oh.'

'Come on, Mum. We can't leave the kids on their own this late,' Chloe begged her.

Nicole shut her eyes for a moment, as if she was thinking about what to do and say next. Rose and Chloe exchanged glances.

'I'll walk back with you,' said Rose. 'I need some air.' She put her arm in Nicole's and helped her off her bar stool. 'Come on.'

Nicole slid off the stool and onto her feet, leaning heavily on Rose as Chloe took her other arm. There was a moment when it looked as if Nicole would fall backwards, but they kept her upright and moved her towards the door, hoping to get her out before anyone noticed.

Rose caught Maggie's eye across the room and nodded her head towards Nicole, to indicate they were taking her home.

'Thank you,' Chloe mouthed at Rose. She was mortified. She had thought Nicole had been drinking the elderflower she'd given her, but she must have swapped it for something else. If she'd had a few drinks before she arrived, it wouldn't have taken much to tip her into incoherence. It never did these days.

They steered Nicole between them as they walked along the road. Luckily it wasn't too far to Kerslake Crescent.

'What an amazing night,' said Rose. 'It was even better than we hoped.'

'I've never seen the pub so busy. It's going to be great,' said Chloe. 'It's going to bring the village back to life.'

'Where did they all come from?'

'Rushbrook's bigger than you think. There's all the little lanes, don't forget.'

'So was it all locals, do you think?'

'I recognised most people, but there were definitely some outsiders.'

It wasn't far to go now. They had reached the turning off that led to Kerslake Crescent.

'You've been a real help to Mum this week, you know,' Rose told Chloe. 'She's such a perfectionist and you've kept her calm. I can't do it because we're too close and we wind each other up.'

'She's amazing. And your grandmother. You're really lucky.'

Chloe darted a look at Nicole to see if she was listening, but she was in her own world.

'I am,' said Rose. 'They are quite a lot to live up to, though.'

They arrived at the front door, and Chloe dug in her pocket for the key. Nicole started protesting.

'Come on, let's go back to the pub,' she slurred. 'The party's not over yet.'

'It will be by now, I'm afraid,' said Rose firmly.

'You've got to be quiet, Mum. We don't want to wake the neighbours.' Chloe put the key in the lock and turned to Rose. 'Thanks so much.'

It was clear she didn't want Rose to come in. That she wanted her to go.

'Will you be OK?'

'Fine,' said Chloe. It was obvious she was used to this. Nicole was swaying forwards and backwards, hardly able to keep her eyes open.

There was an awkward silence.

'Listen,' said Rose, keeping her voice down. 'If there's anything you want to talk about, I've had a bit of experience with . . .' She wasn't sure what to say. She didn't want to frighten Chloe. 'People who drink too much. Who might have a bit of a problem.'

'Thanks,' said Chloe. 'She just gets a bit carried away every now and then, that's all.'

She turned away, plainly not wanting to talk about it. Which gave the game away, thought Rose. That was all part of the conspiracy. The covering up. The pretending everything was all right. Now was not the time to go in hard, though.

'Like I said,' she repeated. 'I'm here if you need me.'

As Chloe closed the door, Rose turned away, knowing she had done all she could do.

43

Maggie stood for a moment on the patio, breathing in the night air. She was hot from running around, and needed a moment to collect herself before saying the final farewells. She couldn't believe the evening had gone so swimmingly. She knew a lot of that was down to preparation, and her amazing team, but there had been a chemistry too, an alchemy you couldn't plan for. It boded well, for that was the magic ingredient that meant success.

She felt a hand on her shoulder and turned. It was Russell, his smile a little wider after a couple of pints.

'Thanks for a great evening,' he said.

'Oh,' said Maggie. 'It's my pleasure. I hope you . . . become a regular. Again?'

'It could become a habit. I was getting to be a bit of a recluse.'

'Well, you know where we are.'

He hesitated for a moment.

'I'd love to do the quiz next week. It's about time I got my brain cells working. But I haven't got anyone to team up with. Could you put me on the waifs and strays team?'

'You can be on my team,' said Maggie, before she'd had time to think about it. She didn't even have a team.

'That'd be grand,' he said. 'I'll be all right if it's seventies rock music or motorbikes. Or pigs.'

'Well, I'll be OK if it's food.'

'All bases covered, then. The trophy's ours.'

He gave a grin, squeezed her shoulder and headed for the door.

She should be working that night. Pacing the floor, making sure everything was perfect. But it was OK, she told herself. They weren't doing dinner during the quiz, just sharing platters. She should be able to supervise and take part at the same time. She was used to doing seven things at once whilst making it look as if she was enjoying herself. Maybe she'd ask Dash and Tabitha to join too – as her guests. And perhaps her dad would come down and be on the team?

In fact, where was Mike? She looked around the pub but she couldn't see him anywhere. She'd seen him talking to various people. Congratulating Tom and Ed. She weaved her way over to Cherry.

'Has Dad gone?'

'I don't think so.' Cherry looked alarmed, and starting searching the crowds. Where was he? There was no sign of him anywhere. No one he had spoken to had seen him in the past fifteen minutes.

She checked her phone. And there was a text from him.

Got an early start tomorrow so I slipped away. But congratulations. What a huge success. x

Cherry stared at the screen. He hadn't said goodbye. He'd shown his face but made his escape before they had a chance to talk about things. The relief she had felt at seeing him earlier faded away, to be replaced by a horrible insecurity. Had he just been paying lip service, knowing that not coming to the opening was a statement too far; that it would alert Maggie and Rose that something was badly wrong? *Was* something badly wrong? She didn't know. He had seemed his old self, genuinely taken by what she had done. He'd been pleased to see her – his kiss had been warm. He had squeezed her hand. Smiled into her eyes. There had been nothing hostile or distant about him. He had been her Mike. Her Trex. The man she'd danced with to 'Nights in White Satin'.

Should she call him? She didn't want to sound shrill or accusatory or needy. She felt confused and anxious. Was this a game? Or a genuine crisis? Or were they simply drifting apart from each other? She couldn't bear the thought of him slipping away. She felt a tingle behind her eyes. She couldn't cry, not in the middle of the pub.

And then a thought made her heart nearly stop. Anneka Harding. Was she behind this strange behaviour? Had he slipped away to be with her? Had he nipped down to Rushbrook this evening as a distraction to put Cherry off the scent? She tried to reassure herself with the memory of how shaken he had been by her reappearance and the anguish she had caused him all those years ago. But maybe if Cherry was out of the picture, there would be no anguish?

She told herself she was being paranoid. This was Mike, the loyal, faithful family man. He was *not* a devious, slippery player.

'Cherry!' She saw Amanda bearing down on her, carrying a tray with a bottle of champagne on it, and several glasses. 'I thought it was time for a toast. You deserve it. All of you.'

Theo appeared at her side, looking apologetic. 'Sorry. I couldn't stop her. Any excuse.'

He smiled fondly at his wife. Amanda looked un-repentant.

'It's not every day your childhood heroine re-does your local pub.'

Cherry smiled. They were fun. And kind. And it would be churlish not to accept Amanda's generous offer. She would call Mike in the morning. Make a plan to set things straight. She didn't have the emotional energy to engage with him tonight. It had been a long and exhausting day, and if Amanda had anything to do with it, it wasn't over yet.

Russell wandered back along the lanes of Rushbrook to the farm. The night sky had a lightness to it, for midsummer never reached the pitch black of winter. The air smelled of pungent elderflower and sweet wild strawberries, and as he turned into the drive there was only the faintest trace of his wards on the breeze.

He felt good. Two pints was just right – any more and he'd wake up with a thick head. And he'd loved watching everyone tear into their hot pork rolls. It was gratifying, knowing that the love and care he bestowed on his charges paid off. He was a good pig man, he thought, and it wasn't often he gave himself praise.

In the kitchen, he flicked on the kettle for a bedtime brew. He looked at his phone and thought he'd try Jen. She might not have left the house for work yet.

'Hey, Dad!' There she was, smiling. Happy to see him. Her eyes widened. 'Oh my God. Look at you.'

'I know.' He held out his arms to display himself in all his finery. She hadn't seen his haircut yet; for the last few times they'd spoken he'd had his hat on.

'What's the occasion?'

'Grand reopening of the pub.'

'Wow. You look a million dollars. Was it fun?'

'It was.' For some reason, he was grinning.

'You've met someone.'

'What?'

'You can't keep the smile off your face. You've met someone.'

'I did meet someone. Yes.'

'Who? What's her name? What does she do?'

'Maggie. She runs the pub. With her mum and her daughter.'

'Ah! Well, that explains why you look so perky.'

He ran his hand through his hair. 'We just had a chat. That's all.'

Jen didn't answer for a while. She was looking at him. 'What's she like?'

He tried to think of the right word. He tried to picture her. Her smile. Her eyes. That dress.

'Sparkly,' he said finally. 'She's sparkly.'

Jen nodded in approval. 'Sparkly,' she said, 'is good.'

At midnight, outside the boathouse, the banks of the river were busy with wildlife under the light of an opal moon. Tiny eyes gleamed; whiskers and feathers ruffled in the night breeze. There was digging and scratching, scurrying and swooping, nibbling and pecking. The river rippled on, minding its own business as ever, a reassuring constant winding through the heart of Rushbrook while its inhabitants slumbered.

Inside the boathouse, Gertie dreamt of a donkey with a hat on, galloping across the field towards her, and laughed in her sleep when she heard it bray.

Rose dreamt of a tiny house covered in a scramble of wild roses, but she couldn't quite place it. She just knew she belonged there.

Maggie dreamt of a warm smile and a hand on her arm and her flowery silk dress in a heap on the floor in front of a roaring fire.

And Cherry dreamt of a rearing horse and a boy with wild curls and no matter how hard she tried to get to him, he was always just out of reach.

44

A week later, on the day of the pub quiz, Mario rocked up in the When in Rome van and jumped out of the driver's seat. He had on a black polo shirt with the company logo, faded denim shorts and espadrilles, a bandana tying back his curls. He hugged Maggie, then held her at arm's length, looking closely at her in concern.

'We're OK, yeah? You and me?'

'Of course we are.'

She patted his arm, realising he was worried he had taken things too far after dinner that night.

'It's the Amarone, you know. It always gets me in trouble.' He gave a quick grin. 'You made the right move, though. I am a way better friend than I am lover. I'm a friend until death.'

She laughed, relieved that he wasn't going to make her feel bad about running out on him. He was very self-deprecating, not arrogant, which he could so easily be. Maybe it was hard being so devastatingly attractive? Maybe it was a curse?

'And you're OK?' He looked her right in the eye to make sure. 'I know how hard it must be, still.'

'It is,' she said with a sigh.

'I hope one day I'll find someone else – someone like you.'

He sounded wistful. Maggie could tell he was being genuine and not trying to hit on her again. And a little bit of her regretted that she hadn't had the guts to go through with her night of passion – sex with Mario would probably have been pretty hot. Her body had been up for it, certainly, as had her mind. It was her heart that hadn't wanted to take part. But he was probably right – he was better as a friend. Without benefits. Say what you like, benefits always changed the landscape.

Nevertheless, even though they had cleared the air, she couldn't quite meet his eye. She had spent the morning working out the table plans for the pub quiz, and matching up contestants, and even though putting her and Russell on the same table had been logistically tricky, she had made sure they were sitting together. There had been something in his dry humour and his warmth and his solidity that she couldn't stop thinking about. Russell was almost the opposite of mercurial, magnetic Mario, but she felt a little guilty, so she changed the subject.

'What have you got for me?'

He threw open the back door of the van with a flourish. 'Braesola. Fennel salami. Taleggio. Gorgonzola. Marinated artichokes. Red peppers. Extra virgin olive oil. Mozzarella. Sun-dried tomatoes with beautiful herbs.' He kissed his thumb and forefinger. 'Pecorino. Ripe fresh figs. Basil.' He picked up a bunch and waved it under her nose.

'Oh my goodness. Winnie is going to go wild for this. Hey, Winnie!'

Winnie was coming out of the front of the pub. She

sauntered over with her apron on and Maggie saw Mario appraising her, taking in her lean physique, her sharp bob, her tattoos.

'This is Mario,' said Maggie. 'He supplies all our olive oil and tomatoes and – well, take a look.'

'A whole Pecorino!' Winnie put out her hand to stroke the pale orange globe lovingly. She looked up at Mario. 'You import all this yourself?'

'My own family put it on the truck in Rome and send it over.'

Maggie raised an eyebrow, not quite sure that Mario's tale of provenance was authentic, but it made a good story and Winnie was entranced. Though more by the food than Mario. Mario, however, was hypnotised as Winnie went through the produce, prodding and sniffing and tasting, firing questions at him which he answered with his usual charm and aplomb.

'You sure you don't want to join my team for the quiz?' Maggie asked him, teasingly.

He shook his head with a wry smile. 'I know nothing about anything. Except maybe football?' He shrugged to indicate his incompetence.

She laughed, but she felt slightly relieved. Mario and Russell at the same table would be more stress than she could handle.

'I think Mario was quite taken with you,' she said to Winnie, as they loaded all the produce into the fridge.

Winnie just laughed. 'He's not my type, I'm afraid.'

'He's a sweetheart underneath.'

'I mean, not my type as in he's a guy.'

'Oh,' said Maggie, blushing.

'Never say never, though.' Winnie heaved the Pecorino

onto the work surface. 'He is pretty hot. I *could* make an exception.'

She gave Maggie a wink.

Maggie cursed herself for being so naïve. But Winnie didn't seem to bear a grudge, and she loved her even more for her feisty, can-do attitude and her passion for food. She made the kitchen an exciting place to be. She had no ego, just boundless energy and enthusiasm, and Maggie was pleased she had taken the risk on her. She just prayed Winnie wouldn't get the urge to take off and travel too soon. Life in Rushbrook was pretty tame, and she suspected Winnie wanted adventure.

She and Chloe spent the afternoon assembling the grazing trays: two on each table of six, together with a bottle of Chianti and a bottle of Soave. Winnie had made fresh rosemary focaccia to rip up and dip into saucers of peppery olive oil, and tiny limoncello tiramisus for after the winner had been announced, to keep the contestants in the pub and stop them heading home straight away.

Maggie watched as Chloe cut up slices of cheese and spread them out carefully on waxed paper. She was really impressed with her work since they'd taken her on. She was conscientious and full of initiative, if a little shy still. She showed genuine interest in why things were done the way they were and asked lots of questions. She was mesmerised by Cherry, and watched, eagle-eyed, as she demonstrated how to arrange a tangle of flowers in a jug, snipping the stems and stripping back the foliage. Chloe copied her to the letter and before long you couldn't tell which arrangement Cherry had done and which one Chloe had done.

She was interested in the food, too. Today, they tried

everything Mario had brought before deciding how to lay it out. Chloe shut her eyes as she tasted. When Maggie asked her which cheese she liked best, she couldn't decide.

'I love the creaminess of that one,' she pointed at the Taleggio. 'But the blue one has more of a tang. Kind of a bite. And I love the crumbly hard one. I love the saltiness. I don't know. I like them all.'

Chloe showed incredible promise. But Maggie was concerned about her. Some days she looked exhausted, as if she hadn't slept, pale, with dark rings under her eyes. She never complained, and was never any less efficient, but there was an air of agitation to her like an electric current. Maggie had seen Chloe's mother on the opening night, knocking back the wine as if her life depended on it.

She had asked Rose about it when she got back from walking her home.

'Chloe says she gets overexcited sometimes and has a bit too much to drink.' Rose made a face. 'I don't think she's very happy, the mum. Something feels a bit off. I've told Chloe she can always talk to me.'

Today, as she spooned cannellini bean dip into earthenware bowls, Maggie wondered what Chloe's home life was really like.

'How's your mum?' she asked, casually.

Chloe looked up at her, startled. She looked trapped, as if she had no idea what to say.

'Good,' she said eventually. 'She's been at work all week so she's probably knackered.'

'She's coming to the quiz tonight, though.' Maggie had put her on the same table as Amanda and Theo.

'What?' Chloe looked up.

'She came in and bought a ticket. She said she loves pub quizzes.'

Chloe was silent for a moment, slicing up a piece of salami with a sharp knife. 'Yes,' she said. 'She's really good at general knowledge. She always gets all the answers on *Mastermind*. We've told her she should go on it.'

Her hands were shaking slightly, and she wiped them on her apron as if they were sweaty.

'Is everything OK, Chloe?' Maggie asked.

Chloe nodded. 'Is it all right for me to go home first, before the quiz? I need a shower and stuff.'

'Of course. You can go now if you like. Just be back by six.'

'You can't come to the quiz, Mum.' Chloe looked anguished. 'Not after last week.'

She'd rushed back home to Kerslake Crescent and found her mother in her bedroom, sitting at the dressing table putting a face on.

'I'm really looking forward to it.' Nicole was looking calm and composed, fresh as a daisy in a Breton top over a chambray skirt. 'And in case you're worried, I haven't had a drink all week. And I'm not having anything tonight.'

Chloe had to bite back a retort. She'd heard that promise before.

'Chloe.' Nicole turned on her stool and took Chloe's hand. 'I'm so proud of you, working there. I'm not going to show you up. And you know how much I love a pub quiz. I want to use my brain. I *never* get to use it any more. This will be the first time I've been challenged for *months*.'

'We said we wouldn't leave Pearl and Otis on their own again.'

'They'll be all right until ten o'clock. We're only down the road. I'll do the quiz and come straight home. It starts at half seven so it'll be over by half nine at the latest.'

Chloe sighed. Pearl and Otis had been savage when they got home after the opening. Otis couldn't resist tormenting his sister, and refused to let her play on the PS5 their dad had bought.

'It's for both of us!' Pearl had insisted.

'You can play on it tomorrow.'

'I want to play on it now.'

'You're too young for this game.'

'So are you!'

They had come to blows. Pearl had been catatonic on the lounge floor when they got back, worn out from hysterics, and had shown them a bite mark on her upper arm that Otis insisted she had done herself. It was impossible to tell who was telling the truth without involving forensics. Chloe had to let Pearl sleep with her to calm her down. She wasn't going through that again.

'Promise you'll be home by ten. Because I have to stay and help clear up, so I might not be back until late.'

'It's a deal.' Nicole put on a pale pink lip gloss and pressed her lips together. She stood up and held out her arms. 'How do I look?'

'Like the perfect mother,' thought Chloe. All she could do was pray that Nicole would keep her promise.

45

At four o'clock, Clive arrived to make sure the sound system was up to snuff. He probably wasn't much over forty, but he dressed like an old fogey, in his cords and a checked shirt with a bow tie and highly polished brogues. He laid out laminated sheets on each table. On them were photocopies of the celebrities, heads of state and historical figures the contestants had to identify for the first round.

'Don't let me see!' said Maggie. 'I don't want to be accused of cheating.'

'Quite right. Cheating is very much frowned upon,' Clive said sternly. 'I know some pub quizzes tolerate all kinds of skulduggery, but not on my watch. I might even have to ask you to turn off the wi-fi to make sure no one googles.'

'I don't think that's a good idea,' said Maggie. 'We'll just have to trust them.'

Clive raised his eyebrows. 'Never trust anyone, is my motto. And my say is the final say. I will not brook any argument. I've done my research and my answer is the answer. I hope you'll back me on that.'

'Of course,' said Maggie, quailing a little at his sternness. But he was probably right to be strict.

'Once people realise the terms of engagement,' he assured her, 'it'll go swimmingly. You have to be stern from the outset.'

'Have you got a tie-breaker? Just in case?'

'I most certainly have. Now, I need to check the Bluetooth for the music round.' He held up his phone. 'It's all on here. Classical, jazz, rock music. Everything from Elgar to ELO. You'll need a very broad musical knowledge to get through this round.'

Maggie felt a momentary pang. That would be Frank's forte. Frank had always loved a pub quiz.

'What would you like to drink during the quiz?' she asked.

'Oh, just fizzy water. I've got to keep a clear head. I'll have a restorative glass of vino when it's all done.'

'I'm very grateful to you for organising this.'

'I love compiling a quiz. Don't worry. This is as much fun as I ever have.'

Maggie could believe it. Funny old Clive. There were rumours he was minted, and his E-type Jag substantiated those rumours. Every village had its eccentrics. As long as he was happy to run the pub quiz, she was happy to have him. They were a great way of bonding the community and bringing people together to have fun. And tonight's would be a showcase for the kind of food and atmosphere they were going to provide. Winnie had decided to make arancini stuffed with Taleggio at the last minute, and Maggie didn't think she'd tasted anything quite so delicious in her life.

She double-checked all the table plans for the tenth

time. On her table were the two Matts, whose general knowledge was pretty sound, and Dash and Tabitha, who she wanted to get to know better. And Russell, of course. She popped his name card casually next to hers.

Just before seven everyone began to trickle in and take their places. Maggie settled the two Matts and Dash and Tabitha at their table. They picked up the laminated sheet and began to peruse the faces.

'Dot Cotton,' said Tabitha, with certainty.

'Catherine the Great,' said the Reverend Matt, prodding her face with a meaty finger.

'Lord Byron,' said Dash, who had a touch of Byronic good looks himself. 'Hello, Chloe.' He smiled as Chloe brought their bottles of wine over to the table. Maybe Dash would have some intel on Chloe's home life, thought Maggie. Not that she was spying, but she felt incredibly protective of her protégée.

Her eyes flickered towards the door every now and again. There was no sign of the sixth member of their team yet. What if he didn't turn up? They'd muddle through, she supposed, but as the minute hand inched nearer to the start time, she became more anxious. She saw Nicole come in, and make her way over to Amanda and Theo's table. She'd put them with another couple new to the village, Bryony and Max, and Cherry.

'Just keep an eye on Chloe's mum,' she'd asked her. 'I think she's a bit of a loose cannon when she's had a few.'

The tables were all filled. The wine was poured. Clive stood up to take the microphone.

'Ladies and gentlemen,' he said. 'Welcome to the inaugural Three Swans pub quiz. We are hoping to make this a weekly event, so any feedback would be gratefully and graciously received.'

Maggie sank into her seat next to the empty one with a sigh. He wasn't coming. She understood why. Russell was knackered after a week on the farm and had chosen a quiet night in with a can of beer and the telly, over the ordeal of having to mix with people and use his brain.

And then the door opened and there he was. He strode through the pub to the seat beside Maggie, quite unselfconscious.

'Sorry I'm late,' he murmured with a smile. 'Pig pandemonium. Welcome to my world.'

46

They were into the third round. Foreign expressions. The second round had been the natural history of Rushbrook, a shoe-in for those born and bred in the village. The incomers realised they had to brush up on their wood pigeons, wagtails and sparrowhawks; their celandines and their clematis.

'What,' asked Clive, with a dramatic pause, 'is the French term for *love at first sight?*'

Maggie instinctively turned to her neighbour to confer, then blushed to the roots of her hair when she found Russell had turned to her. They stared at each other for a moment, then shrugged. Neither of them knew. The Reverend Matt leaned forward and spoke quietly.

'It's *coup de foudre,*' he said, and reached out to pat his husband's shoulder with a smile. 'I should know.'

'How do you spell that?' Maggie looked down at the answer sheet, still pink. Matt took the pen from her and wrote it down.

Coup de foudre, thought Maggie. Is that a thing? Could you really fall in love at first sight, without knowing anything about the other person?

Something was happening to her, she thought. She couldn't take her eyes off Russell. His broad arms. That shaggy hair. The smile that was part shy, part supremely self-confident.

Lorraine in the shop had come into her own for once. Maggie usually avoided her gossip, but she had asked about him, as casually as she could.

'He was a traffic cop, up north somewhere.' Lorraine had waved a hand to indicate an area that could have been Yorkshire, Lancashire, Cumbria, Northumberland. 'Married to the job, apparently. His wife left him. He doesn't seem to have got over it. Bit of a recluse. Nice enough though. Why?' She had looked at Maggie beadily. 'Are you interested?'

'Just curious,' said Maggie. 'We're going to be stocking his meat.'

'Well, he's good to his pigs. No one can argue with that.' Lorraine smiled. 'And you know, I think he could scrub up quite well, if he made the effort.'

He certainly could, thought Maggie. He intrigued her. He seemed vulnerable, yet radiated strength. He was a mass of contradictions.

Perhaps divorce did a similar thing to grief, she thought. Chopped you up and put you back together differently, so you were never quite yourself again. You became tentative, risk-averse, yet also brave and indomitable. In some ways, she had never felt as strong as she did now – taking over at The Swan had been an incredible challenge. But in other ways, she felt as if she would never be the same. That she would never be the passionate, carefree, loving Maggie she had been with Frank. She felt as if she was driving around with the handbrake on, terrified to release it in case life ran away with her.

Maybe Russell felt the same? Maybe he had *his* hand-brake on, afraid to be hurt? Maggie understood how it was easier, not to take risks.

But what if someone was worth the risk?

'What,' Clive was asking, 'is the Latin term for *in wine there is truth?*'

The Reverend Matt sat up straight, for of course he knew the answer again, but he didn't want to hog the answering and come across as a know-it-all. Luckily Tabitha pitched in.

'*In vino veritas,*' she said, picking up her wine glass with a grin, and Maggie scribbled it down.

Russell leant over to whisper to her. 'I've been bloody useless so far.'

'Don't worry, your turn will come,' Maggie whispered back. 'No one knows everything. Except Reverend Matt but that's why I chose him.'

'I hope so. I feel like a dead weight.'

'You're not,' Maggie reassured him, patting his arm. 'Not at all. Wait for the music round – it's up next.'

She could feel the hard muscles under the softness of his shirt. She took her hand away hastily and took a swig of her Soave. She saw the Reverend Matt looking at her and turned her head to look at Clive and listen attentively to the next question.

'What is the German term for *head over heels?*'

At the end of the first four rounds, Clive announced a forty-five-minute interval for food.

This was easy, thought Nicole, as the rest of the table she was on disappeared off to get drinks and go to the bathroom. Not drinking was a doddle once you put your mind to it. She'd been nervous when she joined the table, but the two couples sitting with her were both new to the village, so she was able to share her local knowledge and tip them off about the best Indian takeaway in Honisham. And Cherry was very welcoming to her, telling her how much they adored Chloe and how well she was doing, which made her heart burst with pride. And the questions were easy. There wasn't a single one she hadn't been able to answer yet, and everyone seemed very impressed. It was wonderful to have a clear head and to use your brain. She smiled over at Chloe and lifted her glass of water, to show how good she was being. Chloe gave a grateful smile back as she began to hand out the grazing platters to each table.

Nicole's eye fell on the open bottle of Soave on their table. Wine with food was almost essential. No, she thought. She had to keep sharp for the final round. They were definitely in the lead, and just one question could mean the difference between victory and failure.

'So,' said Amanda, sliding back into her seat having been to the loo. 'Tell me about you.'

'Oh,' said Nicole. 'There's nothing to tell.'

'I can't believe that. What do you do?'

Nicole chewed the side of her thumb. 'Nothing really,' she said, finally. 'I've got a job doing some cleaning for the Safari Lodges. But apart from that...'

Amanda frowned.

'But you're super smart. Anyone can see that.'

'I was an English teacher at Meadow Hall. My husband left me for one of the mothers. It kind of all fell apart.' She made a face. 'I couldn't face all the gossip. So I resigned. And then I lost my driving licence as well.'

'Ouch,' said Amanda, wincing.

'I know. I hate myself for it. But it's impossible to get a decent job round here if you can't drive. Though I love working for Dash and Tabitha.'

'It does seem a waste, though.'

'When I get my licence back...' Nicola gave a wan smile. 'Or I've thought of private tutoring. I'm going to try that for the new academic year. I do know my stuff.'

'I can see that.' Amanda put a hand on hers. 'Take it from me. I've been around the block a few times. Things will get better.'

Nicole managed a smile. 'Hopefully.'

Amanda picked up the wine bottle and offered it to Nicole, who shook her head.

'No, thanks,' she said. 'I'm working early tomorrow.'

'So where do you live?'

'Um... Kerslake Crescent,' said Nicole, grateful that the newcomer probably wouldn't have any idea of its reputation.

'You are kidding me?' Amanda shook her head in amazement. 'What number?'

'Five?' said Nicole, her heart sinking.

'Oh my God. That's the house I grew up in. Me and my five brothers and sisters. Can you believe it?'

'Really?' Nicole couldn't. How could this glossy, successful, smart woman have begun life in Kerslake Crescent?

Amanda sighed. 'We had a tough old time of it. My mum died when I was ten. My dad was the postman. And he did odd jobs in the village. He was the handyman up at Rushbrook House. He worked all the hours he could. I guess maybe that's where I got my drive from.'

'You're a TV producer, right?' Nicole asked. 'That must be fascinating.'

'Oh no. Not really.' Amanda waved her hand dismissively. 'It's like running a glorified creche. As long as you keep everyone fed, you're winning.'

She threw back her head and laughed, and Nicole joined in. She was having a great time. Good conversation, a bit of stimulation and some attention. That was all she needed. She didn't need drink. She needed to get out more, that was all.

During the interval, after the grazing platters had been devoured, Russell went off to the bar to fetch more drinks, Tabitha and Dash were chatting with another table, and Maggie was about to go and find Cherry when the Reverend Matt took her hand in his.

'This has been a wonderful evening. You've brought the village back together. I wish my Sunday services were as popular. Perhaps Clive could be prevailed upon to swell the congregation.'

Maggie laughed. 'He's in his element.'

'It's good to see people venturing out. Russell, for example.'

'Yes.' The very mention of his name flustered her.

The Reverend leant forward. 'It would be all right,' he said, 'to dip your toe in again, you know. It's not a betrayal.'

Maggie lowered her lashes and tried to look demure.

'I'm not ... I don't ...' She couldn't think of what to say. Matt nodded, understanding her discomfort.

'Just go gently,' he said. 'And you know where I am. God doesn't have to come into it. I'm a safe pair of ears.'

And he stood up, disappearing off into the crowds. Maggie watched after him in astonishment, mixed with fondness. How kind and perspicacious he was. Probably the two most important things in a vicar. She hoped that no one else was as eagle-eyed. She looked around. Never mind eagle-eyed, they were all pie-eyed. The pub quiz looked to be a roaring success. It was just gone nine and the joint was jumping. Clive was in his element, being congratulated and slapped on the back. She thought it was probably the most social interaction he'd had for months, but she felt pleased. Wasn't that what a local was for, bringing people out of their shells?

She walked back to her table and slid into the seat next to Dash, who had come back to his seat. 'I think we're in with a chance of winning,' he said. 'The Matts are ferocious. Is there anything the Rev doesn't know?'

'I don't know if I should be seen to be on the winning team,' said Maggie, suddenly anxious.

'Oh, I don't think anyone would mind,' he assured her.

'Well, if we do win, I'll put my prize back into the ring.'

'That's very honourable.'

She hesitated for a moment before lowering her voice. 'Can I just ask – I know Chloe's done a bit of work for you. Is everything all right at home, do you know?'

He frowned, looking uncertain.

'Honestly, don't answer if you don't want to. But I'm a bit worried about her.'

He took a sip of his pint before answering. 'I know. She's an absolutely lovely girl. We're very fond of her.' His eyes flicked over to Nicole. 'Nicole's a complicated character. She's super bright, you know. She shouldn't just be cleaning for us. And when she's on it, she's great. But...'

He made a face. He was trying to be discreet. Maggie understood that you had to be careful what you said in a village like Rushbrook. Once you'd divulged a secret, you couldn't hide it again.

'Do you think she's got a drink problem?'

Dash looked at his pint. 'It's hard to say. We all overdo it from time to time, don't we? And she's got a lot on her plate, bringing up three kids on her own. I get the feeling the dad isn't much help. Just buys them Playstations or iPads every now and then. But Chloe definitely seems to have too much responsibility.'

'That's what I thought,' said Maggie. 'She seems to look after all of them.'

'Yes. And she seems very anxious a lot of the time. They all rely on her far too much. Even the bloody hamster.' Dash sighed. 'But what can we do? It's a very fine line between protecting and interfering. And Nicole is very...' He searched for the right word. 'Evasive. But also so capable. On a good day, you would have no idea there was anything wrong.' He looked across at the table where Nicole was demurely sipping mineral water.

'Hmm,' said Maggie, not sure if she felt better now her suspicions had been confirmed, or worse.

Dash put down his glass. 'I'm so pleased to see how well Chloe's doing here. And you're great role models for her. It's what she needs, I think.'

'Thank you. We're very invested in Chloe's future. She's a valuable part of our team already. We'll do everything we can to help her.'

'Good,' said Dash. 'She's got a lot of potential, that one. I'd love to see her flourish.'

Dash and Maggie exchanged looks, so much unsaid but so much understood.

The final round was tense. In the end, they had to have a tie-breaker. It was between the Reverend Matt and Nicole, both of whom had been nominated by their tables. The two of them stood up while Clive read out the final question.

'Closest answer wins,' he said. 'How many minutes is the total running time of the 1972 film *The Godfather*?'

The Reverend Matt put his hands to his head while he thought.

'A hundred and eighteen?' he ventured.

Nicole tried to focus. It was definitely more than two hours. She'd seen it several times. She ran through the whole thing, trying to estimate. She reckoned just short of three hours, to get through all that betrayal and revenge.

'A hundred and sixty-four?'

Clive held the answer in front of him, teasing the room while he waited to announce. He finally put them out of their misery.

'A hundred and seventy-eight minutes,' he said, and held out his arm to Nicole. 'We have a winner.'

Nicole beamed as she sat back down, and everyone on her table congratulated her, patting her on the back.

'How did you get so close?' asked Amanda.

'It's one of my favourite films. I went through every scene in my head and made an educated guess.'

She felt a little bit shaky. She wasn't used to so much attention, and the thrill of winning had filled her with adrenaline.

A moment later, Theo was holding out a glass of champagne for her. He was the sort of man who made champagne appear from nowhere.

'Just one,' said Amanda. 'You deserve it.'

She *did* deserve it, thought Nicole, stretching out her hand. Just one. Just one glass. After all, she couldn't remember the last time she had drunk champagne.

Maggie was relieved that their team didn't win. The trophy went to the brazenly named Wisteria Winners. Amanda and Theo had bought a bottle of champagne to celebrate, and were congratulating her on a great evening.

'Better than any London night out,' declared Theo.

'Moving here is the best thing we ever did. I wish we'd done it sooner.'

'We've got friends for the weekend so we're going to have dinner here tomorrow. And maybe Sunday lunch,' Amanda told her. 'But I'm not angling for special treatment,' she added hastily.

Maggie made a mental note to make sure they *were* cossetted, because she knew they had the potential to be very valuable customers.

Across the room, Chloe's face fell at the sight of Theo topping up Nicole's champagne glass. Her mum looked as if she was having fun, chatting with the Bannisters, laughing, looking carefree. It was already after ten o'clock but she couldn't face the thought of reminding her of her promise to be home on time. It wouldn't be fair to drag her away – she'd done so brilliantly winning the quiz. Nevertheless, she felt let down. Yet again, it was going to fall to her to be the responsible one. She made her way over to Maggie.

'I'm really sorry. I need to go home. I can't leave Pearl alone with Otis. Not after last week. They'll just fight. She gets upset and she's only twelve. I've told Mum she can't leave them after ten o'clock. Pearl should be in bed and she won't go to bed if there's no one there.'

'It's OK, we can manage without you. You've done an amazing job tonight. Honestly, don't worry.'

Chloe's forehead wrinkled and her cheeks flushed with worry.

'Are you sure?'

'Of course! See you tomorrow.' Maggie reached out and gave her a reassuring hug, then watched as Chloe took off her apron and went to put it in the kitchen before hurrying off.

Maggie was concerned. It shouldn't be on Chloe to take the responsibility for Otis and Pearl. Should it? She glanced over at Nicole, who was animated, clearly enjoying her win. She was talking to Clive now, who looked as if all his Christmasses had come at once, for Nicole was very beguiling. Chloe had made reference to how tough her mum found it, being on her own and without a proper job. 'Dad just does exactly what he wants with Elizabeth,' Chloe had said, 'and Mum really struggles.' *Struggles*, thought Maggie, was code for *drinks*. It was so easy, to take refuge in a bottle when things got tough. A six o'clock sharpener could so easily turn into a binge.

Maggie felt for Nicole. She knew better than anyone how the rug could be pulled out from under you. She had been lucky to be surrounded by people who loved and supported her when Frank died, and maybe Nicole didn't have that luxury. And there were times, Maggie knew, when she had leaned heavily on Rose for comfort. So she wasn't going to judge her too harshly.

And although Nicole wasn't her responsibility, Chloe was, and they would be there for her, to support her and give her advice. That was the kind of boss she wanted to be, thought Maggie. Caring. Open. Proactive, when appropriate. She never wanted to see any of her staff struggle.

As she made her way back to the table, Russell was standing up ready to leave.

'Are you off?' she asked, disappointed.

'Pigs don't give a flying monkey's if you've had a late one,' he said ruefully, and she laughed. 'But I'm really glad I came. I have to admit I'm out of practice on the socialising front.'

'My job forces me to be social,' said Maggie. 'Or I'd be on the sofa every night in my pyjamas. Though I can't actually remember the last time I went out just for fun.'

Even Mario had been work-related, she told herself.

'Well, us being on the same team fuelled the village gossip, anyway.' He rolled his eyes with a smile. 'Three people asked me if we were an item. What are they like?'

'Oh, I know. Doesn't it drive you mad? Can't they mind their own business? Don't they understand that we're single because we want to be? Honestly!'

He was nodding. 'I mean, the only thing we've got in common *is* we're both single.'

'Well, quite.' Maggie frowned. 'Though we don't know that, do we – we might have loads in common.'

Russell looked at her. 'Are you a fan of Hawkwind, then?' he asked, deadpan.

Maggie laughed. ' "Silver Machine"? It's a classic. Though I have to admit I'm not familiar with their entire back catalogue.'

Was this flirting, wondered Maggie? It felt like it. Light-hearted teasing banter, back and forth. Both of them making eye contact. Both of them smiling. She felt a rush of impulsivity.

'Why don't we go on a date to find out if we *have* got anything in common? That would give them something to talk about.' She panicked as he looked puzzled. 'A pretend date, I mean.'

'A pretend date?'

'Just for fun. I actually really miss going out. Sometimes I want to go out for something to eat or go to the movies and I realise it's just boring old me for company.' Oh God. She'd put her foot in it. He was looking at her aghast.

But then he grinned.

'Why not? We can fuel the village gossip and have a laugh into the bargain.'

'We could keep it up for months.'

'Yeah. What do they call that? Friends *without* benefits.'

Maggie shrugged. 'Just friends will do.'

'Yes, but they don't have to know that. And then we won't get endlessly asked *have you found anyone yet?*'

Maggie rolled her eyes. 'Oh yes. If I had a penny for every time someone asked that . . .'

He put his hand out. 'It's a deal.'

She took it, laughing, remembering the first time she had met him and taken her hand away.

'So – when?' he said.

'I can only really do early in the week. We don't do food Monday and Tuesdays . . .'

'Do you like bikes? Motorbikes?'

'Um, I don't know. I've never been on one.' Maggie was embarrassed at how sheltered she seemed. How very uncool.

'I was going to take mine for a run over the moors. Maybe stop for a picnic somewhere? Monday afternoon?'

Maggie's tummy turned over at the thought of being behind him on a motorbike. Her mouth felt a little dry. That was definitely out of her comfort zone. But why not? Why shouldn't she have an adventure? A thrill went through her and she smiled.

'You're on!'

'I'll pick you up at two.'

369

'What do I wear?'

'Jeans. Boots. Something with sleeves. I'll bring you a jacket and helmet.'

Her stomach turned over. Was this reckless?

'I'll be ready.'

He gave her a wink and moments later he was out the door.

Friends without benefits, thought Maggie. The perfect arrangement. Surely the butterflies in her stomach were the thought of going on the back of motorbike for the first time at the age of forty-seven? There was a first time for everything.

47

It was Lorraine from the shop who gave them the heads-up, as always the first in Rushbrook to know when anything was afoot. She phoned the Three Swans first thing on Tuesday morning and Maggie answered.

'You're in one of the big papers!' she told her gleefully. 'A review. A good one, too. I've saved you three copies. I've cut one out and put it up in the shop.'

Maggie felt a rush of affection for the shopkeeper. Her heart was in the right place, despite her penchant for gossip and conjecture.

'I'll send someone down for it.'

'There's a parcel here for Cherry too.'

Maggie texted Chloe to see if she could pick up the papers and the parcel on her way in. As soon as she arrived, they spread the paper out on the biggest table in the dining room, all clustering round: Maggie, Rose and Cherry, Winnie and Chloe.

Maggie read the review out loud.

Somerset these days seems to be full of people with no discernible job but happy to pay more than £300 for a

square metre of wallpaper. This is not my tribe. But I've just been to stay with very dear friends who've just bought a house in the tiny village of Rushbrook. My heart sank when they suggested going to dinner at their local pub. 'It's just been done up,' they cried.

Britain is full of gastro pubs bought by enthusiastic wannabe landlords who splash about a bit of Hague blue, find someone to supply them artisanal sausages and watch the pounds roll in, only to go bust a few months later because actually they have no idea about hospitality, catering or profit margins.

The Three Swans in Rushbrook was bought recently by a mother, daughter and granddaughter trio. If you're a boomer bloke like me, you probably had a poster of Cherry Nicholson stuck to your bedroom wall. She was the chick on the motorbike in silver hot-pants we all grew up fantasising about. Now, however, she is the respectably clad front of house and the driving force behind the pub. She saved it from development, much to the gratitude of the locals who are thronging there.

Cue Farrow and Ball, quirky objets d'art and interesting lighting. Though Nicholson has a surer hand and a better imagination than most; it's like walking into the home of your schoolmate with the really cool parents. And there are dogs everywhere. I tripped over the vicar's pug on arrival. Cherry's daughter, the redoubtable Maggie with a background in food PR, runs the kitchen with a rod of iron, two miniature wire-haired Dachshunds in her wake. Granddaughter Rose is in charge of the gardens and the de rigueur rescue chickens.

The food is nothing special. Unless you like thick chunks of ham with a ginger marmalade glaze, perfectly fried eggs and your chips crisp on the outside and marshmallow fluffy on the inside. Or a pie with French-polished pastry, hiding chicken and leeks coated in a perfectly piquant mustardy cream. Or feather-light treacle sponge drenched in vanilla-flecked custard.

There's a dizzying array of craft beer on tap. And Melchior cider is like drinking liquid toffee apples and will make you do things you shouldn't with people you shouldn't. No wonder everyone seems to know each other in here. I met a television producer, the local rat-catcher, the vicar and his husband. It's *Cider with Rosie* meets Babington House. Or like being in an episode of *The Archers*.

As I stumbled out, the full moon was reflected in the black treacle of the river. An owl hooted. I was intoxicated, bewitched, enchanted. I'm not a jealous person. I have arguably the best job in the world. But I left feeling envious of my friends. The Three Swans is the pub we all want on our doorstep. I hope and pray it stays exactly as it is.

'Oh my God,' said Cherry. 'We couldn't have paid for a better review. But who is Adam Best? When did he come in? It must have been Saturday. That's when we had the ham on.'

'He said his friends had just bought a house in the village,' said Maggie. 'It must have been the Bannisters.'

Amanda Bannister, thought Cherry. Of course. The

Bannisters were just the sort of people to know a restaurant reviewer.

'This is going to be a turning point,' Cherry told them all. 'But well done everyone for getting us this. It's down to you all. I am so proud of our team.'

She opened the package that Lorraine had sent down with the papers. It was Catherine's planting plans. She'd asked Mike to put them in the post, the last time she had phoned him after the opening party.

'Why did you disappear like that?' she'd asked him, trying not to sound needy.

'I had an early start. You were really busy. I didn't want to distract you.' He stuck to the story in his text.

'You could have said goodbye.'

'Sorry,' he said, not sounding it.

'What did you think? Of the pub?'

'Amazing,' he said. 'But I knew it would be. How could it not be, with you lot behind it?'

She felt slightly mollified by that. Maybe he was just being considerate? It had been a whirlwind of a night. Now, she looked down at the planting plans and saw a scrap of paper attached. She turned it over, wondering if he might have sent a note of some sort. But it was a compliment slip from the university with his name printed on it. Her heart sank. When had their relationship plummeted to this? A bloody compliment slip? Even if he was trying to use them up before he left, that was a pretty damning indictment of the distance between them.

She ran her fingers over her mother's tiny writing, wishing yet again that Catherine was still here, that she could sit at the kitchen table with a cup of tea and share her troubles. She sighed. She'd take the planting plans up to Amanda. Thank her for the review, or at least get her to pass on their thanks to Adam Best.

'I'm going to pop these up to Wisteria House,' she said. 'Rose, can I tell Amanda you'll help with the garden?'

'Of course,' said Rose. 'I'd love to. Just ask them when they want me. Don't let them leave it too long at this time of year or it will run away with them.'

Once Cherry had left, Chloe hovered anxiously, plucking up the courage to speak to Maggie and Rose. How had she even thought for a moment that working here was going to pan out? She couldn't manage the stress, of hoping each day that things were going to be calm enough for her to get away and do the job she had come to love. Worse, she couldn't manage the tension of looking at the big oak door whenever she was at The Three Swans, wondering if Nicole was going to come in.

Nicole had done her best to reassure her when Chloe had a go at her for breaking her promise after the quiz.

'The kids have to learn to get on,' she insisted. 'They're old enough to look after themselves.'

This was true, though it didn't seem fair on Pearl, as Otis always managed to wind her up. Maybe she was being overcautious, thought Chloe, though she was only trying to protect her little sister. And Nicole had sworn to be back by ten.

'You promised me you wouldn't drink,' Chloe reminded her.

'But we won. It would have been rude for me not to have a glass.'

She'd had more than one, for sure, but there was no point in arguing.

On Sunday, Nicole had tried to win Chloe round. She'd started talking about Chloe's outfit for the prom, pulling up outfits online to show her. But Chloe had no interest in the prom. She'd moved on from school. And then Nicole had got upset.

'You're punishing me,' she complained.

'I'm not. I don't think I'm even going to the prom,' said Chloe.

'You have to go, darling. It'll be fun. You'll get to see all your friends. Come on, let's make you look like the superstar you are.'

Chloe had ended up sitting next to her mum and looking at endless photos of Hollywood actresses in reams of satin and lace. And it had actually been quite nice. Exactly the kind of relationship she longed for. Mother and daughter having some quality time together. Miraculously, they had got through the whole of Sunday drink-free and had settled on an outfit that Nicole promised to make for her. And Chloe knew she would look amazing. That Nicole would make her look like an A-lister, because that was what she was good at. Making things look better than they really were.

But Chloe couldn't take the strain of keeping up appearances any more. She would rather bow out now than have the job snatched away from her when she let them down again.

'Can I have a word?' she asked Maggie, who was sitting writing out menu plans ready to discuss with Winnie. Rose was sitting next to her, finishing a coffee, and looked up at Chloe, concerned. Chloe wanted Rose to be there too. She'd been so kind to her, the night they'd taken her mum home.

'Of course.'

Chloe took a seat at the table next to them. The review was still spread out. She'd been part of that. She had served that table on Saturday, when they came in for dinner the night after the quiz, and made sure their every need was tended to. She'd treated them like royalty, and they'd given her a twenty-pound tip, pushing it into the pocket of her apron, so she knew she'd done well. But she had still held her breath all evening, watching the door.

'I'm really sorry,' said Chloe. 'I don't think this job is working for me. I know I'm booked in for a few more shifts but I can't come in after today.' She looked down at the review, the words blurring through the beginning of tears. 'Sorry,' she said again.

Maggie frowned. 'I don't understand, Chloe. You're so good at what you do. And everyone loves you.' She tapped the review. 'This table made a point of telling me how great you were on Saturday when they left.'

Chloe shrugged. She couldn't find the words to explain, or a believable excuse, so she kept quiet, praying that Maggie would let it drop. There was silence for a moment.

'What can we do to keep you here?' said Maggie. 'I'd do anything. Whatever it takes.'

Chloe hung her head. 'I can't stay. I just can't.'

Maggie looked over at Rose, appealing for her help.

'Is this because of your mum, Chloe?' Rose asked,

putting a hand on her arm. 'Is this because things are difficult at home?'

She'd been asked this question so many times before. *How are things at home?* well-meaning teachers would ask, in that special sugar-coated voice. She'd always managed to reassure anyone in authority that everything was fine, and been super-careful for the next few weeks to be diligent, on time, not look too tired. Which was exhausting in itself.

And somehow Nicole always got it together. She would turn up at parents' evening in a chic trouser suit with a satin shirt, her hair sleek and shining, her make-up immaculate, proving to the school, to Dad, that she had got everything together. She would ask all the right questions, allaying everyone's fears.

Why couldn't she be that mother all the time? It was as if she was two people. Chloe had learned to dread watching Nicole slide from one to the other as soon as she reached for the bottle. There had to be an answer; a way to stop that happening.

Something told her to trust Maggie and Rose. Something told her they might be able to help her find a way out of this mess.

'I think,' she said, 'my mum's an alcoholic.'

She didn't think. She knew. She'd looked it up often enough. Analysed the behaviour and counted the bottles. Gone onto the support sites, raking them for advice and strategies. But she was always too scared to reach out. Instead, she kept quiet, and tried to be the mother her mum wasn't for Otis and Pearl, and tried to keep Nicole happy so she didn't drink so much.

'Oh darling,' said Maggie. 'That must be incredibly tough for you.'

'I'm worried she's going to lose her job with Dash,' said Chloe. 'And then she'll drink even more. And I'm worried...' Tears gathered in her throat, holding back the words. Now she'd starting telling them, she couldn't stop everything spilling out – words and tears all in a big jumble. 'Otis keeps getting into trouble at school. And Pearl's so anxious all the time, and she's obsessed with her hamster, and she can't ever bring friends home in case Mum's had a drink and I don't think I can do it all any more.'

She took in a deep breath to calm herself.

'Chloe, you shouldn't have to do it all. Look at me.' Rose leaned in and looked into her eyes. 'None of this is your fault or your responsibility.'

Chloe gulped and nodded. 'I know. But I'm scared.'

'There are support groups who can help you. I know it feels as if you are the only person in the world going through this, but you're not. And there's help out there. The most important thing is to make sure you do what you want to do with your life.'

'But I can't. Someone's got to look after Pearl and Otis.'

'If we can get you the support you need, things will get better. Otis and Pearl aren't babies. They can help too. I think you've been doing everything for so long everyone thinks that's normal. Including you. And it's not fair.'

Chloe couldn't look at either of them. She felt full of shame, and panic that she had in some way betrayed her mum. Now she'd spoken the words, they were out there, and she didn't feel in control any more. She'd opened Pandora's box. What if—

'Chloe. Look at me.' Rose's voice was firm but kind. 'I'm going to help you. And you can trust me.' She put a hand on her hand. 'I promise you can trust me.'

Chloe finally found the courage to look up. 'Thank you.'

'There's something else I want you think about.' It was Maggie talking now. Chloe looked wary. 'I'd love to take you on as an apprentice. There's a catering course at the college – the one that Winnie did. You'd split your time between college and working here, then hopefully stay on with us. We would get Winnie to mentor you. You are just the sort of person we want on our team, Chloe. I don't want to lose you.'

Chloe shut her eyes. She felt overwhelmed. It was too much to hope for, that her past and her future might be sorted out, just by being brave enough to talk to the right people. She was terrified too. This was a huge step. She told herself she couldn't carry on as things were. She couldn't keep covering for her mother and fighting for her own place in the world. She'd been about to walk away, but she'd taken the risk of trusting Maggie and Rose.

Chloe chewed her thumbnail, nerves churning her stomach. She could close down now and back away from this job and carry on just as she always had. But enough was enough.

'I'd like that,' she said. 'I'd like that very much.'

48

Cherry hovered on the doorstep of Wisteria House, staring at the door knocker in the shape of a lion's head that her father's patients had used so many times. It was odd, to have to knock on the door of the house that had been her home for nearly seventy years. To not just push it open and run up the stairs to her bedroom. She lifted her hand and tapped just loud enough to be sure that if anyone was home, they could hear.

Amanda opened the door, and her face lit up when she saw who it was. She was in camouflage jogging bottoms and a sweatshirt, her feet bare, her hair tied back in a scrunchie and no make-up. But she didn't seem bothered.

'Cherry!' She stepped back to let her past. 'Come in. Come in. I've just made a cup of coffee. Oh God, don't look at anything. We're still in a total pickle – we had friends for the weekend and they've only just gone.'

'That's partly why I've come.' Cherry stepped into the hall. It smelled different. Of Jo Malone – there was a huge three-wick candle on a console table, burning away. And there were boxes everywhere. Shoes and clothes spilled out of them. Amanda could see Cherry taking in the chaos.

'God, don't look. Half of this is on its way upstairs. But we've had such fun since we got here, we haven't got down to unpacking. Honestly, we are like kids in a sweetshop. We should have moved out of London ages ago. But you have to wait for the right time, don't you? Come into the kitchen.'

Cherry followed her down the hall. The kitchen looked as if a bomb had hit it. More boxes half unpacked. A ravaged cheeseboard and rafts of empty wine glasses. Breakfast things piled up in the sink. What looked like the remains of a roast were in a tray on top of the Aga. And countless bottles.

'Don't think less of me,' said Amanda. 'We were up till four. Theo's going to clear it up when he gets back from running the others to the station.'

Cherry laughed. 'I'm not going to judge. But I've come to say thank you. For the amazing review. I'm guessing you were behind it.'

Amanda nodded.

'I didn't say anything to you at the quiz. Just in case. Adam is very hard to please. But everything he wrote was from the heart. You've done something special, Cherry. Sit down, sit down.'

She whisked away a basket of croissants and two dirty plates.

'Well, we can't thank you enough.'

Amanda sat down opposite her.

'Do you know, it's the least I can do. I can never repay what your parents did for me. Especially your mum. She knew exactly what we needed, especially us girls.' Amanda gulped. 'You have no idea how she changed our lives. She made us cakes. She taught us how to knit. She plaited our hair. She made us tidy our rooms and take care of ourselves. I mean, Dad was amazing but he only remembered to make us have a bath about once a week. He didn't neglect us. It was just impossible for him to do it all and put food on the table. Your mum had the time.'

'I suppose, as the doctor's wife, that was her role. To help where she could.'

'She went above and beyond. It was your mum who made sure I got to grammar school. She made me come here every week. She coached me to get through my eleven-plus. Dad didn't have the time. It didn't even occur to him that I might have it in me.' There were tears glittering in her eyes as she pointed out the window to the garden. 'She'd sit me out there and go through everything. It was there that I learned I could do anything I wanted. That I could be anything I wanted. That's why I bought this house when I saw it come on the market. I would never have dreamt I could live in a house like this, when I was little. But here I am. And it's all thanks to your mother.'

'I never knew that,' said Cherry. 'I knew she helped people. But I never knew what a difference she made.'

'I worshipped her,' said Amanda.

'Me too,' said Cherry, and suddenly it was all too much. Sitting in this kitchen, without her mum pottering about, filling the teapot. The pressure of getting the pub up and running. The strain of her relationship with Mike – not being sure what he was thinking, or what their future was. Suddenly she found herself dissolving into tears.

'Oh God,' said Amanda. 'I didn't mean to upset you. I didn't think. I know it hasn't been long. Shit, I'm so tactless. Theo's always telling me—'

'It's not that,' said Cherry, trying to wipe away her tears. 'It's lovely to hear what she did for you.'

'Then what is it?'

'It's Mike.' She took a piece of kitchen towel Amanda was handing her. 'I should never have bought the pub. I did it on impulse. It seemed like such a good idea. But it's put our relationship under a lot of strain. I'm not sure it's going to survive.'

As soon as she said the words, she realised that was her fear. That Mike was drifting away, and she might never get him back.

'Now listen.' Amanda sat back down and looked at her sternly. 'What the three of you have done is incredible. That review proves it. And if Mike can't handle it, he's not the man I thought he was. And just for the record, he didn't take his eyes off you all evening at the opening. He still adores you. Trust me.'

'Oh,' Cherry gulped. She felt foolish, breaking down in front of this woman she barely knew, even though they went back more than fifty years. But something in Amanda's spirit spoke to her. She had an indomitable feistiness, mixed with a warmth and a wonderful sense of humour, which made Cherry trust her judgement. And hearing about the influence her mother had upon her made her feel even more connected. She had a feeling Amanda was going to become a close friend. Life was strange, she thought, thinking back to the little bespectacled girl hanging over the fence.

'You just need to talk to him,' said Amanda. 'Lay all the cards on the table. Reassure him you still love him. There is room, you know, to do something you're passionate about and keep your relationship alive. It takes a bit of practice to get the balance right sometimes.' She grinned. 'Theo's trying to make me step back a bit so I can enjoy life here, and I'm gradually coming round to the idea. I'm going to do more work behind the scenes rather than on set. I know once I've made the break, I'll get used to it.' She plunged the cafetière. 'You need to talk to him and find a way to make it work.'

'You're right,' said Cherry. 'I've lived and breathed the pub over the past few weeks and haven't given him any attention. Not that he's needy. Not at all. But I guess I've always been there.'

'Split the difference,' said Amanda, passing her a coffee cup. 'Or find a way of getting him involved.'

Cherry couldn't help laughing. 'I've kind of left it a bit late,' she said. 'To try and get my work/life balance right. I've never had a proper career before. I'm nearly seventy.'

'You're kidding?' said Amanda. 'Yeah, I guess you are. I'm knocking on the door of sixty. But I don't think age matters these days. You can do whatever you want, whenever you want.'

'Hmm,' said Cherry. 'But you can't, though. Not if there's someone else involved.'

'You can,' said Amanda, unrepentant, and Cherry smiled at her determination. Catherine would agree with Amanda, she thought, thinking back to her mother in this very kitchen, urging her to do something for herself.

Which she had. But now it was time to go back to Avonminster and talk to Mike. Claim back the heart of the man she loved. She hoped it wasn't too late.

49

Admiral House felt reproachful as soon as Cherry walked in. *I miss you*, it seemed to say. *I miss the noise, and the laughter, and clack of Maggie's high heels, and the thump of Gertie's Converse, and the scuttle of Fred and Ginger's nails.*

The house had never known quiet, really. But now there was an eerie silence. And there was no sign of Mike. She'd wanted to surprise him. She'd brought lunch for them to have on the balcony, for much as she loved the pastoral beauty of Rushbrook, she'd missed that view, that sweeping gorge and the bridge across it.

He wasn't anywhere to be seen. He wasn't in his study or the kitchen. She ran up the stairs to the drawing room and gasped. He had taken it over completely. All the furniture was pushed back and there were canvasses everywhere. Huge canvasses covered in splashes of red paint, crimson and scarlet and burgundy, which at first seemed abstract. But when you stood exactly the right distance away, it become clear they were human hearts, the anatomy apparent amidst the chaos of the swirls, and in the centre of each one, a silver dagger. They were strangely beautiful, the paint thick and layered up. Cherry felt afraid for a moment. These were angry paintings. She could feel the fury radiating off them. The emotion that had driven him. Yet they were brilliant too. Raw and energetic, but technically impeccable. Every brushstroke, every dot of paint, had a purpose.

She checked her watch. Half eleven. He could have popped out anywhere. He'd probably be back by lunchtime.

The doorbell drilled through the air, and Cherry jumped. She ran down the stairs to the front door. Outside was a young man in a grey suit, clutching an iPad and a sheaf of glossy brochures.

'Yes?' smiled Cherry, wondering if he had got the wrong house.

'Eamonn Cross? I'm here to do a valuation. This is Admiral House, right?' He stepped back to check the slate sign to the right of the door.

'Yes, but . . . I don't think we've booked a valuation?'

'It must have been your husband I spoke to. Hang on.' He rummaged in his iPad to try and find the name.

'OK,' said Cherry. 'Well, he's not here, so I guess he's not expecting you.'

But just as she spoke, she saw Mike hurrying along the street. He arrived a little out of breath.

'Sorry to keep you waiting. I couldn't get a parking spot. Literally the only downside of living round here.' He looked at Cherry, flustered. 'I didn't know you were coming.'

'No,' said Cherry. 'What's going on?'

Mike looked like a small boy who had been caught doing something he shouldn't.

'I thought it would be useful to have the house valued,' said Mike. 'There's no commitment.'

'No commitment at all,' said Eamonn cheerfully. 'It's always good to know what you're sitting on. In case you want to release some equity or downsize.'

Eamonn was looking between them, hoping he wasn't going to lose the valuation. This wasn't the first time he'd been asked to do one behind someone's back. It was an occupational hazard.

Cherry took in a deep breath. There was no point in protesting. 'Why don't we let Eamonn have a wander round and see what he thinks? While we have a chat?'

'Absolutely,' said Mike, relieved as he held out an arm to show Eamonn the way in.

A couple of minutes later, Cherry and Mike faced each other in the kitchen either side of the island. Unlike Wisteria House, nothing in here had changed. Cherry felt as if she had only stepped out five minutes ago.

'What are you doing?' asked Cherry. 'You can't put the house on the market without asking me.'

'Of course not. I wouldn't do that,' said Mike. 'But I wanted to know what it's worth before I figured out what to do next.'

'Next?'

'This isn't a home without you in it. I've been rattling around here while you've been down in Rushbrook.'

'It's not for ever!'

'How do I know that? You haven't involved me in any of the decision-making.' He shot her an accusatory glance. 'You just came home one day and presented me with a fait accompli.'

'I know. And I'm sorry. It was an impulse purchase,

but it turned it to be a great decision.' She went to take the review out of her bag to show him. 'Look. A fantastic review in today's paper. Six paragraphs.'

Mike picked up the cutting. She saw his face soften as he read it.

'That's wonderful. I don't wish you anything but success.' He put the cutting down on the island. 'But I need to get on with my life. It's obvious that your plans have changed. That it's not going to be about us any more.'

'That's exactly why I came here today. To talk about it.' She corrected herself. 'Us.'

'It's too late, Cherry.'

'What?' Panic clawed at her. 'What do you mean?'

Was it Anneka? Was he heading off to LA for a season in the sun?

'I feel lost.' Mike held his hands up. 'Retiring is a big ordeal for me. I'm scared. I've worked nearly every day for fifty years and it's all about to come to an end. Until the party, I was excited. I was excited about us being together and making a new life. We've always been a team, and I knew with you behind me I could reinvent myself and we'd create something amazing. But it turns out that wasn't what you wanted. You waltzed off to Somerset with everyone I love, leaving me all on my own to figure out what to do with myself.'

'Hold on—'

'No. Let me finish. I came to that opening night and I felt invisible. I had nothing to do with it. It was you and Maggie and Rose – even Gertie had more to do with it than me. You cut me out. Maybe because of a moment of indiscretion after too many glasses—'

'We've talked about that.'

'Yes, but I still feel as if that was the reason for you doing what you did.'

Cherry could see that he was on the verge of tears. She had never seen him cry, except the night before Frank's funeral. Mike was giving the eulogy, and he'd broken down while trying to rehearse it. He had said it was better to get it out of his system. He had read the eulogy perfectly on the day.

'Mike. I'm so sorry—'

'I'm going to Berlin.' He looked at her, trembling but defiant. 'I'm meeting somebody about an exhibition. And I'm going to try it out for size. See if it's somewhere I'd like to live. Maybe start looking for an apartment to buy. If we do end up selling.'

Cherry tried to think. They hardly ever argued, so she didn't know how to handle this outpouring of emotion. Besides, everything she thought of saying made her sound like a hypocrite. She couldn't tell him not to be rash and impulsive, because that's what she had been when she bought The Swan. She couldn't tell him they should talk it over first because she hadn't allowed him that privilege. He was right. She had cut him out.

'Let's go for lunch,' she said. 'There's room for us both to do what we want, and to be together.'

'It's too late, Cherry.' Mike repeated, this time looking at his watch. 'My flight's at four.'

Did he mean too late for lunch? Or too late full stop?

There was a cough in the doorway. Eamonn was standing there. He held up his iPad and gave them an enthusiastic smile.

'I've got a rough idea of price,' he said. 'If you'd like to have a chat.'

Cherry picked up her bag. The only thing to do was be dignified and call his bluff by giving Mike his head. Let him go to Berlin. A change of scene might help him put things into perspective. She could see there was no point in trying to talk him now.

'Your paintings,' she said. 'They're amazing. Are those the ones for the exhibition?'

He stared at her.

'Yes.' He gave a twisted smile. 'I thought I'd call it "Stabbed Through the Heart".'

She winced. Even if it wasn't true, she'd asked for that.

'I'm going to go,' she said, calm but not cold. 'I can see you're upset, and I can see why. Let's talk when you get back from Berlin.' She smiled at Eamonn. 'By the way, I know exactly what this is worth. I know what I paid for it and I know what I spent on it. So don't try and reel us in by overvaluing.'

And she walked out of the kitchen.

In the hallway, she paused for a moment, leaning against the wall. Her knees were shaking. She looked around at her pride and joy – it looked as fresh as the day it had been finished. This was her house. Their house. Their *home*. Had she jeopardised this, and Mike, for the sake of the review in her handbag?

50

Nothing had changed, thought Rose. Of course it hadn't. She hadn't been away that long.

When Cherry had told her she was driving up to Avonminster for the day to see Mike, Rose had jumped at the chance of a lift. As she walked into the Soul Bowl, she felt the sweet rush of familiarity at the brightly coloured walls with the mural of Avonminster; the sound of reggae bouncing out of the speakers; the clusters of people standing around chatting. As always there was a mix of old and new faces already sitting at the trestle tables, playing chess, puzzling over the crossword, drinking tea.

Through the hatch she could see Shona in the kitchen, and smiled as she remembered Aaron complaining about her food. He'd just been trying to flatter Rose. Whatever Shona was cooking smelled delicious; the scent of onions and spices drifted towards her, making her mouth water.

Across the room, Aaron caught sight of her and his face lit up with delight. He bounded over and gave her a huge hug, pulling her tight into his chest. He didn't know his own strength, she thought.

'Let go,' she laughed. 'I can hardly breathe.'

'Tell me you're coming back,' he said.

'I'm just here to visit,' she said. 'I've missed you all.'

'Well, that's good timing. Because I've got something to show you.' He looked gleeful, bouncing up and down with unsuppressed energy.

'What is it?'

'Come with me.'

She followed him outside, intrigued, as he led her around the side of the warehouse to the garden. There, with his top off, looking as fit as a fiddle, was Gaz, digging out one of the raised beds.

'I thought Gaz was just the man for the job. Turns out he's got quite green fingers.'

He raised a hand to wave at Gaz, who dropped his spade and came running over. He slowed up as he came nearer, looking a little sheepish.

'Bloody hell,' he said to Rose. 'Last time you saw me I must have been steaming. I owe you one.'

He was jocular on the surface, but underneath, the seriousness of what had happened that night lingered. He paused, not sure what to say. What did you say to someone who had got to you just in the nick of time?

'It's really good to see you,' said Rose. 'You look all right.'

He grinned, wiping his hands on his cargo shorts. He looked a different person from the comatose figure lying on the bed that evening. He'd filled out, and caught the sun, and the sweat on his face was from hard toil, not the effort of not drinking.

'I tell you what,' said Gaz. 'Whatever you said to Shell that night worked magic.'

'Really?' Rose hadn't been able to recall her conversation with Shell without feeling anxious.

'We're not back together,' Gaz added hastily. 'It's a bit late for that. But she lets me see the little one whenever I want. And as long as I can do that, it's all gravy.'

Rose felt overwhelmed with relief. 'I'm really pleased.'

'I'm going to my meetings as well. Three times a week.' Gaz grinned proudly. 'And that little unicorn. Skye carries it with her everywhere. Whenever I have a wobble I think about it, and remember what I nearly lost.' He laughed at himself. 'Bit daft, I know.'

'Whatever works,' said Rose, who could barely breathe for wanting to cry.

'I better get on. We've got a load of manure arriving later.' Gaz nodded his head towards Aaron. 'He gives me all the best jobs. Shovelling shit.'

Aaron raised his fist towards him in a gesture of solidarity. 'I'm looking out for you, buddy.'

'I can't believe it,' said Rose, watching Gaz head back over to the raised beds and get back to work. 'He looks a different person.'

'He's in a much better place. And I've told him to call me if he's ever having a bad time.'

Rose looked at Aaron, wondering if she could ever be a tenth as good as he was. How did he do it, be so smart and cool and nice? So many successful people didn't have room for anyone else, but Aaron seemed to have space in his heart for everyone.

'I want to talk to you about something,' she said as they fell into step, heading back to the Soul Bowl. They reached the wooden table and bench outside. Aaron sat down, and Rose sat opposite him. 'I want your advice.'

'Sure.'

'I've had this idea,' she said. 'Gertie's going to school in September, so I need to figure out what I want to do with my life. The thing is, I love gardening. Growing stuff. Being outside with the elements. But I love people too. Helping them. Making a difference.'

Aaron nodded. 'You have incredible empathy, Rose. And you don't judge.'

Rose shrugged off his compliment. She didn't like praise all that much. 'Anyway, I couldn't choose between them.' She held up her hands, as if to weigh the difference. 'Plants and people. They're both rewarding in their own way. And then I thought – why couldn't I combine them?'

Aaron looked puzzled. 'How?'

'There's this thing called horticultural therapy. Using gardening to help people's mental health.'

'Oh. Yeah. I guess it makes sense.' Aaron nodded over to Gaz. 'Case in point.'

'Exactly. It's perfect for addicts in recovery. Or people with depression. It's got so many benefits. It gets people out into the fresh air. Gives them a purpose. So I thought I'd train. To become a horticultural therapist.'

Rose looked at him expectantly. She wasn't sure what answer she wanted from Aaron, but she needed to look at the idea from all angles. She trusted his judgement more than anyone else. She knew Maggie and Cherry would support her in whatever she decided to do because their support was unconditional. But Aaron would give her an objective opinion.

'It sounds like the perfect career for you.' Aaron nodded his approval. 'I mean, you've got the ideal name for a start.'

She laughed. 'I'm going to do a horticultural course at the college first. Then I can charge proper money to do people's gardens. I do need something to live on.'

'Sounds like a plan.'

'Then I need to get some counselling skills. I can do that part time at college while I work. It's going to take a while, but I guess anything worthwhile does take time. I'm a bit behind everyone else, but I think I can catch up.'

She looked at him. Aaron put his head on one side, smiling.

'I guess that doesn't leave you any time to come back here?'

She sighed. She looked around her. Helping out here had given her the germ of the idea. What had happened with Gaz had cemented it. It had given her the courage to reach out to Chloe too, even though at times she had doubted herself. She was learning to trust her instincts, and to encourage people to trust her too. Now she was trying to find a way to harness it all. It was a puzzle, and of course all the pieces didn't quite fit.

'I don't know how I can. College and work and Gertie and The Three Swans...'

'I would pay you, to spend a day a week here. It would be good experience.'

He was gazing at her, more intently than he ever had before. She remembered the night of the opening – he had looked at her like that then. She couldn't be sure what he was thinking. She wondered for a moment if...

No. Of course not. He was way too cool for her. What would he see in her?

He put his hand over hers.

'You know how much I think of you, don't you?'

She stared back at him. Their fingers entwined. For a moment, the world stood still under the heat of the sun. She felt giddy and confused. This wasn't what she'd expected. What did he mean? She didn't want to make a fool of herself by misinterpreting his words and assuming something when he was simply being kind.

'Rose,' he said, leaning forward. 'I need you. I need you in my life.'

The heat shimmered on the tarmac. Music floated out from the door of the Soul Bowl. She could smell his cologne. Citrus. Salt. She imagined her skin on his. She looked at their hands. His strong fingers wrapped in her little paw.

His overture rocked her. How easy it would be, she thought, to be pulled into his world. An exciting world, certainly, of success and money and status and a certain glamour, as well as the philanthropy that made him such a wonderful person, and one she could be a valid part of, for they agreed on so many things.

But the time wasn't right. Not yet. She was starting to build a world that she was at the centre of, that she was in control of, that had her future at the heart of it. A life that was the best it could be for her and Gertie. Being with Aaron might put that off kilter. And although she thought the world of him, being with him dazzled her a little. She had to get the balance right first.

But she didn't want to lose him.

'I don't think I'm ready,' she said. 'Not yet. Can you wait?'

He squeezed her hand, not answering for a moment.

'Of course,' he said eventually. 'I'm not going any-where.'

'I need to sort my life out. I want to be the right person. For you,' she said.

'You've always been the right person for me,' he smiled. 'But I get it. You need to be the right person for *you*.'

Of course that's what she meant. And of course he understood.

Behind Aaron, she saw Cherry's car draw up.

'I have to go. My grandmother's here,' she said, but she didn't move. He ran his thumb over her wrist and she wondered if he could feel her pulse. It would be too easy to just fall into his arms and take everything he had to offer. She'd spent enough time relying on other people. She had to make sure her future was solid, and that she could stand on her own two feet.

'That night in the garden, I wanted to kiss you so much,' he said.

She laughed, remembering how much she had wanted to kiss him too, but had panicked. 'It was Midsummer's Eve,' she told him. 'Do you know the poem?'

'No,' he said. And she told him.

> *'Rose leaves, rose leaves*
> *Rose leaves I strew*
> *He that will love me*
> *Come after me now.'*

He smiled. 'Don't make me wait too long,' was all he said.

When they got home, Rose fetched Gertie from Dandelions and they went down to see how the chickens were getting on. They were so much bolder and braver than they had been when they first arrived, striding out confidently, basking in the sun. Their feathers were already starting to grow back, covering over the bald patches of pink on their poor little bodies. Rose helped Gertie scatter some chick crumbs for them, then went to see if there were any eggs.

She felt at peace here, in the sun, the soothing sound of the hens singing away to each other, Gertie chuntering away to them. As she sat there, watching her girls venture further from the coop, stretching themselves out, interacting with each other where once they had been wary, kicking up the dirt, she thought about what had happened that afternoon. It was thrilling, and overwhelming, but at the same time she reflected on how Aaron made her feel safe, for she trusted and respected him more than anyone, apart from her own family. He would be good for her.

As soon as she was ready. She had a lot to organise, a lot to arrange, but knowing Aaron might be part of her future gave her the courage to take the next step.

51

'Oh. My. God.' Maggie heard the bike before she saw it. She was standing in front of the pub, a trifle self-conscious, wondering if she had chosen the right outfit: old faded Levis, chunky suede boots and a baggy Rolling Stones sweatshirt, her hair tied in a plait at the side. Practical, certainly, for a motorbike ride and a picnic on the moors. Did she look like a rock chick, or did she look like mutton?

It didn't matter, she reminded herself. This wasn't a real date, just a charade, a bit of fun for two people who weren't ready for anything more serious. Nevertheless, she felt a thrill go through her as Russell roared into the car park and came to a halt in front of her. The bike seemed huge: a sculptural tangle of silver, black and red metal. He swung his leg over the saddle and got off, removing his helmet and shaking out his shaggy hair, loping over in his leathers.

'Hey,' he grinned. 'All set to jet?'

'I think so,' said Maggie, feeling a tiny bit of doubt creep in. This was real. She was going on the back of a motorbike. A big one.

He opened his pannier and handed her a helmet and a leather jacket. 'Stick those on,' he said. 'And let's go.'

She fumbled with all the fastenings, trying to put them on, her stomach churning, wondering if it was too late to back out. The bike looked much bigger than she had imagined, a huge silver exhaust to one side.

'What is it?' she asked politely.

'Ducati 900SS,' he told her, but he could have said anything, as it meant nothing.

'It's gorgeous,' she said, not sure what the right adjective was to use, and thinking that liking its colour probably wasn't a cool thing to mention.

He just nodded. 'Ready? Hop on behind me and just hold on. Try and relax and go with me. When I bend, bend with me. It's all about balance.'

Shit, thought Maggie. She was going to be like a sack of potatoes on the back. This was going to be totally humiliating.

'OK,' she managed to squeak, her mouth dry.

'Don't worry. You'll get the hang of it. Just tap me on the shoulder if you want to stop.' He gave her a grin. 'Right, let's give the village something to talk about.'

He climbed back on, and Maggie got on behind him, feeing rather inelegant. She found it disconcerting being so close to his leather-clad solidity, but she could hardly inch away. She rested her hands tentatively on his waist.

And then suddenly the bike roared into life and they were off, gliding across the car park and onto the main road through the village. It was faster than she could have imagined – or at least it felt like it; he wouldn't be going over the speed limit, after all. She reminded herself he'd been a traffic cop. If she was going to go for her first motorbike ride with anyone, he was the best choice, but she was so terrified, so tense, she couldn't see if anyone saw them as they roared through Rushbrook.

The tarmac beneath rushed past them. She wanted to shut her eyes, but that would be worse. They went over the bridge on the outside of the village, and she thought her stomach had been left behind. They reached a bend in the road and he leaned over to take it and she tried to go with him, hoping and praying she wasn't going to upset the balance, even though it was counterintuitive to lean over.

There was a straight road in front of them and he went up a gear. She didn't think she could take the stress of the acceleration, the speed, the horrible sense of being completely out of control. One false move and it would be all over. Just touch him on the shoulder, she told herself, and it will stop. You will be safe.

But she didn't want to chicken out. They were heading out towards the moors now, following the river as it hugged the side of the road. She started to relax a tiny bit. Started to second guess when he was going to lean to one side or another. The tightness in her throat started to ease and the panic subsided. She actually started to breathe. Fields, trees and hedgerows flew past. Houses loomed up then disappeared behind them. They travelled on and she eased her grip, relaxed the tension in her legs. On and on they drove, eating up the miles, the sun in front of them, urging them onwards.

Eventually they passed over a cattle grid and the wilds of Exmoor lay in front of them, acres of undulating ground smothered in gorse and heather which seemed to spread out to infinity. There seemed to be no one else for miles, nothing but the swallows swooping overhead. For a moment, Maggie imagined she was the wild and passionate Lorna Doone, riding across her family's ancient land to escape her arranged marriage. Her grandmother Catherine had given her the book when she was young, and she had read it over and over in the spare room at Wisteria House when she went to stay.

And now Russell was taking a tiny road off the main track, riding down towards a stone bridge stretched across a shallow river. He pulled into the side and stopped, taking off his helmet.

'Here we are,' he said. 'The perfect picnic spot.'

Maggie jumped off the bike. Her legs felt a bit wobbly from the tension, but she felt giddy with relief, and exhilarated by the isolated beauty of the spot.

'Is this still the Rushbrook?'

'It is. We've just followed the river over the moors. You could walk back home along it, if you wanted. Come on.'

She followed him down to the grass by the edge of the river. The water was shallow, burbling happily over the flat stones. Dragonflies hovered and darted in front of their eyes. She breathed in the air, sharp with the scent of gorse and the earthy drift of pony. They sat down, and Russell pulled refreshments out of his pannier: a giant sausage roll each, and a bottle of apple juice which he poured into tin mugs. A simple picnic, but every bite and every sip was delicious, perhaps because she was grateful to have survived the journey.

'I don't think I've ever been here, even though I spent most of every summer in Rushbrook with my grand-parents,' Maggie admitted. 'It's glorious.'

'This is where I come when I want to be alone,' Russell told her. 'When I want to think. You know.'

'I do know,' said Maggie. 'Though I actually hate being on my own. I crave people. Being on my own makes me panic.'

'It's people who make me panic. Most people,' he added, looking at her, and she blushed, not sure what he meant. 'I had enough of them in the police. It was part of the job, you know, to work out how people tick. And I saw a lot of things I didn't like. I had to get out before I lost all faith in human nature. Divorce didn't help, on top of it all. My daughter says I've become a miserable bugger.'

'Oh,' she said. 'I found the opposite. People were amazing to me after Frank died. I couldn't believe how kind they were.'

'Well,' he said. 'Maybe you can help me restore my faith.'

They locked eyes, and she was hypnotised. She couldn't deny how drawn to him she felt. He was strong, still, a slab of sturdy Yorkshire stone. But there was vulnerability there too, in his confession. He had been hurt.

Suddenly his eyes lit up and he nodded behind her.

'We've got visitors,' he laughed, and she turned to see a pair of Exmoor ponies staring at them from a few feet away. It broke the tension, eased her inability to know what to say.

When he'd finished eating, he folded his leather jacket up for a pillow and lay back with his arms behind his head. He had on a black t-shirt, and she could see the chiselled curve of his biceps. She was overwhelmed with an urge to lie down next to him, to rest her head on his chest so she could feel his heartbeat through the thinness of his t-shirt. But instead she lay down at a respectable distance, feeling the heat through the dry, springy grass underneath her.

They lay there for a while, staring up at the sky, the clouds drifting gently above, the sound of the river dancing past.

'This is heaven,' he said, making her jump. 'It's nice to get away from the pigs. Not that I don't adore every single hair on their chinny chin chins.'

'So why pigs, anyway?' She was intrigued to know more about his story.

'Pigs are great. I've always loved them. I lived near a pig farm when I was a kid and helped out in the holidays. So I already knew my stuff. And it was always my dream, to have a little smallholding when I left the police.'

'So it's a dream come true?'

'I guess so. Life's got a nice rhythm to it. Pigs let you be yourself. I love looking after them. It's the selling bit I hate. But I have to make money, otherwise there's no point. I find it hard, though. Being pushy.'

'I can help you with that.'

'What?'

'It's what I do. Well, what I did. Marketing. Sales targets. Distribution.'

'Oh.' He sounded pleasantly surprised. 'Well, if you can give me some sort of kick up the arse. My daughter's always going on at me to be more business-like.'

'The big mistake is ticking over without any strategy.'

He laughed. 'That's exactly what I'm doing. I haven't got a clue.'

'I'll lick you into shape.'

'I'll look forward to that.'

His voice sounded sleepy, and she wasn't sure if the teasing note in his voice was innuendo. The sun was beating down on her, but it was a heat from inside that was making her bones melt. She turned her gaze to look sideways at him. His eyes were tight shut. She could see the rise and fall of his chest and felt a sudden, visceral longing.

'Are you thinking what I'm thinking?' His voice made her jump.

'Um, I don't know.' Probably not.

'We ought to head back soon. Those pigs will be ravenous.'

She didn't want to go. Ever.

'I'm ready when you are.'

She sat up and grabbed a bottle of water, slaking her thirst, and he stood up and shrugged on his jacket, blocking the sun. She could see his bare stomach as he lifted his arms. She looked down at the ground, thinking she might have to throw herself in the river or she would spontaneously combust. She gathered up the remains of the food and tidied it away.

'Well, it's been lovely,' she said, thinking how prim she sounded.

'Aye,' he said, putting everything back in the pannier.

The sun seemed to slip in the sky, turning it to a deeper petrol blue. A small pony standing nearby gave a dismissive toss of its head, as if in solidarity with her, as if to say, 'You win some, you lose some.' Maggie tried to swallow down a sense of disappointment, telling herself that there had been no expectations, that the deal had always been no strings, no benefits.

As she climbed on the bike behind Russell, the leather of his jacket scorched her, even though she tried to keep a sedate distance. She longed to lean right in and mould herself to his back. As the bike roared away, leaving a trail of dust on the moor, the audience of ponies scattered and Maggie clung on to his waist, concentrating on trying to stay alive.

Russell's bike swooshed over the pale gravel in front of The Three Swans and came to a standstill. Maggie felt a little self-conscious as she slid off the seat behind him. It was nearly six and before long the bar would be coming to life as people dropped in for a riverside aperitif or an after-work sharpener, but luckily there was no one there yet to see her rather inelegant scramble. She shimmied out of the jacket and helmet Russell had lent her, conscious that she was looking less than her best as she shovelled them back into his pannier. When she went to thank him, he was holding his helmet under his arm, his legs astride the bike, his hair perfectly tousled, looking infuriatingly cool and collected.

'Thank you,' she said, 'for a lovely afternoon.'

He didn't reply. He just looked at her. Then the side of his mouth lifted into a teasing smile. And she saw his eyes glimmer, as if someone had tipped a tube of sparkly glitter into them. She took in a sharp breath. She could feel electricity shoot along their eyeline, backwards and forwards, drawing her towards him.

For crying out loud, just kiss him, a voice in her head said. He wasn't looking at her as if he was dying to get away. He'd be long gone if he wasn't waiting for her to do something. She remembered that protective barrier that widowhood put around her. The one that even Mario respected. She had to make the first move.

Just as she found her nerve, and moved forwards to kiss him, Chloe came round the corner, ready to start her shift. Maggie stepped backwards, awkward, laughing nervously. She couldn't be seen *in flagrante* in the pub car park by her youngest member of staff. It was totally inappropriate.

'I'll see you soon, then,' she said instead.

'Yes,' he said. 'Very soon, I hope.'

And he gave her a wry grin and a little shrug, as if acknowledging that if it wasn't for Chloe, things might have taken a different direction. She smiled back as he slid on his helmet and started the engine. It roared through her. She watched him drive away, her heartbeat gradually lowering, slightly dazed, utterly bewitched and feeling more alive than she had done for a very long time.

Maggie headed back into the pub on trembling legs. Inside, she saw Cherry sitting at a table, her head in her hands. Her pace quickened as she walked towards her mother, filled with alarm.

'Mum?'

Cherry looked up, her face drawn, her eyes filled with anguish.

'I can't do this any more,' she said. 'I've made a terrible mistake.'

'What?' Maggie sat down next to her and took her hands. 'What is it, Mum? What's happened?'

'It's your dad,' said Cherry. 'I've been so selfish. I didn't think about him at all in any of this, and . . . I think I've lost him, Maggie.'

'Don't be ridiculous. He's Dad. He adores you.' Maggie couldn't imagine any scenario where Mike would turn his back on Cherry.

'I've pushed him too far.' Tears sprang into Cherry's eyes. 'He's had enough.'

'Have you had a row?' Her parents never rowed, thought Maggie. And Cherry never cried.

'Not a row exactly. But he's thinking about putting Admiral House on the market. Doing his own thing. He's gone to Berlin.'

'For good?' Maggie looked appalled.

'To see someone about an exhibition. But maybe for good. I don't know. But I need to do something.' Cherry looked around the pub. 'This has been amazing but it's not worth losing Dad for. I belong with him. He's right – I left him out in the cold. I got carried away with this... crazy impulse purchase and forgot what really matters. Us. Me and him.'

'You can talk about it. You still love each other.'

'Of course we do. But I don't think there's room for me and Dad and the pub in our lives. I'm going to have to sell. Not straight away – I want a few months' profit first to get the best price—'

'Wait,' said Maggie. 'You're doing it again. You're moving too fast.'

'I'm terrified of losing him.'

'You won't. I know you won't.'

'But this is all-consuming. And I need to be with him.'

'So let me take over.' Maggie was calm. 'I was already thinking that you wouldn't want to be here indefinitely. And that the logical thing would be for me to buy you out. So why don't I do that sooner rather than later?'

Cherry blinked in surprise.

'How?'

Maggie's eyes flashed with determination. 'I might not be able to buy it outright. But if we could come to some arrangement... maybe if you kept a share... I've got the money from selling Tine. And I could sell the house in Avonminster. There's no mortgage on it. It's gone up in value a lot since we bought it.'

'But it's your home. And Rose's home. And Frank's...'

'I'd have to talk to Rose, of course. But it's just four walls. I can't cling on to it for ever. If I use it to build a new life for us, then that's good, isn't it? We can take Frank's spirit with us.'

Cherry didn't speak for a moment. She looked down at the table, thinking it all over, crunching the numbers, analysing the implications and practicalities, all the time trying to push down her panic. She could not lose Mike. She could not lose the man she had spent nearly all of her life with. But she couldn't snatch away her daughter's future for the sake of her own. Or, indeed, Rose's. Rose and Gertie had woven themselves into the fabric of Rushbrook.

Could Maggie's suggestion be the solution? Cherry could remain a sleeping partner. Keep a share. Still be involved, but not responsible or tied to the day-to-day running. She could free herself up so she could live the life she and Mike had imagined for themselves: enjoying a sense of adventure and new beginnings.

'Mum,' Maggie said. 'I feel as if this is the right place for me. I've loved putting a team together and making it work. Winnie and Chloe and the others. I'm not letting all that go. And I love being back in Rushbrook. It's like home for us. I can build my future here. It makes me feel . . . happy. Content. I never thought I'd feel that again.'

Maggie didn't mention what had just happened outside with Russell. That was the icing on the cake – the promise of romance and fun and fizz with someone new. Her tummy flipped at the thought.

Cherry was smiling through the remnants of her tears. 'If that's what you want, we'll find a way to make it work. For all of us.'

'I'll speak to Rose. Her security, and Gertie's, is the most important. But she seems much happier here too.'

Cherry nodded. Her panic and anguish had subsided a little. She could see a clearer picture. But there was still something worrying at her. Something she needed to deal with sooner rather than later. She couldn't take a risk with the thing that mattered the most.

'Do you think,' she said, 'you could manage here for a couple of days without me?'

Maggie nodded. 'Yes. As long as you're back by the weekend? I think we could hold the fort.'

Cherry smiled. 'I can be back by Friday evening. All hands to the pump. Literally.'

52

Organising a new life, Rose was starting to realise, was all a bit chicken and egg. What did you start with first? She had made a list. Everything on it was part of the puzzle and the key to her future, but one thing depended on another, logistically, and it made her head spin.

Maggie had spoken to her the night before, about the possibility of selling the house in Mountville. Until recently, the prospect of such an upheaval, such a drastic change, would have sent her into a spin. But somehow, it felt as if the time was right to let go, for both of them. They held each other, mother and daughter, and shed a few tears at the thought of passing on the place they had called home for so many years, the place that had been home to the man they both loved. But they couldn't carry on living there out of sentimentality.

'It'll be tough,' said Maggie. 'Clearing everything out, and saying goodbye. We were all so happy there.'

'But we'll be happy here,' said Rose. 'I know we will. And Dad would think it's a good idea.'

'He would,' agreed Maggie.

And now Rose had a ream of practicalities to tackle. Her first call was to the local education authority.

'My daughter's registered to start school in Avonminster, but I moved to Rushbrook over the summer,' said Rose, her stomach fluttering with nerves because this really mattered. 'I wondered if there was a place free for Gertie at the primary school in September.'

She had to answer several questions from a woman whose tone didn't give her any hint as to whether it was likely. Eventually, after leaving her on hold for several minutes, the woman came back on the line.

'You,' she said, 'are very lucky indeed. There is one space left.'

Rose felt jubilant. She knew that you didn't always get into your local school; that places were sought after. Fought after. People moved house to be in the right catchment and even then it wasn't a dead cert.

'Thank you,' she managed, and arrangements were made for her to be sent the registration forms, and a uniform list. She'd seen the children in their jolly red jumpers and couldn't wait for Gertie to join the throng. She had already made several friends at Dandelions who would be going to Rushbrook Primary. The school was completely different from the one in Mountville she had put her down for, but she'd had long enough to think about whether this was the right place for her daughter, and she decided it was. It would mean a slower pace of life, but Rose shut her eyes and imagined walking Gertie along the road, the two of them kicking at conkers, and it felt right.

Then she went back online and searched for the college in Honisham. She read through the details of the course again. Horticulture, Gardening and Landscape Design. Every time she read it, she became more convinced that this was what she wanted to do. Propagation, pruning, pesticides... she longed to learn more. She imagined the garden at The Three Swans a year from now, totally transformed, an abundant vegetable patch, a potager brimming with herbs and edible flowers, fruit cages bursting with raspberries and blackcurrants for Winnie to plunder. And perhaps a local client list: Amanda Bannister was definitely interested in her helping at Wisteria House, and Lorraine had told her there were lots of newcomers in the area who had no idea about where to start in the garden and were always putting ads up for help.

Rose envisaged a kind of mentoring scheme for newbie gardeners, where she would empower people to take control, turning to her for advice and guidance when they needed it. Developing that side of the business would go hand in hand with her horticultural therapy. She thought her career would probably evolve, that the answers would come as she gained knowledge and experience.

It felt like what she was meant to do: growing, nurturing, caring... sowing seeds.

She typed her details into the application form and pressed send.

Then she picked up her phone to look at the card she had photographed on the board outside the village shop. The one next to their own advert.

BARN CONVERSION TO RENT
AT DRAGONFLY FARM

*We have a small two-bedroomed barn conversion
up for rent on our cider farm.*

*It's light and bright and well equipped with clever
storage space.*

*We would like to rent it to someone local, to fit in
with our ethos.*

For more information, call Tabitha Melchior

There was a photo of a tiny red-brick barn with floor-to-ceiling windows at the front. Rose could imagine sitting there with a cup of tea in the morning, breathing in the scent of apple blossom while Gertie munched on toast and shouted out her spellings.

She made an appointment to view it at four o'clock that afternoon, praying that she counted as a local. After all, she had been christened in Rushbrook Church, more for Catherine's sake than anyone's, for Frank and Maggie weren't great believers. She wasn't Rushbrook born and bred, but her heart and soul were here. And the fact her family was running the pub must count for something.

'Oh my God, of course you count,' Tabitha told her that afternoon as she led her into the yard. 'I just didn't want to let it to someone from London who was going to use it as a weekend bolthole. I want a real person who has a life here. Now, the rent's low because we're still doing a lot of building so it's a bit of a mess. This is the cider barn' – she pointed at a new building, long and low and sleek – 'and we're gradually converting the old barns and

415

stables into a mix of workshops and residential. We've just finished this one and I have to admit it's my favourite because it's tucked away in the corner. You'll have Lola and Gabriel and Plum and Inigo next door – Gabriel's my cousin and they moved here from London a few years ago. And there's no garden, but you're welcome to ramble about in the orchards any time you like.'

'Mummy,' said Gertie. She had gone absolutely rigid, her eyes round, pointing a finger.

'What is it, darling?' Rose bent down and followed Gertie's finger, to see what she was pointing out. And she began to smile.

'A donkey,' whispered Gertie, overwhelmed. 'The donkey, look.'

'Oh yes,' said Tabitha, catching Rose's eye and winking. 'Whoever lives here has a very important job. They have to feed the donkey for us. It's part of the contract.'

The barn itself was very compact. A living space with a small kitchen area with hand-made units, a fridge and a washing machine. Two bedrooms and a sleek shower room. There were white walls and oak floors and several cubby holes for storing things.

Rose could barely swallow or speak. She wanted it so much, it hurt. It was going to take her a while to get her business up and running, especially if she was at college, but she had some money her grandmother had left her. She'd had it earmarked for a car, but she thought that for the time being, she wouldn't need one. She had her bike, which she could bring down from Avonminster. Gertie's school was walking distance; there was a bus to the college.

She had enough for six months' rent. Enough to tide

her over for the time being. She wanted it so badly, a space she could call her own, a space she could begin to be herself.

'What do I have to do?' she asked Tabitha. 'Are there other people interested? Do I need references? Or a credit check?'

Tabitha gave her a strange look. 'You're Catherine Nicholson's great-granddaughter,' she said. 'You don't need any of that. As far as I'm concerned, it's yours if you want it. Only don't forget the donkey clause, or you'll be out on your ear.'

Rose and Gertie walked back down the long drive to the road back to Rushbrook. The dragonflies that gave the farm its name zigzagged in the air around them, as if escorting them. She pulled her phone out of her pocket, staring at the screen for a moment. She felt elated by everything she had achieved. A school place for Gertie, a college place for her, a new home . . . Phase one of New Rose was firmly in place, and to her surprise she wasn't feeling any of the anxiety she had feared. Somehow with each mission ticked off the list, she became stronger and more confident. Was it Rushbrook that had helped her fears subside? The Three Swans? Or was it simply time?

Or was it the thought of Aaron waiting for her? Had that been an incentive? Suddenly she longed to tell him what she had achieved in such a short space of time. She wanted to hear his voice. She wanted to touch him.

'Phase One is complete!' she texted him. She paused for a moment before typing out the rest of the message. 'Lunch at the pub on Sunday?'

It was agony waiting for his reply. They reached the little stone bridge that crossed the river on the way back into the village, staring down at the water as it burbled along. She felt the twin buzz of a text in her pocket. Beep beep. She pulled out her phone, her mouth dry. He might have changed his mind about waiting. What if he had? Suddenly she realised how important he was to her. He was the last piece of the puzzle.

'I'll be there,' he said, followed by a line of emojis: hearts and roses, and a knife and fork at the end.

Rose smiled as a pair of swallows swooped in front of them in the bright summer sky, joyful and carefree.

The puzzle was complete.

53

Amanda stood outside 5 Kerslake Crescent and felt the years fall away. If she narrowed her eyes a little, she could replace the uPVC windows with the old Crittal ones that had once been there, and visualise the red wooden door with the peeling paint and the crazy paving on the path and the overgrown grass. She could remember her feet squeezed into metal roller skates, and clomping to the road at the front to whizz up and down for hours, awkward and inelegant. She could remember music blasting from the upstairs window: 'Hey Jude' and 'Sunshine of Your Love' and 'Lily the Pink', which made them all roll around laughing. It had been a tough house to live in: ringworm and cold custard with skin on top and ice on the inside of the windows and hand-me-down clothing. There were rarely any hugs, but it wasn't that there was no love. It was just that once her mother had gone, they weren't sure what to do with it. They were competing to survive, hide their grief, and get their dad's attention, of which he didn't have much.

Wisteria House had been a haven, and Catherine Nicholson had undoubtedly been her saviour. Amanda was eternally grateful for the help and encouragement she had been given, and knew just how blessed she was to have had such a rewarding career – both creatively and financially – and now to realise her dream, with a man she trusted and loved.

And now, it was time to pay it forward a little. On the night of the quiz, she had recognised something broken in Nicole. She had seen the weariness in her, and the wariness, but also the flash of joy when she had won the tie-breaker, as if for a fleeting moment she actually meant something.

She knocked at the door, wondering if Nicole had seen her and if she might pretend not to be in. But to her surprise, she answered. She looked older than she had the night of the quiz, draped in a baggy black sweater and jeans and her hair scraped back. She looked weary and wary.

'Hello . . .' she said, in the tone of voice of one expecting trouble.

'I hope you don't mind me calling in,' said Amanda. 'But after we met at the quiz, I had an idea. I've got a proposition.'

Nicole looked surprised, but there was something so buoyant and upfront and open about Amanda. She didn't invite suspicion, just curiosity. She was a person who made things happen, and that was very beguiling. So she let her in.

'Please excuse the mess.'

Actually, by the usual standards, the front room wasn't that messy today. Nicole had managed to clear the surface detritus when she got up, thank goodness – the plates and the abandoned homework and Otis's Pokemon cards, and at least the curtains were open. The sun was shining in and showed the dust on the telly and the streaks on the windows, but the cushions on the big sofa were plumped up and the throws neatly arranged and it looked if not pristine then at least homely.

'God, this is nothing compared to when we Fryers lived here,' Amanda said cheerfully. 'We used to peel all the wallpaper off and scribble everywhere. There was no carpet. And for some reason there was always Smash everywhere. Little clumps of mashed potato squashed into everything. I'm still a bit of a slattern, to be honest. This is immaculate by my standards.'

Nicole found herself laughing. 'Sit down. Coffee?'

'I've had my coffee quota. But thanks.' Amanda flopped onto the sofa. 'I wondered if you might be able to help me. Don't look so worried – I think you might find it fun.'

'OK,' said Nicole, sitting in the rocking chair adjacent to the sofa. 'Tell me.'

'I'm supposed to be taking a back seat so me and Theo can spend more time here. I don't want to be a hands-on producer any more. It's an eighty-hour week. So I'm going into development and I need to look for projects. But the one thing I'm short of is time. I get sent rafts of books from scouts and publishers hoping for a television deal. I couldn't read them all if I stayed at home for the rest of my life, and you never know which one is going to be The One.' She leant forward, her eyes smiling. 'What I need is someone to read them all for me, and do a synopsis. And maybe a paragraph or two on whether they would be suitable for adaptation.' She smiled brightly. 'And I thought of you, and your love of books, and your teaching background, and I thought it might be up your street?'

'You are joking?' Nicole looked shocked.

'Oh God. I hope I haven't offended you?' Amanda looked worried. 'I do have a habit of jumping in with both feet if I have a brainwave. I just thought—'

'I would absolutely love it!' Nicole said quickly. 'I can't think of anything I would love to do more. Spend my days reading? It's a dream come true.'

'I'd pay per book. Not a massive amount, but enough to make it worth your while. And the more you read, the more you'd make.'

'I'm a fast reader. So be warned,' Nicole laughed. Suddenly the years rolled off her. There was joy in her face, and light in her eyes.

Bingo, thought Amanda. She had learned to trust her gut, and knew on instinct that Nicole was bright, and would pick up on what she needed quickly.

'We need a meeting,' she said. 'So I can talk you through the kind of projects I'm looking for, and the qualities I need in a book. A strong hook, a unique concept. Compelling characters. The potential for a sequel.'

'I get it,' nodded Nicole.

'So do we have a deal?'

'But how do you know?' said Nicole, still rather overwhelmed. 'Whether I'd be any good?'

'It's my job,' said Amanda. 'To suss people out. To know what they're good at. To spot talent. I'm never wrong.'

Nicole stared at Amanda in awe. She was so sure of herself. So full of certainty. If she could have an ounce of Amanda's self-assuredness, she could better herself. She was being given a golden opportunity. She should grab it with both hands, learn as much as she could from this amazing woman, try and steer herself up and out of the mire she was wallowing in. Maybe this was the turning point she needed?

She held out her hand. 'It's a deal,' she said.

When Amanda had gone, Nicole sat down and tried to take in what had just happened.

She couldn't mess this up. She recognised Amanda as a person who rewarded endeavour and talent. After all, Amanda had overcome adversity and got herself out of this very house under her own steam, ending up with a glittering career and Wisteria House. If she could do it, then Nicole could. Not just for her, but for Otis and Pearl and Chloe.

She knew she would need help. She knew there was support out there. She had refused to reach out for it before because she wasn't ready. Whether she'd reached rock bottom yet was debatable, but she'd seen something she wanted, something that gave her the strength and courage to make a drastic change.

Before she could change her mind, she picked up her phone and dialled the doctor's surgery.

'Hello. I'd like to make an appointment to see someone, please.'

When the receptionist asked what it was about, she paused for a moment, breathing in.

'Alcohol dependency,' she answered, as clear as a bell. 'I have alcohol dependency.'

'No problem,' came the reply. No judgement. No shocked tone. 'Let me see when I can fit you in.'

Later that afternoon, when Chloe came in from her lunchtime shift, and before Pearl and Otis were home, Nicole sat her down and told her she had made a decision.

'It's OK,' she told her daughter when she saw the anxious look on her face. She realised that was how Chloe looked most of the time, and felt a stab of remorse. She was sixteen. She should be carefree and living her best life. 'It's a good thing. I think you'll be pleased.'

'As long as you're not sending us to live with Dad.'

'Absolutely not,' Nicole promised. 'I need your help, that's all.'

'Oh,' said Chloe, thinking that she'd given quite a lot of that already. 'Sure.'

'I've hated myself for a long time,' Nicole told her, 'for being weak, and useless. I hate myself for breaking every resolution I ever make, before I even make it. And there's only one thing that makes that hate go away. When I'm drunk, I'm amazing. I can do anything. I can be the best mother in the world. For about five minutes.' Her face seemed to melt, her eyes and mouth turning down, tears flowing down her cheeks. 'But by then it's too late.'

'Oh, Mum...' Chloe could feel her heart breaking for her mother.

'I've made an appointment to see my GP,' Nicole told her. 'They will get me help. But I have to be honest.

I have to tell them everything. The whole truth. So I wondered if you would come with me? To make sure I tell them everything and that I don't lie. I don't trust myself,' she added for good measure. 'I know all my own tricks. I can't be answerable to just myself.'

It was a critical moment. Chloe could easily turn away from her. Nicole held her breath.

'Of course I'll come with you, Mum,' said Chloe. She went to sit next to her mother, picked up her hand and stroked the back of it. 'And I know you can do it. It'll be hard, but I've got your back.'

Nicole sighed. 'I get so tired sometimes,' she said. 'Of being me.'

It was tangible, her weariness. She could barely hold up her head or lift her limbs. Chloe put her arms around her mother's shoulders and felt how frail she was.

'I do love you,' she said, squeezing hard.

'I know,' said Nicole. 'But I know it's difficult to love me sometimes.' She sighed. 'And I love you more than you can ever know. I'm sorry. For being so . . .'

'Shhh,' said Chloe. There was no need for her to say any more. With Rose's support, Chloe knew she had the strength to lift her mum up and help her become the person she deserved to be, the mother she deserved to be. They both knew it would be a long journey, difficult and dangerous, but Nicole had taken the first step.

'And thank you,' said Nicole. 'I know without you, this family would have fallen apart. I was only able to behave like I did because you were there to pick up after me. It was unforgiveable.'

'Mum, it's cool.' Chloe nestled into her. She poked her in the ribs, playfully. 'Just finish making me that prom dress, and we're all good.' She was desperate to lighten the tone. She didn't want to talk about it. The strain, the fear, the darkness. The tiredness. Nicole's head dropped onto her shoulder and she pulled her in tighter.

Her mum.

54

Cherry arrived in Berlin late on Tuesday night. She felt a little like a Cold War spy. She had booked herself into a small, unassuming hotel near Mike's. His flight details and hotel booking had come through to her phone, from the time when they had set up a shared diary to make their lives less complicated. Either he had forgotten or didn't care if she knew his whereabouts.

She got up early the next morning dressing in jeans and a white t-shirt, sneakers and a trench, repacking her backpack. It contained everything she needed for two nights away.

She had only booked into this hotel for one.

She set the satnav on her phone and strode through the streets of the wakening city for about half a mile, coming to a halt outside an imposing white Bauhaus building wrapped round the corner of two streets, its rows and rows of windows winking in the sun. Like so many buildings in Berlin, it had reinvented itself – once the HQ for the Hitler Youth, it was now a glamorous and edgy hotel.

She pushed open the door and walked in. It might have intimidated a lesser person than Cherry, but she wasn't overwhelmed by opulent light fittings and street art. She knew all the tricks. And whilst an English hotel might have worn its hypercool with a certain aloofness, the staff here weren't at all snooty and the other guests seemed relaxed, not in the least bit up themselves. She loved it on sight. There was a knack to making people feel at home, even when they were very far away, and this place had nailed it.

She knew Mike's habits like the back of her hand. He would have woken early, gone for a run, followed by a very long hot shower. By now he would be having a coffee, soaking up the atmosphere, reading the guidebook, deciding where to go for the day.

She found him in the club bar, where breakfast was served. Like the lobby, it was oozing glamour – floor-to-ceiling metal windows, high stools in eau de nil velvet, round tables with curved banquettes, glittering chandeliers. Chic wait staff moved amongst the tables, clad in black aprons. And although it felt like a nightclub, and it was only nine o'clock in the morning, it didn't feel seedy. It felt alert, the guests soaking up the atmosphere and readying themselves for the day ahead. There was a smell of rich roasting coffee and baking.

Dotted around the room were people having breakfast meetings, chatting over movie deals, ad campaigns, property development. It gave Cherry a thrill. There was a creative buzz in the air that was infectious and she felt excited by the possibilities that lay in front of her. The promise of Berlin. A city that had been torn apart but had mended itself, with dignity and pride and style.

He was there, sitting at a small table for two near the windows, snug in a club chair, his nose in a book, as she had predicted. Her heart turned over as she saw him sip his coffee – double espresso, half a teaspoon of sugar. He had his rubberised backpack next to him, and she knew what would be in it: sketchbook, pencils, water, camera, SPF50, scarf, beanie, cashew nuts, a tube of Colman's mustard. He would already have bought a book of metro tickets. Mike got himself organised with military precision and then left everything to chance. He would have familiarised himself with every inch of the city, but would see where fate took him. If he found somewhere he liked, he might stay there all day, hanging out in the cafés and bars, talking to strangers. Or he might walk and walk and walk. He travelled with an open mind.

And Mike certainly looked as if he belonged here. She realised everyone in here would probably know his work, even if they didn't recognise him. She felt a little burst of fond pride.

There was room in their lives for both of them to do what they wanted.

Together.

'Can I help you?' A charming waiter hovered in front of her, smiling. She pointed over at Mike.

'I'm joining the gentleman over there. Would you bring me a pot of coffee?'

'Sure. Give me two minutes.'

It would only be two minutes. She wouldn't have to ask again. It was that kind of place.

'Actually,' she put a hand on the waiter's arm. 'Could you bring us two glasses of champagne as well?'

His eyes widened in conspiratorial delight. 'For sure.'

She walked over to Mike, her heart beating a little

faster, nerves in her tummy. He looked up at she arrived at his side.

'Jesus Christ.' He looked as if he had seen a ghost. He dropped his book. Then got to his feet. 'Jesus Christ, Cherry.' He touched his heart. 'You've nearly given me a heart attack.' Then he started to laugh. 'What are you *doing* here?' He ran round to the other side of the table and pulled out a chair for her. 'Oh my God. I can't believe it. Sit down. What's going on. Shit.' He suddenly looked panicked. 'Is everything OK?'

'Yes. Oh yes, God, sorry. Don't panic. Everything's fine.' She sat down, and he sat opposite her. 'I just needed to see you.'

They stared at each other for a moment. The altercation at Admiral House faded into the background. The tension of the past few weeks. Somehow, being in a totally different space made their differences disappear. They couldn't help smiling at each other. He was pleased to see her. She was pleased to see him.

She swallowed.

'I need to ask you something.'

Mike put up his hands. 'Go ahead.'

She paused for a moment. This was a big question. The biggest she would ever have asked anyone in her life.

'I know this is going to come as a complete shock. Even bigger than me turning up here. And you don't have to answer straight away.'

He shrugged, holding up his hands as if to say, 'How can I answer if I don't know what the question is?'

She smiled.

'Will you marry me, Mike?'

He looked thunderstruck.

'What?'

'Will you marry me?'

'Oh no,' he said. 'You do not get to pull that one on me. You've come all this way to ask me the one question I've wanted to ask you for years but didn't dare. You always said you didn't want to get married. You were adamant!'

Cherry had always told Mike that they didn't need to get married. That they would be there for each other for ever without an antiquated ceremony. And he had agreed – it was the times they had lived in, all free love and lack of convention and not wanting to be shackled by marriage vows.

'I know. And I'm not going to say something glib, like it's a woman's prerogative to change her mind. But I have changed my mind. Things have happened that have made me see things differently. They've made me realise how wrong I've been.'

'No,' said Mike. 'Sorry, I'm not having it.'

Cherry felt a chill around her heart. She had misjudged everything. Her grand gesture had backfired. He wasn't interested. He wasn't going to forgive her.

And now, here was the waiter, holding out two glasses of champagne on a tray, the tiny bubbles shooting up through the liquid. He looked at their faces, wondering if perhaps he had interrupted an argument. 'You ordered champagne?'

Mike gestured to Cherry. 'Did you?'

Cherry nodded, not feeling as if she could send the drinks back. The waiter set the glasses down gently and retreated.

Mike stared at Cherry, then picked up his glass.

'Well,' he said. 'Since you're here, we might as well get one thing straight.'

Oh God, she thought. He's got someone else. She gripped the bottom of her glass, tensing herself for the worst. But suddenly Mike's face broke into a wide smile, that same wide smile he'd had the day she'd first seen him at the stables.

'If anyone's doing the asking round here, it's me,' he said. 'Cherry Nicholson, will you marry me?'

They drank their champagne and wandered out hand in hand into the streets of Berlin. They decided to go full tourist and took the Hop On Hop Off bus around the city, getting off wherever took their fancy. They saw the Brandenburg Gate and Checkpoint Charlie, and the infinite grey concrete slabs of the Holocaust Memorial.

In the Museum of Terror, Cherry looked at a photograph of three female prison guards in a concentration camp, having a cigarette break. They looked so young and carefree, whilst behind them the huts they were guarding contained untold horror.

'I bloody love this city,' said Mike, as they climbed back up to the top deck of the bus. 'After everything it's been through, it's come out with attitude and creative energy. Living proof that anyone can reinvent themselves if they try hard enough.'

Cherry slipped her hand into his. There was a vim she realised she hadn't seen in him for a while. Perhaps, with the death of her mother, she had overlooked his agitation at his impending retirement. Now they were allies again, they could take stock and plan their future. There was room for all of their ambitions, she thought. But the most important thing to remember was that they were all on the same side. Her and Mike and Maggie and Rose and Gertie. They were not at war.

They had lunch at an opulent restaurant overlooking the river, all dark wood and moody lighting and louche, over-the-top art. A suitably decadent place to celebrate a long overdue engagement. They had white asparagus and wagyu steaks smothered in Café de Paris butter. And more champagne.

'Maggie's selling her house,' Cherry told Mike. 'She's going to buy me out. Though I'm going to keep a share. It is The Three Swans, after all. I'm not putting all that energy in and not reaping the benefits. Maggie's called me Head of Lampshades.'

Mike laughed. He knew better than anyone that Cherry was so much more than that, but they all loved teasing her. 'What about Rose? And Gertie?'

'Rose and Gertie,' said Cherry, 'are moving to Dragonfly Farm. Gertie's going to Rushbrook Primary, and Rose is going to college in Honisham.'

Rose had texted her the night before in great excitement, and Cherry had felt a fierce pride in her granddaughter for taking control.

'Maybe I was wrong all along,' said Mike. 'Maybe we should have kept Wisteria House?'

'No,' said Cherry. 'That would have held us back. We've all learnt a lot. About ourselves. About life.'

'Shit, that reminds me,' said Mike. 'I need to cancel a viewing.'

'What viewing?'

He looked sheepish. 'I was just looking. A loft

433

apartment. In a factory.' He pulled out his phone and scrolled through his emails.

Cherry put out a hand to stop him. 'Don't cancel it,' she said, smiling. 'Let's go and have a look. You know that's my favourite thing in the world.'

'Looking at wildly unsuitable property?' Mike laughed. 'OK. The appointment's in the morning.' He looked at her. 'You are staying over, right?'

'Damn right,' said Cherry. 'I hope you've got room?'

He certainly did. The room at the hotel was plush and luxurious, with a huge velvet bed and sweeping curtains and subdued lighting. Cherry took pictures of every little detail, never off duty, while Mike went for another run to burn off lunch before they went out for dinner.

Cherry was lounging in the middle of the bed when he came back.

'I'm going to grab a shower,' he said, and threw something onto the bed next to her. 'You better take a look at that. See if it's your thing.'

She sat up, confused, as he disappeared into the bathroom, and reached out for whatever it was he'd thrown. A box. A little black velvet box. And inside, a ring. A ruby, cherry red, in a square Art Deco setting flanked on either side by a row of diamonds. Simple, discreet, with a hint of thirties Berlin. She took it out of the box with a smile. She had not realised, at the age of nearly seventy, how very pleased a ring would make her feel. There was nothing like a romantic gesture.

When Mike came out of the bathroom ten minutes later, Cherry was fast asleep in the middle of the bed, a smile of contentment on her face, and the ring on her finger twinkling in the evening light.

'This, as they say,' said Cherry the next morning, 'is right up my *strasse*.'

The apartment was in a leafy area of Friedrichshain. It wasn't huge, but it felt spacious, open plan, with exposed brick pillars and full-length metal windows looking out onto a little terrace. They'd walked there from the hotel, passing little shops and bars and galleries on the way.

'Aren't we wasting our time?' asked Mike. 'I wanted to go to Museum Island.'

'We can go there later. It never hurts to look,' said Cherry. 'I get some of my best ideas viewing properties. It's always inspiring. It's like a peep into another life. A life that could be yours if you wanted.'

They stood here now, holding hands, looking around the light-filled space.

'It's funny,' said Mike. 'It feels as if I've been here before. But I definitely haven't.'

Cherry looked at him. 'That's because it feels like home. It feels like us. I can see our paintings on the walls.'

Mike rolled his eyes fondly. Cherry was doing what she always did. Drawing him in. Painting a picture. But she was right. He could imagine the photo that had cemented their relationship hanging, unashamedly, on the far wall. Berlin wouldn't judge it. Berlin understood context. Berlin understood better than anyone how things were done in the spirit of the age. They had learned not to hide things, but to learn from them.

Cherry felt a familiar leap of excitement. Possibilities. Adventure. Change. A challenge. She recognised it as a sign that she shouldn't ignore. It was her gut telling her this was a good idea. It had never, ever been wrong.

She cleared her throat.

'How much?'

Mike told her. 'I thought we were just looking. I thought we were playing?'

'You like it, though. Right?'

'I absolutely love it. I mean, what's not to like?'

'So . . . if we sold Admiral? We could afford this and have some left over.'

Mike looked at her, a smile spreading over his face. 'What? We can't.'

'Why not? I mean, you were the one who booked the viewing. There's no smoke without fire. You must be interested in life here.'

'I love this city. It excites me. It makes me want to create. It makes me feel alive.'

'Well, me too.'

'It's not that simple.'

'Of course it is. You just have to have the balls.' She looked fierce.

'Oh yeah,' he said. 'I'm talking to the woman who bought a pub on a Monday morning. Just like that.'

He could talk about it now. He could laugh about it. She'd been right, though it had come between them. That had been his fault. He'd been stubborn, wallowing in his own insecurity. He could see that now.

'So what do you think?' Cherry held out her arms. 'It's wonderful, isn't it?'

Mike looked at the polished concrete floor, the high ceiling, the light flooding in. He could feel his creative energy flow back in. A positive energy, not the anger he'd been using to paint of late.

'Yes,' he said. 'But—'

'But?' said Cherry, feigning indignation. She came up to him with her arms crossed, her eyes dancing. 'Have you learnt nothing from me? Haven't you learnt that there is nothing more exciting, more invigorating, more life-affirming, than an impulse purchase?'

55

'I think,' said Maggie, 'I'm falling in love.'

The eyes she was gazing into were wise and kind, but with just a gleam of mischief. She was transfixed.

'It's impossible not to, really.' Russell was standing next to her, gazing at the sow with equal adoration. She had not long given birth to a pile of piglets who were snoozing next to her in the afternoon sun. 'She gave birth outside, under the stars. It was too hot to stay in. That makes me so happy. Knowing she knows what's right for her, and letting her do it.'

'That's wonderful.' Maggie was charmed by his pride. And he was right to be proud. His farm was beautifully kept; his pigs content. He had given her the grand tour, talking her through everything he had done. She could see how hard he had worked, and what a commitment it was. A way of life.

She looked down at his arms, leaning on the top of the fence, bronzed from working outdoors. She pushed down the urge to move closer to him.

'So – what do you think?' he asked.

He wasn't being pushy. She had offered to give him an

appraisal – the same one she would offer to any client, free of charge, before they took her on.

'I think there's huge potential to create a quality brand. But you need to expand to make it really profitable and not just a glorified hobby. You'll need more staff. You can't possibly do it all by yourself. You need a name. A catchy name that's easy to remember, that restaurants can reference in their menus. What we could do is draw up a three-year plan, with sales targets, an investment plan and a strategy for—'

She broke off. He was staring at her, but he wasn't really listening. She could tell.

'You're not listening.'

'No.' He smiled, that slow smile that made her tummy turn over. He was looking straight into her eyes. She could see exactly what he was thinking. The same as her. Yet she knew it was up to her to make the first move.

So she did. She stepped towards him, placing her hands on his upper arms, feeling his strength. And then she kissed him, placing her mouth over his until their smiles matched and their eyes were so close that their lashes were almost tangled. He lifted his hands up to her hair, teasing the strands apart with his fingers, running them up to her scalp. She leaned right into him so she was pressed against his chest, relishing its hardness, feeling his arms close around her.

Eventually she pulled away, breathless, laughing.

'I wanted to do that all afternoon, when we went to the river,' he said. 'But I didn't think it was gentlemanly. Given the terms of our agreement.'

'I think those terms have gone right out of the window,' she said. They stared at each other.

'What do we do now?' he asked. His hand was stroking the back of her neck, kneading away the tension, making her melt. She felt wanton, and slightly shocked by her animalistic response.

There wasn't time. Not now. She had to get back to the pub before long. She couldn't leave anything to chance in these early days. Not that she didn't trust Winnie or the rest of the staff, but it wasn't fair to leave them to it.

Besides, she didn't want to rush things. Her body was urging wild abandon, but her brain reminded her that she needed to be cautious. This was a small village. Russell was on her doorstep. And even though her instincts told her he was a good person, there was nothing wrong with taking it slowly. She owed it to herself.

Besides, wouldn't it be even more delicious, to savour the experience? Revel in the anticipation?

'I have to go soon,' she said. 'But how about a second date? A proper date.' Then she laughed. 'Or an improper one.'

He laughed a warm, treacly laugh that slid its way deep inside her. She held up her hands and he laced his fingers in hers and they kissed again and he ran his mouth along her jawline and down to her neck, his stubble grazing her skin, and she tilted her head back, thinking she might melt into a puddle of molten silver right in front of him.

'An improper date,' he said. 'Just tell me when. I'll be waiting.'

After service that evening, Maggie sat at the bar once everyone had gone, Fred and Ginger snoozing under her stool. She poured herself a glass of Malbec, and sat sipping at it, thinking over the events of the afternoon, savouring the memory and thinking about Russell and the kind of man he was.

He was funny. He didn't take himself too seriously. He was obviously a hard worker. And someone who knew how to realise their dream. But sensitive too. She had been right to take it slowly, for they were both in thrall to the obvious attraction that had sprung up between them and neither of them could afford to be hurt. But it was time, to take a risk on each other.

The thought gave her a delicious thrill. She had thought she would never feel like that again. Although it was a very different feeling this time round, which was a good thing. A different chemistry. She knew she would never find another Frank. She could never replace him. But now it was time to put him to one side, gently. To make a little bit of space in her heart for Russell.

She pulled her notebook out of her bag, and found the page where she had last written. She put today's date, and began writing.

My darling F,
Thank you, for teaching me that my heart is big enough for more than one person. There is still room for you in there. You will never, ever not be deep inside me, guiding me, encouraging me, taking the mick... But for now, it's time to draw the curtain. I need to learn to love again, in a new way.
Thank you, my darling, for understanding. You will always be my world, my universe, but for now it's time for me to travel to another country. I cannot stand still for ever. I need to take those bold steps into unknown territory, without

you holding my hand. I'm scared, but I'll have everything you taught me to help me.

For now, this is my last letter to you. If it's a bit smudgy, that's my tears. Thank you, for being there even when you're not. I love you.

Maggie xxxx

Epilogue

Rushbrook had welcomed in September reluctantly at first, not wishing to let go of summer, but by the end of the month they had decided they suited each other very well. The sun was lower in the sky and it seeped through the branches of the trees as they turned their plumage to russet and burnt orange and gold. The cold morning air had a hint of wood smoke, foreshadowing the onset of winter: soon the days would shorten and the clocks would go back. The Three Swans had moved from botanical cocktails, garnished with Rose's borage and mint, to hot buttered cider to be drunk by the fire. It was time for digging out hats and scarves and wellington boots. It was time for making damson gin and plum jam and apple chutney. Before they knew it, it would be Hallowe'en, then Bonfire night – then Christmas!

In the kitchen, Winnie swore softly as a blob of cream slid off the side of the cake she was decorating. Fillets of pork with blackberry and apples were bubbling in the oven, and a tray of pommes dauphinoise was waiting to go in. She was more nervous about this lunch than anything she had cooked before. She had truly found herself at The Three Swans, under Maggie and Cherry's direction, and had grown in confidence, but it mattered to her that this was the best meal she had ever produced. A gesture of recognition and appreciation for what they had done for her.

In the dining room, Chloe was putting the finishing touches to the table that would hold just twelve for the wedding breakfast before more guests from the village joined for cake and champagne at teatime. As she tweaked the last linen napkin and adjusted the cloth, she told herself that everything was perfect. She was one month into her course at the college, and she was loving it. She, too, was profoundly grateful for the support she had been given by Cherry, Maggie and Rose. Her mum was a different person, throwing herself into the opportunity Amanda had given her, and she hadn't had a drink for over two months. The difference in Pearl and Otis was remarkable: they were much more settled now they had their mum's full attention.

Up the road, a procession was making its way from the church to the pub. The Reverend Matt stood smiling in the doorway watching them go. It had been an absolute joy to bless the union of Cherry and Mike, who had tied the knot officially at Honisham Registry Office earlier that morning, but had asked him to do the honours in a discreet ceremony afterwards. It had been a small congregation, but his words had been as heartfelt. And he and Matt would be joining them all for the celebratory wedding breakfast later at The Three Swans. The pub and the church, he thought. The mainstays of Rushbrook. Of course the pub would always have a bigger congregation, but he was not a vain man. He was simply there, whenever he was needed, by whoever, and today his role had been a particular privilege.

Cherry and Mike led the procession, Mike in a blue linen suit, his silk tie decorated with tiny tyrannosaurus rexes. Cherry had hesitated before cutting into the lace of her mother's wedding dress, the one she had found in the attic at Wisteria House, but she had heard Catherine's no-nonsense voice telling her to put it to good use, so she had made a long trailing skirt which she wore with a cherry red velvet blazer: the outfit was sleek, streamlined and sumptuous. She carried the last of the dahlias from Wisteria House: deep burgundy and copper and chocolate.

Amanda and Rose had harvested them the day before.

'I'm completely obsessed with gardening now, thanks to you,' Amanda told Rose. 'Every time I get on the train to London I feel resentful. I can't wait to get back. Get my hands dirty.'

Behind Cherry and Mike was Cherry's brother Toby, who had travelled down from York, then Maggie and Russell. Russell had panicked about being an intruder at the wedding breakfast, but Maggie had shushed him.

'I'm afraid,' she told him, her eyes dancing, 'you're as good as family now.'

He'd been to Exeter to buy a suit, and Jen had examined him on Facetime earlier that morning and given him five stars.

'I'm so proud of you, Dad,' she said. 'And I can't wait to meet Maggie.'

She was coming home for Christmas, and he thought how wonderful it was going to be this year, compared to last, when he had eaten lunch alone. The thought of waking up on Christmas morning with Jen in the house and Maggie in his life filled him with a joy he hadn't felt for a long time.

Behind them, Gertie was sitting on Aaron's shoulders, drumming her tiny black patent Doc Martens on his chest, but his smile never faltered, for Rose was by his side in a pink satin dress and a huge straw hat. Aaron was falling in love with Rushbrook and the contrast it gave his fast-paced, urban lifestyle. He found any excuse he could to slip away from Avonminster and spend time with Rose and Gertie in their little barn, so much cosier than his bachelor apartment.

Chloe and Winnie choreographed the wedding breakfast with military precision: smoked trout with beetroot, the blackberry and apple pork, a local cheeseboard with Winnie's seeded sourdough. Every last morsel was declared delicious. There were toasts and speeches, and glasses raised to absent friends. And when the rest of the guests arrived – Amanda and Theo, Dash and Tabitha, Lorraine from the shop, Clive – the cake was brought in to rapturous applause: a towering black forest gateau coated in shards of dark chocolate and topped with dark red cherries.

When the cake had been devoured and tiny glasses of apple brandy from Dragonfly Farm were being poured, Cherry slipped out of the door and back up to the churchyard. Evening was drawing in as she made her way over to the familiar white stone, and laid her wedding bouquet in front of it.

'I wish you were here,' she said to her parents. 'I think you'd be very proud. Of all of us.'

And she kissed her fingertip and pressed it to the cold marble, the dahlias glowing in the fading light. A breeze ruffled the lace of her skirt and she thought she heard the faint whisper of her mother's voice.

'We are, darling. We are . . .'

Discover your next uplifting read from
VERONICA HENRY

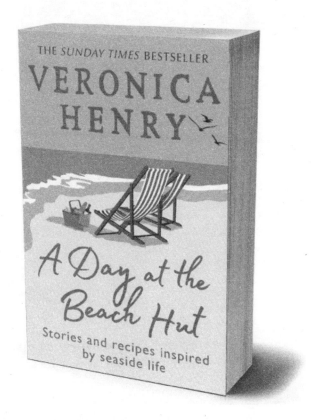

**Escape to the coast with this delicious collection
of short stories and beach-hut inspired recipes**

On a shimmering summer's day, the waves are calling,
the picnic basket is packed, and change is in the air.

It's just the start of an eventful day for a cast of
holidaymakers: over one day, sparks will fly, the tide will
bring in old faces and new temptations, a proposal is
planned, and an unexpected romance simmers...

**Return to Everdene Sands, where the sun is
shining – but is the tide about to turn?**

Robyn and Jake are planning their dream wedding at the family
beach hut in Devon. A picnic by the turquoise waves, endless
sparkling rosé and dancing barefoot on the golden sand...

But Robyn is more unsettled than excited. She can't stop thinking
about the box she was given on her eighteenth birthday, and
the secrets it contains. Will opening it reveal the truth about her
history – and break the hearts of the people she loves most?

As the big day arrives, can everyone let go of the
past and step into a bright new future?

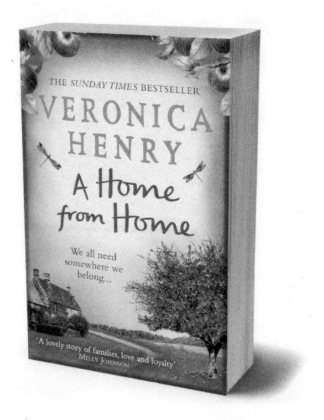

Sunshine, cider and family secrets...

Dragonfly Farm has been a home and a haven for generations of Melchiors – arch rivals to the Culbones, the wealthy family who live on the other side of the river. Life there is dictated by the seasons and cider-making, and everyone falls under its spell.

For cousins Tabitha and Georgia, it has always been a home from home. When a tragedy befalls their beloved Great-Uncle Matthew, it seems the place where they've always belonged might now belong to them...

But the will reveals that a third of the farm has also been left to a Culbone. As the first apples start to fall for the cider harvest, will Dragonfly Farm begin to give up its secrets?

Credits

Veronica Henry and Orion Fiction would like to thank everyone at Orion who worked on the publication of *The Impulse Purchase* in the UK.

Editorial
Harriet Bourton
Charlotte Mursell
Lucy Brem
Sanah Ahmed

Copyeditor
Clare Wallis

Proofreader
Francine Brody

Audio
Paul Stark
Jake Alderson

Contracts
Anne Goddard
Humayra Ahmed
Ellie Bowker

Design
Tomás Almeida
Joanna Ridley
Nick May

Editorial Management
Charlie Panayiotou
Jane Hughes
Bartley Shaw
Tamara Morriss

Finance
Jasdip Nandra
Afeera Ahmed
Elizabeth Beaumont
Sue Baker

Marketing
Lynsey Sutherland
Helena Fouracre

Production
Ruth Sharvell

Publicity
Maura Wilding
Alainna Hadjigeoriou

Operations
Jo Jacobs
Sharon Willis

Sales
Jen Wilson
Esther Waters
Victoria Laws
Rachael Hum
Anna Egelstaff
Frances Doyle
Georgina Cutler